Chapter One

BETHANY WAS STANDING on a field of stars.

Looking down, the stars were below her and even between her feet. The floor felt solid, but the array of bright twinkling dots in a variety of colors told every sense that she should be falling through the void of darkness.

When she raised her gaze, stars were on all sides and everywhere above her head. At least the firmament was still. Sometimes, under the spell of the Weaver's Breath, starlight would form long dizzying lines. Panic could set in, along with dread that she would never escape this terrible, overwhelming, awe-inspiring place.

But she was in control. She had her staff in hand, crowned with a metal orb that was somehow fashioned in layers, like the petals of a flower bud. Over her brand-new emerald-green dress, decorated in silver stars, she wore the soft gray cloak of a diviner.

Her training was now a part of her. This wasn't a separate place from the real world. She was just seeing what no one other than a diviner had an opportunity to see. This was the real world. This was the tapestry.

Lifting her chin and squaring her shoulders, she walked the path of stars. She pulled her staff toward her; the pattern of lights around her changed. When she rotated her staff, the heavens moved and familiar constellations came into view.

Even as she worked, under the spell of the Weaver's Breath, flashes of remembrance tried to distract her.

Diviner Trask's face appeared in her mind's eye, with his stern expression, neatly combed black hair, and short pointed beard. Her teacher spoke in his crisp, authoritative voice. *We are aware that your mother is unwell. . . You have performed well in your studies, some would say extremely well. . . You have been offered a place in the household of Esk. . .*

Bethany levered her staff, shifting the swathes of stars, searching for the most important constellations of all: the ones that would lead her to her destination. She knew why her buried consciousness was anxious about the journey. She was on her way to Esk right now.

Xander's sharp-featured face came next, with his intelligent, gold-flecked brown eyes watching her as they sat side by side in the atrium at the Observatory in Everlast. *Bethany, I*—She spoke at the same time. *You've been a good friend, Xander.* He flinched like she had slapped him. *Friend?*

Bethany slowed her movements on the path of stars. She had to concentrate. This wasn't a time to make mistakes.

The warmth that came from Charlton, with his bright blue eyes, messy gray hair, and careworn face was always a source of comfort. *You know that I will miss you too. But you always know where you can find me. And I promise you I will keep a close eye on your mother.*

But then her father's face interrupted, with his thinning white hair and patrician features as he fixed her with his penetrating stare. *You are here to learn the true purpose of your new assignment. Listen to me and listen carefully. . . The Conways will soon be hosting the fielding, as you know, and this fielding is of particular importance. I need you, Bethany, to be my eyes and ears. If any trouble is brewing, I want to know it. From either Declan or my son. . . As for Julian, his role in the fielding should be a minor one.*

Bethany realized she was gripping her staff too tightly. Julian. Her half-brother. Heir to the Eternal Empire. All she wanted was to stay away from him.

She tossed her head. This was her time. Her new life was about to begin. She reminded herself about what Diviner Brooks, guardian of the Argent Arch had said. *What you need to know is that without my recommendation, you would not be in your position, no matter what the palace says or does. Divination is our business, not theirs. . . You will do well, Diviner Sylvana. We all expect great things from you.*

With a final sharp movement, Bethany pulled the stars in front of her closer. She made her final adjustments. Then, with a cry, she cut the air with her staff. The sound of the gateway peeling open was a fiery

2

sizzle. A diagonal line of pure light sliced across the darkness, which she maneuvered, widening and enlarging until she was ready.

A shimmering black doorway lay in front of her, like a glistening mirror of darkness.

It was time.

She took a steadying breath, and then stepped through to the other side.

✦

Bethany left the portal fighting unsteady feet and blurry vision. The Breath of the Weaver had her firmly in its grip.

With stone below and an open sky above, she made sure she had both feet firmly supporting herself. She had to show she knew what she was doing.

Tiny droplets of rain tickled her cheeks. Although it was daytime at Esk, the gloomy gray sky made it feel like twilight. As with all functional gateways, she had studied the Star Temple, but this was her first time actually here.

A five-pointed star made from stone slabs formed the gateway. At its midpoint was the raised triangular frame she had just emerged from, which was about as tall as two men standing on each other's shoulders. The star formation pointed backward, with a stairway between the two legs at its base, in the direction she was facing. It wasn't a large gateway, and wouldn't be able to accommodate carts or wagons; even horses would be difficult to manage.

As the drizzle continued, she pulled the hood of her diviner's cloak above her head. She searched in all directions, peering through the light rain. To a diviner, time was everything, and she had come at the appointed hour. Wasn't someone going to greet her?

There was nothing to do other than walk toward where the steps led down to ground level,

A young man appeared on the steps, startling her.

Looking up at her, he was about her age, clean-shaven and elegantly dressed, with a slim build and intelligent eyes. He wore a coat with a high collar but was bare-headed, with water plastering his brown hair to his forehead and trickling down his face.

"Diviner Sylvana?" He didn't wait for her answer; she was here at the right time, after all. At the same time, she saw he was tense. Agitated. "My name is Caden Conway. You will have to forgive me. Today is not an ordinary day. Please, come. I can take you to the manor but then I am needed elsewhere."

"What happened?"

"An accident. You can ride?" When she shook her head, he made a sound of surprise. "No? Very well, you are quite slender, you can ride up with me." He glanced at the knapsack on her shoulder. At least the oilskin exterior would protect it from the rain. "Is that all you have with you? Pass it over here." He waited for her to hand the knapsack over. He then beckoned her onward as he led her down the steps, to where two horses were waiting, along with a pair of uniformed men she assumed were guards by their swords and bows.

The rain picked up force. No longer was it a light patter; it was slamming down hard enough to make the horses whinny.

Caden turned back to her, calling above the rain. "It doesn't rain often in Esk, not in summer, but when it does. . ." As he spoke, he climbed up onto one of the horses, settling himself before holding out a hand to help her up.

"Put your foot in the stirrup and your hand on the pommel here. Yes, that's good. When I pull, come up and sit in front of me. Get ready. Here we go." He heaved; he was surprisingly strong, and knew what he was doing. "There we are. Good. Shuffle back a little? You will be safe here inside my arms. Hold on, we'll just get your foot out of the stirrup I will be needing that. All set? Take hold of the pommel there. Yes, that's it. Here we go."

Caden gave a cry as he snapped his reins and his horse moved straight into motion. Bethany grimaced at the initial jolt. She had seen plenty of horses in Everlast's busy streets, but she had never had an opportunity to ride herself. She tried to lift her body with the upward heave of the animal beneath her, even as she felt awkward inside the young man's arms.

"How are you doing? I'll start slowly and then we can pick up speed." Caden kept looking to the side, glancing in the same direction. His thoughts were obviously elsewhere.

"What was the accident?" she asked.

She could easily hear him, as close as his face was to hers. "You know about the fielding?" She nodded. "A great deal of construction is underway. A viewing stand for spectators collapsed." His voice was grim. "A worker is buried within."

She stared out into the rain. She tried to imagine working to save a man from a stack of heavy beams and timbers while the heavens continued pummeling the people at work.

"The rain probably weakened the foundations," he continued. "Apologies for the unusual welcome. Normally, we would have all come to meet you at the Star Temple. Please don't feel bad. This is just unfortunate timing."

He seemed distracted but kind enough. It would be hard to welcome a newcomer to the estate in the circumstance.

"Father said you are from Everlast?" he asked.

"The west of the city."

"I studied there for a year. Shared a tiny dormus with three others. Is it still as busy?"

"Always," she said, picturing the market and the streets thronging with passersby, hearing the shouts and, perhaps unsurprisingly, remembering the smells. "How long ago did your last diviner leave?"

"Paxton? Quite recently. His decision to retire came suddenly. Mother and Father were disappointed, but grateful of course for his years of service." He paused. "Ready to pick up the pace? You seem to be managing well."

Bethany tried to keep her worry to herself, but was surprised when the change in the horse's faster gait became rolling and far less bumpy. She began to relax and take more note of her surroundings. The horse kept climbing the wide road, which fortunately was gravel rather than mud and sheltered with trees on both sides. Caden continued to glance to the side.

"Where does the estate start and finish?" Bethany asked.

She could hear a smile in his voice. "I would need a map to show you. Even on horseback, it would take days to ride its length."

She bit her lip. She was obviously more comfortable in a city, rather than the countryside. She would have to apply herself to learn about this strange new world she was in.

After a time, the rain eased off, then stopped altogether. Droplets clung to the branches of the surrounding trees, falling to splash in the little puddles below. The sun emerged, its light softening the whitening sky. Summer's heat returned, bringing warmth and moist, sticky air.

The horse bounded onward, climbing up the incline until the road finally leveled off. Ahead, a structure took shape—or perhaps multiple buildings, shaped like a pair of towers. Grassy fields stretched out on either side, dotted with white and yellow wildflowers.

Caden and Bethany approached a set of gates flanked by two tall towers, each adorned with intricate vines and flowers etched in stone and flowing gracefully down to solid pedestals. Passing between them, Bethany caught sight of the grand structure beyond and couldn't stop herself from gasping.

The manor loomed ahead, impossible large, as though a simple house had been scaled up to monumental proportions. It stood at the end of the road, proud and imposing, its several stories dwarfing her old compound back in Everlast. Window after window lined the facade, so numerous she couldn't guess what lay behind them, whether shared quarters or bedrooms, kitchens or washrooms. In front of the building, a graveled courtyard surrounded a central walled garden where a silver birch tree spread shade over the flowers below. It was everything a noble house's manor was supposed to be.

And she was going to be living here.

The entire journey she had kept wondering about the worker, hoping that perhaps he had already been rescued. And yet, despite the news of the accident, the sight of the manor made her excited. This was going to be her home. She would have a place here. She wasn't a student anymore.

Determination filled her, along with her mother's admonishing voice. She would soon be meeting the lord and lady. She would have to work hard and make herself useful.

The gravel outside the main doorway was fine enough to crunch beneath the horse's hooves as Caden pulled up. The two broad wooden doors were polished and carved, and a large wooden sign above them announced the name of the manor: *Fernley.*

As Bethany moved her head to take in the whole building, a face appeared in one of the upper windows, disturbing a white curtain when it ducked back in. A child? Perhaps a girl? Whoever it was didn't look again.

Caden dismounted. He helped her down until she was firmly on the ground. "Welcome to Fernley Manor. Now, I am afraid I have to be leaving you. Wait here and someone will come in a moment."

He backed away, giving her a quick bow, and then strode away quickly, taking his horse with him, until he disappeared behind a corner of the building.

"Are you Bethany Sylvana?"

Bethany turned to see a girl standing right behind her. With light brown hair, freckles, and an impish face, she stood in trousers and tunic rather than a dress, and looked to be about thirteen.

"You were watching me," Bethany said. She nodded toward the window. "From up there."

"Perhaps," the girl said airily.

A smile tugged Bethany's mouth upward. "You must be Isabelle."

"I am supposed to call you Diviner Sylvana."

"Pleased to meet you, Miss Isabelle."

"Just Isabelle. Only people who want me to do as I am told call me that." Isabelle changed topic abruptly. "There's been an accident. Father said he didn't want me to see. It's because the man might be dead. Or dying. That's what he said, anyway. Troy said Father doesn't want me in the way. "

"I heard." Bethany turned to face the direction Caden had gone. She could wait here for a steward to take her to her quarters. Or she could find out what was happening in the fields. Did they have healers with them? Depending on the worker's injuries, perhaps someone with special skills might need to be found. "How far away is it?"

"Just a few minutes on a horse."

She glanced down; Isabelle was wearing boots. "And on foot?"

"A few minutes more."

"Will you take me there? I might be able to help."

"Why? Are you a healer?"

"No." Bethany crouched down to look into Isabelle's eyes. "I am a diviner. I can't heal, but there are other things I can do."

✦

Bethany's boots were muddy as she followed Isabelle along a graveled path, heading deeper into the estate. The sky darkened once more, rumbling with thunder as they walked through a copse of trees toward some broad fields.

Loud voices and groaning timbers filled the air as they emerged from a stretch of trees, and soon they were heading for a collection of people gathered near a disorderly stack of beams. A cleric in white stood with his back to her, poised, bag at his side, but with his skills evidently yet to be called upon.

"Heave!" a loud male voice called.

The men hard at work were trying to use a beam as a lever to pry the heavy mess apart. As Bethany neared, she watched about a dozen of them in all, red-faced and straining hard.

"It's no use, Lord Conway. We need more men. And a functional pulley."

From the way his chest was heaving, a well-dressed older man was working as hard as anyone else. Swarthy and weathered, with stubbled cheeks and streaks of gray in his bushy brown hair, he had heavy eyebrows, which gave him a fierce expression as he scowled.

"Lord Conway!" someone cried from deep in the pile. "He's talking!"

"Can he move?" the swarthy older man demanded. Watching him, Bethany knew she was looking at Lord Kendrick Conway.

"No, he says he's pinned down. Finding it hard to breathe."

Bethany turned to Isabelle. "Wait here." She continued walking toward Lord Conway, and it was only when she glanced back that she realized that, despite her instruction, Isabelle was still following her. By then it was too late.

"Isabelle? What are you doing here? I told you to stay in the manor."

"Lord Conway?" Bethany called.

He leveled his gaze on her, clearly distracted. "Eh? Who are you?" He gave her a quick, absent inspection. "Just stay back, we're doing our best. There's nothing here you can do."

Isabelle piped up. "She's the new diviner."

"What?" Kendrick's brooding eyes shot to Bethany again. This time, he noticed the staff. His focus moved, onto her diviner's cloak

"Diviner? But you're so young." He caught himself, but the words came out nonetheless. "Ahem. Pleasure, Diviner Sylvana. I'm sorry we weren't able to welcome you, but we have a situation—"

"That's why I'm here," she said quickly. "Are you able to move the timbers?"

He shook his head, his attention still held by the pile. "Not as things stand. The pulley broke. It was the only one strong enough."

A map of the empire appeared in Bethany's mind, along with everything she had learned about every province and large town. "Sedgeford has builders and engineers. The Hexagon is in the middle of town. I can be there in minutes, if someone can get me back to the Star Temple."

"Sedgeford?" Kendrick stared hard at her. "But you just arrived. Don't you need to rest?"

She met his gaze. "I can do this, Lord Conway."

He paused, continuing to ponder, and then made his decision. "Troy!"

A bare-chested young man came forward, red-faced and dirty, with mud on his leather boots and trousers. After working at the pile of timber, mingled sweat and rain glistened on his muscled torso. He was handsome, with dark blond hair and a square jaw.

"Father?"

"This is my son, Troy," Kendrick said. "Troy, this is Bethany Sylvana, our new house diviner."

Troy rested his blue eyes on her for a moment. "Diviner Sylvana."

"Troy, I need you take Diviner Sylvana to the gateway and escort her to Sedgeford." Kendrick stopped speaking, then called out to someone else. "Caden! Over here."

Caden left the group of men he was with. Unlike when she had seen him before, he was also bare-chested, and much leaner than his older brother. "Father?"

"This is Diviner Bethany Sylvana—"

"We already met." Caden gave her a nod.

"Ahem. So you did. In any event, I want you to go with them in case you are needed." Kendrick drew in a deep breath. "Horses!" he bellowed. "Where are the horses?"

Moments later another pair of boys in uniform dragged a pair of horses over to the group. Troy was already dressing himself in a tunic, before climbing up onto one of the horses' backs.

This time, Bethany knew a little more about what to do, and when Troy beckoned over to her, holding out a hand to pull her up, she put her foot onto the stirrup. He was strong enough to settle her in front of him surprisingly swiftly. Caden was already mounted, and as soon as they were ready, both brothers kicked their horses into a fast run. Bethany barely had time to take the saddle's pommel and brace herself.

As Caden took the lead, Troy turned back, spying a uniformed steward. "Hallam?"

"Master Troy?"

"Have a wagon waiting at the Star Temple!"

"I'll see it done."

Caden dug in his heels, spurring his horse to a faster pace, and as Troy gathered speed to follow his younger brother, Bethany turned her mind to gateways and travel.

Chapter Two

BETHANY WAS AGAIN WALKING on the path of stars, but this time she wasn't alone. She glanced back at her two wards. After leaving their horses at the Star Temple, all of them were now on foot.

"Follow behind me," she instructed. "Keep walking to stay with me, but come no closer than ten paces."

The two brothers' eyes were open but blank. As she checked on them, she couldn't help contrasting them. Older and younger. Light and dark. Strong and slim. They were both good looking, each in his own way. In this place, they had their lives in her hands.

Focus!

Returning to her task, she used her staff to maneuver the stars. The familiar constellations came into view and she adjusted, even as she fought the churning in her stomach.

With a hard slice, she opened the gateway at Sedgeford. "Stay with me," she called. "Step through the portal. Make sure you are right behind me when we go through."

✦

"How many beams?" the builder asked.

"Eight, I think," Troy said. "Dark hard wood. Heavy. Each a foot thick. Perhaps thirty feet long."

As Troy and Caden explained the situation, Bethany waited behind them. Troy knew his way around town, taking them straight from the Hexagon to this builder's workshop. Fortunately, the accident at Esk had happened in daytime, and the workshop was open. The sun was also shining, which contrasted fiercely with the gloomy weather in Esk.

Caden cleared his throat. "It was nine," he said firmly. When Troy frowned at him, he scowled back. "I counted."

"Stars alive. . ." The builder, a burly man with rosy cheeks, shook his head. "The problem is this is Esk we're talking about. Usually we send heavy goods to Esk the slow way, via the road." He glanced at his companion, who was a little older with a bald head and might be his brother. "We would need the big pulley. A cart to carry it. Draft horse." He swore. "The Star Temple at Esk doesn't allow for horses. Have to use manpower. Hard carts and the like."

The two builders didn't look hopeful about their ability to help. Troy ran a hand over his face. Caden stood with his brow furrowed.

Bethany brought to mind what she had seen at the Star Temple. Back at the Observatory, she had learned about Esk's gateway, but she was glad now that she had taken the time to make her own assessment. "Bring everything you need to the Hexagon," she said. Everyone turned toward her, worry written across their faces. "Even horses. Let me worry about the rest."

✦

Fatigue slowed Bethany's steps. Her staff felt heavy, in that same way it had during her final test. She almost stumbled when dizziness struck her hard; it was only the halter of the draft horse in her hand that stopped her.

Pale dots sped past her, tiny little stars, so fast she couldn't make sense of them. She drew on her last reserves of energy, closing her eyes and counting.

One. Two. Three. Four. Five.

She opened her eyes.

The stars had slowed, but still they were moving too quickly. The rules were clear. This was her third time traveling in quick succession, which was something she wasn't supposed to do without dire need. Was she taking too big a risk? A man's life was at stake, but if she faltered now, she would doom two master builders and their team of workers, not to mention the draft horse she was leading, and finally, the two Conway sons.

She turned back to check on her wards. They trailed her in a group, as instructed, but she would feel better with some tighter organization.

"All of you, walk in two files, side by side, ten paces behind the horse and cart."

With blank expressions, they all moved as instructed. Troy stood beside Caden. The two builders from Sedgeford came next. Last of all, the team of six strong workers followed to complete the group.

She faced forward once more, her shoulders and jaw tense. The horse plodded along; she knew from Carina's stories that draft horses were generally manageable even when they weren't in a placid state, and this one was under the same spell as her wards. The cart rolled on a star-spotted nothingness that made her queasy when she looked back at the wheels.

Carina. She again saw the look in her friend's eyes after she had tumbled through the black opening at the Crystal Dome.

But this wasn't the time for rumination. She was a diviner. People were depending on her. She had work to do.

She narrowed her eyes at the stars, working with her staff, making sense out of the chaos. The heavens became familiar. She pulled some stars forward, turning her staff, and then brought the end down and back.

At this time of day, at the Star Temple in Esk, the heavens should look just so. She paused to assess the arrangement in front of her.

Nodding to herself, she pulled the end of the tunnel forward. She sliced downward, splitting the air apart to create an opening. She widened and refashioned the opening until she was facing a tall black rectangular mirror. Until she walked through, she wouldn't know what was on the other side.

She called back to her wards. "Stay together. All of you. Now follow me."

✦

The change was jarring, abrupt.

Bethany stepped out onto the flat stone surface of the Star Temple, dragging the halter of the draft horse with her. Still under the spell of the path of stars, the animal plodded along, content to go wherever she wanted it to. The cart rolled straight onto the stone platform.

She knew to keep moving, even as she checked over her shoulder. Of her group, despite her light head and the burning at the back of her throat, she was the only one alert and awake for the arrival. Her training came to the fore. She heard Diviner Aurelia's voice:

. . .there is a process of adjustment after arrival. The same applies for your wards, even though they won't have seen what you have. They

will be disoriented. It is a time of weakness. If you are expecting conflict, guiding guards or soldiers, you will see the danger first. And your voice is the one that must alert them and shock them into action.

Behind her, past the cart, Troy and Caden exited the portal, and then the two builders from Sedgeford. The workers came last of all, and she counted them. One. Two. Three. Four. Five. Six.

As soon as everyone had safely arrived, she raised her staff and twisted it. With a sizzle and a whispering snicker, the gateway closed behind them.

"Stop," she instructed.

Her training had prepared her. She knew what was about to happen.

Everyone shook themselves, even the horse, as her wards all woke up from the strange state at the same time. The draft horse bellowed a loud whinny. Troy hurried forward, crying out for his brother to help him. The two builders called orders as they gathered their crew.

Atop the crowded temple, the draft horse tossed its head, forcing her to tighten her grip on the halter. She heard more shouts from the direction of the bottom of the steps.

"Diviner. Please. Bethany? Let us do this part."

Troy was addressing her as he took her hand, attempting to pry her white knuckles free from the halter.

The best thing she could do was get out of the way. Checking she was safe to leave the area, she hurried down the steps to stand back and watch the commotion. Soon the men were all working together to lift the heavy pulley out of the draft horse's cart and carry it between them down to a waiting wagon. The cart was unfastened. Unencumbered, the horse itself was helped down the steps. Men bellowed commands to each other, the builders and their team from Sedgeford easily cooperating with the men from the fields.

"Easy. Easy!"

"Get her up!"

"That's it. A little more. Hold it. Wait! All right, lift together. One. Two. Three!"

With a loud clunk and rattle, the men settled the pulley into the second waiting wagon.

"Quickly!" Troy cried. "Get it moving!"

Bethany had just traveled to Esk, and then to Sedgeford, and then back to Esk again. She had done everything to be as fast as possible. And despite the heavy weight of her body, with so many people all united in the same endeavor, and the wagon trundling up the road, some men walking, others riding horses, she knew she had to go with them.

Before she could take a step, a dazzling multitude of stars burst across her vision. The fiery pain in her head forced her to put two hands to her temples and close her eyes. Unable to help herself, she weaved, putting out a hand as she felt she might fall.

A hand gripped her shoulder, steadying her. She heard a woman speaking in a tone that was kind, compassionate, but also firm. "That is enough for today, young lady."

She opened her eyes. Someone was with her: a slender woman, a few inches taller than her, with long pale blonde hair she wore in elegant twists. As the woman watched Bethany, her concerned blue eyes conveyed both warmth and the depth of intelligence. She wore a dark blue dress with golden embroidery, and a spider on a chain decorated her neck: the symbol of the Great Weaver as the shaper of fates.

"I am Anthea, lady of the estate. You have already met my husband Kendrick." Lady Anthea's voice became rueful. "My apologies for the terrible welcome. Unfortunately, as you well know, we have a minor crisis here that you arrived straight into."

Bethany managed a deep nod. "It is my pleasure to meet you, My Lady."

Anthea smiled and reached out to take Bethany's hands. Somehow the gesture wasn't forward, simply kind. "I thank the Great Weaver that you are here. We are in dire need of your skills." She let out a breath. "To be without a diviner, right before the fielding. Not to mention what happened today." She smiled again as warmth returned to her face. "We are most happy to have you."

Bethany cleared her throat. "I hope to be worthy of the honor."

Anthea wrapped her long, delicate fingers around Bethany's hands and squeezed. "Now, as I said, you, my dear, have done enough. Let us leave the men to their work. I will show you to your quarters and you can have a much deserved rest. I could not imagine Paxton doing what you just did. I know something about your calling. I am surprised you are even standing. Now, come with me. I insist."

Anthea kept her grip on Bethany's hands as she led her in the direction of Fernley Manor.

◆

The hour was late—late enough that Kendrick didn't even know what time it was. He was weary to the bone, but the hard work had been worth it. Relief had lifted a heavy weight from his shoulders.

Standing in the hallway, holding up a lantern so his wife could see, he hung back and waited while Anthea walked toward Bethany's door.

Anthea gently knocked, waiting for a moment, before quietly opening the door.

"Bethany?" Anthea asked softly. "Are you awake?" A pause told Kendrick that Anthea had received an answer. "You should know. . . the man who was trapped. . . he survived and is now back with his family. He and his family, they have a message for you."

Kendrick's throat was suddenly tight as Anthea paused again, before continuing.

"Thank you," Anthea said.

Chapter Three

A BRIGHT, RISING SUN told Kendrick it was going to be another hot day. He stood in the graveled courtyard out the front of the manor with his wife beside him.

"Busy morning," Anthea murmured.

"All mornings are busy," Kendrick replied, unable to keep the weariness out of his voice. "I wish I could remember when it was otherwise."

His senior steward Hallam had just left, having been issued with a rapid series of instructions about the eventful day ahead. Before Hallam, the master builder had explained to Kendrick and Anthea how he planned to get his work back on schedule. The new builders from Sedgeford had agreed to stay on for a while and help. Deliveries were expected. More money too. Anthea was behind with her accounts. Yesterday's accident had turned out as well as could be hoped for, but along with the unexpected bad weather it had all led to the loss of precious time.

"Father? You asked for me?"

Kendrick turned to see Troy striding briskly toward him.

"I did. I need you to meet the wine seller on the road and escort her here to the manor. Remember, she is traveling by road, not gateway.

Show her where everything is and help her unload."

Troy headed off just as Kendrick spied Caden dressed in riding boots and leading his horse away.

"Caden," Kendrick called. He sucked in a breath to shout louder. "Caden!"

Caden looked back with guilt in his posture. Anthea glanced at Kendrick; she could see it just as clearly. Kendrick waved, beckoning his youngest son over. Caden trudged over with a roll in his shoulders, resigned and more than a little irritated, bringing his saddled horse with him.

"I was just going for a ride—"

"Where is Isabelle?" Kendrick cut him off.

"Isabelle?" Caden raised an eyebrow. Scanning the area around the manor, he nodded in the direction of the stables. "There she is, feeding the dogs."

Kendrick finally caught sight of his daughter's smaller figure. Soon she was walking away, her task completed, leaving behind the scurry of feeding dogs.

"Isabelle!" he roared.

Unlike Caden, she at least hurried over. He didn't like to think about what she would be like when she was Caden's age.

"Father?" Isabelle asked.

"Go and take Caden's horse back to the stables. I want you to unsaddle and water her."

"Why?" Caden protested.

"Because you have other work to do. I need you to take some of the servants and pace the length of the jousting lists. I only want straight lines, and I will check."

Caden scowled. He opened his mouth then closed it. "Yes, Father."

"Caden?"

"Yes Father?"

"Do you still want more sword instruction? If so, you will only get it if I hear no more complaints, and that includes complaints written all over your face."

Caden squared his shoulders and walked away. Meanwhile Isabelle led Caden's horse to the stables, chatting to the animal like she was a friend.

And then they were all gone, leaving Kendrick and Anthea alone in the courtyard, under the rays of morning sunshine. Everyone had their duties. The comparative silence after the hectic morning and frantic previous day was a blessed relief. A new sound filled the air: the music of chirping birds.

Kendrick let out a breath. "Ah, peace. Even a minute is worth something."

"It was an eventful day," Anthea said, and for a brief time they both remembered. "Tell me. What do you think of her?"

"Our new diviner?"

She raised an eyebrow, her voice dry. "Who else, husband?"

"She's certainly young."

"And pretty."

Kendrick glanced at the manor's upper levels, even though they had no chance of being overheard.

"She is going to send the boys mad," Anthea said.

He pretended to be pensive, scratching his stubbled jaw. "Maybe we should send her back," he said, as if considering.

"Maybe we should," Anthea said, smiling slightly. "Someone could get himself into trouble."

"Well. . . I suppose trouble does run in the family."

"You?" Anthea laughed. "You were too busy fighting."

"I had my own encounters with the ladies," Kendrick protested.

"A stolen kiss, or something more?"

Kendrick smiled. "In truth, a few dances. One or two looks across crowded rooms. I have said it once, and I will say it again." He took his wife's hand and raised it to his lips. "I only have eyes for the jewel of my heart."

Anthea's smile broadened, and she leaned forward to give him a quick kiss, brushing her lips against his. "There is a poet in there somewhere. Buried under an old set of armor, a rusty sword, and a very large pile of horse manure."

Kendrick laughed loudly. "And you call me the poet."

Anthea gave a curtsy, before gradually she sobered. "Seriously, Kendrick. As long as we can keep the peace between Troy and Caden, she could really make a difference. Paxton was loyal, and we love him, but the girl has. . ."

"Initiative?" Kendrick replied.

"Courage," Anthea said.

Kendrick turned to face the manor. He had asked the corpus for someone dedicated and yet young enough to grow with his family. Perhaps they had actually listened.

Loud shouting from the direction of the fields broke his reverie. His builders had new help from Sedgeford, and were hard at work. Today, he planned to leave them to it. If there was a problem, they would say.

"Tell me," he asked his wife. "Do you still think it was the right thing to do?"

"The fielding?"

He nodded.

She considered for a moment. "Troy and Caden are both of an age where they need to gain attention and prove themselves. And it won't hurt for Isabelle to be noticed." She glanced at him, amused. "Don't give me that look." She paused. "And you?"

"In truth, I wish I had resisted you more." He rested his eyes on her spider necklace. "It feels like too much of what happens next is out of our control."

She clasped her hand around the silver symbol. "You know as well as I do that everything is the Weaver's hands. It is not for us to understand her plan."

"We each have our own threads, my love. I want the best for our boys, but it is the quiet life for me. I would take down the Star Temple, piece by piece, if I could."

She smiled. "You would not."

"Oh? Watch me. Let me just find a hammer big enough."

He pretended to turn away, before Anthea grabbed his hand, laughing.

◆

Bethany awoke in an oversized bed, wide and heavy, with a soft mattress and thick, luxurious linen. She blinked slowly, her gaze drifting up to the ancient beams that crisscrossed the rafters above. For a moment, she lay still, the unfamiliar surroundings stirring her mind as she pieced together where she was.

She sat up, looking around. Her quarters were the size of her entire dormus back in Everlast. She had a door at the back, with her own personal washroom. A chest hugged the foot of the bed. Multiple wardrobes gave her far too many places to store her few possessions. A cushioned chair sat in front of a dressing table and mirror.

What would her mother make of all this?

Hearing voices, she left the bed and went to the window. She drew the curtains apart, just a little, until she had a view of the courtyard outside the front of the manor. Kendrick and his wife stood together, talking, giving instructions, engaging their children one after the other. Troy came and went, heading for the stables. Dark-haired Caden had to give up his horse, which was led away by his younger sister, before he strode away in the direction of the fields. Kendrick and Anthea looked in the direction of the manor's upper levels, and she almost felt like they had focused on her exact window as they discussed something. Kendrick and his wife laughed. He pulled her toward him by the waist and kissed her on the lips.

The Conways were good people, Charlton had said.

Hearing seven bells chime from some distant room, she started—she had work to do. Leaving the window, she changed out of her bedclothes and dressed herself in one of her favorite new dresses, which was a shining sky blue, decorated with a swathe of silver stars, and short-sleeved to take advantage of the warm summer weather. After washing her face, she brushed her long hair and styled it with a silver clasp set with the symbol of a star.

She stopped and looked around. Her diviner's staff rested in the corner, near a polished wooden stand for hats and coats in the shape of a tree. Her gray cloak draped from one of the tree's branches; she decided to leave it where it was.

Three knocks sounded on the door.

After a hurried glance in the silver mirror on the wall above the dressing table, she called out. "Yes?"

The door opened, and Lady Anthea peeked in, seeing Bethany dressed and ready.

"Ah, Bethany. You are awake. Breakfast is often informal here. Cook has laid out a few things downstairs. Oh, I should have asked. I may call you Bethany?"

"Yes, My Lady, of course. Thank you. I was just on my way down." She smiled apologetically. "I am used to meditation at dawn, and here I am waking up close to seven bells."

"Please," Anthea said. She entered the room all the way. "The last thing you should do is apologize. It was a difficult night. I expected and hoped you would rest longer. Traveling the gateways is hard work, and that is just for those of us who never see what is actually in there."

"You see it, My Lady. You just don't remember it."

Anthea's eyes sparkled. "Ah, but if you don't remember something, then did it really happen at all?"

As Bethany smiled, she studied the older woman, this time in the bright light of morning. Today Anthea wore a brown dress that complemented her straight blonde hair and blue eyes. Cut low and embroidered, the dress was both feminine and dignified, just like the woman who wore it. The spider necklace lay flat against her skin, just above her breasts.

In turn, Anthea was taking in the staff with the orb on top in the corner, and the diviner's cloak draped on the frame, before returning her attention to Bethany.

"I have heard the training is hard, and not all survive. But you are driven. My friends in the corpus say you show strong promise. And more importantly, you work at your weaknesses and turn them into strengths."

Bethany wondered who Anthea had spoken to. Trask? Aurelia? Surely not Gallow. No one had ever said anything like it to her.

"I was surprised when our diviner, Paxton, retired. It is true, travel takes its toll. But I suppose it was the suddenness of it."

Bethany knew who must have influenced Paxton's decision. She already hated starting her new role with a secret to hide from the Conways. She hadn't exactly agreed to share what she learned with her father, but if the emperor asked her directly, what was she supposed to say?

"It is true that travel exacts a toll," she said carefully.

"My husband once had a difficult passage through the gateways. The memory still affects him now. You should probably know, he doesn't like to travel much. Well, I should say it as it is . . . he doesn't like to travel at all." Anthea smiled. "That doesn't mean we will not keep you hard at work. The coming weeks are going to be busy to say the least. Travel to and from the Star Temple. Supplies coming in from afar. Fortunately most days it is goods arriving here, rather than the other way around."

"I want to help in any way I can."

"Yes, you have shown that already. And as for bringing a draft horse and wagon through the Star Temple." Anthea smiled even as she shook her head. "No one has ever tried that before. Perhaps a quieter day might be a good place to start. Today I have organized riding lessons, if it suits you?"

Unable to hide her reaction, Bethany felt excitement bring a flush to her cheeks. She was going to learn to ride a horse. "That would be wonderful. Thank you."

Anthea's rueful smile created dimples in her cheeks. "Wait until you have difficulty sitting down after a morning in the saddle. Later, I will have some letters for you to deliver to the Wheel."

The Wheel of Klare was a hub that enabled information to be quickly sorted and distributed to other gateways. Bethany had traveled there as one of the gateways in her final examination. "I can take your messages directly—"

"The Wheel is best," Anthea interrupted. "You would be traveling the gateways for a week." Her eyes crinkled with mirth. "I send a lot of letters."

"Yes, My Lady."

"Also, Paxton taught Isabelle geography and cartography, as well as writing and numbers, and also about the tapestry. I assume you will be able to instruct her in the same manner?"

"It would be my pleasure."

"Excellent. And finally, if you sense an arrival at the Star Temple, or hear a clarion, you will of course alert either me, my husband, or Hallam, our senior steward, whom I will soon introduce you to. Hallam and I keep a list of scheduled arrivals, whether by road or gateway, but we especially need to know about anything unexpected."

"Of course."

Anthea paused, inspecting Bethany again, and then nodded. "Apply yourself, and you will do well here, Bethany Sylvana."

Chapter Four

THE MANOR WAS QUIET, with the lunch time bustle fading away as the individual members of the household disappeared to attend to their afternoon duties. Bethany sat with Isabelle in the conservatory, diagonally opposite from her younger companion.

The afternoon sun shone on the other site of the manor, and the conservatory was both cool and pleasant. Planters filled with shrubs and flowers lined the glass walls and, overhead, dark green vines enshrouded the transparent ceiling. The air smelled moist and fragrant.

"Now," Bethany asked, "what did Paxton usually teach you?"

Isabelle was staring at the table, but she looked up. Her expression was one of manufactured innocence. Tugging at the locks of hair framing her face, she pretended to think.

"Hmm. . . All sorts of things, I suppose. About Everlast and all the different people who live there. About what it is like to be a diviner and to travel through the gateways." She tilted her head at Bethany. "I think I would like to learn about you, and what you were doing before you came here."

Bethany hid a smile. "Your mother mentioned maps and geography. Letters and numbers."

Isabelle waved a hand. "I know about all that already."

Bethany's smile grew. "I have an idea. You can ask me three questions. And then I will ask you ten questions. And we will go on like that."

Isabelle brightened.

"Now, what would you like to know about first?" Bethany asked.

"I have three questions?" Isabelle curled her hair around her finger. She met Bethany's eyes. "Where are you from?"

"I am from Everlast."

"I knew that. That's not what I meant. I heard somebody say you must be from the Far Reaches."

"Well, my mother is from the Far Reaches. From a place called Loriastris. My father is a Dymantine."

"Does that make you half and half?"

"I don't feel half and half." Bethany smiled. "I would say that I am from the Fabric District. I am from Everlast. There a lot of people in Everlast from all over the place, so it isn't just me. I am from Dymantus, one of the Inner Territories. And finally I come from the Dymantine Empire."

"And you are from the planet Kaspar."

Bethany's smile grew. "Correct, just like you. However it wouldn't feel right to say I come from the Far Reaches, even though I always love learning more about my own past and where my mother grew up. I have never actually been to the Far Reaches."

"Hmm," Isabelle said slowly. "My parents say they come from two worlds. They weren't allowed to be married, but they did it anyway."

"They told you that?"

Isabelle nodded. "It's something to do with the nobles and their orders. They say that I'll be able to marry who I want."

"Whom," Bethany corrected without thinking, hearing her mother's reprimand.

"What?"

"It doesn't matter. We can worry about it another time."

After a moment, Isabelle shrugged. "What was it like growing up in Everlast? I've never been there. They say it's huge."

"Your third question," Bethany said. "Everlast is the capital and it's big, even bigger than you might believe. I didn't leave my district very often, a little like you here, so maybe that helped me make sense of it. My mother worked hard. I suppose we both did. She is. . . was. . . a seamstress."

"What happened to her?"

"You have asked your three questions, Isabelle. Now it's my turn."

Bethany opened the workbook on the table in front of Isabelle, turning to the first of many empty pages. With a reluctant sigh, Isabelle picked up her quill pen.

As Isabelle readied herself, Bethany wriggled in her seat. As time passed, she was becoming increasingly sore from the morning's riding.

"Now," Bethany said. "Let's see where you're at. What can you tell me about a right-angled triangle?"

✦

Bethany sat cross-legged on the Star Temple's main platform, with the steps descending just in front of her. Her eyes were closed as she focused on her breathing. Her diviner's staff lay across her lap.

She had so many new memories to make sense of, and yet she was able to bring about a state of calm in moments. Her thoughts wanted to flit and bounce around, forcing her to dwell on what had already happened and what might happen next, to explore her reactions and feelings. But now wasn't the time.

She instead explored her breathing.

In. . . Out. In. . . Out.

She made herself aware of the trills of the birds in the nearby forest. She experienced the warmth of the sun on the exposed skin of her arms.

"Is she asleep?"

She opened her eyes to see Troy and Caden both watching her as they stood by the bottom of the steps. Both young men wore comfortable clothing, with high boots, trousers, and tunics loose at the arms and neck. Troy's flaxen hair was a little disheveled and his hands were dirty, whereas Caden's darker hair was more neatly styled.

"Sorry," Troy said. "We didn't mean to wake you."

"What are you doing?" Caden asked curiously.

Bethany remained cross-legged. She wasn't irritated; she had allowed plenty of time to meditate, and they were only showing interest in what she was doing. "This is part of what I need to do to get to know this gateway," she explained. "Then, when someone travels here, I will be able to sense them coming."

Troy rubbed his chin. He gave his younger brother a perplexed look. "How?"

"The tapestry resonates. . ." she tried to find the right words, "it hums, like the strings on a mandolin. Part of becoming a diviner is sensing and responding to the vibrations, and then learning how to shape them."

"Is it the same when a clarion sounds?" Troy asked. "Do you need to know the gateway?"

"Exactly the same. A diviner can send a pulse to a gateway, a little like knocking on a door, but I won't hear it if I don't know the gateway, and I wouldn't be able to send one either. That's why I'm here."

"What about the staff?" Caden asked. "Is it special? Or will any staff work?"

"It's special."

Bethany climbed to her feet. From her position at the top of the steps, she faced the pair of brothers. "Do either of you have an iron crown?"

Caden pulled a coin out of a pocket. "I do."

"Throw it to me," she said. "Watch."

Caden flicked his thumb and she focused on the coin as it sailed toward her, flipping over and over. She allowed it to bounce off the stone, and then she thrust out her staff.

The coin clinked as it stuck to the metal orb.

"The staff is magnetic. Among other things."

"Impressive," Troy said.

Bethany pulled the iron crown away from the orb, needing some force to detach it. She flicked the coin back to Caden, pleased at her dexterity in front of the two young men.

But then, as Caden caught the coin out of the air, something occurred to her.

"Hold on," she said with a frown. "You grew up with a diviner in the household. Didn't Paxton tell you these things?"

Troy opened his mouth and then closed it. "Well. . ." he said hesitantly. He looked like he was trying to suppress a grin. "He did, but not in the same way you are."

Caden didn't even try. His lips spread in a crooked smile. "I think she might have found us out, brother."

Bethany put on a cold expression. "I have work to do. I am sure that you both do as well."

"Wait," Troy said quickly. "I actually did come down here to ask you something."

"Ask me what?"

"I've won several prizes for horse riding. If you like, I can give you some extra lessons?"

Caden pretended to splutter. "More riding lessons? Don't you remember how sore you were when you learned? Allow her some time to recover." He shook his head, before leveling her with an earnest expression of his own. "I could take you on a tour of the estate? I know some pleasant walks."

Bethany couldn't remain angry. She smiled, as the two young men continued to look up at her. "As I said, I am busy."

The sound of a horse whinnying made the brothers turn toward the manor. Isabelle was riding down the path, easily bobbing up and down with her mount's rolling motions before she pulled up. One day, Bethany would look like that on a horse.

"Father is asking for you both," Isabelle said. "He thought you might be here. He said to leave the poor girl alone." She put a hand to her mouth. "I don't know if I was supposed to say that last part."

Bethany nodded in the direction of the manor. "You heard the lady. From the sound of things, play time is over."

She didn't know if she had gone too far, but Caden laughed out loud. "Well said, Diviner Sylvana. I suppose we will see you at dinner."

Caden gave her a little bow and turned away. Troy's blue eyes lingered on her before he left too, and she was facing their backs as they walked beside Isabelle upon her horse.

She shook her head and then sat down again. With the gateway at her back, she set her staff across her knees, closed her eyes, and the rest of the world vanished from her mind.

Chapter Five

BETHANY WAS DREAMING. She sat at a polished table and tried to eat a fish from a golden plate, but the fish was still alive and flopped about in a frenzy. Across from her, Lord Kendrick Conway was asking her something, eyebrows together, becoming more and more insistent, but she couldn't concentrate. Meanwhile, her elegant cutlery kept sliding away from her fingers when she tried to pick it up.

Her dream shifted.

She was passing a doorway, glancing in to see Lady Anthea praying at the manor's chapel. When Anthea turned Bethany's way, her eyes were bleeding red tears.

Another shift.

Trees whisked past her as she rode a maddened horse. She tumbled from the saddle and fell down, down, to fall into the waters of a raging river. When she swam to the bank and climbed out of the water, there she was, up on horseback again. She had companions. Up ahead, on two dappled mares, Lord Kendrick and Lady Anthea kept drawing away from her, and she kicked in her heels as she struggled to keep up with them. Then something bumped her from the left, and there was Troy, deliberately knocking into her, trying to ruin her balance. Another bump came from the right; Caden grinned with mischief as he charged his mount into hers. A high-pitched voice kept calling her name, and there was Isabelle, standing in the road, directly in her way. Isabelle screamed. Bethany was about to gallop directly into her; in moments her horse's hooves would churn the girl into the mud. The scream was like the ringing of a bell.

She gasped as her eyes shot open.

For a time she didn't know where she was. It was sometime in the middle of the night. She was staring at long dark shapes: black rafters crossing the ceiling. Sweat coated her skin. Her bedcovers were rumpled. The sound of Isabelle's piercing scream remained, a remembrance she was struggling to dispel.

Wait. Something was actually happening.

It began as a low hum that rose in pitch. Her stomach felt it first, before the sensation grew and spread throughout her torso. It was something real, strong enough to penetrate through her slumber. There truly was a ringing, but felt inside her bones, within her body. The humming vibration continued to spread from her head to her toes. The tone climbed higher and then fell.

This was something she had learned about in her classes. She and the other students had stood in the Crystal Dome and experienced the pulsating up and down, in and out, of a gateway making an announcement.

What she was feeling was called a clarion. She was the Conways' house diviner. The Star Temple was under her care. Responding was one of her duties.

From her position on her back, she swiftly rolled over to throw herself out of bed. She threw on a dark brown dress. Grabbing her diviner's cloak, she gathered it over her shoulders and also took hold of her staff. She then headed out of her room, along the hallway, and down the wooden stairs, hearing each step creak as she descended with quick but quiet footsteps.

The manor was dark and still. Stars lit up the night sky outside the windows and the moon cast a silvery glow. She put on her riding boots and opened the main door. After departing the manor, she headed straight for the stables.

The clarion was no longer sounding. Most likely, whoever had sounded it was coming to the Star Temple, and was already on their way.

She heard the gentle snorts of the horses before she saw them. Opening the wooden gate, she entered the stables and passed several strong horses on the way to her smaller mount. The gelding snorted, pawing at the ground when he noticed her coming, and she opened the gate to take him by the halter and lead him out.

The blanket was in the same place it always was, and she laid it on her horse's back. The saddle came next, and she cinched the girth under the gelding's belly. She then led her horse out of the stables and out into the open.

Aware of time passing, she nonetheless remembered her instruction and checked the girth a second time. She then took a breath and grabbed hold of the pommel. When she put a foot in the stirrup and mounted up, she was pleased when she didn't wobble. She held the reins firmly, nudging the horse's flanks with her heels as she made a clicking sound with her mouth. The horse was well-trained. At her gentle urging, he began to walk.

She now followed the road to the manor's lower gate. Between the two towers, a pair of guards in uniforms stood watching her approach.

"Lady?" The younger of the pair spoke up. Tall and rangy, he had an odd habit of squinting. "Is there trouble? Do you need an escort?"

"A clarion," she said. "I'm heading down to the Star Temple to find out who it is."

The rangy guard exchanged glances with his older companion, who was gray-haired, with a thin beard stretching from ear to ear.

"Hold on," the bearded guard said. "We'll get you a few men from the guard house."

"Thank you, but I can manage well enough on my own," she said.

"It is better if some men go with you," the rangy guard said.

Bethany didn't want to miss the new arrival at the Star Temple. She was only just developing an affinity for the gateway, and didn't know how long it had taken for the clarion to break through her slumber.

"There are guards down at the Star Temple," she said. "I would rather not wait."

The rangy guard hesitated. "Very well. As you wish." He indicated that the road was hers.

"Never forget, we are here for your protection," the bearded guard said, tapping the stag insignia on his uniform.

"Thank you," she said.

With rising urgency, she nudged her horse at a walking pace through the gate then dug in her heels a little harder. Her horse gamely picked up the pace, shifting to a trot, and then she urged him on to a canter.

She moved her body with the horse underneath her, the way she had been taught. The trees lining the road passed swiftly on both sides. The route descended, and soon the clearing containing the Star Temple lay at the bottom of the road ahead.

Another pair of guards manning the gateway were already on their feet, hands on swords as they watched her. "Lady? Is anything amiss?"

"I don't believe so," she answered, quickly but clearly. "I heard a clarion."

"At this hour?"

She dismounted and tied her horse to a tree. As she finished and hurried toward the Star Temple, her skin tingled. The tingling grew stronger; now that she was developing an affinity for Esk's gateway, this was what she would feel anytime someone used it.

The two guards with her warily watched the Star Temple from the bottom of the stairway. She remained a short distance behind them.

"Be ready," she instructed. "The gateway is about to open."

The moment she finished speaking a flash of light accompanied a sizzle. A diagonal tear opened in the air, within the span of the triangular stone frame. The gash became a black hole, which widened, turning and changing shape. The mirrored doorway grew in size to become a tall rectangle, shimmering with stars before someone stepped out.

He was a middle-aged man in leather boots and black clothing, with a diviner's gray cloak on his shoulders and a staff held vertically in his hand. Drooping eyes gave him a long-suffering expression, and his brown hair was more than a little tousled.

She waited, but no one else came. Aware of her duties, she climbed to the stop of the steps to greet the newcomer.

The diviner glanced from side to side, perplexed. He raised his staff to keep the gateway open.

"Welcome to Esk," Bethany said.

The weary-looking diviner continued to search, frowning as he looked at the watching guards. "My apologies. . . I know where I am, but where is Diviner Paxton?"

"My name is Diviner Bethany Sylvana. I am the Conways' new house diviner."

His face registered surprise. "Oh?" He took in the guards' uniforms. As a member of the corpus, Bethany didn't wear house insignia. "I have instructions to deliver this to Diviner Paxton and no one else." He hesitated, before displaying a scroll. "Either to him or to the lord and lady."

"Very well. Would you like to come with me to the manor?"

He cast a quick look back at the shimmering black portal. "You are the Conways' new house diviner?" He again took note of the guards. And after all, Bethany had been here to greet him. "I ask that you deliver this as instructed. It must go straight to the hand of Lord Kendrick or Lady Anthea."

"The choice is yours. . ." Bethany said. "You may also wish to come to the manor to rest."

"Rest." He grunted a short laugh. "If you knew my master, you would know the word does not enter his vocabulary. I thank you, however, my prompt return is expected."

"And your master is?" she murmured, more to herself than anyone else, as she inspected the seal. The stylized emblem displayed a spider straddling a star, but didn't know the noble houses well enough to place it.

"Lord Declan Quinn of Graystone. Lady Anthea's brother." The diviner gave a resigned shrug. "He tends to work late at night. I must be on my way. Good evening."

"Good evening."

The diviner turned back to the darkness contained in the triangular frame, and a moment later, he was gone.

She held the scroll gingerly. She had almost certainly just met Declan Quinn of Graystone's house diviner. Her father's words came back to her. *If you sense trouble, I must know it.*

The seal was intact. There was no way she could break it.

And she wasn't even sure if she wanted to.

✦

Bethany slowed her horse to a walk as she rode through Fernley Manor's lower gate. The rangy guard was missing, but she smiled at the bearded older guard, who gave her a nod and wished her good night.

The moon had drifted higher. Visions of her bed came easily to her mind. But as she neared the manor, where silver light glowed upon the courtyard, her eyes widened, for out the front was Lord Kendrick. He was pacing back and forth, evidently waiting for her. Turning and spying her, he called out to someone on the other side of the courtyard: the rangy guard who had been missing back at the gate. He said something to the uniformed guard, who called back a reply.

Kendrick beckoned her over to where he stood. She reined in and dismounted carefully, relieved when both her feet were on the ground. As she turned to face him, his grim expression made her stomach tighten. Why was he here? And why were his eyes so cold?

He didn't immediately say anything. His face was like stone as he looked at the scroll in her hand, long enough to note the spider and star insignia.

"My wife's brother works into the night. If you can call it working. He also has a flair for the dramatic. And little concern about the nighttime routines of others." He put out his hand. "Give it to me."

Bethany handed over the scroll.

Kendrick raised his voice. "Farrell? Take her horse back to the stable, would you?"

"Of course, My Lord."

Kendrick waited until the guard and horse were both gone. He held up the scroll. "We can leave this in the lady's study. She can open it in the morning." He stared into her eyes. "Now, you and I need to reach an understanding."

Bethany's stomach gave another lurch when she heard the tone in his voice. She had heard him have cold words for his sons, but never for her.

"Forgive my plain speech, Bethany, but I know that your father is missing or dead. At any rate, he abandoned you and left you to your mother to raise. She is now blind and nearly half of your income goes to buying the medicine she needs. Do I have that right?"

She nodded.

He raised his voice. "And yet you go out at night, on your own, without an escort. What do you know of this country and the creatures that lurk in the darkness? You are still a newcomer here. You are a part of my household, which means you are my responsibility. Your safety is important, to me, to my family. The world is not a safe place."

"I heard a clarion—"

"I don't care. If you go out at night, take an escort with you. My men will follow your orders. They have instructions to do so. For as long as you are my house diviner, you are part of my family. I am responsible for you. No harm will come to you as long as you are under my protection. Do you understand?"

"Yes, Lord Conway."

"Good," he said. "Now get yourself back to bed."

✦

"Kendrick?" Anthea called. Crisp morning light filled the manor as Kendrick followed Anthea's voice, coming to a doorway to find her seated at the table in the conservatory. Looking up, she beckoned him over. "Come over here. We need to talk."

He could guess what she wanted to talk to him about, especially when he saw her brother's message in her hand, but he still had yet to learn its contents. He reluctantly entered the conservatory. Facing east, it was always a little too warm in the morning, which meant that whatever she was saying, she didn't want to be overheard.

"We need to talk." Kendrick repeated the phrase as he took a seat at the table. "The words that make a chill go up and down my spine."

As he waited, he heard Isabelle and Bethany's voices from upstairs. Poor Bethany; he wondered how she ever managed to find time for herself. Isabelle seemed to follow her everywhere.

He rubbed the stubble on his chin. "I hope I wasn't too harsh on her." He had already told Anthea about the previous night. "In truth, she has settled in well."

"Hmm? Bethany?" Anthea was re-reading her brother's message. "I doubt you would be. You are always soft with women. I do agree about her settling in. She is clever and works hard. The children like her."

"The children. . ." Kendrick thought about his sons. "Perhaps a little too much sometimes."

Anthea still sounded distracted. "Some healthy competition might be good for the boys. They need to show themselves well at the fielding."

"As long as they know their boundaries."

"They do. I have spoken with them." Her expression was serious as she met his eyes. "At length."

"Hopefully the poor girl doesn't realize—"

"Kendrick." Anthea held up the paper. "We need to talk about this."

He sighed. "Very well." From her expression, his wife was thinking hard. "What does it say?"

She handed him the paper. "Here."

He took the scroll and read the contents quickly. The message wasn't long. But as expected, it dispelled any thoughts of a relaxed morning. His hand holding the message fell to the table as he worked to understand the implications.

"He says that it's true," Anthea said. "Rigel met a woman while campaigning in the Far Reaches. Not only were they together, they were married, before Rigel even became general. . ."

Kendrick finished for her, "And they also had a child."

Anthea nodded. "But Declan does not yet know who the child is. Nor has he found the mother. Aside from what people have told him, he has no proof at all."

"More rumors, then."

"Kendrick, this is Declan. We both know he is not prone to wild speculation. If he says it, he believes it."

"If he reveals this, at the fielding. . ." Kendrick's brow furrowed. "He wouldn't, would he?"

"He is my brother. He has no wish to cause us trouble. We simply have to get through the fielding, with our sons knighted and our estate in one piece. As far as I can see, at this moment, this message doesn't change anything."

"I understand his motivation, but surely he knows we could be talking about some boy living in a tiny village in the Far Reaches? How old would the child be anyway?" Kendrick stared into the distance, unable to prevent himself from working it out. "Let's see. Rigel became emperor over twenty years ago... the child would be at least that old. Very well, then. Not quite a child after all. But who is to say that he—or she— would make a suitable emperor? Declan should instead be trying to replace Julian with someone with broad support. Perhaps a man like Agapon."

"You know what Agapon is like. He would never abandon the fight in Jaynia. Blood is blood, Kendrick. This is the succession we are talking about."

"True. But you understand the point I'm making." Kendrick held up the message. "What does your brother want us to do with this?"

"Ask questions, of course."

"Questions. . . We would need to be discreet."

"In the extreme."

"And what should we say to him in reply?"

"Isn't it clear? He wants our promise of help."

"Very well. We will promise him to make some enquiries of our own. We will also ask that he refrain from any open action until after the fielding. Agreed?"

Even as Kendrick finished speaking and Anthea nodded, he heard Bethany and Isabelle's voices much louder now as they headed down to the manor's ground floor.

"Bethany?" Anthea called.

Kendrick heard Bethany's voice in the distance.

"Wait here," she said.

A moment later Bethany came to the conservatory's doorway. Isabelle appeared behind her; his daughter had completely ignored Bethany's instruction.

"Can I help, My Lady?" Bethany asked.

"I need you to deliver a message to Graystone."

Bethany nodded. "The Stone Circle of Graystone. Of course."

Anthea was already scribbling. She muttered to herself as she wrote. "Enquires. . . very discreet. . . no action. . . after the fielding. . ."

Anthea wrote some more, finishing with her name, before rolling the paper and tying it with a brown ribbon. She then took a stick of brown wax she had on the table and went to one of the lamps to light it. She returned to the table, flattened the scroll and dripped the wax onto the paper. Finally she squashed the wax with her personal seal, leaving an impression of a stag with a branch in his mouth.

"Here," she said, passing the scroll to Bethany. As Bethany took the message, Anthea met her eyes. "Right away, please. And do not place this into any hand but my brother's. Wait there for his reply."

"Will I be staying long?" Bethany asked.

"No longer than you need to. Take an escort." Anthea raised an eyebrow at Kendrick. "Troy?"

"Eh?" Kendrick was still worried. "Troy is busy getting feed for a thousand horses."

"Take Caden," Anthea said to Bethany. "You should find him in the archery field."

Chapter Six

BETHANY AND CADEN RODE together to Graystone Abbey. They had just traveled to a completely different part of the empire in no time at all, and yet Bethany felt almost clear-headed. She had slept well in her comfortable bed, and as she bobbed up and down on her horse, the cool mountain air dispelled the lingering effects of the Weaver's Breath. Caden also appeared to be in good spirits, pleased to have a reprieve from his training.

Together, they climbed a winding trail on a hillside. The abbey couldn't be missed, high and forbidding as it clung to the side of a jagged peak. A gray sky spread above, heavy like a smothering blanket, with clouds moving on the hard wind.

Bethany turned her head, surprised to see how far they had come, and how small the stone circle that served as Graystone's gateway now appeared. Past the ring of monoliths, the rolling landscape of northern Weiland was just like she had imagined: rugged and windswept, filled with sheep and cattle, with plenty of scrub but not much in the way of trees.

"Impressive, isn't it?"

Caden was focused on the abbey, which grew larger as they climbed the road. It looked nothing like the temples and cathedrals she was familiar with from the Corpus District in Everlast. Instead the abbey was made from dark stone, with multiple levels rising to points that mirrored the shapes of the surrounding mountains. Black gates rivaled the great gates at the Nexus's main entrance. Above the gates, tiered battlements with walls like rows of teeth climbed one above the other.

Glancing her way, Caden noticed her wide-eyed stare. "Uncle Declan told me it's an old fortress repurposed to be an abbey. And now it is something different again, and he has turned it into an archive. He has gathered more than a million books inside. Not just any books either. Important ones."

With its brooding appearance, Bethany didn't find it hard to imagine vaulted rooms inside, filled with bookshelves stacked high. "Why?"

"He thinks the empire is doomed. He has written an entire book about it. He's incredibly intelligent. Everyone says so."

Bethany winced when she timed the movements of her gelding poorly. In contrast, Caden rode easily beside her on a beautiful black mare. His riding costume was elegant, and with his brown hair combed and face cleanly shaved, he looked every inch the lord's son. In keeping with the cooler climate, beneath her gray diviner's cloak Bethany wore a long-sleeved dress in deep crimson with stars embroidered on the collar.

"What does your father say?"

"Father would say what everyone else says. The empire is eternal. Seven centuries is a long time."

"Eternity is a lot longer."

He nodded. "You understand. People say Uncle Declan speaks only of doom, but perhaps he is just a realist, perhaps he is only being wise. If he were ever proved right," he gazed up ahead, "his archive could mean everything to the people trying to rebuild."

"Is it true he lost his son?" She had learned all about the duel from her father, just as she had also heard it discussed around Fernley Manor. They would expect her to be curious.

"My cousin, Bryan. We never saw a lot of each other, but that doesn't mean it's easy to bear. They outlawed duels for a reason. People drink too much and someone dies."

She decided to change the topic. "What does it mean, that your uncle is the head of an order?"

"You know about the three orders?"

"Only a little."

"The Blacks, the Reds, the Blues. . . the Wardens, the Crusaders, and the Guildsmen. My father belongs to the Wardens, and no doubt when the time comes Troy will join him too. The Wardens stand for caution. . . for holding onto the past, never making big moves, for feeling the way forward with care."

From the little she knew about Lord Kendrick and his personality, it didn't surprise her to hear which group he belonged to. "And the Crusaders?"

"The Order of Crusaders—it is as pompous as it sounds. The Reds are all about military conquest, about expanding the borders of the empire. They see the empire as a civilizing force, to be imposed by necessity upon the barbarians outside."

From Caden's words, he wasn't enamored by either group he had described. "What about the other group, the Guildsmen?"

"The Blues are all about embracing change. Sometimes you have to reinvent yourself in order to go forward. Sometimes holding onto the past can make you blind to the fact that the present has changed forever. Our enemies could make new advances that make their weapons or tactics superior to ours. We have to be mindful of progress."

"Which group does your uncle lead?"

"The Blues, of course. If you read his book, you would know he couldn't be anything else. He believes the empire can't last another fifty years."

"Fifty? For that to happen—"

"There is no guarantee it will simply keep going. When gateways fail, we don't know how to repair them. You would know that. We should be learning, studying, trying to make new gateways, rather than rely on the ones the Eidar left us. We've been at war in the Far Reaches for decades. Now we've got these Veldrians on the southern border, and whatever we are telling them, they haven't gone away."

"They also haven't attacked—"

"Imagine if they found out about the fielding. How would they react? We should have reformed the Armies of the West years ago. Now, it might be too late. Everything moves so slowly. People like my father aren't helping."

Caden broke off now that they were nearly at the abbey. Bethany was relieved; she didn't want him to say anything he regretted, and she kept her own mouth closed.

As they slowed their horses, she tilted her head back to look up at the nearest tower to the gates, which was broad and black, encircled by balconies and displaying open slots for archers. Flags snapped in the wind: a wheel against blue, alongside the empire's gold and crimson crown on a field of purple. Soldiers watched from high above, but they were small, too distant to make out faces. The abbey's gates were wide open. She was traveling a little behind Caden as he led her straight through to the open yard.

Graystone Abbey was even more impressive from within, and she was only seeing the foremost part of it. She entered an area open to the elements, framed by stone walls with multiple climbing stairways. The tower she had already seen wasn't the only one; there were at least half a dozen more, some of them even taller.

Caden dismounted, and she followed suit, taking one foot from the stirrup and throwing her leg over until she slid to the ground. She glanced around. It was her best descent yet, but there was no one else to notice.

Youths came forward to take their horses, boys in gray uniforms whom Caden completely ignored. Then Caden's expression changed, and Bethany turned as a lean man came through an archway with his arms held wide open. He was tall and thin-limbed, with combed hair the color of ash and a high forehead. Like Caden, he was clean-shaven and wore high leather boots and black clothing.

"Caden! Unexpected, but in a wonderful way. It is good to see you, lad."

Caden grinned as he and the older man embraced, clapping each other on the back. "You too, Uncle Declan."

"And who is this?" Declan made a show of looking surprised to see Bethany. The hood of her cloak was back, revealing her glossy copper hair, held back with her clasp in the shape of a star. With her staff in hand, there was no doubting who she was. "What happened to Paxton?"

"He retired," Caden said.

"Right before the fielding?"

"Uncle. . ." Caden was smiling but he spoke with an admonishing tone. "You know everything that happens in the empire. Don't pretend you weren't already aware."

Declan didn't contradict his nephew. His eyes twinkled as he also became amused. "I can see the expression on your father's face when Paxton told him."

"Worse even than that." Caden grinned. He indicated Bethany. "This is Diviner Bethany Sylvana."

"My Lord." Bethany bowed her head; he was the lord of Graystone, and she was in his domain.

"Hmm. . ." Declan considered. "Let me guess. Loriastris?"

She was surprised. "My mother, My Lord. I was born in Everlast."

"A pleasure to meet you, Divine One." He smiled when he noticed her confusion. "Did you know that's once how we addressed diviners, not two centuries ago?" He turned back to Caden. "Now, I have been expecting a visit, perhaps from my younger sister in person but I suppose she is busy. Is this a long stay? I would love to show you my archive." He rested his eyes on Bethany. "You would love my archive. I have volumes even the corpus thought lost to the past."

"We cannot stay for long, I am afraid." Caden glanced around. "Aunt Meredith? Is she here?"

Declan's expression became strained, which perhaps said a lot; he seemed the type to be adept at hiding his emotions. "Your aunt is home at Ashton Manor, Caden. I will send her your regards."

"Please do. Tell her I wish her well." Caden started, remembering the message. "Here. We came to bring you this."

Caden nodded at Bethany, who handed him the sealed scroll she had brought. "My Lord," she said as he took it.

"Thank you," Declan said solemnly.

"Mother said to wait for your reply," Caden said.

"Well then, if that is the case I can make your visit last as long as I like." Declan gave a dry chuckle, waving a hand. "My jest. I know you both have duties to attend to. Very well then. Let us see what you mother has to say."

He broke the seal, unfurling the scroll to read swiftly. Whatever he was thinking as he read, it wasn't revealed on his face.

"Hmm," Declan said, lowering the scroll. "Very well, Caden." His tone was still light, but his eyes had tightened. "It appears my own sister doesn't trust my discretion." He paused, before reaching a decision. "Please. Both of you. Come with me."

He led Caden and Bethany through a doorway and up some steps, made of the same dark stone as everything else. After following a broad corridor with a ceiling twice their height, they came to an open door. Declan beckoned for them to follow him into the room as he sat at a desk and slid over a piece of paper to rest on the surface in front of him.

Unlike some other studies Bethany had visited, there were few books. Instead, a sideboard lay covered in sealed scrolls, each neatly arranged, one beside the other. The desk in front of Declan had paper, ink, and multiple quill pens. As Declan swiftly wrote his reply to his sister, brow furrowed, making neat little letters, she had no difficulty seeing him working late into the night.

She remembered his house diviner, the man with weary eyes and disheveled hair. She was only beginning to learn how fortunate she was with the Conways.

Declan finished, rolling and sealing the scroll with gray wax to make the imprint of a spider straddling a star. He handed his reply to Caden.

"There," he said. "Your parents and I are in agreement. Discretion is the word, as they should know me well enough to count on. I am sure that the fielding will be a success." He cleared his throat. "Now, I do realize you need to be going, but can I convince you to stay a little longer?" He raised an eyebrow at Bethany. "A diviner's work is not easy. My food isn't quite as good as what they serve at Fernley Manor, but it is certainly passable."

"Thank you," Bethany said carefully. "I am ready to travel." She turned toward Caden.

"Apologies, Uncle, but Mother was clear," Caden said regretfully. "It is always good to see you."

"Very well, very well. . ." Declan let out an elaborate sigh. "Back the way you came, then."

Returning to his feet, Declan ushered them from the room. Soon he was once more descending the steps, leading them out to the graveled yard where, after being fed and watered, their horses were soon brought out.

"Until next time, my boy. Good luck with the fielding. You are a full-grown man now. I have no doubt you will do well."

Caden blushed at the praise, giving his uncle another embrace before he climbed up onto his horse's back.

"And a pleasure to meet you, Diviner Sylvana," Declan said.

"My Lord," Bethany replied.

As she and Caden walked their horses through the abbey's imposing gates, and dug in their heels to put on speed, she reflected upon what she had learned.

Declan Quinn didn't seem as difficult as people made out. He had lost his son. He obviously cared about Caden. Instead, he seemed clever. Energetic. Perhaps somewhat manipulative.

He wanted to hurt Julian. But Julian was the emperor's son—his heir—and there probably wasn't much that he could do.

Chapter Seven

AS THE FIELDING BEGAN, Bethany had never been so busy.

Throughout the morning of the fielding's first day, Esk's gateway was in constant use. Bethany's skin tingled so much she wondered if people thought it strange to see her shivering in the height of summer. Most of the high-status arrivals came through the Star Temple, and she was there nearly all the time, greeting lords and ladies and their retinues, offering respite to diviners. She directed newcomers to the fields, along the roads that were now decorated with large white stones on both sides, where others would help them find their tents and pavilions. Dressed in a variety of costumes, from wealthy finery to soldierly splendor, they came to seek position for themselves or their sons and daughters, for the excitement of the spectacle, and to learn how their status compared with their compatriots in the seating. They came for the fun, to make wagers, to eat hearty food and to drink wine and ale. To make new friends. To show up old enemies.

For many, however, the fielding wasn't about pleasure; it was work, the pursuit of their military profession. A great deal of effort had been going on behind the scenes. Making an army wasn't something that could happen overnight.

Bethany now stood in front of the Star Temple, waiting for the next group of arrivals and rubbing her arms in a vain attempt to dispel the sensation on her skin. The gateway peeled open. The rectangular doorway took shape, and a diviner stepped out, calm and focused, staff held high as he led his group.

The diviner's hood was back, revealing black hair curling to his collar. As he checked on his wards, the young man was tall, with pale skin and a sheen of stubble on his sharp jawline, the faintest shadow to match the shade of his hair. Most noticeable were his deep brown eyes. Even as he called back to his followers, his gaze returned to the area ahead, searching.

He spied Bethany at the bottom of the steps. All of a sudden his expression changed, lighting up.

"Xander!" she called out without thinking.

He leveled her with a broad smile as she remembered her duties and bit her tongue; she should instead be greeting the people he had brought with him. Fortunately they were still dazed, unresponsive as the effect of travel worked its way through them.

Xander was leading a delegation from the corpus. Trailing behind him, shaking themselves as the haze of travel cleared, came at least a dozen black-robed confessors. The foremost was an ancient man, lean and straight-backed, with a pattern of white lines like a woven lattice on his robe. Seeing the pattern—the warp and weft—Bethany's eyes widened, even as the elderly confessor blinked away his confusion to focus on her waiting figure.

She cleared her throat. "Welcome," she said, placing her palms together. "Welcome, confessors of the corpus."

"Divine One," the ancient confessor at the front acknowledged.

"Please, come this way," Bethany said.

Xander had paused on the temple's platform, so that Bethany was waiting off to the side of the stairway as his group descended. Clearly in charge of his companions, the ancient confessor looked again at Bethany, and his serious gray eyes met hers. With his quiet assurance and smooth, ivory skin, he projected an aura of both serenity and wisdom.

Once they were all on ground level, she indicated the beginning of the road marked with white stones. "Please follow the white stones to the fields. A steward at the top of the path will direct you onward."

"Thank you, Divine One," the ancient confessor replied solemnly.

The old man in the striking robe departed, along with his followers, leaving Bethany out the front of the Star Temple with her mouth open. "Was that. . .?"

"The high confessor, Roman Valaeric," Xander said as he came up beside her, a little awestruck himself. "He decided to come early, so we didn't have much time to prepare. I think he did it on purpose."

Bethany was still struck by the strange sense of calm she had felt in the high confessor's presence. Unlike some of the lords, or her father, she hadn't felt worried about how she was being judged. Instead, she had felt like she could trust him. And she had only been with him for seconds.

"I knew you were working for the corpus . . . but to guide the high confessor. . ."

"Apparently he likes to give his trust to the new diviners."

"Even so, they chose you. . ."

Turning back to Xander, she forgot all about the high confessor. She couldn't believe he was standing here in front of her, just the two of them, alone. Her heart felt like it was rising through her body and she found herself wanting to smile. She was conscious of her own hair and clothing; she had brushed her copper hair until it was straight and shining, and with the hood of her diviner's cloak back, she hoped it looked as well as it had when she fashioned it in the mirror. Her long-sleeved dress was her favorite: sky blue and figure-hugging, with a swathe of stars across her torso. Under his gray cloak, Xander wore a shimmering silver tunic decorated with a crescent moon above his heart, embracing a star in the same shade.

For a moment neither of them spoke. There had been no warning; she hadn't known she was about to see him, and in the unique circumstance they hadn't even embraced.

"How. . . how are you?" she asked.

"I'm well. I wasn't supposed to be working but I begged a favor." He gave her his familiar crooked smile. "I've always wanted to go to Esk. Seeing you was just a happy accident."

"You horrible person," she said, but she was laughing.

His expression became serious. "Honestly, I haven't been able to think of anything else. It's good. . . really good to see you. I've missed you." He looked like he was about to say something else but then corrected himself. "I know you must be busy. I won't take much of your time. How is it all going?"

"Exciting. Frantic. Nerve-wracking. Surprising. In truth, part of me can't believe I've been given so much responsibility. And we've only just begun."

"You'll make it through. You always do."

She cleared her throat; she could feel color come to her cheeks, not just at his words, but at the way he was looking at her. "How long do you have?"

He became crestfallen. "I'm returning right away."

"Oh."

She watched his face, and then his eyes changed, their brown shade twinkling and sparkling with golden flecks.

"Bethany." He grinned. "It's me. I don't have long, but we both know I'm allowed some time to rest."

She gave him a playful slap. "I have some time until the next arrival. I will sense it, anyway, when they are about to come."

He surprised her by taking her hand. "That path," he asked, nodding toward a trail that left the clearing containing the Star Temple, "where does it lead?"

"To the lake."

"Is it a pretty lake?"

"Beautiful."

"Good. Then how about we go for a walk?"

✦

Xander released her hand as soon as they started walking. Her disappointment made her study his face, but he was simply concentrating on his footing. Together they followed the forested path, stepping between roots and crunching pine needles underfoot. Rippling water appeared through the trees and the forest opened up as they emerged onto the grassy bank of a small lake.

Xander stopped for a moment, closing his eyes as he inhaled. He released his breath, opening his eyes at the same time. "By the stars, it's good to be out of Everlast." He turned to her and smiled. "And to be with you."

A long low log rested by the waterside, and without any communication between them, they moved to sit side by side. She turned her body at an angle. Would he take her hand again? She didn't know, but she knew she wanted him to.

The sun glowed on the treetops and sparkled on the shifting waters. Xander asked her about her new life. She asked him about his. He surprised her by saying she seemed happy, and she realized perhaps she was. When she asked him about his family, he was obviously proud that his position and income had helped return his family's trading business to a solid footing.

After a time, there was silence, and he took another slow breath. "It is beautiful here. . . no one could ever doubt that." He smiled and shook his head. "I can still barely believe you got this position."

She changed the topic. "You sound like you live on your own?"

He nodded. "I have my own dormus, near the Corpus District. I wouldn't be able to do my work if I was out in Westhill." He hesitated. "I . . . I went to see Carina."

Her breath caught. She turned to face him directly. "And? How is she?"

He didn't reply immediately, staring out at the lake for a time. "She sits in a chair, by a window, and rarely speaks. When she saw me, it was like she didn't recognize me. I asked her questions, if she was well, that sort of thing. She said she was fine. I mentioned your name. . ."

Bethany watched him carefully, waiting upon every word.

". . .and she gave me a little smile, as if she were remembering. And that was it. That was all that passed between us."

Bethany reached out and took his hand, giving him a brief squeeze.

Meanwhile he continued to rest his troubled gaze upon the lake. "I saw her, but I still miss her. Does that make sense? I miss the old Carina. She's gone now. And no one knows if she will ever return."

"I just wish they had let us see her, right after it happened. We were her friends. I don't know. . . perhaps we could have helped her."

"It was cruel. I don't care. That's how it feels to me."

"I don't know if they really knew what was best for her, but I have to believe she would have wanted to see us. To know that we cared about her and were there for her." She cleared her throat. "Thank you, Xander. I haven't had a chance—"

"I know that. Everyone knows that. Have you even had time to go back to see your mother?"

She shook her head.

"I saw how it affected you when Carina. . . when she left. I'll never forget how you were in the library. I was worried about you."

"In truth, I still feel frustrated. Doesn't it bother you? We graduated, but there must be more than what they taught us. Why can't we build a gateway for ourselves? How is it that a stone circle and a staff can warp the tapestry—?"

"—Bethany. . ."

She spoke more rapidly. It was rare these days that she had an opportunity to talk about the diviner's craft. "Have you noticed how different one gateway is from another? Some are like this, some like that. To solve the problem of building them or repairing them, we need to learn about them, to understand them. . . that makes sense, doesn't it?

"Of course—"

"—For example, the light ones, the gateways that are just a circle of thin stones . . . what would happen if the stones were even thinner? Or just sticks in the ground?"

"I have a feeling that wouldn't work."

"Why?" Facing him, she spread her hands.

His smile faded and he shrugged. "I don't know."

"We're heavier than sticks in the ground. Have you ever noticed how you can feel the people near you, as well as the gateway, when you first open it? Especially if you know them. That seems to make the effect stronger. Is that why they make us do our final examination with someone we know well?"

"I suppose it could be. . ."

"Imagine if we could make the gateways we need, rather than build the empire around what's already there. Imagine if we could build gateways here, there, on the frontier, deep in enemy territory . . . the possibilities are endless. It would change everything."

Xander was watching her with his head tilted. "Fascinating. . ." he murmured.

"What?"

"It is also people who change everything."

She nodded. "True. We say that everyone who has ever lived or died makes a thread on the tapestry. We all have a shining light. We all warp the tapestry, by our actions, by the effect we have on others." She stared into his eyes. Surely he had experienced and wondered about the same things she had? "Have you sensed it?"

He met her gaze, unblinking. "I can sense it in you right now."

She broke his stare to frown in the direction of the lake. Talking to Xander, another diviner, was forcing her jumbled thoughts to make enough sense for her to describe them. "Gateways are there to tell you exactly where you are. You can't go somewhere without leaving somewhere else behind. Our task is to connect two different places. . ."

"I'm right here," he said.

"Hmm," she said, brow furrowed. "A gateway tells us which way is north, south, east, or west. . . Where the sun may rise or set at a certain time of year. When a particular star or constellation might be in view. It is a kind of calendar, as much as a way to orient ourselves. Maybe that is all it is." She corrected herself. "No, that can't be all. A gateway also warps the tapestry. Gateways are always solid, heavy—or at least built near something else that is."

He raised an eyebrow. "I think I'm with you."

She shot to her feet, leaving the log to move to the grass by the edge of the lake. "I have an idea. Let's do a test. Stand up."

He reluctantly left his position to come over to her.

She maneuvered his arms, so they were flat at his sides. She then moved to stand behind him, so she was facing the back of his head. "Close your eyes. Promise me you will keep them closed."

"Very well." He paused. "My eyes are closed."

"Now. I am going to spin you around. I want you to keep your eyes closed the entire time, and don't open them."

She turned his body, spinning him around and around. She counted as she did, and when she reached a dozen turns, she brought him to a halt. After again admonishing him to keep his eyes closed, she turned him in the opposite direction, until even she had lost track of how many times she had rotated his body.

"Now, I am going to let go of you and step away. What I want you to do is open your arms up at your sides, so they are pointing toward your left and right. Keep your eyes closed."

Following her instruction, he opened up his arms. She could see that as he held his eyes closed, he was frowning, wondering what she might be trying to do.

"Now turn, until your nose is pointing due north. Your left arm should be pointing to the west, and your right arm to the east."

"How am I supposed to know?"

"Guess," she said firmly.

Shaking his head, he moved first one way, then another, until he had settled on an orientation.

"Now open your eyes."

Xander opened his eyes and checked the sun and sky. He made a sound of surprise. "A lucky guess?"

"I don't think it was a guess at all. I think we all have something inside us that can help us find our way. It's a little like when you wait for an hour to pass, and when you think it has, your guess is correct to the minute."

He glanced at the sky again, but when he spoke, his tone was puzzled. "I am afraid I still don't see the point you are trying to make."

"What if gateways are just there to help us? To make something difficult a lot more achievable? If we can orientate our position ourselves . . . if we can sense the passage of time and know the season and the stars and the exact location of our world compared to the sun . . . if we can warp the tapestry not by weight, but by the fact that we have agency, and we are living creatures who all have an outsized effect on the world around us. Maybe then . . . maybe we wouldn't need gateways at all."

"I think I understand a little about what you're saying, but I don't know if a person could have the same effect on the tapestry as a pyramid."

"Why not?" She walked over to him, and now she was close behind him, close enough to feel the warmth from his body. "It's like when two people are really close. We feel connected, even when we're apart. If I trust you, and I don't know where to go, I don't need to know anything at all, I can simply follow you."

"But what does it all mean?"

She screwed her eyes up tight. "I don't know. But there is definitely something there."

"I agree," he said. And there was something in the way he said it that made her quickly open her eyes again. "There is something there."

He turned all the way around, and he was staring at her intently, his chest rising and falling, even though he hadn't been exerting himself at all.

Her mouth went dry. Something was going to happen.

"Bethany . . . Do you remember when we last saw each other?"

"Of course I do."

"You said something about us being friends."

"I know."

She knew exactly why she had said it. But at the same time, she wanted his warmth, his touch. She wanted him to be more than a friend.

All of a sudden he was closer than he had ever been. His face inched toward hers. The movement was slow, hesitant. His head was tilted. She looked up at him, and moistened her lips.

Their faces grew closer. . .

Her lips pressed against his. . .

And then they were kissing.

Her heart raced and her skin tingled, but this was a different kind of tingle. It made her feel as if she were sizzling like a flame. She felt warm from head to toe. As Xander's arm went around her back, he pulled her close, and she hugged into him, never letting her lips move away from his.

Chapter Eight

BETHANY FORGOT ABOUT gateways and nodes. About the fielding and the lords and ladies of the realm. About her father and his worries and about Julian and Declan. About her mother and her failing health.

All she knew was that she was in Xander's arms, and she didn't want their kissing to stop. He made a slight sound, a kind of muffled moan, and pulled her closer. She didn't stop him.

Her hand traveled up and down his back. She touched the black locks at the base of his neck. He cupped the back of her head and stroked her long copper hair.

Beside the lake, near Fernley Manor, part of Esk, in the region of Umber, Bethany Sylvana was having her first kiss.

He kissed her for long enough that she knew he wanted her. This wasn't some fleeting fancy; they were friends, and he wanted it to be something more. She kissed him to tell him she was ready.

Her knees felt weak. He was partly supporting her weight, and she was glad for it.

But then her skin tingled. And this was the kind of sensation she had been experiencing all day.

She broke off the kiss, pushing his shoulders back, panting. "Wait." Her head turned to the side, in the direction of the Star Temple. "Someone's coming. I have to get back to the gateway!"

"Bethany—"

"I can't let them arrive without me there."

She tried to run but he grabbed her hand, holding her. He gently pulled her back toward him. He kissed her again, and she couldn't help herself; she kissed him in return. But she broke it off once more.

"Bethany . . . I need to know how you feel."

Even with them both panting, she smiled. "As I was saying, the thing about gateways is. . ."

With a mock cry of anguish he pulled her in for yet another kiss. Again she was forced to disengage.

"Hopefully you can guess." She smiled at him. This time she was the one who kissed him, but it had to be a brief one. "Now, I have to do my work."

He grinned and tried to hold her hand but she slipped free. He reluctantly followed as she half sprinted, half-dragged him along, heading along the forest trail to the clearing containing the Star Temple. They held hands the entire way, but then when the trail finished, he knew to let her go.

Just in time, she returned to her place in front of the temple. The gateway opened and another group exited, led by a diviner she didn't recognize. A short distance away, Xander stood and watched, just another diviner. She greeted them and sent them to the fields along the trail of white stones. As soon as they were out of earshot, Xander came back over to her.

There was something in his manner that reminded her: he had never been someone who would simply go along with what someone else said. "Just tell me this. How long until the next group comes?"

Part of her duties was to know the gateway's schedule, and part of her training as a diviner was to be skilled at remembering facts, locations, and numbers. "There's a brief gap. A little under an hour."

"Then I have an idea. I am a young man and you are a young woman. Over there," he nodded, "right now, a fielding is underway. Tell me, Bethany Sylvana, have you ever been to a fielding?"

"No. . ."

"Neither have I. There won't be another for years. What do you say? Come with me, and I promise you I will get you back here in time."

She hesitated. The offer was more than tempting. For a time she stood facing the direction of the fielding. Everyone else was enjoying the event, while she was trapped here at the gateway.

"You promise?" she finally asked.

"I promise."

As he grinned at her, a welling feeling of excitement climbed her body. She couldn't help a smile creeping up on her own face, as his enthusiasm sparked her own.

"We can take off our cloaks, leave them here by a tree . . . " he said, reaching for the clasp at his neck.

"As long as I'm back here in time."

"You will be," he said. "Come on. We don't have long. Let's go."

✦

Bethany dragged Xander along by the hand, heading straight up the hill.

"You look like you know where you're going," Xander laughed.

Bethany wasn't wasting time as she led him up the road lined with white stones that led to the fields. The sun was already high. In the distance, the silhouettes of the viewing galleries grew taller as they reached level ground and made their way closer.

She grinned at him. "We don't have long, and I've had some time to get to know the area."

The path soon joined the broad road for those who were traveling overland. There was only one way to go, and more people soon filled the approach to the fields. Some of the arrivals rode horses, but most were walking. There were more men than women, but that didn't mean that colorful clothing was absent, and girls in bright dresses and nobleman in garish tunics traveled along with the uniformed soldiers and commoners in smocks. A dozen men in chain mail walked ahead; from their furs and coarse clothing and black hair tied like horses' tails, they might be mercenaries come to offer their services. Bethany looked over her shoulder; farther behind them half a dozen men in coarse brown tunics carried tall longbows and quivers on their shoulders.

Kendrick and his family would be busy, and as long as Bethany made it back to the gateway in time, she didn't have to worry about being recognized. In her sky blue dress, aside from the pattern of stars, she could have been just any other young woman attending the fielding, come to see the competitions and enjoy the dancing, feasts, and revelry. Xander's glistening silver tunic was striking, but many nobleman were clad in their own finery.

At any rate, it didn't matter. If anyone saw that they were diviners, no one would guess they were supposed to be working. Diviners were inevitably involved with wars. Nobles had their own house diviners. For a short time, Bethany was free, liberated. In the time she had, she intended to enjoy herself.

The closer they neared the fielding, the more her head moved from side to side. Colorful pavilions designated the emperor's private section, close to the main parade ground. Another area of tents housed the nobles and the people they had brought with them: sons and daughters, stewards and servants, men-at-arm, and military advisors. Most distant of all was the multitude of tents—a temporary town—for all the soldiers and common folk, including those working at the fielding itself.

The path of white stones led them onward to the busiest area of all, with streets and alleys between rows of market stalls and larger buildings set up as dining and drinking halls. The competitions were scheduled at a number of locations, all of them out of view. In any event, the fierce contents to win accolades in jousting, wrestling, horse riding, archery, and sword fighting wouldn't begin until after the opening ceremony.

The sound of music now reached them; warbling and jingling that came from the sprawling market. A tambourine clanged and pattered, along with pan pipes playing merry trills. Loud voices called out. A woman's raucous laughter mingled with a man's hearty guffaw. Meat was roasting somewhere. The trail of white stones ended, and now the ground was churned up by the passage of feet, but the mud was something to be shrugged off and accepted, and nobody seemed to care.

The number of people kept growing. She had grown up in Everlast, in the busy Fabric District where commoners and laborers mingled with the wealthier patrons come to tend to their clothing. But she and Xander were now about to enter the first of many paths framed with stalls on both sides—and the fielding was something altogether different. A pair of grizzled soldiers stood with a trio of plump ladies in jewels and dresses, all eating the same skewered meat, all watching the same trio of jugglers. Two gray-haired military men scowled at a pair of children racing along the crowded lane between stalls. Half a dozen foreigners with heavy accents bargained with a vendor displaying a gleaming sword.

Bethany stopped to stare open-mouthed at Xander as people pushed past them to get into the market. There were so many things to see, it was almost overwhelming.

"Ever seen anything like it?" he asked. As she shook her head, he grinned. "Me either." He raised an eyebrow. "Well? It's your fielding. Where are we going first?"

A round of applause from somewhere inside the market drew her attention. "That depends."

"On what?"

"Are you hungry?"

"I could definitely eat. Unfortunately for me, it's lunch time back in Everlast, but midmorning here in Esk."

She laughed. "Xander, this is a fielding. Come on. Let's find some food, and we'll see as much as we can on the way."

Together they plunged into the market. Almost immediately, Bethany had to let go of Xander's hand as she was forced to slip between two groups of people. But then when they were through, he took her hand again, and her heart beat a little faster. Two things were happening at the same time, which was strange and exciting. They were passing stalls, looking this way and that, seeing shining swords and vicious axes at one, pikes and halberds at the next, and a bewildering variety of long and short bows after that. They watched the trio of jugglers, lithe men in patchwork clothing who danced and cavorted, performing somersaults and never losing a ball while the occasional onlooker tossed a coin into a hat on the ground. The music shifted as they left behind the troupe with the pan pipes and tambourine to approach a lively mandolin player.

But something else was happening. Xander occasionally rubbed his thumb against her palm. When she brought something to his attention—a mustached man with a fat mottled snake coiled around his neck—she squeezed his hand. They stopped to peer along an intersection between different lanes, and when they did, they stood close together, bodies warm and touching.

"I can see people eating over there," she said, nodding toward an area up ahead. Even as they looked, the smell of food greeted them, inviting them onward.

"Lead the way," Xander said.

After taking the turn, they skirted a roped off area where a horse trader was parading a charger, a powerful black stallion big enough to carry the heaviest knight in armor. A soft whinny came from beside them as a middle-aged woman in a brown smock led another horse through the market. At the end of the path, one of the great dining halls was visible as a raised up wooden platform with a rail at waist height, and already a number of men and women of all ages and stations looked to be drinking wine and ale, mead and stronger liquor.

At another corner, half a dozen young men—and one giant of a woman—stood at a notice board to view the detailed information about when and where they would soon be competing. In a wider space, a bearded man in polished plate armor checked his horse's hooves.

Finally they reached the row of food stalls. Bethany turned back to Xander and smiled. The smell of so many different kinds of food, all at the same place, was enough to make her stomach rumble more loudly than she might have wanted it to. The vendors employed a number of cooking techniques, most involving hot coals. An old woman's sign announced she was selling boiled dumplings filled with spiced meat, which she cooked in a simmering pot of water. At another stall, a number of sausages on long skewers dripped sizzling fat into the bed of embers below. An oversized cauldron bubbled with meat and barley stew. Honeycakes lay piled up on a wooden counter, where nearby, two young women in summer dresses laughed as they took healthy bites. A fat man used a special tool to deftly flip onion pancakes on a flat iron cooking plate. A popular stall sold cured meats and cheeses, along with loaves of freshly baked crusty bread.

Bethany and Xander kept walking, pointing out each different item to each other, torn by what to try. But then Bethany stopped when something caught her eye, before she picked up her pace, walking at twice the speed.

She came to a halt at a stall where a middle-aged man with graying dark hair was filling a stone oven with fresh hot coals. Finishing his task, the vendor noticed her standing with Xander, even as he rolled a ball of dough out on the floured surface in front of him, tossing in a handful of herbs and spices, before making a flat shape with the special curl she knew well. With a copper tone to his skin and gentle green eyes, his appearance marked him as someone from the distant provinces.

"Young lady?" the vendor asked. With a smile on his face, he glanced at Xander, and then back to Bethany. "If you haven't tried flatbreads from the Far Reaches, today is your lucky day. However—perhaps you have—and if so, you will know the treat you are in for."

"I have." Bethany nodded toward Xander. "However I can guess that my friend here hasn't."

"Friend?" Xander raised an eyebrow, but his eyes were twinkling.

"Special friend," she said with a mischievous smile. "Have you tried them?" He shook his head. "My mother used to make them when I was little."

"When I saw how quickly you came over, I thought you must know from experience." The green-eyed vendor grinned. "Trust me, mine are among the best." He rolled a second ball of dough, fast in his movements, before tossing the two flatbreads into his stone oven. "Two flatbreads?" Bethany nodded. "Coming right up."

"With butter?" she asked.

"Is there any other way?"

"No," she said with a smile. "How much?"

"Ten coppers each."

"Let me pay—" Xander began.

Bethany held up a finger. "Xander Cole. . . Whose fielding did we say this is?"

"Well . . . yours?"

"Then let me pay. You can pay next time." Finding the coins in a pouch in her dress, she handed them over.

"Thank you, young lady." The green-eyed vendor took the coins. "I couldn't help overhearing. Your mother made them for you, you say? Where is she from?"

"Loriastris."

"Ah, the land of emerald forests. I hail from Darian, myself. Hope to get back there, one day."

The vendor laid out two large sheets of paper. He then used his small shovel to pull first one flatbread, and then the other, from his oven. He laid each on its own piece of paper, then spread butter from a pot onto them both. Last of all, he sprinkled some salt, before folding up the papers to hand the packages out.

"Here you go. Enjoy the fielding, and I hope the two of you never forget the importance of a special friendship." He said the last with a sparkle in his eyes, before turning to the next waiting customer.

Bethany and Xander moved away to have a little space to enjoy their food. Unable to wait, Bethany took a large bite, first tasting the salt and butter, before savoring the smoky, crisp, chewy flatbread and then the herbs and spices. Her eyes were closed. Her mother's food; the food she grew up with; by the stars, she had missed it.

She opened her eyes as she swallowed, to see Xander standing with eyes closed himself, as if he had forgotten where he was. He didn't even open his eyes as he took a second bite, and she had to say his name.

"Xander!" He opened his eyes, mouth half full and a guilty expression on his face. "Well? What do you think?"

"What do I think?" He shook his head. "I have never tasted anything so delicious."

A short distance away, the green-eyed vendor smiled and glanced over at them, even as he served his next set of customers in a growing queue. Bethany took another bite and swallow, the smell of butter, bread, and spices bringing back as many memories as the taste.

She couldn't stop herself from eating it, taking salty, buttery mouthfuls, until it was all gone.

"Your mother could cook like that?" Xander asked, awestruck as he looked regretfully at his empty paper, before taking her paper to put them both into a basket provided for the purpose.

"Well, we didn't have a stone oven. But she could cook like no one else."

"Did she teach you? Because one day—"

She punched him in the arm, laughing, before something occurred to her.

"What?" Xander asked, watching as the color drained from her face.

"What time is it?"

Xander paled. Like her, he didn't need a clock to know that they had only minutes to get back to the gateway. "I'm sorry, I know I said I would get you back in time—"

"It was worth it." She turned her head. "There's a quicker way out." She pointed toward a gap between stalls that would lead to open ground. "That way. Come on. We have to hurry."

✦

Bethany was breathless as she reached the Star Temple. The hairs were rising on her arms; someone was coming, but she had made it, if only just in time.

"They aren't here yet, but they soon will be, and they are going to keep coming," she said. "You have to go now."

Xander checked that they were alone, before pulling her into a kiss. He held her close, arms around her waist and back, even as weakness entered her limbs. She reluctantly pushed him away. But even as the tingling grew stronger, she leaned forward to kiss him again.

"Go," she said. "Now."

He squeezed her hand. "Come and see me. Back in Everlast."

"I will."

"Promise me."

"I promise. Quick. You have to go now!"

"And if I don't want to?"

"Xander!"

He hurried over to her and brushed her lips with his own, but then he kept moving. He ascended the platform, raised his staff, and summoned his own gateway.

He stepped through the shimmering black doorway.

And then he was gone.

Chapter Nine

IN THE MORNING the worry was about the arriving people, but then, all of a sudden, the fielding was underway.

Kendrick was tense. The opening ceremony was scheduled for noon, and the sun would soon be in the middle of the sky. This was the first of the key events, with the knighting ceremony and oath of fealty scheduled for the same time tomorrow.

From his seat in the high gallery, the tallest and most important of the viewing galleries, he leaned forward. As befitted his role, he sat in the center seat, in the highest row available to a lord of the empire. Above and behind him, however, was a barrier and then the emperor's personal section, which gave this viewing gallery additional stature.

He shuffled in his uncomfortable military uniform. He was finding it difficult to remain still, even as people found their seats around him. A few ladies looked disgruntled and a couple of lords scowled as they whispered in their wives' ears. But in the main, there was more decorum in the pretense that wherever someone sat in relation to everyone else was as it should be, and certainly meant nothing at all.

And a pretense was what it was. The seating in all the galleries, whether filled with clerics and confessors or military engineers and builders, followed the same pattern. The men and women with the highest status were in the top tiers, then continuing, until down at the front were the people with the lowest rank. Additional nuance came into play with respect to the extreme ends and positioning near the stairs. All Kendrick knew was that he was glad to be able to leave all that worry in the capable hands of his wife.

People. Everywhere he looked, there were people. With the opening ceremony soon to begin, most numerous of all were those who didn't occupy the viewing galleries at all. Down below, along both sides of the parade ground, crowds milled in heaving numbers, held back by rope fences. Most of them were the empire's soldiers, whether new recruits or veterans, but there would also be bowmen from among the peasantry as well as mercenaries from foreign lands. One of the biggest risks was that fighting would break out, but the emperor's personal soldiers, Imperial guardsmen, patrolled the fences. Distinguished by their white cloaks and shining armor, few would cause them any trouble.

Kendrick could barely believe it. From his high position, he could see tens of thousands of people. And here he was, the host.

From a wider perspective, the viewing galleries stood in rows, like upright houses facing each other across an unusually broad avenue. Meanwhile, against the parade ground, in front of the viewing galleries, the fenced jousting lists had been sited so that the contests could be seen by all. The jousts were what many had come to see. With lances at the ready, armored men on horseback would charge each other at speed, and some might even be killed.

Kendrick was trying hard not to think about that part.

As lords and ladies continued to find their seats, he turned his attention to the collection of purple and gold tents located close to the parade ground, from which the emperor was going to appear. There was some movement, but the time had yet to come. and he turned his gaze toward another area, more distant from the parade ground.

The sandy oval-shaped arena was already set up for the horse riding, with jumps and obstacles ready to test both horses and riders. His two sons had a unique advantage: they had been able to practice on the very grounds where they would be competing. For them, this was home. He felt no guilt about the privileged position; if it kept his boys alive and helped them secure a future, then all his hard work would have been worthwhile.

At the very back of the fields, the archery range presented a row of straw targets with concentric rings dyed red and white. And off to the side, past the arena, were the pits for sword fighting and wrestling. He remembered Troy and Caden, red-faced and brawling while Isabelle watched from the scaffolding. It was only a few months ago, but it already felt like years.

He nodded to himself, as pride welled up inside. It had been difficult, putting this all together, but look at all they had accomplished.

A loud laugh from somewhere below brought him back to the gallery. With most seats now filled, it was strange to see nobles from different orders side by side. In the Marble Court each order occupied its own area, but here, everywhere around him, were familiar faces from among the Reds, the Blacks, the Blues. The three heads of the orders each occupied the same row he did, with their closest allies arrayed around them.

There was Declan now, leaning forward in his seat to speak with the man in the row in front of him. Declan's wife Meredith hadn't made it to the fielding, which wouldn't have been a surprise to anyone. Farther down the row, past Declan, was the guffawing figure of Gavin Arturius, leader of the Crusaders, a yellow-haired man with the barking, soldierly manner of a typical Red.

Much closer to Kendrick, at his left-hand side, Anthea was speaking with the curly-haired woman beside her. His wife finished whatever she was saying and then glanced at him, watching for a moment.

She leaned in to whisper. "I know a smile would be asking too much, but try not to scowl, dear."

He tried to smooth his expression. "What did she have to say?"

"Lord Vine will be judging the jousting. Apparently he is fair."

He nodded. "I would agree with that."

On Kendrick's other side, Tristan Benedict, leader of the Wardens, leaned forward. Plump and smiling, he looked elegant in his military dress, and as usual the oversized gold ring on his finger proudly displayed the black shield insignia of the order he led. "You should have asked me who was judging, My Lady," Tristan said, looking past Kendrick at Anthea. "I could have told you."

"Ah," she replied with a smile. "But did you know that Lord Vine's cousin Sir Niall is sick with congestion, and therefore had to withdraw from competing?"

"Sir Niall has withdrawn?" Tristan's eyes registered surprise and then admiration. "No I did not. I stand humbled, My Lady. This improves the odds for your sons, eh, Kendrick?" As Anthea returned to her conversation, Tristan leaned in closer, so that only Kendrick could hear him. "Look, Kendrick, I know you're probably still angry about the vote. I honestly don't think you had a choice, and look now at the honor you've brought not just your order, but your entire family. I mean this, with all my heart. Take a good look around. No one else could have done what you have."

Kendrick leveled Tristan with a long look. There was only one thing he could do; sometimes things turned out the way they had to be. His frown softened, and he reached out his hand. With a relieved smile, Tristan shook it. "I appreciate that, brother," Kendrick said.

"No, my brother. Thank you."

"Look!" A voice called out from below. "It's starting."

A trumpet blasted a brief triumphant melody. In the parade ground below, a herald rode from place to place, extremely agile as he reached an area and reared his horse back to kick the air, before putting his trumpet to his lips and blowing again. He continued, completing a ride around the perimeter of the broad space below, until there was no set of ears he would not have reached.

Kendrick hadn't realized how much of a din there was around him until it all settled, the last loud conversations dying away to murmurs and then an expectant silence.

The herald rode to the very center. Kendrick had to appreciate the man's set of lungs. When he called out, Kendrick heard him distant but clear.

"The Dymantine Emperor, Rigel Regus Livius, declares this fielding underway!"

More trumpeters came into view, until they were lined up along both sides of the parade ground to blast again and again. A huge white horse came into view, pulling a chariot, as it entered to become the focus of all attention.

Kendrick glanced at Tristan, who returned his apprehensive expression, but neither of them spoke. Rigel had always prided himself on his soldierly background, rising to become general during the early wars in the Far Reaches. Kendrick and Tristan both knew, and as did many other nobles present, that the emperor would insist upon entering on horseback. The sight of a chariot was more than surprising.

The rumors about the emperor being unwell must be true. How serious was his condition?

All heads were turned the same way, and like Kendrick they were focusing hard on the emperor as he came into view. But from their vantage, the emperor looked the same as ever. Rigel stood tall and regal on the chariot's platform, waving and smiling, with the thick ruby-studded circlet on his head: the Crown of Blood and Gold. He was at least driving the chariot himself and clutched the reins in one hand while he held the other high. His clothing was in white and gold, while his purple cloak flew dramatically behind his shoulders.

Kendrick knew every element of the opening ceremony. Next would come an escort of Imperial guardsmen, the emperor's personal soldiers.

But instead, another man appeared, on horseback this time, following the emperor to enter the parade ground.

Riding a beautiful white destrier, a warhorse so big it made most other horses look like ponies. Julian was bare-headed, and with the summer sun high in the sky, his golden hair glowed as if he were wearing a cap of metal. The crown prince was tanned, athletic, and youthful, and shared his father's patrician features. He wore armor, beautiful steel plate that glistened silver, and a jeweled scabbard dangled at his side. As soon as he was well in view, he drew his sword to ride with one hand and hold the point of the blade high into the air.

Kendrick exchanged a worried glance with Anthea. She knew the proceedings as well as he did, but neither of them said anything. Julian would have planned his unscheduled appearance, and must have told the guardsmen to hold back. Had Rigel been aware of the change?

And it wasn't just Julian who seized the attention of the vast number of gathered people. Another chariot appeared, this time driven by a soldier, who stood beside a slender dark-haired woman. Samara had the eyes of tens of thousands of men all on her, and from her broad smile as she waved, she had no problem with all the attention. She had fashioned her dark hair into a braid, highlighting her high cheekbones, and wore a garment somewhere between a dress and a stylized suit of armor made of shining golden fabric. However unlike a set of armor, her garb revealed as much olive skin as it concealed, and the dress plunged at her neckline, where she displayed a ruby on a golden necklace. Cheers from male voices swelled up from below, much louder than those so far.

At last the ceremony unfolded as expected, as the emperor's guardsmen came next. Huge men in armor with gold trim, they marched in unison to their commander's loud bellows, to which the guardsmen roared responses. Veldon Marx, the huge commander with the close-cropped white hair, issued the calls from up front as he marched with an oversized sword on his back. Kendrick didn't know Veldon Marx well, but he had heard the stories. The man was regarded in equal fear and awe by the soldiers in his command.

Next came High Confessor Valaeric and his retinue. The black robed men and women passed in a group, stately and somber as people in the crowd held up clasped palms and called out for blessings, to which the high confessor responded, raising his hand toward the crowd.

After the confessors was a delegation from the University, white-clad clerics who in Kendrick's mind represented one of the best things about the empire—the fact that if someone became sick or injured, there were knowledgeable healers available to help. Clerics did their work for a fee, of course, but in many cases the fees were absorbed by either the corpus or the local nobility.

High Diviner Gale Azren and dozens of diviners with gray cloaks represented the Observatory, and as the elderly diviner with the stooped frame and immense white beard passed, along with so many others with orb-tipped staffs, Kendrick's thoughts turned to Bethany.

Her duties were linked to the Star Temple, and out of the tens of thousands of people here, she was the only one without a seat or even a designated standing area. He hoped she had a chance to enjoy herself for some of the time at least.

Then something changed in Kendrick's viewing gallery. All the lords and ladies turned, facing the rear, as they rose to their feet and applauded. Anthea climbed to her feet, and Kendrick stood beside her. Everyone looked on as the emperor, the crown prince, and the princess all took their places in their private section above. Up close, Rigel appeared a little hunched but when Julian tried to aid his father the emperor waved him away.

Emperor Rigel met eyes with Kendrick and nodded, and although he had been hoping and almost expecting it, Kendrick felt a flush of pride as he bowed back. The special favor would be noticed. Perhaps it was all worth it. Everyone would know who Troy and Caden were. Even little Isabelle too.

The clapping continued, and then slowly, one by one, the nobility of the realm returned to their seats.

There was already movement down below. Two armored knights had taken up positions at either end of the jousting lists. The knight on the left had green decorations on his horse, along with a matching tabard over his armor and green pennant on his lance. The knight opposite, on Kendrick's right, was clad in yellow, with his darker horse dressed in sunny colors like a village girl at a summer feast.

An announcer's voice rose, calling the names of the competitors, but behind Kendrick the emperor fell into a bout of coughing and Kendrick missed their names. No one reacted, even as the emperor continued to rumble, until finally his cough calmed down.

The two riders raised lances. A trumpet gave a strident note and they charged at each other, moving from trot, to canter, to gallop as they leveled their lances, aiming them at their opponent even as they hefted their shields to protect themselves.

Beside Kendrick, Anthea tensed and then gave a jolt as the two men crunched together in a flurry of motion that made it difficult to gauge the outcome.

The green knight was down. The yellow knight turned his mount at the end of the jousting list, riding to the front of the gallery to salute the emperor. The loser climbed to his feet, staggering for a time as he walked over to fetch his horse and lead it away.

Tristan spoke into Kendrick's ear. "How many jousts today?"

"Twenty-five," Kendrick said. "Every fifteen minutes during daylight."

The next competitors were already preparing themselves. In the time between jousts, people in the viewing gallery were beginning to leave their seats to head elsewhere.

"When are your sons having their turn?" Tristan asked.

"Tomorrow, in the morning. Just before the knighting ceremony."

Tristan shielded his eyes, gazing farther into the fields. "I think I shall watch the horse riding. Baden Lynch's nephew is competing and I want to have a word with him."

"It's true, then?" Kendrick asked quietly. "He is to be named overall commander?"

"Yes, Lord Marshal Lynch it is, but keep it quiet."

Kendrick couldn't help making a sound of disgust. "If you had seen the things I saw in the Reaches. . ."

"Listen to me, my old friend." Tristan leaned even closer to Kendrick. "Look at them all. Go on." He nodded toward the tiers below them, where everyone was talking in murmurs, exchanging gossip, asking favors. "There is going to be endless maneuvering in the coming days. I know you and Lynch aren't friends, but today is also about your sons. Show civility, and he will do the same. We both know that when it is your sons' turn, you will want the new lord marshal watching. I'm going to go and see him now. You should probably come with me, before he gets too busy. "

Despite Tristan's low tone, Anthea was giving Kendrick a meaningful look. Kendrick sighed. It had been a long time since he had fought in distant wars. But some of the acts he had seen, especially from his own side, he would also never forget.

"You will be fine here alone?" he asked Anthea.

"Kendrick," she said dryly. "Lady Glenda is here. Yes. I will be fine."

Accepting the inevitable, Kendrick stood. He bowed to the emperor, as did everyone who found or left a seat, and followed Tristan from the gallery.

Chapter Ten

ZHUANA LEANED OVER Garric's bedside, about to pull the linen higher on her son's slight frame when he gave an anguished moan and rolled over. His arm shifted position, revealing his right hand as he clutched the bedcovers.

Garric's skin was the same as it always was, dark and smooth like hers.

But his fingernails . . . they were all entirely black.

Her heart skipped a beat. And then she was breathing hard. No. It couldn't be. Her eyes were open wide. Please, Mother . . . please, no. She grabbed his hand, uncaring of the fact she might wake him. Each and every fingernail as black as coal. She yanked the linen from his body and seized his other hand. Five shining black fingernails greeted her.

She stumbled backward, staring down at her son.

The darkness had come . . . and now it had reached the person she loved more than anything else. He was going to lose his life—everything he was—in the most horrific way imaginable.

"Zhuana!"

The powerful male voice bellowed from somewhere outside. Shaken, terrified, she turned to the nearby door and opened it.

From her position in the doorway, she found herself facing the city of Veldria's main thoroughfare. Maven Dresk stood out in the open street, surrounded by flames that licked up the walls of the crowded shops and houses. Veldria was burning. Maven was lit up in the flickering glow, revealing his muscular body, bald head, and ugly, misshapen nose.

"Look what I have for you!" he cried triumphantly, lifting something up to display it.

He was holding a head, gripping it by the hair on top. The face was grimacing. Zhuana clutched the door frame. The head belonged to her dead husband, Barrix. Flaps of skin hung down at his neck. Blood dripped down to the cobblestones. His green eyes—the same color as her son's—were wide open and stared straight into her soul.

"He was a strong warrior, Zhuana. I didn't like him, but I respected him. Who is there now to protect you?"

"I can protect myself," she whispered.

Maven acted as if he hadn't heard her. "And it is true, I did call you a mangy dog. In truth I have on occasion said much worse." He turned the head close to his own face, as if they were having a conversation. "You fool, Barrix. You didn't have to call me out—then I had to challenge you. And now look at you."

"I will never know why the Mother let you win," she breathed.

"Really, Zhuana? I think we both know why—because one day I am going to be king, and a stronger ruler than you. You escaped the keep when your father died, and my chance was taken away. Since then I have been biding my time. Your son is your weakness." He sneered. "And now look at your little boy. . ."

She heard a strange sound behind her, a snicker and hiss. She whirled and a creature was slinking toward her, a reptilian figure with curled claws for fingers and glistening scaled skin. The creature had red eyes with black slits for pupils, two holes for nostrils, and a thin-lipped mouth, which was parted to display its pointed teeth.

The creature grabbed hold of her leg. . .

✦

Zhuana cried out as her eyes burst open. The summer air was sticky and her bedlinen was soaked and tangled. Early light glowed at the shuttered windows. She always slept alone. Lost in the throes of her nightmare, there had been no one by her side to wake her.

She blinked as reality overcame the terror. She wasn't in Veldria. Her city was gone. She had burned it to the ground to create a barrier between her fleeing people and Torian Varlish's great army—an army cursed with the darkness, and almost certainly lost to its fate.

She had taken her people to the only place they might be safe, to the Eternal Empire, which was rich and powerful, with libraries of books and people with knowledge. She was in her fortified camp on a hill, where a gorge defined the border, with the Imperial city of Lexia on the other side.

Throwing herself out of bed, she went straight to the doorway that opened into the next adjoining room. All she could think about was her son. And there he was; Garric was fast asleep, with the sound of his heavy breathing filled the small space. She rushed to his bedside, peeling back the covers to examine his hands and fingers.

She knew what she would see—the druids checked everyone to a rigorous schedule—but her shoulders still slumped with relief when she saw his nails untarnished. She released his wrist and her son sleepily rolled back over.

Veldria was lost. The land of Grendal had also fallen to the darkness. The first slinking creatures had even made it across the badlands—to be met by a hail of arrows from the people she had left in waiting.

But the darkness had yet to reach her here.

She returned to her own chamber, fully awake now. It was time to ready herself for the day. As she moved past the dresser and the polished bronze mirror, her reflection flickered at the edges of her vision.

Brown, penetrating eyes looked back at her, but they were eyes filled with worry. After her nightmare, urgency made her gnaw at her lip. Her long tresses had yet to be woven with diamonds, but she had more important matters on her mind.

"Queen Zhuana?"

Zhuana turned her head toward the closed door. The voice belonged to one of her handmaidens.

"Enter."

The door opened to reveal a flaxen-haired girl who stood at the threshold and spoke with her gaze deferentially down on the floor.

"Well? What is it?"

"Elder Alric is searching for you, Highness."

"He is, is he?" Zhuana's eyes narrowed. "Very well. You may go."

"My Queen." The girl bowed and left.

Zhuana glanced at the mirror once more. Her mouth was set in a thin line. The darkness was coming. She was now planning to summon her war council. Her frown deepened as she reached for the first piece of her body armor.

✦

Zhuana took long strides as she passed through the main camp. The morning air was fresh but already the sun's rays were fierce, promising a hot day to come. She glanced from place to place as she headed for the druids' section. Around her, people were going about their business, which for most meant preparing for war. Bundles of arrows made neat piles. Flasks and water bladders filled an entire area, containing the firewater that gave her warriors both courage and endurance.

She had now spent all of her gold. The empire's greedy traders were happy to take it, and once Alric had the raw materials, he and his fellow druids had brewed their potion in great quantity. The horses were all fat, well fed, and ready to ride.

As she approached the area where the druids did their work, she smelled smoke, but this was of a different kind than wood smoke. This smoke was bitter and sharp, and when she neared the door to Alric's workroom, its presence made her eyes water.

She threw the curtain aside. Alric was with another druid, watching as the younger man stirred a bubbling cauldron. Alric dipped a ladle into the cauldron and inspected the contents, even though from Zhuana's position her nose and throat were already burning.

"Not long now," Alric said. "You know what to do next." He must have noticed her frown but didn't obviously react. "Ah, My Queen."

"Let us talk outside," Zhuana said. She waited impatiently for Alric to join her and then strode away from the area. After passing through the broad gates, she found a vacant space outside the encampment, somewhere to talk without fear of being overheard. "I am the queen, Alric. You do not send for me."

"I promise you, My Queen, I did not send for you. I have been eager to speak with you, that is all. Perhaps I made my urgency too clear. . ."

They were under the open sky, a short distance outside the palisade protecting the camp. The Imperial city of Lexia was clearly in view from their position. "Well? What is it?"

"I have learned something from one of the empire's traders—"

"The empire's traders. . ." She shook her head and scowled. "They have been mocking us, even as they take our money. Their information has been worse than useless—" Alric gently cleared his throat, causing her to trail off.

He surprised her by coming in close and lowering his tone. "This one has no love for the empire. He is the same trader who told me that the prince was not seriously injured in the fight in the gorge, no matter what he claims in his missives. He gave me a tiny piece of information and once I had it, I took him aside and used fear to learn all there is to know." He paused, his sunken gaze meeting hers. "Does the word *fielding* mean anything to you?"

"Fielding?" She raised an eyebrow.

"It is a word that describes a great mustering, a gathering of a special kind."

"A gathering of what?"

He continued to stare into her eyes. "Of soldiers, My Queen. Of noblemen and knights, soldiers and mercenaries. Of horses and merchants. Of dealers in weapons and armor. These fieldings only come around every few years. The emperor himself always attends. The crown prince too."

"The crown prince. . ." She glanced at Lexia. "And when is this fielding?"

"My Queen. . . This fielding is taking place right now."

She hissed, unable to stop herself. "Julian is at this gathering . . . right now?"

"Yes. And there is more. It is always a military event, but this fielding has special importance. The imperials. . . they are using it to assemble an army."

A fiery sensation clawed at Zhuana's belly, bringing heat to her face. "And what is it they intend to do with this army?"

"You and I . . . we both know the answer to that."

Her head again snapped to the side, toward the gorge at the border and the city that lay beyond. "This fielding. . ." she said in a tone as cold as ice, "they tried to keep it a secret but they failed. What you are telling me, Alric, is that right now, as we speak, the emperor and Julian are hosting a great gathering to form an army and drive us away."

"That is exactly what I am saying, Queen Zhuana. Others will confirm the truth, now that we know the questions to ask. But some things now make sense, would you not agree?"

And with that, she knew negotiations were at an end. There could be no alternative to her next course of action. In a way she was relieved, now that there was no other path. If she could have come to terms with the empire, she could have saved lives—many of them. But the empire chose otherwise.

"Do you think they ever meant to negotiate?" she asked to herself as much as the druid.

"Their Marble Court is a hive of buzzing bees. What is agreed one day may change upon the arrival of another. We will never know what they were planning when we first arrived here at the border." Alric paused, and when she looked his way, there was fire in his dark, deep-set eyes. "One thing I do know, however, is that we have to act quickly, while we can still catch them off guard."

Zhuana had been toyed with, deceived, betrayed. All the laborious conversations with Julian Malventus, all the delays and wasted months.

She remembered the messages describing the severity of his wounds and pleading for just a little more time.

Her people knew her, her druadan knew her, just as she knew herself. She may be slow to anger, neither ruled by her head nor her heart. But when her wrath was raised, like tinder added to smoldering coals, nothing could stop her.

Julian was going to pay a price for his duplicity. The empire would suffer. And Julian most of all.

She was going to make sure of it.

"This means war, Alric. Now or never. While they are still unprepared. While there is still time."

In this distance, the Imperial city beckoned, waving at her, taunting her. A well-trodden road now connected the settlement to her encampment. Lexia lay open. Exposed. Vulnerable. Compared with the numbers she commanded, the city's garrison was tiny.

"The time for an accommodation is past. When this is all over, I will occupy the Imperial Palace as empress, and then we will see if they still call us barbarians."

Chapter Eleven

KENDRICK GLANCED AT ANTHEA'S HANDS. As she sat beside him on the viewing gallery, she looked composed, but she was twining her fingers in the way she only did when she was extremely anxious.

Summer's heat had risen. Today, the second day of the fielding, saw the women in the gallery fanning themselves with pleated paper. Meanwhile there were already pockets of red-faced men, laughing and talking loudly, in the throes of too much ale or wine.

Kendrick decided he needed some water. He grabbed the mug on a table by his knees and tilted it back. But he almost spat when warm ale filled his mouth. After glaring at Tristan's empty seat, he quickly returned the mug to its place, with no other choice than to grimace and swallow the mouthful he had.

Along with the sounds of the crowd, thudding horse hooves and crashing lances reached his ears. In the lists below, the jousting continued, as it always did during daylight. Earlier in the morning, an unlucky young man had been killed, although Kendrick had been with the horse riding and hadn't seen the incident first hand. Another twelve horsemen were injured badly enough to be forced to withdraw from the tournament. When the current round ended, the remaining competitors would continue charging at each other until only one victor remained.

A trumpet blared. The next two men rode at full speed with long poles pointed at each other's torsos. Kendrick had done his fair share of jousting as a younger man, and had won his own handful of golden medals. Now, despite the obvious parallel with the skills of war, the whole thing seemed like madness.

Soon he would be watching his sons, who were scheduled close together. Then, afterwards, the contests would pause for another spectacle in the parade ground: the knighting ceremony, with Troy and Caden among the young men granted the honor. With nearly two hundred new knights to ordain, the high confessor's arms would be busy delivering the accolade, touching his ceremonial sword to one set of shoulders after another.

There was also something new below, a platform at one side of the parade ground, where a great banner displayed the Imperial colors for all to see. After the knighting ceremony, the next part of the fielding had also been planned in detail: the public oath of fealty.

At exactly midday, bells would toll, the viewing galleries would empty, and the central parade ground would fill with the great number of gathered nobles. The emperor would stand in front of the Imperial banner and received his due support, in full view of the great host of onlookers, as his nobles dipped onto one knee and offered their sword and service, and most of all, their undying, unwavering loyalty.

Behind Kendrick, both the emperor and Julian were absent, with the gallery's highest section empty. Rigel's health was becoming discussed in hushed tones, and Kendrick turned his attention to the colorful section of pavilions near the end of the parade ground, where the short distance meant the emperor and his family could easily come and go. One pavilion stood out from the others, grandly decorated in gold and purple. The emperor might choose not to attend the knighting ceremony, but he certainly wouldn't miss the oath of fealty. Whatever he was doing now, he would show himself soon enough.

"Kendrick." Anthea's voice seized his attention. "Declan isn't here. Have you seen him?" She had leaned forward to look along the row, but her brother's seat was empty.

Kendrick frowned. "Not since this morning." Declan was Troy and Caden's uncle, after all, and it was strange to have him absent at this all-important moment.

"Look," Anthea then whispered, nudging Kendrick. "Troy. Over there."

The previous joust had finished and the lists were clear. Anthea wrapped a hand around her spider necklace as Troy came forward on horseback, dressed from head to toe in plate armor but with his visor up so that Kendrick saw his eldest son's square-jawed, handsome face, set with determination. Troy's bay mare had been brushed until her coat glistened in the bright sun, and she wore a fringed skirt in dark red. A matching crimson plume decorated Troy's helmet.

The announcer, a heavy-set man with a set of lungs to match his size, sucked in his chest and bellowed.

"In red, Troy Conway of Esk." He indicated with his arm, pointing. "In gray, Sir Jarryd Fry of Laurel."

Troy's opponent appeared at the other end of the list. Kendrick's son was tall, but the man he would be facing was a full head taller and already several years a knight. A mountain of a man, he was clad in chain mail from head to toe, with a gray tabard on his torso and the dressing on his oversized horse also in the same shade. An open circle in his chain revealed his face, which was red and scowling. Sir Jarryd had taken a third place medal once before, and would be eager to improve on his record.

Kendrick sensed people looking his way but he ignored them. He heard a man's voice from somewhere on a lower tier: "By the stars, look at him. He's huge."

Anthea bit her lip. "You said he was big, but Kendrick. . ."

"You know I couldn't influence the selection."

Her hand came out, and Kendrick grabbed it in his, as she gave his palm a hard squeeze. Below, the two competitors readied themselves at either end of the long white fence. They brought their padded lances up, horses ready and facing each other. In moments, they would race along the fence and each would try to knock the other man off. The man still on his horse at the end would win acclaim. His downed opponent would suffer shame—or worse.

With his lance tucked under his right arm and shield stuck to his upper left arm, Troy saluted his opponent. Sir Jarryd gave a more casual wave, barely raising his arm.

Kendrick's heart quickened. He tried to moisten his lips. His wife's squeezing hand grew tighter. Troy's expression became fierce, and for a moment Kendrick couldn't believe this was the same son he had taught to skip stones on the lake as a boy. No matter what happened, he told himself he was proud. Troy had been practicing for months. As long as his eldest son lived. The force coming from that huge man and his lance would be immense, and could cave in a man's chest in a direct strike. No. He couldn't think about that now.

The trumpet blared. Troy cried out, kicking his horse straight into a gallop. Kendrick and Anthea both leaned forward. In seconds both horses were galloping, faster and faster. Sir Jarryd adjusted his lance. Troy did the same. *Here it comes.* They were about to collide. There could only be one victor.

Troy's lance missed as Sir Jarryd swerved. Troy took a hit, rocked to the side as his opponent's lance struck his shield a glancing blow. Neither man was unhorsed. They continued their ride until they reached the end of the list, and reduced speed to turn around.

Anthea's lips were moving in a silent prayer. She clasped one hand around her necklace, the other gripped Kendrick's. She was no longer trying to keep her composure, but all eyes were on the contest below.

Sir Jarryd kicked into a gallop before Troy was ready and Kendrick swore. Troy quickly corrected his mistake and in moments was charging toward his opponent. A distant part of Kendrick observed his son's skill. Troy had his lance in good position. Sir Jarryd's red face looked angry.

Horse hooves thundered on the dirt. The rumble grew louder as the two charging riders reached full gallop. Lances inched upward, then to the side, padded points trying to find their mark. Racing at formidable speed, the two competitors each tried to swerve but also bring his lance to bear on his opponent.

This time, when the two collided, the crunch was sickening. Still clutching each other's hands, Kendrick and Anthea both shot to their feet. A loud roar came from all quarters as Troy tilted his body, narrowly dodging his opponent's weapon. Meanwhile Troy's lance evaded Sir Jarryd's shield to slam into the bigger man's torso. Kendrick watched as Sir Jarryd was propelled from his horse in one of the most dramatic unseatings in the fielding so far.

Troy wobbled but kept his seat, and slowed before reducing his horse to a walking pace. A great roar came from the spectators in the standing area. Around Kendrick, lords and ladies clapped and cheered. Several men in the gallery were up on their feet. Troy's face was flushed as he rode until he was directly in front of the high gallery. He raised the tip of his lance to salute the emperor's empty seat, but Kendrick knew he was seeing his mother and father both in the gallery, standing as they cheered his performance.

Kendrick and Anthea exchanged relieved glances. Anthea was shaking her head, letting out a long breath. Everyone who was on their feet sat back down and Kendrick and Anthea followed suit.

After a short time Kendrick leaned in to murmur. "Shame for the emperor not to see."

"Look." Anthea directed his attention to a tall man, plainly dressed in brown leather, standing out front of the viewing gallery. Easily picked out by his shaved head and severely cut gray-speckled beard, Baden Lynch stood close to the white fence, where he would be able to watch the jousting up close. "Our new lord marshal definitely did. Thank you, Kendrick. Whatever you said, he looks to be on our side."

The next two bouts passed without serious injury, as another two aspirants made their way to the next round and another two young men found themselves defeated. Then Anthea reached out to squeeze Kendrick's upper arm.

"Wait," she said. "Look. There he is."

As Caden walked his horse forward, he also had his visor up. A few brown hairs poked out from his helmet, fluttering in the breeze, and this time Kendrick was struck by how young his son looked—he was just nineteen, after all. For Kendrick, the impression was strange; here his son was, in plate armor, in the view of thousands of spectators as he prepared to battle an opponent in a conflict not far from real war. And yet all he could see was his little boy, who had always been bested by his bigger, stronger older brother.

If Anthea's grip had been tight before, now she was holding Kendrick's palm with enough force to make his fingers hurt. She didn't look his way, instead focusing on Caden intently, as if her will could affect the outcome of the contest.

The announcer called out, "In black and white checks, Mandel Drey of Engel. In blue, Caden Conway of Esk."

Caden and his opposite were about evenly matched in size, although Caden's frame was slighter compared with his broader, stockier opponent. Caden's chestnut horse complemented the blue coloring of the fabric skirt and the blue pennant that decorated his lance.

Mandel was also older than Caden, perhaps in his late twenties. His black horse, dressed in black and white checks, matched his painted black plate armor, and he looked confident, with an easy manner, smiling as he waved to the crowd and rode his mount to the starting point.

Caden ignored the onlookers completely as he waited with his horse in position, lance stretched out before him. He lowered his visor, ready to start.

The two competitors saluted each other.

The trumpet sounded and the charge began.

Caden cried out loud enough for Kendrick to hear, kicking his horse hard as he forced his chestnut horse into action. Mandel was a moment slower, but he leaned forward to launch his larger horse in motion. Within seconds the two riders were galloping toward each other.

Time slowed.

Caden's lance wobbled to the side, and then he over-corrected. Mandel leaned at an angle, preparing to dodge when the collision came.

"Come on," Kendrick whispered. He had his jaw clenched, eyes focused. "Come on." Unable to stop himself, he was again on his feet, with Anthea standing beside him.

Caden improved his lance's position, putting the padded tip at the exact place it needed to be. At the same time, Caden weaved to the side, so that Mandel's lance pierced the empty air.

The slam of contact was loud enough to make the people in the gallery flinch.

The strike was perfect, as Caden's lance punched into his opponent's torso, throwing him from the back of his mount. A roar came from the spectators, accompanied by cheers from all directions.

"Did you see that? A perfect strike! First pass." Kendrick was shouting as he hugged his wife's shoulders. People from the lower tiers looked back at Kendrick and grinned, but he ignored them.

"Kendrick," she laughed. "Kendrick!"

Caden slowed his horse, riding slowly over to the high gallery. But before he reached it, he raised his visor to smile at someone out of view. It was only then that he halted in front of the gallery to salute the absent emperor and grin up at his two proud parents.

Kendrick and Anthea both smiled and clapped, hands in the air as Caden rode away. But as soon as he was departing, they both leaned forward. In the direction of their son's gaze, there was Bethany, in her diviner's costume, along with a few other spectators, watching from down on ground level.

"Did you see that?" Anthea asked, raising an eyebrow.

Kendrick nodded. "I saw it. I'll have a talk with him later." He wasn't at all surprised to see Bethany watch his sons compete. Caden, on the other hand . . . The boy had to realize that everything he did was scrutinized and potential fuel for gossip.

"Hmm. Perhaps it can wait. Let us not spoil his victory. It is not too often that Caden shows up Troy. Bethany is a part of our household, after all. And as for Caden, I have no doubt that at tonight's feast there will be several young ladies all eager to meet him."

Kendrick stretched and shook his shoulders, still on his feet. He hadn't realized how tense he had been. He wanted the fielding to be a success . . . but he needed his sons to survive.

He turned back to his wife. "The knighting ceremony isn't far away. Can you believe it, our two little boys both about to be knighted?"

"Not little anymore."

"You know what I mean."

"All I can say is I am looking forward to when this is all over."

"The fielding, or our boys risking life and limb?"

"I think you know the answer."

As Kendrick chuckled, something down below caught his attention: an Imperial guardsman in a white cloak talking to someone on the ground. His brow furrowed. The guardsman was speaking with Bethany.

Shortly after, the two of them left together.

Anthea was also looking in the same direction. They watched until Bethany and the guardsman were out of view.

Anthea's words echoed his own thoughts. "I wonder what that is all about?"

Chapter Twelve

BETHANY ENTERED THE DARK PAVILION, trying to make sense of the furniture and objects in the sudden change, from brightness outside to the swift absence of light. She made out a huge bed, draped with linen, and heard coughing, as the figure on the bed moved.

"Ah, Bethany," a hoarse voice spoke. "Please, leave us." The guardsman escorting Bethany bowed and left without a word. "You too." This time he was addressing the blonde woman in white cleric's robes by his bedside, who also bowed and departed. As the cleric passed close by, Bethany recognized the woman's heart-shaped face from when she had met her father in the Nexus gardens.

She was now with her father, the emperor, alone. The pavilion was big, and this main section had just the one wide, open space. She could guess what her father wanted, after their last conversation. Whatever was said, unless they raised their voices, they wouldn't be overheard.

"As you can see, I am more than a little unwell. I was hoping the country air would do me good. The travel certainly did not. Perhaps I should have asked you to guide me, eh?"

As her eyes adjusted, she made out her father on the bed, watching her with dark, somber eyes. Blankets covered his body to his waist. Pillows supported his back. He appeared to be fully clothed, wearing a fine silk tunic rather than bedclothes. His thin white hair was neatly combed. Yet his state of dress couldn't change the fact that he looked pale and red-eyed, with a sagging, weary face.

He coughed again, wiping his mouth with a piece of cloth. "You seem to be doing well in your new position with the Conways. Tell me, daughter. Are you enjoying life as a house diviner?"

"I like my work," she said cautiously.

He gave a rasping chuckle. "I have no doubt that Fernley Manor is a more pleasant place to live than that poor little dormus in Everlast." When she didn't reply, he cleared his throat. "Now. You will no doubt remember the last time we met. I asked you to be my eyes and ears, and in particular to help me prevent any kind of conflict, caused by either my son or Declan Quinn of Graystone." He watched her for a moment. "I know Declan has been busy. Tell me, Bethany, what is it you have learned?"

She hesitated. What should she say? She didn't want to betray Kendrick or Anthea's confidence. Nor did she want to get them into any kind of trouble. Not that they had done anything wrong. The Conways' loyalty was self-evident.

Remember. Julian didn't know who she was. One day she would be free. And in the meantime, she was going to build something for herself, her own future, with good people like the Conways, with Charlton, and perhaps even Diviner Xander Cole.

"I think Lord Declan is looking for something."

He continued to watch her intently. "Go on."

"I don't have much to tell you." She was speaking the truth. "All I know is that two weeks ago, the lord and lady received a message from Lord Declan in the night. Whatever the message said, they were surprised and wrote a quick reply. They said something about being discreet, and whatever it was, they also asked him to take no action until after the fielding."

"Ah. . ." he said, nodding to himself. "And in your view, what is that Declan is searching for?"

She could only reply with honesty. "I couldn't even hazard a guess."

"Truly?"

"Truly. I don't know what they were discussing. I've told you all I know."

"Very well. You have passed my test. Listen to me well, Bethany. Before you came here, just now, I finished a conversation with Declan of Graystone. He told me to my face, in this very pavilion. He was standing where you are now. I know what he has been searching for."

She waited; it was strange that he was sharing so much with her, which was something he had never done before.

"You," Rigel said. As he stared directly into her eyes, with terrible intensity, her heart skipped strangely out of time.

She swallowed. "I don't understand."

"Declan Quinn of Graystone is looking for you, Bethany. He wants me to find an alternative successor to Julian, and as a result he has been digging into my family and into my past. He discovered some things about my time with your mother. He felt he knew enough to ask me directly, which forced me to face some truths I have long been denying."

He noticed her stunned expression and waved a hand. "I confirmed your existence. He does not yet know who you are, nor even if you are man or woman. You could say that I had no choice, but there is always a choice. When he asked, I told him."

She spoke without thinking, "But he could find out more—"

"He almost certainly will. However I made it clear that I will not have my hand forced. Instead, I asked him to wait, and here you are now. He didn't find you, Bethany. I found you myself, when you showed yourself capable of earning a place at the Observatory and passing the many trials to become a diviner. I believe that right now we are feeling the force of the Great Weaver bringing the threads together." He beckoned. "Please. Come here."

She approached the bed, and up close, the shadows under his eyes were heavy, as were the wrinkles around his mouth and in his forehead. His skin was gray, almost translucent, yet his wits were as sharp as ever, his voice thin but as incisive as a razor.

"I realize I have not always done right by you. Perhaps it is this wretched illness, or perhaps it is the flaws in my son's character, flaws that now make me regret that I never kept you closer. Whatever it is, I find that my eyes feel open for the first time." He paused, regarding her, and then his attention moved to a sideboard, which he pointed to with a finger. "Get me that letter over there."

A silver platter lay on the sideboard, with a piece of paper on top. She headed over. The paper was open and unfolded, beautifully bordered with lines and swirls and the Imperial emblem, the Crown of Blood and Gold, centered at the very top.

"Take it. Bring it here. It is not for me, it is for you."

She took the paper, brow furrowed as she brought it back to the emperor's bedside.

Without waiting for her to read it, he continued, "It is a written statement, a deposition if you will, a proclamation that I am your father and that you, Bethany, are my daughter. You probably know that my marriage to your mother was annulled when I became emperor. According to law, the annulment in no way takes away from the fact that when you were born, you were of course fully legitimate."

She looked down at the paper. Long lines of text were neatly arrayed in elegant, spidery writing. "I don't understand. Why now? What is it you want from me?"

"The written statement is merely a show of faith. The words are in my own hand, as is the signature."

At the bottom of the paper, there it was, her father's full name, Rigel Regus Livius, written in sloping cursive letters. There would be records in the Imperial archives—among them her mother and father's annulment. Together with her father's statement, no one would be able to accept anything but the truth.

But it was a truth she didn't want at all.

"The reason I am talking to you now is because the moment may soon come for your existence to be revealed. Never fear. I would be there beside you, helping you to adjust. You grew up with nothing. Your world was one of poverty. But this is your chance, for you to be a part of my world, the world of wealth and power. You carry yourself well. Your connection to the corpus would grant you many supporters. As for the blood of the Far Reaches . . . well, the wars in the Reaches have gone on for long enough. Perhaps we could turn that to our advantage."

She stared down at the letter. How was she supposed to answer him? "I hope you can understand. . ." she spoke slowly, then looked up to meet his eyes. "I am happy where I am. To be honest, I don't want to be part of your world at all."

He didn't become angry; instead he gave a short laugh. "Ah, Bethany. Sometimes you do remind me of your mother. Listen to me, however. I am well aware that you have taken nothing from me. Unlike my son, who has had every advantage possible. And perhaps that is your strength. Perhaps you are destined for great things. I have two children. My son is feckless, whereas my daughter is intelligent, brave, and resourceful. The past is but a memory. The future is what we are talking about now."

Holding the paper, she tried to conceal her feelings. Her mother raised her. Her mother told her stories at night and taught her letters and numbers. Her mother taught her well enough that she was able to further her own education, and become accepted at the School of Divination, and not just survive, but to apparently impress some of her teachers. She couldn't even distill her mother's parenting into a simple collection of experiences. Her mother was the reason she knew how to sew a seam, to make her way in the world, and to understand values like compassion and loyalty.

"But . . . Julian. . ."

"He has the wife he wanted, much to his disgrace. No matter what happens, he will inherit wealth and privilege. You are his half-sister. I am hopeful that the two of you would have a natural bond with each other."

Her last encounter with Julian came to her mind—the sneering look on his face, his blazing eyes. Events were spiraling out of her control. She had to do something to stop this—

She opened her mouth but the emperor threw himself forward on the bed, hand on his chest as he coughed with savage movements that racked his body. His coughs became rapid, as he sucked in breaths between them.

And all of a sudden, she and her father were no longer alone. The blonde cleric hurried to the emperor's bedside, a golden chalice in her hands. A second cleric, stern-faced and frowning, took Bethany's hand, shaking his head, leading her away as more clerics entered the area.

She had no choice but to allow herself to be taken from the emperor's bedside. She still held the sheet of paper, and quickly folded it and put it in a pocket.

In a space between coughs, the emperor called out hoarsely. "Bethany . . . Bethany . . . We will speak again soon."

✦

Samara circled Julian, checking the folds of his clothing, making sure that nothing was out of place. She moved a few strands of his golden hair. Meanwhile Julian stood frowning; she had asked him to stay still, and it was only now that he understood why.

"Excellent. You cut a fine figure." She pursed her lips then nodded to herself in satisfaction. "Not long now my love. Soon you will be raised up high, with all eyes on you. You will stand proud and tall, with the Imperial banner behind you. The high confessor will call upon them to bend the knee. When they give you their oath—"

"Stop, Samara," Julian said with a scowl. "You are acting like he has agreed to it. Enough. Unless he has had a sudden change of heart, it is not going to happen."

She put her hands on her hips. "But why would he not delegate to you? He is more than just unwell. Listen, would you? You can hear his coughing from here."

"You do not know my father. It is no use. It does not matter how many times I ask him."

"That was back in Everlast. But anyone can see that the travel has affected him badly. . . He is not well, Julian. The oath is an important part of the fielding. More than that, it is *tradition*. To not have the oath would be unthinkable. And there is nothing strange about the emperor's heir accepting it on his father's behalf. I know my history, and it has happened many times before. Surely he knows—"

"I am telling you. How many times can I ask him if I keep getting the same answer? He will never agree." He shook his head. "As I told you a long time ago, this is a fool's quest. We should not stay here a moment longer. We may as well go home."

"He must have a better reason than that he is likes to do it himself." Her eyes narrowed. "You are his son. What is his problem—?"

"He is a stubborn old man. That is the problem. He has always accepted the oath himself, and so that is how it must be."

"But you are his heir and successor," she persisted. "Why would he not want to give you this honor? You won the vote but it was close, far too close for comfort. Doesn't he realize you need other people to see that he supports you? This fielding, this is the occasion, nothing could be more public. You need this."

"It does not matter, Samara. I told you this would be the case, but you would not believe me. Listen to me. I will say it again, clearly. My father will never agree."

"No," she said, crossing her arms in front of her breasts. "We are not going home. Everyone is here. Your father is ill, all you have to do is look at him, let alone hear him coughing all day and night. I am seriously worried for his health, as you should be too. He has to see reason. He is in no condition to accept the oath. He just has to be convinced. You are his designated successor. A fielding always has an oath—"

"My Lady?"

As a new voice interrupted Samara, she and Julian both turned. A cleric stood framed in the light at the doorway to their pavilion. She was one of the clerics tending his father, a pretty blonde woman with a kind-looking face.

Samara raised an eyebrow. "Yes?"

"Lady, you wanted to know you if his condition changes. He has worsened, I am sorry to say."

Samara stared into Julian's eyes. "Go to him. Talk to him again. He has to see that he is in no state to leave his bed."

Julian bit his lip, even as the cleric waited at the pavilion's entrance. "I should go and see him. He really is quite ill."

Samara turned back to the cleric. "Has he said if he will be attending the knighting ceremony?"

"It is doubtful, Lady."

"Thank you. You may leave," Samara said to the cleric, who bowed before departing.

With worry tight in his stomach, Julian went to the pavilion's entrance, shielding his gaze first toward his father's grand tent and then the nearby parade ground. Young men were arranged in orderly rows, on their knees as the black-robed high confessor stood in front with his ceremonial sword in hand. On both sides of the parade ground, well-dressed lords and ladies were massed and waiting.

He turned back to Samara. "Midday is nearly here. Surely he can see for himself? Everyone is waiting. If he cannot make the knighting ceremony, how will he summon the strength for the oath?"

"Julian, ask him again. You are his only child. He has to see reason. Listen to me, my love. . ." She came over to stand beside him, staring straight into his face. "This is the hard part. The oath itself will be easy. You will stand high, in front of the Imperial banner. The high confessor will call for the nobles to bend the knee, and that is what they will do. They will swear allegiance, and everyone else will be watching. All of them including my father have to bend his knee, Julian. We have to force him to accept that you are going to be emperor. And when it is done, no one will be able to take it away from you. Go to him. Be strong. Do it now. Make your father see reason."

Chapter Thirteen

THE EMPEROR'S PAVILION couldn't be missed, decorated as it was in purple and crimson and gold. Julian strode straight up to the entrance. He set his jaw. He was the crown prince, dressed in full regalia to prove it, with a gold-trimmed cloak and jeweled scabbard at his side. He was young and strong, with golden hair and the fire of a man in his prime. The two guardsmen at the pavilion's entrance might be twice his size, but he had faced the Veldrians at the border and won.

"The emperor is resting, Prince Julian," said the younger of the pair, a brawny soldier with a shaved head. "He asked not to be disturbed."

"Let me inside," Julian said, narrowing his eyes. "My father is in poor health. I want to see him."

The two guardsmen exchanged glances, as the young soldier rubbed his hand over his hairless crown. The older gave a slight nod to his companion.

"Very well," the younger guardsman said. He stood aside and then parted the pavilion's draping curtain. "Here you go, Highness."

Julian entered and the curtain fell behind him. He blinked as he found himself in the pavilion's vast interior but in unexpectedly low light. As his eyes adjusted, items of furniture came into view: chests, clothing stands, benches, and dressing tables. But it was the immense bed in the center that dominated the space.

He approached slowly, footsteps heavy. He held his breath. Surely his father was still alive? As he neared, he heard a labored exhalation, and his shoulders slumped with relief.

"Julian. . ."

"Father."

Julian turned his head when someone in white stepped forward; the blonde cleric from earlier was hovering at the back of the area. "Please, leave us," Julian said to her.

"You may go," Rigel said. "Leave me with my son."

Julian waited until he and his father were alone. "Father . . . how are you?" He approached even closer, his eyes now used to the low light. "You have to know. . . everyone is worried about you. . ."

His father was well-groomed and clothed, but with blankets covering half his body, and his skin was pale, with barely any color at all. With a reddened cast to his shadowed eyes, he looked truly awful.

"I will be better soon enough, Julian. Perhaps now is not the best time for us to talk. Let me have my rest. There will be time for talking later."

Julian stood with legs apart. His conversation with his wife was fresh in his mind as he stood firm and cleared his throat. "I regret disturbing your rest, Father, but the knighting ceremony will soon be done, and the nobles are already gathering. As you know, the oath of fealty is an ancient tradition and an important part of any fielding. Please. Let me be your delegate. You can continue your rest. You are unwell—"

"Enough, Julian," Rigel said wearily. "I have not yet made the announcement, but there will be no oath of fealty, not today. The oath can wait until I am feeling better."

"But when will that be?" Julian's brow furrowed. "Father. We are speaking of tradition. At every fielding there is an oath—"

Rigel moved to sit up taller against his pillows. He leaned forward, which appeared to cost him an effort. Then, after taking a difficult breath, when he spoke, his mouth twisted with displeasure. "Listen to me, Julian. When I ask you to stop this, that is what I want you to do. For once, do as I ask. Why can you not give me that much?"

"Father, we both know you are unwell. Why can it not be my turn—?"

"—Julian," Rigel snapped, with the sharp, cutting quality he had inherited from his time as a commanding officer. "Very well then. This is what your insistence gets you. I no longer ask that you leave me alone to my rest. Instead, I want you to go home. It will be better for you if you do."

"Go home?" Julian demanded. "I may be your son, but I am a child no longer, as surely even you can see. Why would you ask me to leave, when I could instead be your delegate out there?" He thrust out an arm to point in the direction of the parade ground. "There would be nothing strange in it. It is part of our tradition that the emperor's successor can accept—"

"Julian! You need to go home. If you refuse me and stay, I promise you, nothing good will come of it."

Julian's face felt hot; his vision tunneled in, so all he could see was his father's narrowed eyes, his scowling look of disdain. "No. It is you who should listen to me. I am your successor. Your representative. I am also your son, your only child. There is no one else, Father. There is only me. Now, for once, give me my due—"

"Julian! Close your mouth and be silent."

Julian stood where he was, nostrils flaring, chest heaving in and out.

"I tried to make this easy for you but you had to use trickery, you and that wife of yours. Do you remember, when I was out on the terrace, negotiating on your behalf? The truth is, when I was speaking with the leaders of the three orders, I was asking for their help. I wanted them to let you down gently. That was my mistake. Because when we sat there and talked, for once we were all in agreement. What I was trying to make sure of was that your confirmation went against you."

Julian stood in place, uncomprehending, his mouth open and closing. His father was wrong. He hadn't just said what Julian thought he had.

"I tried talking to you. You have no idea how I tried. You had too much opposition allied against you. After your marriage to that woman, and your duel with her brother, you made too many enemies. You were going to lose the confirmation. I sat you down and I told you. It was supposed to be done with. But you . . . you and that wife of yours . . . you had to scheme and scrape through anyway. And do you know what? That only made me believe it all the more. An emperor cannot lead using manipulation and lies. There will be no oath of fealty. I would rather not have one at all. I do not want you to be my successor. I have not wanted it for a long time."

While Rigel was speaking, Julian's face had felt hotter, and hotter, until he was standing with his fists bunched at his sides. "I am your only child!"

"You suffer from weakness of character. The empire deserves a better ruler than you."

"You despicable old man—"

"You are nothing but a spoiled child." Rigel's voice became cold as the grave. "And you are wrong, boy. You are not my only child."

Julian was stunned into silence.

"I am telling you the truth. There is another. Someone in the shadows, someone I believe may be eminently more suitable than you. I tried to let you down lightly. I tried to make it so that it was the nobles who refused you, rather than your own father. But you left me no choice. Now go home, Julian. We are not having an oath of fealty. Instead we are going to make an announcement. It will be better for you if you are not here when it is made." He called out. "Guards!"

A guardsman came to the pavilion's entrance. "Emperor?"

"Fetch me Declan Quinn of Graystone."

"At once, Emperor."

The guardsman's face disappeared, as Julian backed away. Julian's eyes were wide. His head was shaking from side to side.

"Go home, Julian. Nurse your wounds. Never fear. I will look after you. You will still have a life of privilege."

Julian pushed his way from the tent. His vision was blurred. He walked in a stumble, with one hand pressed over his heart, even as he thought he was going to be sick.

✦

Julian couldn't bring himself to enter his own tent. He stood outside and tried to call out, but his voice came out like the last breath of a dying man. All he wanted was his wife. He wanted nothing more than to go home.

Home. The thought suddenly occurred to him. When someone else became emperor, it would no longer be his home.

"Samara. . ." From outside the pavilion, he tried again, searching for his courage. "Samara!"

She came to the opening, grabbing his arm as she took one look at his face. "What? What is it?"

"It's over . . . my father . . . he. . ."

"Tell me," she insisted. "What happened?"

"My father . . . he is taking it away from me. The succession. He is talking to your father right now. They are going to make an announcement. . ."

Samara's head whirled. She stared hard toward the emperor's pavilion. Julian followed her gaze, and as they watched, the two guards peeled the curtained opening to allow someone inside to depart. Declan's tall, lean frame appeared as he left. His expression was grim, more than deadly serious. He walked toward the parade ground, as if nothing could hold him back.

For Declan to have already finished his conversation. . . he must have been lurking close by. Perhaps Julian shouldn't have been surprised.

The look of fierce determination remained in Declan's stride as he headed to where the nobles were already assembling. Meanwhile, in the same direction, the knighting ceremony was over. The nobles were all gathering in the open field, waiting for the emperor to make his appearance on the platform, in front of the Imperial banner.

"Wait here," Samara said.

Julian tried to catch her hand, even as she hurried toward Declan. "Wait. Samara! What are you going to do?"

She called over her shoulder. "He's my father. I'm going to make him see reason."

She shifted from a walk into a run. Watching, gnawing at his lip, Julian followed after her. Declan was passing the last few tents in the Imperial section. In the area surrounding the platform, the nobles were all milling and speaking amongst each other; they hadn't yet noticed anything unexpected.

Julian put on speed but Samara had already caught up to her father. She said something. Declan snapped a quick reply. She grabbed his arm. Declan shook her off. Resuming his fast pace, Declan left her behind, and then he was crossing the parade ground. He headed directly toward the crowd of curious nobles; clearly he was going to climb up to the platform.

Samara's expression was distraught as she turned to race back in Julian's direction. But she went straight past him, leaving him where he was, not far from the platform and the gathered nobles. She rushed straight for the emperor's pavilion, and with a start he understood what she was doing.

She couldn't stop her own father. And so she was trying to reason with the only man who could change what was about to happen. At the emperor's tent, she spoke to the two guards outside, and then she swiftly entered.

Hearing a loud, crisp voice, Julian focused again on the platform. Declan stood tall, the subject of all attention, with the Imperial banner behind him. From where Julian was standing, he could see and hear everything.

"Nobles of the Dymantine Empire. Please. Come in close. I have something to discuss. Something that affects us all. . ."

Julian swallowed. The empire's nobles were all gathered in front of the platform. When he was denounced, their eyes would all turn to him. And he would be ruined forever. The stain of his shame would be something he could never remove.

Declan raised his voice. "I know we are here for the oath of fealty, however our emperor sends his regrets, as he is suffering from a minor illness. He has asked that I be here in his stead." He paused, sweeping the crowd with his gaze. "Our emperor and I have been discussing our Eternal Empire's future, the collective future of us all. He is well aware of what I am about to say to you now, and I announce it with his blessing."

The nobles stirred, but there was barely a sound from the crowd. Meanwhile, Declan's voice had the power to reach them all.

"I bring momentous news," Declan called. "Our emperor just confirmed it to me. In light of this news, our assembly must be—"

Declan stopped speaking.

A woman's wail was loud enough to be impossible to ignore. Across the parade ground, around the tents and pavilions, heads all turned in the same direction. The powerful wail became louder. Julian recognized the voice. Surely the wail couldn't be coming from. . . His eyes shot wide open as he stared at the emperor's pavilion, not far away, in a privileged position near the parade ground.

Among the nobles, people exchanged fearful glances and muttered. The woman's strident wail went on and on.

Julian heard a male voice shout. Armored soldiers came running. Within seconds, Imperial guardsmen crowded the area around the emperor's pavilion, along with clerics in white robes.

Julian recognized the young blonde cleric in white as she burst from the pavilion to stare toward the parade ground. She hurried, almost skipping, until she was speaking with the high confessor, Roman Valaeric, recognizable by his striking black robe. The high confessor was an ancient, white-haired man, with pale skin and an aura of calm serenity. But as the cleric led him toward the emperor's tent, he came with uncharacteristic haste.

As Julian remained in place, it was as if he was inside a shadow, a witness to events but unable to be seen by anyone. At the same time, no one else was moving, not the nobles, not Declan Quinn on the platform. The high confessor spent some time in the emperor's tent, but then emerged soon after.

The high confessor stopped to scan, as grave as Julian had ever seen him. He stopped searching when he finally spied Julian, and then he walked in one obvious direction—directly over to him.

The high confessor came to a halt. He didn't immediately speak; he simply stared into Julian's eyes. "Our emperor is dead."

The high confessor took hold of Julian's hand. As the old man gently pulled, Julian allowed himself to be led toward the gathered nobles. When they reached the platform, the high confessor stopped at the bottom of the steps. The high confessor, who counted votes and led proceedings at the Marble Court, glanced up at Declan, obviously waiting. Declan's expression was unreadable as he reluctantly descended so that Julian and the high confessor could take his place.

The woman's wailing never stopped. It had subsided, but now it rose up again.

Soon Julian was beside the high confessor up on the platform, as the high confessor faced the crowd and opened his arms wide. With the sea of faces arrayed in front of him, Julian stood stood white-faced and numb. The faces all blurred in his view as his eyes became unfocused.

"Nobles of the Eternal Empire! Together we must grieve." The high confessor stared up at the open sky. "Our emperor is dead. Rigel Regus Livius is on his way to the stars."

And then the high confessor took Julian's hand and raised it high.

"Our new emperor stands here now. All hail Julian Malventus Livius!" The high confessor called out in a clear voice. "May his name last throughout the ages!"

Julian told himself to do something; he had to force himself into action. He was in view of the empire's nobility. Whatever happened next, it would reverberate for years to come. He refocused his eyes. He moved to stand soberly, with legs apart. He lifted his chin and held himself with pride.

A stentorian voice called out, belonging to an Imperial guardsman. "Nobles of the realm, the emperor is dead. Long live the emperor! On your knees! All hail, Emperor Julian Malventus!"

And then, one by one, the nobles on the field all sank down to the ground. The effect rippled out, noble after noble sinking to one knee and looking up, until every person present was down. There were no exceptions. Kendrick Conway. Tristan Benedict. Baden Lynch. Gavin Arturius. All of them bent the knee.

Julian's head moved. Standing near the platform, Declan looked as shocked as anyone. He had to be thinking hard, and in the end, he had no other choice.

Declan had one of the most bitter expressions Julian had seen on a man, as he set himself down on one knee.

"All hail, our new emperor!" the high confessor called again. "All hail, Emperor Julian Malventus!"

The echo came from all around him.

"All hail!"

The woman's wailing went on and on.

Chapter Fourteen

CONFESSORS WALKED IN WIDE CIRCLES around the emperor's body, incense in their hands that they held up and then down, leaving smoky trails confined within the broad pavilion. Softly intoning passages from ancient texts, the confessors prepared for the emperor to become a star, a great node on the tapestry, watching down on his beloved empire from a high point in the sky.

Within the confessors' circle, Julian leaned over his father's body. He brushed back his father's white hair and kissed him on the forehead. His father's eyes were closed, as if he were sleeping.

"Even with him here, this doesn't feel real," he murmured. "It feels like a drama . . . or a dream. I keep expecting him to walk in and laugh at what fools we all are."

He placed his hands over his face, rubbing the skin up and down. There were so many emotions swirling around inside him, but most of all, he felt numb. Ignoring the black-robed confessors and their mumbled chants, he turned toward Samara.

"When . . . when do you think?"

Her eyes were red and her dark hair was disheveled. "I walked in and he had already. . ." She cleared her throat, "He was already gone." She stared at the emperor's body, her hand over her mouth. "At first, I didn't even know I was screaming."

"Didn't the clerics. . . ?"

"There was no one here when I entered."

"I. . ." He was aware of the confessors nearby. "Even after everything, I wish I was here for him. He was all alone. No one was here with him . . . at the end, I mean."

"I know how you feel. It's understandable. We can't control these things. It is a blessing that he passed in his sleep."

Julian closed his eyes, thinking hard before opening them. "My father is dead. Our emperor is dead." He shook his head. "This is going to going to send shockwaves throughout the empire. And beyond."

"People may test your power."

"They can scheme all they like. It is done, now. They will all have to fall into line."

"Nonetheless, as soon as we get back to Everlast—"

"Not now, Samara. No more maneuvering, not here, not now. This isn't the time or place."

She paled, but she nodded.

And Julian couldn't help wondering.

He tried not to, but it was impossible. Could his wife have had anything to do with his father's death? Surely not. The timing though. . . some will think she did. They would never voice it out loud, of course, not even to their most trusted allies. But in the privacy of their homes, away from prying eyes and listening ears, they would wonder if his wife was a killer, and not just any killer, but the murderer of their emperor.

When he watched her now, still in a state of shock, of course the idea was absurd. She was hugging her body, face haggard, looking fragile in her gauzy dress. Everyone knew how poor his father's health had been.

He returned to his father's body, reaching down to clasp his hand. Rigel had never been one to hold hands, and his palm felt cold and dry. He hoped that wherever his father was, he was at peace.

Peace. . .

Some people just didn't allow peace to flourish. Declan wouldn't let go of his hatred. Did he know about the existence of this other child? Julian had wanted to doubt the truth of his father's words, but he wouldn't lie, not about something like that. In his heart, he knew that there was another. *Someone eminently more suitable than you.*

Declan had never stopped his plotting, but whatever he had been about to say, whatever tricks he intended to deploy to take back what was already agreed, his bold endeavor became pointless—with the emperor dead, Julian automatically assumed the throne.

Declan had bent his knee. And now he had fled back home to lick his wounds. Would Declan ever give up on his scheming? In his heart, Julian knew the answer.

Julian had won. He was now emperor. And yet he couldn't help working through the rapid events of the day. What would have happened if his father hadn't died? Declan would have pressed the assembly to change the law and hold another vote. Julian would have lost the succession. His father would have remained emperor, but the process would have commenced to find a new successor. And Julian? He would have been forced into hiding, after losing too much standing to have even the slightest hint of power.

When the time was right, Julian had to deal with Declan Quinn, once and for all.

His father's body was motionless, expressionless, utterly still. As the confessors' murmured chant filled the silence, Julian understood how close he had come to complete failure. Ever since Julian was born, his father had worked hard to see his son follow in his footsteps as ruler of the Eternal Empire. Illness had twisted his thoughts, that and the manipulations of Declan Quinn, but his father didn't mean the things he had said. Instead, Julian would be a strong, powerful emperor—that was the legacy that he intended to honor.

Samara's voice broke through his reverie. "What happens now?"

"The presentation of the rank and file is moving forward to tomorrow. Some decisions we will simply have to rush. We will say the parade is a tribute to the emperor, and it will be, while at the same time the Armies of the West will be given some sense of order."

"And?" she asked, after a few moments had passed.

"And what?"

"Listen to me, husband. Do not wait long for the coronation. We cannot trust them. You know that."

"Samara, we cannot have a coronation and a funeral at the same time—"

"I realize that—"

"—his passing must be mourned. I am already emperor, and I have just lost my father." He frowned at her, then returned to his father. He kissed his brow again. "Farewell, Father. I will live up to your example. The empire will be strong. The empire will be whole. I give you my promise that it will be so."

Chapter Fifteen

AT THE END OF A FRAUGHT DAY, Bethany lay on her bed in Fernley Manor and stared up at the ceiling.

Her father was dead. Gone. He had departed her life forever.

Any bargains they had made were gone too. She didn't have to work for him, or be his eyes and ears among the diviners. Other than Declan Quinn, no one knew she existed, and Declan didn't know who she was. With luck, the idea of Rigel's second child would be forgotten, and she would be free to pursue her own destiny.

And yet she knew better to rely on luck. Her future was now more uncertain than ever. If Declan could find out the truth, then so could Julian. If Julian did learn about her, what would he do with the knowledge? She anxiously explored one outcome after another. Should she go and see the new emperor, before he found out on his own? No. Her intuition told her that was the last thing she should do. She didn't just have to worry about herself, she also had to think about her mother.

Julian knew that she had visited his father at the Nexus. She was house diviner to the Conways, an important noble family. If he learned the truth—that she was Rigel's daughter—the pieces would fit. He would believe it; he would know it to be true.

How would he react?

Her eyelids fluttered, becoming heavy. Her worries persisted, but even they couldn't keep her awake. She was weary after the long, difficult day, and sleep gave her no choice as it settled its heavy weight upon her.

Her dreams were strange. Her father was a corpse, and yet he was sitting on the armchair in the corner of her bedchamber. He had her knapsack on his lap, and was rummaging through it, until he withdrew a sheet of paper. Holding it up, he kept pointing at the text, mumbling something unintelligible as his dead eyes stared without seeing.

Then her mother was crouched by her bedside, whispering quietly in her ear while she slept. "Never take anything from him," she whispered. "Never owe him anything."

Bethany's skin tingled, jolting her awake.

A crystal tone was making her head hurt. The chiming sound gradually faded, echoes falling away. She was exhausted, worn out by ragged emotions. Her mind was foggy. But then the strident note came again, setting her teeth on edge. The peal slowly descended. Then it came again, loud enough to create a strong burst of pain between her temples. As sharp as the note was, she wasn't hearing it with her ears, but inside her mind.

The strident peal was a clarion, sounding at the Star Temple. She was hearing it again. And again. And again.

She sat up as blood rushed through her body. She shook herself and then threw her body out of bed. In moments she was dressed and wearing her gray diviner's cloak. Grabbing her staff, she raced to make her way downstairs. Fighting away the last tangles of sleep, she left the manor through the main front doors and hurried along the graveled path toward the lower gates.

The two uniformed guards there were watching her, and she recognized the younger rangy guard as well as the bearded soldier beside him. Kendrick had told her his men were under her orders. She also remembered him addressing the rangy guard–Farrell, his name was.

"Lady?" Standing and alert, Farrell squinted at her . "What is it?"

"I need both of you to come with me to the Star Temple."

The two men exchanged glances. Farrell touched his brow. "Of course. We'll just need someone to take our place up here."

"Quickly," she said. "And bring horses."

The clarion pealed again as she paced back and forth impatiently. She had never heard of such a thing, a clarion sounding over and over. Only a diviner could send the signal. She had no idea what it meant.

A whinny made her spin on her heel. The two guards had returned, both up on horseback as they led a third horse by the reins. Without a word, she hurried over, grabbing the pommel to put a foot in the stirrup and pull herself up. As she settled herself, she turned back toward the guardhouse where two more uniformed men were coming her way on foot.

The clarion's piercing tone again made her grit her teeth. She waited for the sound to fall. The two newcomers were now close enough to hear her.

"Wake Lord Kendrick," she called. "Tell him there might be danger at the Star Temple. He needs to be ready for anything. "

She then tugged her reins to guide her horse toward the Star Temple, at the same time digging in her heels to get her mount moving. Her horse leapt gamely forward and soon she had the two mounted soldiers following close behind. She passed through the gate towers and shifted into a canter, traveling at speed down the graveled road. A crescent moon lit up the area. Trees swished in the summer breeze. Before long, far ahead, moonlight shone on the clearing containing the gateway.

There was always another pair of guards posted at the Star Temple, and the two men in uniform stood at the foot of the steps, heads turned toward the road. As she reined in and slid off her horse, one of the gateway's guards called out to her.

"What is it, Diviner? Is there danger?"

Her two trailing companions dismounted as well. The presence of four armed soldiers was comforting, although she had no idea what was coming.

"Something might be coming. I don't know what," she said. "All I can say is we need to be ready."

"You heard her," Farrell called to his fellows. "This is her domain, not ours. Draw swords!"

All four guards immediately drew their weapons, filling the night air with the sound of scraping steel.

Bethany headed closer to the Star Temple. She and the men with her were all in a row, with her standing front and center. Together they faced the bottom of the steps that divided two of the points of the star-shaped structure. Up past the stairway, even in darkness, she could make out the immense triangular frame on the broad stone platform above. She made a decision. "We should get closer."

"Are you certain that's wise?" Farrell asked.

She met his eyes and nodded. "Remember, aside from the diviner, whoever comes through will be disoriented as they arrive."

She climbed the steps, focused on the triangular opening. As the clarion screamed inside her head, she winced, resisting the urge to clutch her temples. She couldn't escape the feeling that someone was trying to warn her. Why did she only have four soldiers with her? She should have gathered more.

Reaching the top of the stairway, she kept moving until the triangular frame was a dozen paces in front of her. She sensed the guards taking positions at her sides as they flanked her. The four soldiers were all watching warily, naked blades held out in front of them.

Her skin crawled, as if a thousand ants were walking over her skin. The tingling grew stronger. She tightly gripped the staff in her hand. She might be forced to use it as a weapon, which was a purpose it had also been designed for.

"Be ready!" she called. "It's about to open."

A bright light sparked inside the stone triangle. The light became a gash, peeling open before it turned and elongated to reform its shape as a tall rectangle. The black mirror shimmered, and the tension grew as the seconds trickled past.

Bethany gasped as a diviner fell out of the gateway.

She was a woman, middle-aged, with a conservative brown dress and gray cloak. As she clutched her staff with white knuckles, she collapsed onto one knee. The hood of her cloak was back, and Bethany's attention was drawn immediately to the top of the woman's head.

The woman had no hair . . . The skin and hair on top of her head had been cut away, leaving raw red flesh. Her scalp was gone. The pain had to be agonizing.

She also wore a collar.

Made of iron, the metal band around her neck was attached to something . . . something still in the gateway. Long chains, half a dozen or more, traveled from the woman's neck to the black portal. As the woman tumbled forward, the chains dragged something along behind her.

The chains pulled several warriors out in a group, strange men who stumbled together through the open portal.

Bracelets encircled the warriors' wrists, connected to the diviner's collar. Leather armor covered their muscled bodies. Curved swords hung in scabbards. Some warriors had tattoos, others shaved patterns in their hair. The strange men were disoriented, emerging through the portal and shaking their heads to clear their senses, confused from their time in the path of stars. The last warrior in the group carried a satchel across his body.

Still on one knee, the diviner looked up. She swept her blue eyes in front of her, seeing Bethany and the four swordsmen standing with blades bared.

She screamed at Bethany: "Don't wait! Kill them!" She then straightened and took her staff in two hands. Whirling against the encumbrance of her chains, she tried to launch the orb toward a warrior's skull. But her body traveled too far with her motion, and she collapsed again, gasping as she sprawled on the ground.

Bethany turned to cry at the guards. "Go!"

Kendrick's soldiers were well-trained, and once they acted, they each moved straight into combat. The bearded guard performed a fast thrust into a warrior's body. Another guard slashed his sword across a warrior's torso, backed up by a companion who stabbed the same enemy. Farrell almost collided into his opponent as he struck twice in quick succession. In an instant, three chained men were down.

The guards threw themselves at their next opponents. A warrior was at the verge of realizing what was happening. He clumsily tried to block a strike, but he was too slow and Farrell's hacking blow took him down. Another newcomer cried out in pain as he fell with a gaping wound in his chest.

But there were still two warriors left. One blinked and shook himself, before narrowing his eyes and brandishing his curved blade. Like his companion with the bag, he now realized he was in a fight for his life.

As the four guards battled the last pair of strange warriors, the struggle reached a new level of frantic grunting and fighting. Bethany stood holding her staff as Kendrick's men lunged and blocked, trying to surround their enemies. The air rang with the sound of blades scraping against each other.

A uniformed soldier went down. Bethany didn't know the man's name. The tattooed warrior who had struck him then whirled and slashed his blade across Farrell's chest, causing the rangy soldier to gasp and stagger.

The bearded soldier and the last guard were embroiled with the warrior with the bag. Instead of joining the fray, the tattooed warrior fixed his gaze on Bethany as blood dripped from his weapon.

He came in a rush toward her.

She stood frozen in place, unable to move. She wanted to raise her staff, but her body wouldn't obey. The tattooed warrior snarled and raised his blade.

A whistling sound flew by her ear. An arrow thunked into the tattooed warrior's body, followed by another, and then two more struck him in quick succession. He jerked with each strike and then crumpled.

There was just one warrior remaining, the man with the bag slung across his body. Even as the two guards worked hard to fight him off, another bowstring thrummed. The warrior with the satchel convulsed as an arrow sank deep into his back. Another arrow sprouted beside the first, making him shudder again, before his knees gave way beneath him.

The fight was over.

The panting guards prodded the warriors on the ground with their sword points, confirming that each man was dead.

Bethany turned. Kendrick stood with Troy and Caden, along with six more soldiers with bows.

"Take care of our men," Kendrick instructed. He was grim-faced as the soldiers with him ran up the stairs. He focused on her and called out. "Are you hurt?"

She shook her head.

"Head back to the manor. You." He nodded at one of the soldiers he had brought. "Escort her back."

Bethany ignored him. She couldn't imagine how much pain the diviner must be in as the woman lay sprawled out nearby, entangled with her chains. Passing the bodies that littered the area, Bethany hurried over to her. Up close, the bare flesh of the woman's scalp was raw and seeping blood.

Bethany crouched. "Can you hear me? What is your name?"

The diviner answered hoarsely. "Shauna."

"What have you just traveled from, Shauna?"

"I am . . . I was . . . house diviner to the governor of Lexia."

"What happened?"

"Dead," she whispered. "All dead."

Kendrick raised his voice. "Ask her what is in the bag."

Shauna heard him herself. "A message. From Maven Dresk, on behalf of the queen. He made me do it. I . . . I tried to warn you."

One of Kendrick's soldiers maneuvered the satchel from the dead warrior's body. He took the bag to open it and peer inside. He immediately recoiled. Kendrick headed over to take a look.

"Who was he?" Kendrick asked, looking back at the diviner.

Shanna spoke softly, "Roos Bannon. Garrison Commander."

"There are clerics here," Bethany said. "We can get you help."

"It's gone," Shauna said.

"What is?" Kendrick asked.

"Lexia. They came so fast. You need to tell the emperor. The Veldrians have invaded."

Chapter Sixteen

THE DAY WAS GRAY AND WINDY, threatening rain, well-matched to the mood in the air. People were massed again, but this time they kept their heads uncovered and voices stilled. The atmosphere was utterly unlike the raucous, competitive atmosphere that had prevailed in the fielding just the day before.

But a lot could happen in a day.

Julian stood and watched from the high gallery, in front of the same seat that had recently been occupied by his father. Below him, as the crowd looked on, confessors in black walked four abreast in a column that made a perfect line through the parade ground. Following behind them was an even larger group of Imperial guardsmen, men in shining silver armor who marched together. Last of all came the late emperor's personal protectors, his inner circle of guardsmen, and then the onlookers stirred as they saw it: the coffin containing the body of Rigel Regus Livius. Four guardsmen carried the litter between them, supported by long poles, where the gilded box of ebony lay draped in the Imperial flag. Directly in front of the litter was Commander Veldon Marx, his great sword held dramatically in the air as he walked, honoring the man he had served for many years.

A muted trumpet played a low dirge, with the player standing by the parade ground as tens of thousands of people watched the funereal march. Mournful silence filled the viewing galleries and fenced enclosures.

As Julian stood, hands respectfully clasped behind his back, he kept his face stoic, even as he was well aware that the news would be spilling around the empire at a faster and faster rate, from past the Far Reaches to beyond the Emerald Sea.

The emperor was dead. The Veldrians had invaded.

He also knew what else people would be saying.

The new emperor was inexperienced.

The Eternal Empire had been plunged into a crisis.

The coffin was now moving past his position. His father had been ill. Had Rigel given any thought to how grave his illness was? Now that Julian thought about it, there had been a certain fatalism in him. By the stars, his father was always so strong. When his time came, his death had been so sudden.

Regret made him sigh, letting out a long, slow breath. His father should never have come to the fielding. Travel through the gateways stressed the mind and body. His father had been away from home when he died, far from the comforts of the Imperial Palace. Worst of all, the terrible illness had affected his father's judgement, making him angry and spiteful, pushing him to say hurtful things he didn't really mean.

Julian had a brother or sister somewhere, he believed that much. But as for Julian not becoming emperor—he had spent his entire life preparing to be emperor. It was what he was born to do. He had the intelligence, the education ... by the stars, he even had the handsome, regal looks. He would try to remember his father as he had been, not as the sick, twisted man he last saw.

He couldn't control things that had happened in the past. His promise was the important thing. His father wanted for the empire to be strong and whole. He would do whatever he had to in order to honor his father's memory.

The sad drawn out notes of the trumpet went on and on. The sound of jingling armor and marching men kept a background tempo, but there was no talking, nothing but quiet from the surrounding people. Regular infantrymen came marching behind the guardsmen, levies drawn from the empire's nobility, this time twenty abreast. In the distance, behind them, horses were now approaching.

The empire had its new army, but it had come with a high cost. Zhuana must have learned about the fielding, leading her to invade, and to send her grisly message. He had been saddened to hear of Roos Bannon's fate. Unfortunately for the commander, it had been his city that the invaders had arrived at the doorstep of.

In any event, the empire had learned a lesson. A diviner could be controlled, just like any man or woman. All it took was the willful application of pain. Messages had been sent to the Wheel of Klare, to be distributed throughout the empire. Gateways were already guarded, but now, across the empire, all gateways, and especially strategic gateways, would be given additional protection.

The man who had signed the orders stood at Julian's right hand.

As the emperor's coffin passed from view, Julian turned to his companion, who had been given a special honor by standing at his side. Baden Lynch, the new lord marshal, was completely bald, with a neatly trimmed gray-speckled beard and a horrific wandering scar on his right cheek. His skin was like the clothing he wore: brown leather, tough and weathered, and his eyes were as dark as ebony. He wore his collar buttoned high, where he had a T-shaped iron spindle dangling on a chain around his neck: the Great Weaver as the Bride of Life and Death.

"Lord Marshal?"

Lynch tilted his head. "Emperor?"

It was still strange to hear his new form of address. Strange, but not unpleasant. "The diviner from Lexia. I think we should speak with her again. I can think of a few more—"

"She died of her wounds. No one told you? If you want to know more about what happened at Lexia, there will be others we can question."

"Ah. I see. Of course."

Julian had only spoken with the woman a few hours earlier. One moment a person could be living and breathing, the next moment the same person could be dead.

Putting her out of his mind, he again glanced at the man beside him. "We all have our reputations. I have heard that you do not get involved in the dirty deal-making of the assembly."

"You have heard correctly, Emperor. I belong to no order. I never vote. My duty is to the empire, and to the Great Weaver who looks over us all."

"As is mine, Baden." Julian used Lynch's first name, but immediately regretted it. Lynch was a man who favored titles. "The orders may bicker, Lord Marshal, but it will be you and I, working together, who will get the empire through this current crisis."

The different units of his new army continued to file past. After the long march of regular infantrymen a stretch of horsemen appeared: knights, men-at-arms, and mounted crossbowmen. Then came archers, followed by spearmen and pikemen. The mercenaries didn't have the same marching style, but there were enough of them to make up a sizable portion of the army.

"How many do we have?" Julian asked. The last time he had confronted Zhuana, he didn't have the backing of an army. This time things would be different.

"Thirty-two thousand, Emperor."

Julian liked it that Lynch had answered so quickly. "How many Veldrians are there again?"

"Over sixty thousand barbarians. Perhaps seventy. But that includes all of them: men, women, children . . . We might be able to use that against them. Worrying about their young is an obvious vulnerability."

Julian frowned, and he didn't take up Lynch's suggestion. He had heard the stories about the man. An emperor should be strong, but there was nothing strong about targeting children. "I will give it some thought. As for our next move, where do you suggest we deploy?"

"Engel would be my choice."

Julian's eyebrows went up. "You intend to abandon the Southern Provinces?"

"Lexia is under occupation. Bavia may have already fallen. If they were to keep moving, Gorvia's capture would be just two or three days behind. It will take us time to set up supply lines and build fortifications."

"And then we fight back."

Lynch nodded. "Yes, Emperor," he said, scratching at the scar on his cheek. "Then we fight back."

"Tell me. What do you make of the Veldrians?"

"They are barbarians. I have fought many barbarians. I will take their measure when I join them on the battlefield." Lynch raised his spindle to his lips and kissed it, closing his eyes as he did. He must have been making a prayer, for it took him a moment to return his attention to Julian. "There is one thing I would like to know, however . . . "

"Yes, Lord Marshal?"

"You know this queen? You have met her?"

"Several times."

"Anything you can tell me about her and their other leaders could be of great benefit. I assume she delegates to a general?"

Julian almost snorted. "Delegate? No. Not Zhuana. Her druadan—their version of nobles—are powerful leaders and warriors. But they follow where she leads. She even fights with them."

"A woman?"

"She is a force to be reckoned with. She is also motivated. And angry. She now thinks I was merely looking to delay her, which is effectively true." He cast his mind back, remembering. "There is nuance. I didn't like negotiating without strength, and so I needed an army to counter her. Perhaps we could have paid her off or formed an alliance against another enemy. But the fact is I needed her to remain in place until the fielding, and then she found out, and here we are. And so, yes, she will be angry. Vindictive. In the way that only a woman like her can be."

"The contest at the border. What can you tell me about these druids and their potions?"

"They have some kind of medicine . . . I watched it work first hand. I don't claim to understand it, but their fighters can keep going when another man would fall."

"And sixty of their warriors, unarmed, defeated sixty of our guardsmen." Lynch didn't frame it as a question, and Julian's irritation spiked.

"No," he said. "Sixty-one of us," he tapped his chest, "defeated sixty of their warriors. They are human. They bleed. In the end, Lord Marshal, the empire will be victorious."

Lynch noticed something behind them, causing Julian to turn. A man was waiting for his turn at an audience, standing patiently with legs apart. With his prominent jaw, brooding eyes and strong, sloping brow, there was no mistaking Commander Veldon Marks for anyone else. The funerary procession was over, and Lord Marshal Baden Lynch now cleared his throat.

"Speaking of victory. I have matters I must attend to. We will speak later, Emperor."

Julian nodded, and after the bald man in brown leather departed, he turned toward the commander of his Imperial guard. Even after Lynch had passed him by, the commander waited for Julian to beckon him closer. It was only then that Marx made his way over.

Julian had always observed Veldon Marx at a distance. It was his father who spent time with the commander of his personal force of fighting men. As the commander closed in, the difference in their size was pronounced. With his arms as thick as other men's legs, wide muscled shoulders and a thick neck, Marx was so tall he couldn't help looking down at Julian.

"Emperor," Commander Marx said in a deep, baritone voice. His icy-blue, deep-set eyes and fierce brow him a permanent look of menace. "I came to see you because it is now time."

The words were enigmatic enough to make Julian frown. "Time, Commander?"

"Time for us to talk."

"I see," Julian said. It didn't appear that the commander was going to waste time with flattery or vague pledges of service. His father had always described him as a blunt instrument, but an extremely effective one. "Then let us talk."

"I would guess that I know you better than you know me, Emperor."

"That may be true, Commander."

"I served your father as a soldier, then as an officer. When he became emperor, I joined the Imperial guard. I made commander at the age of thirty-five. That was fifteen years ago. You were a boy. Now you are a man. I have had the opportunity to hear of your exploits many, many times."

Julian wondered where the commander was taking the conversation. "And?"

"I think I know what kind of emperor you are going to be. You have always known what you want. You are not the type to be ruled by others. In that sense, you remind me of your father."

Julian was pleased, but he tried not to show it in his face.

Marx continued, "But as I said, I do not believe that you know me. It feels right to tell you a few things about myself."

The commander never broke a smile, and never altered expression from what appeared to be approaching a scowl. His voice was harsh as well as direct.

"Your father and I always agreed on one thing: the empire must be strong."

"You should know that I feel the same way."

The commander leveled Julian with his cold, flat stare. "The empire stands for stability. Without stability there is only chaos, and chaos means death and disorder on a scale we see only in nightmares. I would kill a hundred innocents if I had to in order to save the empire. A hundred babes in arms."

Julian gave a slight smile. "Well, I shouldn't expect—"

"Emperor, I am not finished," Marx said, and Julian's mouth snapped closed. "You are the emperor, the head, the person who must be respected if the empire is to last. When you are wrong, you are still right. The seeds of doubt must never be allowed to bloom. Do you understand me, Emperor Julian? I served your father . . . "

Surprising Julian, the commander sank to one knee, before tilting his head back and looking up to meet Julian's eyes. Even on one knee the man was huge.

" . . . and now I am here to serve you. I place my men at your disposal. Command me, and it shall be done."

Julian chose his next words with care. What Commander Marx was saying was important to him. The loyalty the man was offering couldn't be bought or won over. From his grave expression, it was simply his belief that if Julian was the emperor, then he was also the empire. Julian had to reply in kind.

"I thank you, Commander," Julian said. "Please, rise." He held out his hand, and the commander took it, returning to a standing position. "Now, there is something I want you to know. You will always have a place at my side, just as you were always at the side of my father."

"That is as it should be," Marx said. "The Imperial guard is yours."

Julian couldn't prevent a shiver, a thrill of pleasure. "Together, Commander. Together we will make our empire strong, and we will keep it strong. There will never be chaos, as long as I am emperor. Nothing is more important than the maintenance of order. Together we will do what must be done."

Chapter Seventeen

IT WAS NIGHT TIME AS KENDRICK stood in the courtyard outside Fernley Manor, facing toward the fields. Lights shone from the nearby manor windows. He scratched at his stubble and pondered the uncertain future ahead for his family.

Like a passing storm, the fielding was over. Esk was left with churned up mud, timber structures, and debris of all kind. Kendrick was left with a sword to sharpen and armor to dig out of his cellar. He had sons to prepare . . . an estate he would soon be absent from. War was always difficult, unpredictable. War changed everything.

And more than anything else, he hated change.

The war was all anyone could talk about. He had now heard enough speculation to make him long for some time alone. What had the Veldrians done with the common people they conquered? After all, they had beheaded Lexia's garrison commander and tortured the governor's house diviner. Surely the empire was dealing with an implacable evil. Didn't the Veldrian fighters drink the blood of their fallen enemies, which was the secret source of their power? How could the empire ever have tried to negotiate? Were the cities in the Southern Provinces now falling, to be burned to the ground, one by one? Was it all becoming ash and blood and bone?

And yet, despite the many things Kendrick had to worry about, there was something that concerned him more than anything else.

Julian was going to be the supreme commander, in charge of everything, including Kendrick and his sons. And when he looked at Julian, Kendrick didn't like what he saw.

He could only worry about what he could control. He should focus his mind on the fact that the new army, the Armies of the West, would be heading south, and that he and his sons would be there to join the struggle.

He sensed movement, as Anthea came out of the manor to join him. "You should eat. Cook can make you something." She waited, but he didn't reply or move. "What's troubling you?"

"Our new emperor. Among other things." He checked that he and his wife were alone. "Have you spoken to your brother?"

"I have."

"He told you?"

"I wish he hadn't, truth be told."

"Rigel was ready to deny Julian the succession. Declan was about to announce it. And then . . . "

"And then it didn't matter," Anthea finished. She performed her own scan of the area, lowering her tone. "I asked him, but he didn't tell me what he plans to do now."

"He won't let go of it. Not even now. He is going to find this other child—"

"Who is younger than Julian, and was never part of the succession. Why go to all the trouble?"

"Because his wife has gone mad and vengeance is all he has. He came close, Anthea. Even now, Declan will have caught the smell of blood."

"I am worried. Not just about him, but about you too. You and the boys." She took his hand and stared up into his face. Raising her hand, he kissed the back of her palm. "Must you really go to war?"

"I wish I could stay, more than anything in this world. But our empire is under attack. We have been busy fighting each other, when we have bigger threats outside. Julian is going to be tested, and we will see what kind of man he is." He turned toward the fields again, shaking his head and remembering. "What terrible luck. His father dies. And yet, by that very fact, he is saved."

"Do you think that is what it was? Luck?" Anthea hesitated and then spoke so quietly it was almost a whisper. "She is no fool—"

"Never say that out loud," he interrupted, again checking in all directions. "Not even to me."

Her mouth snapped closed and Kendrick changed the subject, moving on from dangerous territory. "I have spoken with Baden Lynch. Troy is being given the command of a small company, a dozen men. Caden is one of the twelve—he is to fight under Troy." He noticed his wife's worried expression. "I know. It's not ideal. But Caden is just going to have to learn how to take orders from his brother."

"And Troy—under whose command is he?"

"The lord marshal's, of course."

"Kendrick . . . Don't jest with me. Not now."

"Don't worry." He smiled and squeezed her hand. "They will both be under my command. I will be there to take care of our sons. They did well at the fielding. Sir Troy and Sir Caden are both going to make names for themselves."

Anthea inhaled, and then let out a breath. She tightly gripped his hand in hers. "Kendrick . . . if Julian knows what Declan did . . . or was about to do . . . "

"He is now emperor," Kendrick said. "He has what he always wanted. We have a mutual enemy, and that should be enough. There is no use in holding onto what might have happened. Now, you're right . . . I shouldn't be staying out here. Let's go tell Sir Troy the news about his first command. It will be good to shed some light into our home."

✦

Bethany was in her chambers when she heard a knock. She had her knapsack on her bed, wide open as she packed. The written statement from her father was visible in an open pocket, and as soon as she heard the knock she pushed the paper down further to slide it out of view.

She straightened, turning to face the room's entrance. "Enter."

Kendrick opened the door but remained standing in the doorway. His face was strange as he glanced at the knapsack and then back at her. He looked like he was wrestling with something.

"Please, My Lord," she said. "Come in."

He came over, leaving the door open. Stopping a few paces from where she was packing, he opened his mouth and then closed it.

"What is it?" she asked.

"Farrell is going to be fine. His wound was worse than it looked."

"I am glad to hear it." She paused. "But that's not why you are here, My Lord."

"I . . . There is no other way to say this. I will need a diviner where we are going, but it doesn't have to be you. I want you to know. My decision is not about your skill . . . to be honest you have impressed us all. It is about the war . . . I cannot in good conscience take you—"

She interrupted. "Lord Kendrick, what do you know about what I do?"

He hesitated. "In truth, when it comes to divination, I know enough to know that I understand very little."

"Traveling the gateways is one of the empire's greatest military advantages, would you agree?"

"It is," he said warily.

"We bring in supplies. Fresh soldiers. We take away the wounded. We make plans to circumvent the enemy."

He gave a wry smile. "It sounds like you know more about soldiering than I do about divination."

"What happens if, just at the wrong time, a key gateway fails? We are depending on it, and then it simply . . . stops working."

He frowned and scratched at his stubbled chin. "That can happen?"

"It has already happened to General Agapon in the Eastern Reaches, and to others before him. I can list three gateways that have failed in the last ten years. The corpus doesn't like it to be discussed, but we have no means of getting them working again. I believe we could be doing more to find out how they function, but at the moment, once gone, they are gone forever."

"You have a keen mind. Even more reason to stay. You will be able to study—"

"I haven't finished," she said. "My Lord." She smiled to soften her words. "If gateways fail, if important reinforcements get lost while traveling, if the enemy finds out a way to resolve the disorientation people feel after travel . . . If and when these things happen, many people will die, and the empire may even fall."

She moved until she was standing right in front of him, staring up into his eyes.

"I have already decided, My Lord. All diviners know we might be called upon in times of war. Our role is one of the most important ones of all."

"But you are young, and your mother—"

"If I went back to Everlast, the corpus would just give me another position. Perhaps I would help move supplies or guide people back and forth from the Argent Arch. I've given it serious thought. I would rather stay with you."

Although she had been smiling, Kendrick remained deadly serious. "Bethany, listen to me. This is not a game. You will be in great danger. You are young and you think bad things happen to other people and never to you. Trust me. Bad things happen to all of us."

"You and Troy and Caden will be the ones fighting in battle, My Lord. You will be the ones in danger. In times of trouble, I'll be the one there for you."

"But why?" He shook his head. "Most sane people would do anything to avoid going to war."

Her lips curved upward. "Do you include yourself?"

"Well, no, but—"

"Being a diviner is what I'm good at. Perhaps I don't trust another to do it as well."

He stared at her, brow furrowed, thinking hard. "Please, Bethany. Let me change your mind. I knew you were young when you became my house diviner. But at that point in time—"

"Not just young, but a woman."

"Yes, well—"

"You cannot change my mind, My Lord."

Even as she spoke, she had motivations he was largely unaware of. The Conways were a powerful, respected noble house. Kendrick was a war hero, and she had heard rumors about his skill as a fighter. The three pillars of the corpus were ruled by the high cleric, the high confessor, and the high diviner. But the corpus was the emperor's body; all of it was under the emperor's command. An emperor who was her half-brother, and who may or may not learn about her existence.

She trusted Kendrick. She felt safe when she was with him. She wanted to remain by his side, even if that meant going to war. And she had meant what she said—she cared about Kendrick and his family; it was her duty to do what she could to see them through the trials to come.

Seeing her determination, he sighed. "Very well. We will be leaving tomorrow, in the afternoon, one of the first groups to travel to Engel. All of my levies will be with us. You will want to get a message to your mother. I suggest you write it tonight, as well as any others you wish to send. Get some rest, Bethany. Tomorrow is going to be a long day."

Chapter Eighteen

ZHUANA STOOD ON THE BATTLEMENTS, atop the outer wall enclosing the city of Gorvia. The arid landscape she was facing was flat enough for her to see a great distance, while around her, bodies lay scattered on the stone and littered the streets behind her. This was the third city she had conquered. The soldiers of the garrison had fought, and they had died. Despite her rapid victories, however, it wouldn't continue to be so easy.

"You wanted to see me?"

She turned as Maven Dresk approached. He still wore his armor, and his bald head and face were spattered in blood, with a wide swathe across his torso. He had dark red on his arms, on his neck below his chin, even under his fingernails. He seemed unaware of the image he made, or perhaps he didn't care.

Perhaps he even relished it.

There was a time when she had seen him similarly sprayed with red. He had just delivered a final killing blow to the man he had been fighting, to send his body tumbling in the dust. Panting, he had stood in place, over his fallen opponent, a gleam in his eyes, knowing it was he who had survived the duel.

She swallowed, thrusting the memory away. The duel was in the past, over sixteen years ago ... even though the blood back then, the blood all over Maven's body, had belonged to her husband Barrix, the father of the babe she had held in her arms.

Maven's cold eyes regarded her, as they had back then. Even without his squashed, broken nose, he was always an ugly man.

She heard a cry, drawing her attention inside the city, down on the ground by the bodies. Warriors from among her people had noticed her and Maven up on the battlements of the city they had conquered. Men clapped each other on the shoulders. Companions called out to each other to point up at their position.

But it wasn't Zhuana's name they called.

"Maven!"

"Maven!"

"Over here!"

They waved at the muscled warrior and cheered when he turned his gaze upon them.

Zhuana revealed nothing, even as she worried about his growing popularity. She had been queen in a period of peace, leading her people in an evacuation, keeping them together throughout their long journey to the empire's southern border.

But people forgot about the wealth and security they had once enjoyed in Veldria. They didn't see the workings of her mind, and know how much she wrestled with different options to find the right path for her people.

Instead they saw Maven: a strong fighter who was always at the front. War and fighting ... they had always been what he was best at.

"Well?" Maven asked. "What is it you want, Queen Zhuana?"

"I asked you here because we need to abandon this idea of using their diviners against them. I have spoken with some of your ... prisoners. There is nothing that can be done about the disorientation on the other side. It doesn't matter what threats you make, or how many diviners you force to take our warriors through the black doorways. The gateways are always guarded. It is too easy for them to butcher our men as they emerge on the other side."

Maven's face was blank. "I have come to the same conclusion. Is that all?"

"Sending that diviner from Lexia was foolish. All it did was alert them to our invasion. We both know I would have stopped you from doing it."

"Respectfully, Queen Zhuana, they would have found out soon enough. I understood you to be looking for vengeance after the way they treated us ... but if I have that wrong?"

Zhuana didn't reply. She instead turned again toward the yellow landscape, stretching all the way to the hazy horizon, and then she changed the subject. "This has been easy so far, would you agree?"

"It is never easy, when you are determined to kill a man, and he is determined to kill you."

"I was in the fighting too," she said flatly. "I am talking about taking these three cities. You may or may not have heard, but our scouts report the building of fortifications at Engel. The new emperor plans to hold the line there, which means the next battle will be decisive. Losing is not an option. We both know it would mean the end of our people."

With the tension between them easing, Maven stared in the same direction she had been looking in, as if he could see across the dusty plain, all the way to the mountainous city of Engel at the other end of the expanse.

He then watched her, gauging her reaction. "I have been questioning the locals. Engel is made of wood. These new fortifications will also have wooden scaffolding."

"Go on."

"I want to take a small force and set fire to the city. To its walls. To its houses. All of it."

She considered his idea. It didn't take her long to reply. "No."

He scowled. "It could win us—"

"I said no. We are committed to either ruling these people or making them enter terms that we will dictate. If we burn cities full of the empire's men, women, and children, they will fight us to the very end."

Maven's voice lowered and his nostrils flared. "Can you not see? We are fighting for our lives no matter which way you see it."

"I am queen," she said, matching his deadly tone.

She saw his hand twitch, located by his side, close to the hilt of his sword. But she and Maven both knew she had the support of the druids and a large number of the druadan—her father's supporters as well as those who followed her late husband. He could strike her down, but if he did, he would never be king. Someone would come for him in turn.

He let out a slow breath, and then his eyes were gleaming as his lips curved in a slight smile. "I saw young Garric in the fighting."

He knew what her reaction would be. "You must be mistaken."

"He is nearly seventeen and we are at war. If he wants to fight, it is his right." He waited for her to respond, but she had nothing to say. "He is fighting with his people. Try to take it away from him and see what happens."

Maven turned on his heel and walked away. Zhuana was breathing heavily; at least where her son was concerned, Maven knew what he was talking about.

Her little son would have been fighting against full-grown men. Garric could fall to an arrow or a slashing wound across his torso. He could die. Yet if it was what her son wanted, she couldn't stop him.

Maven was right. And she could only hate him for it.

✦

The scene outside Gorvia was surprisingly calm after the city's violent conquest. Cactus and spiky grass decorated the dusty landscape, where warriors and horses crowded around the city's numerous wells, waiting in the shade for their turn to get some water. A distant pile of corpses buzzed with flies. As Zhuana took long strides on the yellow dirt, a boy led a horse in the opposite direction with a Veldrian fighter's body sprawled out on its back. The hot wind blew at her dark hair, pulling loose strands across her eyes.

Garric was washing his face from a trough. Her son splashed his cheeks and straightened, lips thinning when he saw her coming. Zhuana kept her face hard and gave him a quick inspection. He had a red cut on his left arm but it wasn't a serious wound. His armor had a new gouge by his hip. As his wavy dark hair dripped down the side of his face, the water was slightly pink, but no, the blood wasn't his.

"Mother . . ." he trailed off. His green eyes were anxious and more than a little guilty.

His hands weren't shaking, which was a good sign. Some people struggled with the brutality of battle, but Garric might have her ability to fight through the blood and violence and the fear that could be overwhelming.

She still remembered her first kill, a raider her father the king made her execute as an instructive exercise. The blood gushing from his headless corpse had disgusted her, but she had slept easily that night—the man had butchered a farmer and his wife and their two young girls.

"You have decided to be a man," she finally said.

He took some time to reply. He glanced around, but where they were, they wouldn't be overheard. "I have."

She kept her face blank. "Then from now on, that is how I shall treat you. If you are going to be fighting in battle, it is also time for you to be seen with me, watching and learning at my side. In battle, you will not yet be as skilled as the warriors you will be fighting alongside. That will come. Until that day, despite your inexperience, you cannot let them forget who you are. You are my son. And one day you will be their king."

His face registered surprise that she wasn't trying to stop him. She was proud of him when he managed to control his childish, awestruck expression, instead nodding with a determined set to his jaw. He was

117

becoming more like his father every day.

"There is more to being a ruler than fighting," she said. "More than warfare. You can defeat your enemies and hold them by your sword point against a wall, but they may be so desperate for your defeat that they will run onto your sword to strangle you. There is power, but there is also restraint. For every action there is a reaction. Do you understand?"

"I think so."

She remembered when he took his first steps, spoke his first words, and rode his first horse. He had grown up without his father, and she was the one who watched his eyes droop closed as she told him stories at bedtime and laughed as he pretended to fight trees with a stick. That time was long gone; she couldn't see him that way now.

At the same time, he was her son. She loved him. How was he truly handling his first experience of battle?

"Were you afraid?" she asked softly. He didn't answer. "Remember, there cannot be courage without fear. We should not let fear dominate us, yet we can still admit it. We can say, yes, I feel fear coming like a snake wriggling up my back. It is there, I acknowledge it, but I am going to get that snake and wrestle it to the ground."

"Mother?"

"Yes?"

His question surprised her, but perhaps it shouldn't have. "Will Maven Dresk be king one day?"

"No. You will be king after me."

"He wants to be king?"

"Whether he does, or he doesn't, it is never going to happen."

"He killed Father. Why do you have to have him on your council?"

"Because giving him a position of power keeps him and his friends as allies, rather than enemies."

He nodded uncertainly, but he was still too young to understand. She also didn't give voice to her next thought.

It was something for her alone.

One day, she would confront her husband's killer and defeat him. If she didn't . . . if there was a conspiracy that was allowed to flourish . . . she and her son might both be killed instead. And whether or not he held the blade, it would be Maven Dresk who brought her down.

This was a thought she kept buried, even to herself.

She was a patient woman. She would choose her time with care.

Chapter Nineteen

BETHANY RAISED HER STAFF HIGH as she stood in front of the oversized triangular frame. She slammed the base on the ground. The Weaver's Breath greeted her nose, familiar yet stomach-churning, bringing a tarry stench and a sickening spell of light-headedness.

She was more used to it now, despite it crashing into her with the strength of her very first time. The world began to hum. She was keenly aware of the people behind her. She was at the head of a long column almost entirely made up of men. All were local to Esk, with coloring ranging from swarthy to pale, and whether dark or blond-haired, young or old, all of them wore their hair cut short. Officers displayed stripes, but they all wore brown uniforms with a stag insignia and scabbards by their hips. Today they were her wards, the people she was going to lead through the gateway.

Each of her wards was unique. They all made up a thread on the tapestry, woven together with other threads, connected to other people, physical objects, structures, and geographical features. Without a world to interact with, the idea of a person's existence was meaningless. People needed somewhere to walk upon, somewhere to live and love. The tapestry wasn't just woven from people and the threads between them. Nor was it a great pattern of gateways and cities and other solid masses that warped it in different ways. The tapestry was everything.

The vibration of the world around her increased. The pulsating was tangible, a humming of threads she could reach out and touch, pull and snap. Strength and power emanated from the staff in her hand. Puzzling thoughts rose to the surface. What exactly were stars? What was the purpose of the universe?

She was becoming too disconnected from the reality she was in. The Weaver's Breath had sent her consciousness spiraling away as she pondered how it was that people weren't as heavy as mountains and yet altered the tapestry in their own way.

Focus. She separated herself into two parts, allowing the awe to do as it pleased, even as she fulfilled her purpose as a diviner.

Her training helped her ground herself. Her physical body was still in front of the triangular frame. Her staff was in her hand, raised up into the air.

She had work to do.

She brought her staff up higher and down across the air, whirling it over and over as she searched for the resonance that matched the pulsating in her mind. The hum grew to fill her as her skin tingled from head to toe. When the staff was in tune with the gateway, she brought the pole down in front of her and slashed it across the air. The air sparked in the triangular frame. A bright line trailed in the wake of her orb. With another series of movements, she widened the gash and elongated it, until the break in the tapestry become a tall rectangle of shiny blackness.

She was breathing hard as she turned back to her wards. "Stay with me. Be ready to enter."

An officer cried out behind her. "Keep order as you enter. Got that, men?"

"Yes, sir!"

She stepped through the portal to cross over into the path of stars.

Shift.

Darkness swallowed her up. She walked along the tunnel, surrounded by bright lights that glimmered against the darkness. The first soldiers entered behind her. To a man, as soon as they were in the tunnel, their eyes became unfocused.

"Stay with me," she repeated. "Keep order. Follow close behind, but leave some space behind me as I walk."

She pressed on, not yet worrying about making sense of the stars that shot past her with dizzying speed. The soldiers came four abreast. There were no horses in the group; they would get their mounts in Engel. Her wards were calm and silent as they kept up with her. Their order looked as it should, but it was never a good idea to relax in the path of stars.

"Keep coming. Maintain formation. Continue four abreast. Remain about ten feet behind me."

At the back of the group, Kendrick and his two sons brought up the rear. She swirled her staff. The gateway at the Star Temple closed. It was now time to get her wards to their destination.

But a surge from the Weaver's Breath made her vision blur. Something in the confusion of glittering white dots forced her to stop. The dizziness grew stronger. Pain flared between her temples. All of a sudden, it took all of her strength just to remain standing.

Part of her was screaming with fear. Once or twice a year, a diviner and his or her wards vanished forever. Her wards were as defenseless as babes. If she failed now, she would doom them all to a terrible death. Panic surged up and down her insides. Her skin felt like she was being pulled in a thousand directions.

She closed her eyes.

Her father's face appeared. His lips were moving, but she couldn't hear anything he was saying, even as she knew what his words were: *You may take my name.*

She didn't want his name. She had never asked for it. What was she supposed to do with the testament he gave her?

Her father's face disappeared, to be replaced with Xander's look of concern. He mouthed another set of words that she didn't hear: *Bethany, find your focus.*

Breathe in . . . Breathe out . . . Breathe in . . .

Calm returned slowly, in fits and starts, in between the pulses of the tapestry. She took control of her fear. She named it, held onto it, and let it drift away.

Once she felt ready, she opened her eyes.

She clutched her staff with both hands for a time, bringing peace to her mind and order to the path of stars. The darting stars slowed down until she could make sense of them. For a time, however, she couldn't see anything familiar. Finally her shoulders slumped with relief. The fish constellation was drifting toward her. Using its familiar shape to orientate herself, she took her staff and pulled the end of the tunnel toward the direction she should travel.

The sight of another constellation—the leaf—made her more confident, and once she had them, she made further adjustments. She walked along the path of stars and brought her staff up, and then across, before twisting it hard to the right. She had studied the stars that should dominate the sky at her destination gateway: the Twelve Old Men at Engel. At this time of day, even though they couldn't be seen, the stars should hover overhead like this . . .

She raised her staff, moved it just a little. Once she was ready, she checked on her wards again. The soldiers appeared just as they should, eyes glazed as they followed her, apparently unsupported by a floor, along the path of stars.

She pulled her staff up, ready to open her gateway. Readying herself, she then sliced open a gash in the air. Sparks accompanied a sizzle. She widened the tear with a series of deft movements, until she was facing another black doorway.

"Stay with me," she called to her wards. "We are now arriving at the gateway at Engel. When you walk behind me, do not stop, keep walking so that those behind you can keep going. Ready. Here we go. Follow the person in front of you."

Leading her group from the front, she stepped straight through the portal—

Shift.

—Smoke enveloped her from head to toe. She coughed hard, bent over, her chest making painful heaves. Enough of her wits remained so that she staggered to the side rather than obstruct the gateway.

What was happening? This wasn't how things were supposed to be.

Hunched over, hand over her face, she attempted shallow breaths. Still coughing, she straightened to scan the area, peering through the dark smoke clouding the scene. Through the haze, the Twelve Old Men came into view. The looming circle of statues meant she had definitely come to the right place. The smoke partially cleared, revealing faces on the statues that were little more than ovoids suggesting heads, along with lengths at the bottom that might be beards. The gateway was positioned on a flat section of hillside, with a slope falling away at one side.

Behind her, dazed soldiers kept coming through the portal. She heard ragged coughs, but they were still docile enough to follow her instructions when she called to them.

"Keep moving—!" She broke off in another cough. "Take twenty . . . take twenty steps forward and move to the side. Clear the way!" The soldiers' figures appeared and disappeared. She was relieved when those in front continued to walk, moving to allowing space for those behind them.

Her eyes were stinging, watering and blurring her vision. She waved smoke away from her face. Voiced barked as the confusion wore off and the soldiers from Esk found themselves in the smoke-filled haze. With the Twelve Old Men on high ground, she spied an area where the slope was clear. Her throat burned as she stumbled, desperate to get away from the clouded air.

Gaining height, she soon realized that whatever its origin, the smoke had found the gateway's dip in the hillside the perfect place to cling to the ground in a thick gray blanket. She heard Kendrick's growling voice call out to her.

"Bethany?"

"Up here!"

A puff of wind cleared the air a little more. Above her position, the hillside rose to become a mountain, and she found herself standing with the gateway just below her and the mountain's tall peak at her back. With the Twelve Old Men in a circle below, the soldiers were all milling about, officers restoring order as they sent the men to the open slopes nearby. Smoke rolled up from the lower ground, constantly climbing, dense and thick like a rising tide. A lengthening plume of the smoke stretched up from far below, with an unlucky wind sending the plume directly toward the gateway.

She stared toward the source of the smoke.

The city of Engel was burning.

Engel occupied an area where the mountains met the plain below. The city was walled and circular, filled with colorful buildings made of wood and stone. Conical roofs topped the houses, which were crowded together, both within and outside the wall. The buildings nearest the center were the grandest, some with several stories, where tall towers shot up as if trying to escape the turmoil.

The fire's progress told a tale. The blaze must have begun in the poorer quarters outside, where the flat roofs were made of timber rather than tiles, for already the area was just charred and blackened ruins. The flames had then caught onto the city's wall and traveled inside, before spreading throughout the entire settlement.

Fire now raged across the city. Flames leaped from house to house. A tower toppled, slowly, inexorably crashing down onto the surrounding buildings. Bright spears danced like vengeful spirits as they burned in a thousand places. Smoke constantly traveled up and outward in a thick, heavy plume, to be pushed along by the wind.

Engel's gates stood wide open. A sea of people streamed from the city. From Bethany's vantage, they were tiny, colorful ants, too far away for her to hear their screams. As for the people still inside . . .

"By all the stars alive . . . " Kendrick's voice came from beside her, his face revealing his shock.

They both tore their eyes from the burning city when a call rang through the air, loud enough to draw their attention back to the Twelve Old Men. Troy was down there, bellowing for all he was worth.

"Enemies! Enemies!"

Another officer's voice joined in. "Form up! Men, all of you. Form up!"

The soldiers from Esk raced toward the slope below the gateway where they could defend such a critical location from attack. But as they moved into formation where the haze was thicker, smoke billowed up again, clouding their group completely. The clash of arms split the air. A man screamed. Steel rang against steel, somewhere farther down the hillside.

Kendrick drew his sword. "I have to get down there."

She grabbed his arm before he could leave. "There's danger here. It's my duty to let people know. If I go to the Wheel, I can alert them."

He thought for a moment and nodded. "Go."

They ran together, but Bethany stopped at the gateway while Kendrick continued past the circle of twelve statues. The sound of steel against steel grew louder, coming closer. Smoke billowed around the Twelve Old Men as she made her way into the center of the circle.

Another man's scream sounded like it was right behind her. Her back itched as she raised her staff high. She turned her orb, heard the click, and then slammed her staff's base on the ground.

✦

Bethany stepped out of her portal to find herself at the Wheel of Klare, the empire's hub for distributing messages and news. The gateway was immense, one of the empire's largest, and shaped like its namesake when viewed from above, with a rim connected to paths that made up the spokes and an expansive central hub.

Located in the middle of a perfectly flat field, surrounded by green grass, most of the Wheel was covered in wooden roofs built by the empire rather than the Eidar. Arrayed along the spokes, dozens of desks all faced the hub where Bethany was standing. Clerks in gray uniforms worked at each desk, concentrating as they sorted messages. Hunched over one of the nearest desks, a diviner in a gray cloak assisted one of the clerks. She was a stocky woman clad in a tunic and trousers rather than a dress, with hair short enough to call stubble. She looked up from her work at Bethany's arrival.

Bethany cleared her throat but then it became a cough. She kept her staff in the air, holding her portal open. "The city Engel is burning. The gateway is under attack."

A widening of the diviner's eyes was the only sign of her shock. "The gateway remains in our control?"

"I believe so. I heard sounds of fighting ... smoke ... " she put her hand on her chest, trying in vain not to cough again, "smoke is everywhere."

"Very well," the diviner said curtly. "We will get the word out immediately. Diviner ... " the short-haired woman paused, waiting for her name.

"Sylvana."

"Diviner Sylvana, do you need to rest?"

Bethany answered quickly, shaking her head. "No."

"You are certain?" The woman frowned. "If you return, will you be in danger?"

"There is always danger, but I have my duty."

The diviner pursed her lips but then nodded. "Very well. Thank you, Diviner Sylvana."

With the Weaver's Breath still working through her, Bethany turned to the black mirrored doorway she had held open. She would pay a price for her travels when the day was done.

She stepped back into the portal.

✦

Bethany was prepared this time, and when she emerged to find herself enclosed by the Twelve Old Men, she swiftly scanned the area.

She was strangely alone. There was no sign of Kendrick, Troy, Caden, nor any of the men they were leading.

The sounds of fighting reached her ears: shouts and cries, hard blows and steel striking steel. Wherever they were fighting, it was somewhere more distant than before. Smoke drifted back and forth as the wind moved unpredictably. She tried to take shallow breaths. She had delivered her warning, and now it just remained to find the group from Esk.

A harsh guttural cry made her head snap to the side.

A broken-nosed warrior with a bald head was striding toward her, a naked steel blade in his hand, coated in another's blood. His harsh voice came again as he called to his companions, half a dozen warriors in leather armor, and pointed his sword at her.

A voice in her mind screamed at her. *Run!* The leather-clad warriors fanned out, and already one was moving to circle behind her. Some were younger, other older, but their eyes were wild and their mouths were open and snarling. This was just like at the Star Temple. Once again she stood frozen in place.

The Veldrians were here. She had no protection.

She couldn't stay where she was. She had to move. *Move!*

At last, the frozen feeling left her.

Her eyes narrowed. Her staff was in her hands. She remembered Madam Mei and all her instruction. There was one time she focused on in particular, a time when Mei had taken the slow dance with her staff and sped up, faster and faster, until the dance became a battle against an unseen opponent. The sensation had been exultant . . . exhilarating.

She turned to face the nearest warrior, a dark-eyed man with curly black hair and a scraggly beard.

Her staff came up, gripped in both hands.

Spinning like an acrobat she whirled, bringing her staff across her body to land the heavy orb into the warrior's torso. The man whooshed as the breath left his chest. She took a step and smoothly continued moving, to bring her staff up again. She put force and speed into her weapon, and it sailed through the air to crunch into the second Veldrian's skull.

The bald warrior with the broken nose was next, but he managed to dodge her blow. He lunged. Quick as a snake, he thrust out a hand to squeeze her neck.

Her staff fell out of her hands. She struggled to breathe. Stars sparkled across her vision.

A sharp pain struck the back of her head.

Chapter Twenty

KENDRICK STOOD ON THE HILLSIDE, searching, eyes roving. There was less smoke, which meant the Twelve Old Men were revealed in detail. But he wasn't looking at the statues, he was trying to find his house diviner. By all the stars, where was she?

In the distance, the city of Engel still smoldered. For the city's residents, the day had been one of terrible tragedy; nothing would be the same again.

He could guess now what had happened. The raiders had been fleeing the carnage they had inflicted upon the city, and for some reason they had come this way and encountered his men. There was a brief skirmish on the hillside, but the raiders fled when seriously challenged, to vanish to wherever they had come from.

Engel's gateway was now well-secured, with a strong perimeter of soldiers holding position. More diviners kept arriving, bringing a steady stream of men and horses. Surely Bethany had done what she had said, and got the word out. After all, many of the newcomers were setting straight off to help the people who had fled the burning city to take refuge—somewhere distant, somewhere they would at least be safe.

Every time a diviner arrived, Kendrick turned to stare, only to feel disappointment when it wasn't Bethany. He wasn't sure how worried he should be.

Troy came over, red-eyed from the smoke. "Orders. We're all to move on to Narzin."

"Narzin?" Kendrick frowned. He shook his head. "No. Our forces can't go to Narzin. There's no gateway."

"It's the nearest city. We'll be traveling onward by road. "

"You know we can't leave. She isn't back yet."

"This comes straight from the lord marshal. The entire army is to form up within the hour. That includes us."

With a scowl, Kendrick took another long, lingering look around the area. How was he supposed to leave, if he didn't know where she was? What could have happened to her?

If she had come straight back as he had expected, he would have seen her by now. She might have needed to rest. Or her superiors might have sent her elsewhere. He had already sent a message to the Wheel with another diviner. If Bethany went somewhere new, he would soon find out.

"Very well. Pass word. Get the men ready to go."

After Troy left, among the newcomers, a familiar figure moved among all the horses and armored men. Wearing a fine cloak with gold trim over his military uniform, the leader of the Wardens contrasted with the other men around him. Plump, gray-haired and jowly, Tristan was energetic as he strode around giving orders, before he noticed Kendrick and waved before coming over.

"Kendrick! What a mess eh? Those poor blasted people. The word is you engaged the enemy."

"Not for long. They weren't looking for a fight."

Tristan shook his head as he looked at the ruins of Engel, eyes roving over the smoking city. "Not the finest start to a campaign."

"Not at all."

"Nor a strong beginning for our new emperor."

Kendrick rubbed his neck; his throat was sore from the smoke, and would probably be for days. "I suppose no one can blame this on him."

"He's the emperor, Kendrick. That's what he is there for." Someone called out to Tristan and he turned away. "Something I need to attend to—"

"Is it true we're moving to Narzin?"

Tristan paused. "Not a good place to hold, but Julian doesn't want to give the queen another two cities—Engel and Narzin—to add to the three she already has."

"It's a bad move. We should be digging in at Meroy."

"Can't say I disagree with you, but orders are orders. See you on the road?"

Kendrick nodded and Tristan returned to his men.

Meanwhile, more soldiers and horses kept arriving through the gateway. As the moments passed, Kendrick waited as long as he could. It wasn't like Bethany to leave him to wonder what had happened, completely unaware of where she had gone.

His younger son was speaking with one of the diviners, a lean dark-skinned man. Caden finished his conversation and caught sight of Kendrick waving him over.

"Father?"

"Any news?

Caden shook his head. "He only came just now from Myra."

Kendrick let out a breath. "There's not much more we can do. Listen. I'm going to leave you here with some men. Wait until midday tomorrow, and then catch up with us on the road. Wherever she is, she may have just been delayed."

"I am sure she's fine, Father."

"I hope so."

The overland journey to Narzin would come with its own troubles.

Bethany would return soon enough.

✦

Bethany awoke to a thudding pain in the back of her skull. Her eyelids involuntarily fluttered. She was slumped with her back against a hard surface and her head down, so that her first sight was pebbles and yellow dirt. She gingerly moved her head, wincing as the rock wall behind her brushed against the sorest part. Tingling pain came from her wrists, forcing her to try to move them, but she couldn't. Her hands were bound behind her back, with what felt like leather cord. She wasn't going anywhere.

Her memory brought her flashing images: the smoke, the bald, broken-nosed warrior, coming in close and snarling as he squeezed her throat.

She was being held prisoner. She might be about to be killed.

Sounds reached her: people talking, laughing, bustling about. The taste of smoke in the air made her swallow, but this was merely wood smoke, along with the odors of cooking meat.

Slowly she raised her head.

Multiple camp fires filled a space between two opposing cliffs. Veldrian warriors were in the process of stripping off their armor and washing themselves from buckets. Others sat by fires, tending flames and turning skewered hunks of meat. A tattooed man in a leather vest made a pained face as he sat on a rock while a companion stitched a wound in his side. There weren't just men in the camp; a woman barked with laughter at something another woman said—both of the pair had faces blackened by soot and curved swords at their hips. One thing she was sure of: these were the raiders who had just set fire to a city full of ordinary men, women, and children.

There were plenty of tethered horses but no tents. A row of bodies lay in the shade of the cliff with cloth draped over them. The Veldrians had taken Gorvia; she already knew that before she had left Esk. In terms of location, she must be somewhere between Engel and Gorvia. The raiders would be looking forward to their triumphant return.

Someone was staring at her.

She turned her head. The bald warrior with the squashed nose was sitting on a rock by a fire. Even as she looked at him, he kept his cold, dark gaze fixed directly on her. He then pushed his knees to climb to his feet.

He came over to crouch in front of her. When he spoke, his voice was harsh and rasping as he spoke Imperial with a heavy accent. "I am Maven Dresk. You are young for a graycloak."

She tried to draw away but there was nowhere she could go; she had to remain where she was with her back against the rock.

"You are wondering why you are here. You are not the first graycloak I have taken. The empire uses you to move things through the gateways. Things and people. I want to find a way to strike at the empire's heart rather than take your cities one by one. But I have a problem. It seems that a man traveling the gateways is weakened at the other end, unless he is a graycloak like you."

Bethany had no intention of helping him. "You set fire to the city?"

"Yes. And then as we were leaving I saw you. It was an opportunity. And here we are. Now tell me what I want to know. You see my problem. I want to find a way to send warriors through with a graycloak and be in fighting form on the other side."

It was an effort to hold his gaze. She had to hope that he would believe her. "You have spoken to other diviners and so you already know. What you are asking for is impossible."

He continued to stare into her eyes. "You do not want to betray your people. But you should know that with the right pressure, anyone can be a traitor."

A chill trickled along her spine .

"Dan Dresk!" The loud call came from a woman with three diagonal scars on her cheek, heading their way on horseback.

Maven straightened, his attention on the newcomer. "What is it?"

"Our scouts just returned. The Imperials are moving their forces to Narzin."

"Narzin?" Maven frowned, before reaching into his leather jerkin to pull out a folded sheet of paper. He swiftly opened it up, revealing a map of the empire's Southern Provinces. Bethany wasn't close enough to read it, but as he traced a route with his fingertip, she recalled her own layout of the empire. Narzin was a smaller city than Engel, bordering the Red Desert, near the coast to the north and east.

"There is no gateway close to Narzin," Maven said, his eyes traveling over the map. "They must still be using the gateway at Engel to bring in men and supplies." He re-folded the map, returning it to his pocket. "We have to tell the queen about the opportunity to strike them while they are out in the open."

He turned to once again consider her, watched her with his sinister, calculating eyes. Her stomach clenched. He might be about to order that she be killed.

"We will bring the graycloak with us."

✦

"My Queen . . . Dan Dresk is approaching. He sent word that he will come straight here."

Zhuana turned to scan the desert. She was in the late governor of Gorvia's council room, located in the highest floor of what would have been called a palace anywhere but the Eternal Empire. She caught sight of a group of warriors riding on horseback to approach the city, a dust cloud following in their wake. Soon Maven and his raiders were entering through the open gates.

The news about what they had done had already arrived.

The man who had spoken, one of her stewards, backed away before bowing to Zhuana and her companions and hurriedly leaving the area.

Zhuana had summoned her council, with the exception of Alric, who was away dealing with some emergency that only a druid would understand. Dan Henwin scratched at his bushy beard. Dan Logrin towered over the group, distinguishable by his topknot and bare, muscular arms crossed in front of his chest. Dana Klara tugged apprehensively at her blonde braid.

Garric was also with her, and from his eyes he looked like he was trying hard to hide his worry. Her son wore dark brown clothing that matched the shade of his hair. As should be the case, he was quiet, and would remain so. The situation was hers to deal with.

Maven had taken his men on their raid without her permission. Everyone would be wondering what she planned to do.

Zhuana was in her fighting garb: black leather body armor and below it a skirt of leather strips. The only nod to form, rather than the function of warfare, were the tiny sparkling diamonds woven into the tresses of her hair.

There was movement at the doorway, and a moment later, Maven strode briskly in.

He was dusty and travel-stained but wore a triumphant expression. When Dan Logrin cheered his name, irritation made Zhuana's jaw tighten, but she kept her face hard and composed.

"Queen Zhuana," Maven said. He stopped right in front of her, legs apart, one fist gripped in the other. He was unable to keep the pride from his voice. "My raid was a complete success—"

"Complete?" She arched an eyebrow. "Nothing went wrong at all?" She pretended to consider. "Tell me. Help me understand. How many of my warriors did you lead on the raid?"

He had the audacity to look surprised at her cold reaction. She remembered giving him a clear command, a command he went directly against.

"A hundred men," he said slowly.

"And tell me something else. How many of my men came back?"

He hesitated. "They were brave but there were risks. Perhaps sixty have returned." He lifted his chin. "But we hurt them . . . badly. We killed many thousands."

Dan Logrin spoke up. Easily the biggest man in the room, his deep voice matched his size. As a lifetime ally of Maven, it wasn't surprising to hear him defend his friend.

"My Queen, to my mind Maven Dresk is a hero, and an inspiration to all of our fighters." Logrin nodded at Maven. "He went out there with just a hundred men, and look at what he has accomplished. He made the Imperials burn."

Zhuana held up a hand. She had no throne, and she didn't have the height of some of the men, but Logrin's voice trailed off.

"I cannot applaud what was done. The people you killed were women. Children. Not fighters, but ordinary families and ordinary workers. This will have consequences. It may look like a strike at the empire, but it will make victory much harder, and a final peace more difficult still."

Maven's face became red. "No one is thinking of peace, Queen Zhuana. We have no choice but to conquer their cities, capture their gateways, and occupy their capital. This is no time for weakness. There can be no place in our hearts for sympathy for women and children. This is war."

Between Maven's red face and Zhuana's stony expression, the tension in the air was palpable. Dan Henwin opened his arms in a placating gesture.

"There are differing views," he said soothingly. "Dan Dresk, no one would disagree that what you did was both bold and valued. The Imperials are no longer able to use Engel as a base. Any plans they had will be in disarray. We all simply think of our fallen, the brave souls who will never return."

Zhuana kept her face rigid, hiding her worry. Henwin was usually her ally. She sensed the mood from the other druadan. Maven had delivered the enemy a blow. Engel was far away, too far for them to hear the screams of the burning people. And they didn't think about the common citizens of the empire, who looked to their nobles for safety, and the nobles themselves, who voted where the wind was blowing. The druadan didn't see how their grand objective was made more difficult. She remembered the words she had given to Garric, about actions and reactions, about putting an enemy's back against a wall. None of them understood the tales that would now be told, or thought about how this war was going to end.

"It is done," she finally said. "How have the Imperials reacted?"

Maven cleared his throat, some of the color leaving his face. "They have been forced to adjust their plans quickly, never a good thing for an army at war. They are now on the run, moving their men and horses to Narzin. We will be able to attack their forces as they travel."

Zhuana addressed her words to the entire group. "We can agree that attacking their forces as they cross the desert is our next move. Before we make plans, however . . . " She returned her attention to Maven. "Your raid . . . I hear that you have taken a prisoner."

"What of it?"

"I want you to bring her to me. At once."

Zhuana had just given Maven Dresk a direct command. There was no hiding it. The other druadan looked from Maven to Zhuana and back again.

Maven scowled. For a time he remained where he was, visibly considering his options. He glanced at the other druadan. Then he spoke in a growl. "Very well. Wait here, Queen Zhuana."

He departed with long, angry strides, and when he had left, Zhuana addressed her gathered council with him absent. "Remember, this is the Eternal Empire we are fighting. You cannot comprehend how many of them there are. Enrage them enough, and even the common people will beg to join the fight against us. I took the measure of the new emperor when we were negotiating. Julian is no fool."

"Negotiated without success," Dan Logrin muttered.

Zhuana took a step toward the huge man. He at least looked apologetic, but she could remember a time when he would never have spoken up. She had to do something about Maven's influence, and soon.

"You do not fight a man without first taking a look at him," she said, narrowing her eyes at the brute in front of her; he knew who she was looking at now. "Believe me. In this war, we will make them fear us. Anyone can murder a child, but we are the Veldrians. We will put terror into the hearts of their strongest knights and soldiers. Would you agree, Dan Logrin?"

Logrin stared at the ground. "I agree, Queen Zhuana," he muttered.

"How about the rest of you?" Zhuana asked, turning toward the others. "Are you ready to fight their armies, to go to battle against a great number of their soldiers? Defeat their armies, and we open up the rest of the empire. Burn their cities, and we strengthen their resolve to defeat us. Do you understand what I am saying?" She moved her gaze from face to face, receiving firm nods in reply.

After a few moments, the druadan stirred. Maven was returning.

Maven now had his prisoner with him, another captive diviner, this time a young woman with long auburn hair and skin in a copper tone. The girl was pretty, with intelligent brown eyes, and a slender frame with just enough curves to fill her snug emerald-green dress. She was bound, pulled forward by Maven as she kept her chin high in defiance.

"Leave us," Zhuana commanded. "All of you."

"Queen Zhuana, she is my prisoner—" Maven began.

"You heard me. This council is over. You too, Garric. I want to be alone with her."

Garric was obviously curious as he appraised the young diviner, who was just a few years older than him and yet knew things he would never understand. The druadan glanced at each other, but then they moved on, one by one, including Maven, who tried to hide his reluctance as he left at the side of his old friend Logrin.

Once they had gone, Zhuana found herself alone with the diviner. She spent another moment appraising the young woman in front of her.

The diviner was bound. Zhuana was armed. The girl would have seen the guards outside the door; running would get her nowhere.

"What is your name, girl?"

"Beth . . . " The young woman cleared her throat, and then spoke firmly. "Bethany."

"Do you know who I am?"

"I believe I do," the young woman said cautiously. "You are Queen Zhuana."

"What is it that he has asked of you?"

The diviner, Bethany, appeared to be choosing her words. "He wants to know if there is a way to take warriors through gateways without them being vulnerable on the other side. I explained that it isn't possible. It's the truth."

Zhuana tapped her lips. "No doubt he will ask you again in a more . . . violent way. Tell me. How are you being held captive? I assume he keeps you bound?"

"I am kept in close sight with my hands tied behind my back. My ankles are often bound too." Bethany stared into Zhuana's eyes. "Do you have the power to free me? If so, then please do it."

"The power? Of course I have the power. But you do not ask me to do things. I am the queen, and I do as I please." Watching the young woman, Zhuana wondered why there was something about her that was strangely compelling. She was distinctive, with her unique coloring, and yet oddly familiar. "What is it about you, Bethany? There is something in you . . . something I have seen before . . . "

"I'm just a diviner, Queen Zhuana."

"No. I have a sense for these things." Zhuana spent another long moment assessing. There was a recognizable fire in the young woman's eyes—not just the steely look of defiance, and not merely the light of intelligence . . . but that wasn't it . . . "If times were different, I would visit the realm of shadows to see what my dreams could reveal." She shook her head. "However there is no time. Instead, I ask that you watch."

As Zhuana stood in front of the young woman, who was several inches shorter in height, Zhuana pointed at her own abdomen, where her belly was covered by her black leather armor. The young diviner frowned, confused. Zhuana continued to look meaningfully at the area below her navel. Slowly she lifted the armor at her abdomen up; she then tugged her skirt of hardened strips down.

Zhuana revealed the thin leather belt she wore concealed, somewhere no one would expect it to be.

Finding the buckle, Zhuana unfastened the belt to remove it completely. She displayed it to the girl, and then showed her the tiny triangular knife in a sheath. As Zhuana knew well, the blade was sharp enough to cut the wisps of hair on her forearm. She kept it that way herself.

"Lift your dress high," Zhuana commanded.

"Why?"

"Do as I say," she repeated, allowing her voice to rise.

Despite her bound hands, Bethany was able to reach down and take hold of the fabric of her green dress, somewhere around the vicinity of her knees. She pulled the material higher, the motion awkward, as

Zhuana's frown deepened.

"Higher," Zhuana snapped. "Above your waist."

Bethany struggled, but she managed to get her dress sliding up, bunching the material in her fingers, until her legs were bare to Zhuana's gaze and she only had her undergarment to preserve her modesty.

Zhuana wrapped the leather belt around Bethany's waist, so that it hung from her hips, drooping a little in the region of her navel. Her brow furrowed with concentration while she tugged and shifted until she was satisfied.

"The knife is at your hip, toward the back," Zhuana said. "You may let go."

The young diviner released her grip on the fabric, letting the dress fall down again. Her eyes were puzzled. "I don't understand. Why are you doing this?"

"For my own satisfaction, for one thing. But also, in your role, you have access to those in power. I want you to tell them that I had no part in the burning of Engel. It is regrettable. Now, Bethany, Diviner of the Eternal Empire. You have been given a tool. The rest is up to you."

Chapter Twenty-One

MAVEN ROUGHLY SPUN BETHANY AROUND, manhandling her over his body as he checked her hands were bound tightly together behind her back.

"Now sit down," he ordered.

She complied, sliding down the wall to rest her back against it. Before he tied her ankles, Bethany bent her knees up to draw her feet closer to her body. He scowled at her.

"It hurts less this way," she explained.

He muttered to himself, but he didn't squash her legs flat again as he tied her ankles with the same thin but strong leather cord.

The guild house Maven Dresk and his followers had claimed was close to the governor's residence. The three storied building was solid and square, with high ceilings and broad stairs and hallways made of stone. Anyone traveling down from the highest level, where Maven had his personal quarters and kept Bethany close, would easily be observed.

Bethany had to be patient. She would watch and learn. Her opportunity would come.

When Maven finished, she wriggled to make herself more comfortable, surreptitiously glancing around. She was in an expansive entertaining area, with divans and recliners and wide windows looking over the city streets. Maven's bedchamber adjoined the space, while the larger doorway led to the main stairwell where corridors branched to other quarters. Rugs lined the floor. The nearby hearth was cold. A broad wooden table and six chairs hugged the window. With summer's heat rising, the shutters were open, but the iron bars made it clear there would be no escape that way.

Maven was facing the window, eyes unfocussed as he pondered something. Whatever it was, he was scowling, so tense he was almost quivering. Bethany heard footsteps and then a tall, lean warrior come to the room. Seeing his sharp, rat-like face and lank hair to his shoulders, she recognized one of Maven's men.

The rat-faced warrior spoke in Veldrian, so that she had to guess what he was saying from his body language and tone. He queried Maven's obvious irritation. Maven gesticulated as he replied, taking the opportunity to vent. The rat-faced warrior shrugged and made a joke that eased some of Maven's mood.

Maven then asked his follower something, and when his rat-faced companion protested, Maven leveled his finger and barked something harshly. Bethany had learned only a couple of Veldrian words during her journey across the desert, but one of them was the word for water. With a reluctant sigh, the rat-faced man set about whatever task Maven had given him, leaving the way he had come.

Maven and Bethany were alone again. With her back to the wall, Bethany kept her hair over her face as she stared at the stone floor. Nonetheless, Maven came over to stand in front of her.

"Your soldiers are unwise to cross the desert. We will ride out at first light and destroy as many as we can."

She replied unthinkingly. "If you burn every city, there won't be anything left to conquer."

He chuckled. "How many cities does your empire have? If it wins us this war, it will well be worth the trouble."

The sound of someone approaching interrupted them. The rat-faced warrior came back to the room, and whatever he had been asked to do, Maven wasn't happy. Along with the word for water, another familiar word was placed in front of it, and they said it more than once. Bethany kept hearing the same utterance; the word for fire combined with the word for water. Maven's subordinate shook his head, saying a name: Alric. Maven raised his voice; there was something negative about the name Alric. Maven delivered a different name: Telric. He issued another command, and again, the rat-faced warrior departed to do his bidding.

Meanwhile, Bethany mouthed the words, wondering if she had heard correctly. *Firewater.*

Maven was distracted, and she took the opportunity to scan the room. Where was her cloak? And more importantly, her staff? They had both been taken from her, but had her captors kept them or thrown them away? She had been wearing the same clothing for days.

"I see something in your eyes," Maven suddenly said. His dark gaze was on her. "Perhaps you are looking to escape. Trust me, girl. You will not find help all the way out here."

"Where is my staff? Have you destroyed it?"

He snorted. "Why would I destroy it, when I might want you to use it on my behalf?"

"Where is it?"

"I have no reason to tell you."

His ugly face give nothing away. It might be in the adjacent room, kept with his other valuables close by him as he slept.

Time passed, and then the sound of footsteps came again. As the rat-faced warrior returned, this time he brought another man with him. The newcomer had yellowed teeth and grubby skin, but wore brown furs and a whipcord belt, different clothing from that worn by most of the Veldrians she had seen.

He spoke in a lecturing tone as soon as he walked in. Filled with self-importance, the newcomer spoke to Maven as if he were an equal, perhaps even a superior. The news he was delivering wasn't what Maven wanted to hear. Again, she heard them mention firewater.

Maven stood regarding the other man with his legs wide apart, fixing him with a glare of displeasure. Addressing the man in furs as Telric, he asked him a short, blunt question.

Telric immediately looked at her.

His greedy gaze lingered for a time, and he chuckled and made an obscene gesture. A strong pressure grabbed hold of her stomach and squeezed. Telric and Maven were now talking about something else. They were discussing her.

The queasy feeling in her abdomen grew stronger. Maven was watching her, his expression pensive. Telric had his yellowed teeth parted. The third man, the rat-faced warrior, watched with an amused expression.

Maven reached his decision. Tapping his chin with a meaty finger, he nodded toward her, and whatever he was saying, he was agreeing to what the yellow-toothed man was asking. He gave Telric his conditions, and the other man nodded again.

Telric now watched her hungrily, eagerly. He said something directly to her, and then laughed, even though she couldn't understand him. The tension between him and Maven had eased. The two men had reached their agreement.

As Telric left, walking with a shuffled step, he called over his shoulder, pointing directly at her. And then he was gone. Maven's rat-faced subordinate said something to Maven and departed a moment later.

Maven came back over to where she was.

"I see you, girl. You look like you know what is coming. Telric and I have struck a deal, but I have asked that he return you unharmed. You look like the fighting kind, but he has some medicine that will keep you quiet."

Dread was like a pit full of snakes in her chest. When she stared up into his eyes, there was no mercy there. "Listen to me." She had to clear her throat. "Don't do this."

"It is done. My men and I used our firewater on the raid. I need more and Telric can get it for me. We ride at first light. It must be tonight. And something else, but that need not concern you."

"Let me go."

"You are a woman, a pretty one, and you are a diviner. Listen to me, girl." He bit off his next words, each one clear and strong. "I am never going to let you go."

Maven walked away to leave her sitting with her heart racing. No one was going to help her. What could she do to help herself? Maven had said something about medicine. Telric was going to give her something to make her weak and unresisting.

A whisper of steel made her head turn. Maven held his drawn sword, and was inspecting the length of the blade. Shaking his head, he laid the weapon down on the nearby table. He shot a look her way, only to see her staring at the floor. Muttering something, he left the room, boots making loud footsteps on the hard stone floor.

She couldn't wait. She had to act now.

Her hands were bound with cord, but she had been tensing and moving them to stretch the leather and create space. The tiny knife in its sheath was behind her hip, several inches from where it needed to be. She tugged on the belt underneath her dress, shifting and shuffling her body at the same time. The belt resisted, tight against her bare skin, but she tried again, and shifted it a small amount.

The patter of footsteps made her freeze. Maven entered the room, to immediately focus on her. Seeing her in place, he nodded, satisfied.

He tossed a whetstone up and down in his hand as he went back to his sword. He took a seat at the table, lying the blade flat on the surface as he began to carefully circle the whetstone over the steel edge to sharpen it.

He had seated himself at the table so that he could watch her every move. If she wriggled or shifted, he would know, and he might decide to check her bonds. She was running out of time. Telric would come for her tonight, Maven had said. The sun had set. There was no light at the window. At the same time, as far as she knew, Maven hadn't eaten.

She needed Maven to move.

Something was happening; she heard shuffled steps. Telric came to the doorway, entering with a wooden crate in his arms, filled with stoppered leather flasks. Liquid sloshed as he struggled with his burden. He headed over to the table and set the crate heavily down on its surface.

Telric looked her way, flashing his yellowed teeth. Her breath caught. Would it be now? Should she try to break her bonds before he gave her something to drink? Her chances weren't good. Even without Maven, Telric's arms were ropy.

Maven took a flask from the crate and pulled the stopper to sniff the contents. He gave the vessel a slosh, sniffing it again.

Telric tore his eyes away from her. He spoke again in his lecturing tone, like a wine seller exhibiting his wares. Maven nodded, satisfied, but then asked another question. She remembered his mysterious description. He had asked Telric for something else.

Telric reached into a pocket, counting out two green-brown buds the size of large coins into Maven's open palm. From the buds' dull green color and their pattern of tiny indented points, they looked to come from some kind of cactus. Whatever they were, Maven clearly thought they were important. He looked down into his hand, his face eager as he closed it into a fist.

Telric said something else to Maven, and then called over to her, to speak for the first time in thick, accented Imperial. "And you, girl. You I will be seeing soon."

Chapter Twenty-Two

BETHANY'S TIME SENSE TOLD HER that an hour had come and gone. Maven had eaten, but rather than leave the room, one of his men had brought him a plate of bread, meat, and cheese, which was now empty on the table beside him. He was utterly patient as he continued to sharpen his blade.

Time was passing. She had to do something.

Clearing her throat, she raised her voice. "What is in the flasks?"

"Magic," he grunted. "Strength and endurance."

"And the cactus?"

He frowned; even as she engaged him, it was dangerous to remind him that she had been watching. "The cactus does not concern you." He raised an eyebrow. "Or perhaps I should feed you a pearl, and you can visit the realm of shadows yourself. It would be interesting to see what a graycloak like you can handle."

She had to get him to leave. "I need some real food to eat."

"My men forgot you. You will have to wait."

"You could have shared—"

"Ha," he barked a laugh. "You go too far, girl. Be quiet or I will gag you."

"Your friend—"

His lip curled. "Telric is not my friend."

"He is coming soon. I'm weak. What medicine will he give me? You seem to want me to live . . . and to be able to do my work."

He gave one last flick of the whetstone across his sword blade, and then set both sword and stone down on the table. Pushing his knees to stand, he came over until he was standing over her. She looked up at him and kept her gaze steady. There was no use appealing to his sympathy. That would get her nowhere. She was a diviner, able to commune with a universe that he knew nothing about.

"Very well. I will find you some bread." He smiled darkly. "I have heard stories about Telric. You are right. You might need your strength for whatever he has planned."

He turned away, and as he walked with a long stride, she watched with all of her attention on his departing footsteps, counting them one by one after he left the room. Soon she couldn't hear his boots at all. They were on the third floor. He might have some distance to go. But he also might give a quick order to one of his men.

She grabbed at the belt beneath her dress and jerked it hard, moving the sheath around until it was located in the small of her back. Then she leaned forward, supporting the front of her body with her raised knees. Her fumbling fingers pulled at the dress, yanking it up even as she rocked and shuffled her body to allow the fabric to move.

The material came up, exposing the belt and the tiny knife. She seized the little handle, feeling it slip through her fingers. After a second attempt, she pulled the knife from its sheath. Its edge was sharp against her finger.

She heard approaching footsteps. But there was no stopping now. She positioned her wrists, and then sliced through the cords binding them as swiftly as she could. She winced as she nicked the tip of her finger. Fear made her movements desperate as she freed her wrists. Her hands tingled as blood returned, but she tried to ignore the sensation as she reached forward to cut the bonds around her ankles.

The footsteps faded away; whoever it was, they were no longer coming toward her.

She unsteadily climbed to her feet.

She was free.

Flight was the only thought on her mind. She had to hurry. But then she hesitated, turning back toward the adjoining bedchamber.

Bursting into action, she ran into Maven's personal quarters. Furniture filled the room: a bed, clothing stand, mirror, wash basin. There—leaning against a wall, near a side table, was her diviner's staff.

She dashed over to grab it and then spied something else. A stoppered leather flask stood on the side table. She stopped, indecisive. With her staff in one hand and the tiny knife in the other, she didn't have anywhere to put the flask.

She made the difficult choice to leave the flask where it was. But then she spied something else: the two cactus pearls the druid had procured, on the side table, beside the flask. What were they exactly? She snatched them and shoved them into a pocket in her dress.

Her cloak was gone; there was no sign of it. She had her staff and wore her green dress. It was more than time to go.

She put her head down and raced from the room, past the broad space where she had been held captive in the corner. Once she was through the doorway, she stopped to get her bearings and search for threats.

The guild house was laid out in nested rectangles, with rooms along the outer rim and a broad inner landing forming the corridor that connected each room together. The landing also functioned as a perimeter to surround the central stairway. She had come this way before, and when she didn't see anyone, she headed straight for the stairs. Running at full speed, she had her staff in one hand, knife gripped in the other. Without pausing, she threw herself down one step after another.

A Veldrian with a scraggly beard glanced up in surprise when he saw her bearing down on him. She threw herself to the other side of the steps. Sprinting past him, she reached the next level, where she would have to navigate another landing.

A shout from the Veldrian followed her.

Now on the guild house's second level, she raced around the landing to reach the entry to the next stairway down. A younger warrior looked determined as he put his arms out to stop her. Without thinking, she slashed down at his hand with her knife. He yelped in pain, but the impact was hard enough to tear the small weapon from her grip. Rather than try to fetch it, she panted hard as she sprinted.

Reaching the next set of stairs, she grabbed a rail to launch herself for the steps, taking them two at a time. She reached the bottom and looked in all directions. On the next landing, she managed to make it all the way around without encountering anyone. Another set of broad steps greeted her as she heedlessly sprinted down them.

She was finally on ground level. There were people staring at her: men carrying piles of linen, a woman holding an iron pot by the handles, a pair of warriors in one direction, an older Veldrian in leathers in the other.

The two warriors spied her first, so she ran in the opposite direction. A branching corridor caused her to stop. Up ahead, the older Veldrian in leathers was running toward her, shouting something as he waved. She felt a puff of wind and turned. A gauzy curtain was blowing over a doorway.

Heart hammering, she put on a burst of additional speed to reach the end of the corridor and yank the curtain to the side. She emerged from the guild house out of the side door into an alley. At the end of the thin lane between the guild house and the fence beside it, people and horses traveled on the open streets. She sprinted in that direction.

Out on Gorvia's main avenue, people were still moving despite the late hour, leading horses by ropes and walking in both directions. Farther away, Veldrians mingled with locals and browsed market stalls. Lanterns up on poles lit the street at regular intervals. In the distance, the city gates lay wide open.

She had stopped in her tracks, turning and scanning, even as she heard loud shouts behind her. Whatever choice she made now would determine whether she managed to make her escape.

Up ahead, a youth was leading a donkey but she kept turning. There—past a couple of burly Veldrians, a long-faced man was leading a horse along the street by the halter. From his loose southern clothing, he was a local, and from the jewels on his fingers, his horse would be better than most, as well as something he could afford to lose.

The cries of pursuit became louder.

She rushed over to the long-faced man, who stopped in his tracks when she grabbed his horse by the halter. She had to hope he was loyal to the empire.

"Please," she panted. "I need your horse."

He scowled and tried to shake the halter free from her hands. "Let go of my—"

She shoved the end of her staff into his abdomen. Breath came out of him as he doubled over, at the same time releasing the horse.

She couldn't see a saddle, only a blanket and saddlebags, and wasn't sure how she would get up onto the horses's back, let alone make it do what she wanted.

The Veldrians chasing her spied her on the street. She had at least three warriors racing toward her, which meant she had no other choice. She threw herself up onto the horse, trying to get her leg to the other side, and at the same time wrapping her arms around its neck.

The horse whinnied, startled, but fortunately kept its feet on the ground. Once she was up, she settled herself and put her feet at the sides where they should be. She dug in her heels, at the same time leaning forward as much as she could to help with her balance. The horse gamely burst into a run.

Wind rushed into her face as she did everything she could to hold on to the horse as it thundered along the street. Buildings of yellow stone passed her in a blur on both sides. She focused on the city gates, hoping they weren't closely guarded.

And then she was riding straight through the gates, to leave the city of Gorvia behind.

✦

Bethany kept her horse running until the animal could take no more. A dozen miles separated her from Gorvia as she turned her head to take one last look at the city. Seeing no signs of pursuit, she faced forward, toward the moonlit landscape of barren sand and craggy peaks. There was little in the way of life: no trees, no scrub, nothing moving at all.

The important thing now was for her and the horse to endure the journey ahead. She settled to a walking pace, her breath misting in the chill desert air, and brought to mind her map of the empire. The army was on its way to Narzin. To get from Gorvia to Narzin, she needed to stay on the thin trail she was following, heading north, hugging the coast as she traveled.

The night passed as she rode for hour after hour. A monotonous, rolling landscape of bald ridges and hills surrounded her, but the stars told her she was traveling in the right direction. Hopefully, when morning came, she would be able to make out the ocean.

Eventually, the sky lightened as yellow tinged the horizon on her right. Up ahead, the first hint of dawn revealed a collection of dark shapes. She squinted until she could make out a tiny village beside a few patches of crops. A circular stone wall had a pulley above it, and she rode toward what could only be a well. Some local children saw her, watching from the front of one of the houses, but she paid them no heed as she lowered the bucket, pulling it up to pour water into the nearby trough for her horse. She then drank greedily with her cupped palms until she had her fill. It was with regret that she mounted up again.

After the village, she found herself climbing ridges, up and down, despite the trail's attempts to navigate the uneven terrain. At the top of a crest, a wide expanse of blue now stretched at her right hand, sparkling in the distance: the Emerald Sea. From her position, it looked flat, with any waves just tiny ripples. The sight of the sun lightened her heart as the golden orb climbed higher above the horizon.

She soon found herself hating it.

After just an hour the yellow sun felt bright and angry. The ferocious heat grew, until she longed for the day to be over. She now understood the lack of vegetation. The searing temperature would drain the moisture from everything around her, withering any shrub bold enough to try to shoot out green leaves.

Her horse's flanks now shone with sweat. Despite Bethany's own exhaustion, she simply had to keep going. Her mouth was as dry as the sand around her. She would give anything to moisten her lips.

She now climbed a long, wide ridge, rising to a height greater than anything around it. The trail led her upward, and she took a slight deviation to reach the summit at the top where she would have a commanding view in all directions.

She reined in, turning her head to sweep the area. More of the same landscape stretched all the way to the horizon: dirty yellow plains, hills, and ridges all turning to the color of rust as the terrain changed in the north, toward the Red Desert. She couldn't see Narzin, not yet. In one direction, everything was desert. In the other, coast, cliffs, and sea. Above her the sun glared down, warning her that the day would only grow hotter.

Something caught her attention. She shielded her eyes. She thought she saw moving shapes, many of them, all traveling in the same direction. But whatever the moving figures were, they had vanished behind a mountain. At the rate they were traveling, they should soon appear on the mountain's other side. She held her breath and waited.

There. As soon as she saw them, her eyes widened.

Thousands of little dots moved at speed, too fast to be people on foot. The Veldrians were riding north, on their way to battle the Imperial army on the way to Narzin. Grouped in a mass of horses, she couldn't believe how many they were. Kendrick, Troy, and Caden, and all the soldiers she had escorted from Esk . . . they were all in terrible danger.

She was Kendrick's house diviner. If someone was wounded, she was supposed to get them to help. If reinforcements were needed, it was her duty to deliver them.

She couldn't even tell them that blood was in the air.

✦

As the hours passed, soon the coastal path from Gorvia would join the wider desert road connecting Engel and Narzin. Bethany and her mount plodded wearily, consumed with the need to keep moving. Meanwhile, she kept an eye out for the road at all times. After this experience, she would never be afraid of riding bareback, but it was also something she would be in no hurry to repeat.

The sun was now falling rather than climbing, but if anything its harsh rays were more fierce than before. Her horse faltered, and then stopped altogether, until nothing she did got it moving. With no other choice, she slid off the animal's back and walked.

She had to hope her mount would recover after some time without her weight upon its back. With the halter in her hand, she almost felt like she was dragging the creature up the long ridge the coastal path was climbing. Her face was salty with dried sweat. She planted down one foot after another. Soon, she would have a good view from the ridge's crest, and if she saw the road, she would be safe in the knowledge that she was getting closer to her destination. A tall boulder stood at the top of the ridge. When she was beside the boulder, she would be able to see the land beyond. The road would be there, just where she needed it to be.

At last, the boulder was a stone's throw away. Then she was almost upon it, pulling the reluctant horse the last distance up the slope. The view beckoned. The road would be there. It had to be.

She stopped in her tracks and stared. Her horse whinnied, wondering why she was holding it so tightly, but she was barely aware of the sound.

The dusty road she had been searching for made a long ribbon, heading west in one direction, farther into the desert, before vanishing into the haze. In front of her, the track she was following continued in the other direction and veered until it joined the bigger road, and continued onward toward Narzin.

She had never seen so many wheeling birds. The scavengers circled each other and dived down from the sky. Their wings fluttered as they fought for space on the ground, shrieking and cawing at each other.

The birds had gathered at the place where the two roads merged. Along with the birds was a multitude of bigger, longer shapes, littered around the landscape, and these shapes were utterly still.

She wanted to swallow but her mouth was dry. Her empty stomach clenched. The shapes . . . They couldn't be what she thought they were. There were too many of them.

"Come on," she whispered hoarsely to the animal beside her. "You'll be going downhill now. It's time for me to get up on your back."

The horse grumbled and stirred, but allowed her to climb back onto its padded back. Once she was up, she nudged the animal forward and even managed a small amount of speed. Riding toward the birds, she descended the ridge, crunching gravel under the horse's hooves as she followed the path until it leveled off.

The shrieks of the scavenger birds grew louder. She had no choice but to pass them by.

She started seeing bodies up close. Flies buzzed. A crow cawed at her as she neared and then flew off, only to return as soon as she had passed. She rode her horse right alongside the battlefield, trying not to look too hard at the grisly sight around her. But she couldn't help it; she stared at a uniformed corpse peppered with arrows. Another body had been torn apart by a sharp blade. A headless corpse was all alone, with no sign of his missing part. Blood had already congealed and blackened as it pooled on the ground or soaked the clothing on the mangled soldiers.

It was obvious who had won the battle, forcing the other force to flee. The bodies were all Imperial. The Veldrians had taken their fallen away.

She kept her horse moving, lips pressed tightly together. Flies were gathering on the dead men's wounds, where arrow shafts stuck out in different directions. These men deserved better than to lie here in the sun. The empire couldn't let them stay where they were. Someone would have to come back to this place to honor the dead.

At least she didn't see any sign of Kendrick or his sons. All of a sudden, she had the strong sensation of being watched. Movement drew her attention; her head snapped around.

A scout was on a hill, a Veldrian warrior watching her from horseback. He looked back over his shoulder to call to someone out of view.

She dug in her heels; it was definitely time to go.

Chapter Twenty-Three

NARZIN HAD THE FEEL of a frontier town that never grew into anything greater. A large port defined the settlement, within the embrace of the houses and workshops surrounding the bay. With no gateway, and the desert impeding travel, traders mostly came and went by ship. Fishing was the main industry, but the raw timber for boats had to be brought in from elsewhere: the Red Desert wasn't known for its forests. The nearest cities were Engel in the west and Meroy in the north, places well served by their gateways. When caravans brought goods between the two cities, they stopped at Narzin, but they didn't stop for long.

A coastal town like Narzin wasn't a place where anyone would choose to turn the enemy, but at the same time, the empire couldn't just keep withdrawing, not with a freshly formed army given the task of fighting back.

Kendrick had moved into a hillside villa facing the harbor. He now sat at a table out on the terrace, a goblet of untouched wine in front of him, while the water in the harbor sparkled and boats sailed the Emerald Sea. With the last light leaving the sky, the distant clouds changed shade, becoming washed with crimson and gold. He was frowning, almost scowling, and even the view couldn't dispel his ugly mood.

The army had suffered a terrible defeat. He had watched his men die around him, struck by arrows from the circling enemies on horseback. All of the fallen were sons and brothers, fathers and grandfathers, men in his care and under his command. Until he regained access to a gateway, he couldn't even send letters to their families. And until the Veldrians were pushed back, he couldn't retrieve their bodies.

The Veldrians had struck hard. The initial shock had been strong, when the horde appeared from nowhere, and then everything was in chaos. The enemy must have traveled a great distance over difficult terrain, in searing heat, and yet their horses still had enough in them to burst into a fast run, all in a great mass. The Veldrians immediately launched an onslaught of arrows before racing away and wheeling to do the same thing again.

From the Imperial side, the infantry knew their business and formed their own shield walls. The empire's archers returned fire and the knights charged, smashing apart the enemy and tearing more than one group to shreds. The Veldrians backed off, but the losses on the Imperial side were horrific. The rest of the journey became a living nightmare, as the army alternated between making best speed toward Narzin and forming up to meet the attacks. The retreating action had continued all the way to their destination, before Narzin's walls forced the Veldrians to back off.

The men were angry. The same applied to the officers. How had they been taken so badly by surprise? The scouts had given some warning, but by then it was too late. Lynch had some experience, but as Kendrick knew well, he wasn't much of a strategist. Distracted by the disaster at Engel, their lord marshal hadn't even been with the main army group.

However there was another man who had been leading them: their emperor and supreme commander, a man had never been tested by war. Julian had become indecisive, caught between prioritizing defensiveness against speed of flight. Kendrick, Tristan, and the other commanding officers had taken the army's leadership into their own hands. The withdrawal had been difficult, but they had survived to reach Narzin.

Now that it was over, Kendrick knew the hearts of men. There was only one conclusion to draw.

Everyone blamed Julian.

As sunset became ever more glorious, Kendrick shook his head, remembering how close Julian had come to losing the succession. If only Rigel could have lived a little longer. If only the vote had gone the other way. If only—

"Father?"

Kendrick turned. "Eh?" Troy had a strangely pleased look on his face, causing Kendrick's frown to deepen. "What is it?"

"I have some . . . news."

Kendrick waited for a long moment. "Well?" he asked. "Out with it, Troy. I'm not in the mood for games."

His eldest son turned. And Kendrick's eyes shot wide open before he leaped to his feet.

Bethany was wearing the same clothes he had last seen her in, with the exception of her missing cloak. The sun had kissed her copper skin so that her face was reddened, with cracked lips and dirty cheeks. Her hair was lank. Her green dress was dusty. She looked weary . . . and more than anything else . . . dry.

"Bethany?" Kendrick shoved his chair away and hurried over to her. Taking her hands, he led her to the table and gave her a chair. "Sit down. What happened?" He leveled his gaze on Troy. "Have you given her some water?"

"Of course."

"Then get her some more. And some food. Quickly!"

Kendrick swiftly sat beside her. He leaned forward, inspecting her face. "What happened? When we lost you at Engel, I thought you might have been caught up at the Wheel. Smoke was everywhere. There was fighting . . . it was chaos. We encountered some of the raiders and drove them away. More men arrived, and they knew what to expect, so I guessed you got the message out. I left Caden in case you returned, but you never came. Then, on the way here . . . " He realized he was speaking in a long rush and drew a breath. "What happened?" he repeated.

"I passed the battlefield on the way here . . . "

His mouth tightened. "Things have gone from bad to worse. A lot of men died."

"I know. I saw."

"Where have you been?" he asked, continuing to stare into her face.

"In the south. I had some bad luck of my own. When I returned from the Wheel, the raiders came and found me—"

He swore. "I should never have let you go."

"It wasn't your fault. No one expected what happened at Engel." She corrected herself. "My Lord."

"Don't worry about any of that. Go on. What did they do to you? Are you hurt? How did you get away?"

"I'm just . . . tired. I was captured by one of their leaders, a man called Dresk. He took me to Gorvia. He and the queen don't seem to get along. I cut through my bonds and stole a horse. The queen helped me—"

"You went to Gorvia? You met the queen?" he asked incredulously. "You spoke to her?"

She nodded. "She gave me a message, to give to the . . . " She appeared to change what she was about to say. "To give to you."

"To me?" He frowned, confused. "How would she know who I am?"

She hesitated again. "A message for the people in charge, I mean."

"This sounds important." He stood up from the table. "I'm sorry but can you walk, just a short distance? I should take you to the lord marshal. He's going to want to ask you some questions." For some reason, Bethany paled, as if he had just said something frightening. "What is it? You went to Gorvia. You met the queen. They need to hear what you have to say."

"Please, My Lord. Perhaps . . . perhaps I could just tell you what she said?"

"This could be important, Bethany. I know you must be exhausted, but I don't think we have a choice."

"Will the emperor be there?"

"He may be. What are you worried about? You have nothing to fear. He's just a man."

"You will be with me?"

"Of course. Come on. I promise you. I will be right by your side."

✦

As Bethany entered with Kendrick, Julian frowned. She saw his eyes move from Kendrick, to her, and back to Kendrick again. "Lord Kendrick? What can I do for you?"

Julian rested his gaze once more on her. Her chest tightened as she waited for him to react, but all he did was raise an eyebrow at her ragged appearance. She began to feel some hope.

He didn't recognize her or know who she was. For the time being, her secret was safe.

Even so, she found herself hiding a little behind Kendrick's broader frame. Kendrick had taken her to the tall building designated to be the army's command center in Narzin. The room was high-ceilinged, with glossy timber paneling on the walls and wide windows at each end, facing the sea in one direction and the desert in the other. Divans and recliners filled a corner, facing the long table where Julian and his wife Samara had evidently been working. The sun had now set, and lanterns in alcoves provided warm yellow light to see by.

Julian was on his feet; evidently he had just been in conversation with Samara, who had papers neatly arranged in front of her, when his steward announced Kendrick and his house diviner.

Bethany's half-brother wore crisp white clothing and his golden hair was oiled and combed. As for Samara, Bethany had never seen her up close, and she was even more beautiful than people said, with olive skin, dark hair in tresses, ruby red lips, and smoky, slightly tilted eyes. She was clad in a sheer pink dress and a thick silver necklace hung from her neck.

A golden goblet rested on the table in front of her.

Bethany's shoulders tensed. Julian's manner was distracted, but he was once again staring at her, and his eyebrows came together. Her coloring wasn't common, even in an empire with a diverse array of peoples, but his deepening frown was making her fear return. Had he remembered her from their brief encounter at the Imperial Palace in Everlast? Back then she had been dressed differently, in the usual clothing she wore when she worked at her shop. Her hair had been a little shorter. It was more than a year ago.

Samara addressed Kendrick, ignoring Bethany completely. "Lord Kendrick." Her eyes narrowed, enough to show her irritation at the interruption. "I assume this is important?"

"Emperor . . . Empress . . ." Kendrick gave a brief bow to each in turn. It didn't escape Bethany's notice that there wasn't a lot of warmth between them. He looked around. "Is the lord marshal close by?"

"Busy fortifying the city," Julian said. "What is it, Lord Kendrick?"

Kendrick was indecisive for a moment before pressing on. "This is my house diviner, Bethany Sylvana. During the fighting at Engel, the enemy captured her and took to Gorvia, before she managed to escape. While she was in Gorvia, she had an encounter with Queen Zhuana."

"Is that so?" Julian regarded her, the corners of his mouth down-turned as he inspected her up and down. "You do look like you have been through an ordeal. And yet, you made it back alive. Tell me, then. What did you learn?"

He spoke dismissively, leaving out her title. Kendrick frowned, and she thought Kendrick might also have noticed.

"Emperor . . ." Bethany bowed her head, before meeting his dark brown eyes. She spoke in a rush. "They are trying to understand how we use the gateways. In particular they want to solve the disorientation people feel after travel. I expect I was going to be tortured. However I was taken before the queen—"

"Zhuana is in good health?" Julian interrupted.

"Yes. At least, she appears to be strong and well—"

"More's the pity," Samara muttered.

Flustered, Bethany stopped.

Kendrick spoke in an encouraging tone. "Go on, Bethany."

"I believe that the queen is at odds with one of her lords, the same man who captured me and took me to Gorvia."

"I see . . . and what is this man's name?" Julian asked.

"Maven Dresk."

Julian exchanged glances with Samara. "I know of him. Anything else?"

"The queen gave me a blade that I used to make my escape. She said that she wanted me to deliver a message. She said to say that she had no part to play in the burning of Engel. It is regrettable, she said."

Julian snorted. "Regrettable? An interesting word, given the thousands of lives lost and homes destroyed." He scowled at Kendrick. "Is that all?"

Kendrick's posture was stiff, his voice low and flat. "I thought the lord marshal might have some questions for her, Emperor."

It was Samara who turned her attention to Bethany. "Very well. Diviner, did you learn anything else? Anything that might help us bring a swift end to this wretched war?"

"They take something they call firewater . . . It is some kind of medicine . . . or potion."

"We know," Julian said.

"Julian, let her speak," Samara said.

"They seem to fight over who gets the potion. Perhaps it's not always in supply."

"Do you believe their supply is running low?" Julian asked.

"I couldn't say for sure."

"But they may exhaust it at some point . . . " he said. "Very well. Anything else?"

Bethany wondered if she should mention the cactus buds, two of which she had taken from Maven Dresk's bedchamber. *Pearls*, he had called them.

Eager to be away from Julian, she shook her head. Surely she had said enough, and now she could go?

"Hmm," Julian said pensively. He was staring straight at her, his penetrating gaze making her more than uncomfortable. "Lord Kendrick . . . would you mind leaving us for a moment?"

Bethany's eyes shot wide open with panic

"I . . . " Kendrick began, his face curled up with worry. But he didn't have a choice. He bowed. "Of course, Emperor."

Kendrick turned and departed, leaving Bethany alone with Julian and Samara.

"Diviner . . . " Julian began, drawing the word out.

"Sylvana."

"Diviner Sylvana . . . " he said slowly. "It took me a moment, but we have met before, haven't we?"

She remained perfectly still, knowing better than to reply.

"You were at the palace, outside my father's quarters. I assumed you were . . . " He cleared his throat meaningfully. "Tell me, Diviner Sylvana. Why were you with him, if my original assumption was wrong?"

Her mouth was dry as she worked to find the right answer. She had to leave him thinking something. "I have worked hard to be where I am, Emperor."

"Oh?" He raised an eyebrow and then smirked. "Ah . . . so it seems I was not wrong after all. You certainly have. Worked hard, I mean. From such low origins, you have risen high indeed. I wonder if Lord Kendrick knows?"

Bethany remained silent, and Julian waved a hand. "Do not concern yourself, girl. You are not worth the trouble. You must have the requisite skills or the corpus would not let you anywhere near the Conways. I believe we are done. You may go." He jerked his chin toward the door. "Did you hear me? Get out of here."

Color came to her cheeks as she turned on her heel and crossed the floor to leave the room. She stopped when she heard him again.

"Diviner?" Julian asked.

"Yes?" she asked quietly, without turning around.

"Try to remain unseen. If the Weaver is kind, I hope to never encounter you again."

✦

Once Bethany was gone, Julian heard Samara's voice behind him. "What was that about?"

"She is a whore . . . " He paused. "Is . . . was . . . I am not sure of the difference. At any rate, I caught her visiting my father, who evidently returned favors by helping with her change in profession."

"Her? Truly?" Samara raised an eyebrow in the direction the young diviner had taken. "One has to admire her. Diviners must possess a great deal of intelligence and dedication, so I have heard."

"Diviners do what they are told. She is nothing."

"Lord Kendrick is obviously fond of her."

"It is no concern of ours. We have other more pressing problems."

He heard Samara sigh. "I wish I did not know how correct you are."

He turned and frowned, surprised as she left her chair at the table to come over to where he was standing. She was strangely sober, worry in her eyes as she resumed the conversation she had begun before Kendrick's interruption.

"As I said, we need to talk. You will remember that I told you to have your coronation quickly."

"I am perhaps a little busy," he said sarcastically. "Just the tiniest amount. A small war, in case you have not noticed."

His wife was dogged when she wanted to be. "You needed to cement your authority while you had it. And now it is ebbing away."

"These setbacks are not my fault."

"You are the emperor, leading the army. Everything is your fault. The Veldrians are winning the war. People are afraid. Frightened people do things they wouldn't imagine in times of peace."

"And? Be clear. What is it you are trying to say?"

"I am saying that your position is more fragile than you seem to realize. These rumors about another child of your father's have grown. Many of your nobles have been bold enough to hold off, rather than join us in our fight against the Veldrians—my father and his allies, to name a few. You and I both know what almost happened at the fielding and so does he. Listen to me carefully. You need to prove that you are a capable emperor, which at the moment means one thing. You need to start winning."

"You think I am not trying? We have had some defeats, but we are the empire. We will turn them back."

She persisted. "You say you will turn them back. And when will that be?"

"We are presently in a poor position. Narzin is a terrible—"

"By the stars . . . no . . . " She shook her head. "Julian . . . Please do not tell me you are planning another retreat."

"Lynch says we might not have a choice."

"Julian, to retreat any farther would make things worse. We both know what my father is like. He will be out there . . . planning . . . plotting . . . trying to bring about your downfall. *Our* downfall. We need to do something to change course."

He scowled. "If you have a suggestion, Samara, then say it."

"Very well. I have been thinking, and I have reached the only logical conclusion. You need to make peace with the Blues. There must be a lasting settlement. This current situation cannot continue."

"Make peace? With your father?"

"Perhaps not with him, but with as many of your other opponents as possible. The alternative is too terrible to think about. You wouldn't even know they were coming for you until you were waiting in a cell to have your head cut off."

Julian blanched, wondering if she was being overly dramatic, but his wife's expression was deadly serious. He opened his mouth, but she interjected, resting a hand on his upper arm.

"I mean it, Julian. You need to start winning, and you need to do it now. First you need a victory, and then you can have your coronation. When that time comes . . . your troubles . . . our troubles . . . will be over." She stared directly into his eyes, increasing the pressure as she squeezed his arm. Her tone lowered. "And then, when the time is right, you can deal with your enemies, one by one. Not from a position of weakness. But from strength."

He instinctively understood the truth in what she was saying. She now spoke in a way he could understand.

"Imagine it," she said. "Imagine the relief you would feel, to have total power, to no longer have to watch over your shoulder or sleep with your eyes open. I will help you get the support you need, to bring them across to your side. But there is something only you can do, you and your lord marshal. No more defeats. You need to show them you can win."

Chapter Twenty-Four

BETHANY SAT CROSS-LEGGED in the villa's central courtyard, a paved square of gardens and fountains. The courtyard was broad and open to the sky, framed by the communal areas, with bedchambers on the level above. She had her eyes closed but she could sense the change in the light around her. It was early, the sun was rising but not yet high enough to reach her.

Her staff lay across her knees. She focused on her breathing as thoughts and emotions bubbled up to the surface. An image came to her: Kendrick's relieved face when he saw her alive and well. It was strange to her now, that at first she had thought him gruff and more than a little intimidating. She now saw him as he really was, a man who wore his emotions openly, with a deep well of protective kindness inside him for those he let into his heart.

As for Julian . . . she planned to do exactly what he had asked of her and stay as far from him as possible. He was now emperor. Her father had wanted to reveal her, but she didn't want wealth or power; she just wanted to be free to live her life.

The war was going badly. Despite its many flaws, the empire was a force for good in the world, and her father had been emperor for a long time, with strong support from his nobles. From the little she knew,

Julian as emperor made things feel more . . . unstable.

Her father's death . . . Julian's ascension . . . the war that had claimed the Southern Provinces. How was it all going to end?

After her encounter with Julian, as she traveled with Kendrick back to the villa, she had taken in the sights around her. Horse-drawn carts trundled past, and hints of soldiers' bodies poked out from the blankets laid over them. A young man in uniform sat on a step in a doorway, cradling his arm in a sling. Whatever had happened to him, blood soaked the bandage around his arm. In an area where market-stalls lined the street, there were empty trays where fruits and vegetables should have been. More men would die, and among them might be Kendrick and his sons. The Veldrians would seize more gateways, cutting off trade and military support from entire sections of the empire. Hungry people would starve.

Everything she knew was under threat. She wanted to play her part.

She opened her eyes.

With her staff across her knees, she took another series of deep breaths, blinking as her eyes adjusted after being closed for so long and the morning began to brighten. Taking her staff, she slowly climbed to her feet.

Once she was standing tall, she took a moment to gather her strength. She didn't need her sore body to tell her she was still weak from her capture and escape. She was about to perform a test.

She commenced the careful dance with her staff, the series of movements she had performed over and over under the Crystal Dome. Stretching her leg in front of her, she inexorably placed down her foot. Turning, she brought her staff across her body. Another step. Staff up and then down, as if striking an opponent as slowly as it was possible to do so.

She was hurting in a dozen places. While her skin was hot, she also felt strangely cold, but she tried to push the sensations aside and lose herself in her movements. She increased speed, just a little. She slashed the staff across the air in front of her. Performing a complete turn, she attacked the place that had been behind her just a moment before. The staff moved constantly, up and down, cutting and striking, from one side to the other. Her eyes were narrowed. She imagined that there were enemies in front of her, and she was knocking them down, one after another.

A pulsing pain began in her head, but she pushed it away. Her limbs were tiring, but she put on even more speed. Her breath whooshed out of her body. Sweat beaded on her forehead. Inhale. Strike down. Exhale. Staff up. She pushed herself hard. She could do this.

The nature of her breathing changed, becoming more like rapid gasps. She clamped down on a sudden burst of fire inside her skull.

Her test had an objective. Could she join Kendrick and his sons in battle? Arrows would be whistling around her. Men would scream as they died. Her thrusts and cuts at the air would be intended to wound and kill. Even as she whirled her body, her vision tunneled in. Perhaps she could—

She stumbled. Her staff fell from her hand to clatter onto the ground. Falling to one knee, all she could do was close her eyes. It was a struggle to keep her wobbling legs from collapsing underneath her. Her body trembled. She grimaced, mouth wide open as she panted, trying to find enough air to fill her lungs.

After a long time, she opened her eyes, and the truth was something she couldn't hide even from herself. She was too weak. She needed more time to recover.

"You diviners can do a lot of damage with that staff."

The voice behind her made her head whirl. Kendrick was watching her from one of the stone benches a short distance away. From his relaxed posture, he had been there for some time. It was early, but he was already dressed, with leather armor covering a long-sleeved gray tunic, black trousers, and high boots. The summons to the walls could come at any time.

"How long have you been there?"

"Long enough. In my time I've seen diviners fight as bravely as any warrior. And more effectively, in some cases. You have it in you, I think. For a time there you had me impressed." His eyes twinkled. "Until the end of course."

Her tone was serious. "I want to help."

He left his bench to come over to her. "I know, Bethany. I know. It's not in you to sit by and let others do the fighting. But as we are both well aware, at the moment, all you would do is get yourself killed. The best thing you can do, for me as well as yourself, is get some rest and recover. We won't always be fighting so far from a gateway, and you are too valuable to lose."

"Valuable?"

He smiled. "Yes, valuable. Like a good horse or a treasured timepiece." His smile faded. "Promise me you will take care of yourself?"

"My Lord . . . You shouldn't be worrying about me."

"I've told you once before. You're a part of my household, which means you are under my protection. You've just been through an ordeal. You need to give yourself time to recover."

She nodded, and he hesitated, as if unsure about what he was going to say next.

Then he reached out to squeeze her shoulder. "Bethany . . . I know you always work hard and do your best. If my daughter grows up to be half the woman you are, I will be a happy man."

✦

Night time found Bethany staring up at the ceiling, unable to sleep.

The day had been strange: quiet for her, terrifying for everyone else. Now and then she heard frantic shouts: barked orders and the thump of running footsteps. Screams drifted on the wind; she sometimes caught the clash of steel on steel.

At the end of the day, Troy and Caden returned from fighting, dirty and blood-stained but alive. Kendrick took a lot longer, but he made it back in time for dinner. The three weary men sat across from her at the dinner table, as the two brothers ate silently, mechanically, not saying much at all. Kendrick had stared into the distance, and she wasn't sure if she wanted to know what he was thinking about or seeing with his mind's eye.

She was now in bed, eyes open despite the late hour. She remembered Kendrick's admonishing words; she needed to rest. At the same time, she felt useless. She had to do something to help.

Giving up on sleep, she left her bed to go to the window. Opening the curtains, she leaned on the sill. Her view was toward the sea and the night sky above it, which was full of stars. Past the streets and the docks, the waxing moon was both above and below, its silver circle reflected in the water. With the current pause in the fighting, the night was blessedly quiet.

She turned her head. Her quarters were plain but functional. The room was much larger than she was used to. Her staff leaned in the corner. Another diviner, a woman of about the same size, had given her a spare gray cloak, which now hung from a peg on the back of the door.

How could she bring her skills to bear? There had to be something more, some way she could make a difference.

She faced the open window as something new occurred to her. There was a mystery still to solve. Troy and Caden had been full of stories about the Veldrians and their firewater. The druids' potion gave the enemy bloodshot eyes. The most savage wounds were ignored as they fought in a terrible frenzy.

But she had spent time with the Veldrians and returned to tell the tale. And when she escaped, she brought something back with her, something that might be important.

Moving to the table at her bedside, she slid open the small wooden drawer. Even in darkness, the two little circular cactus buds were easy to make out.

She took one of the pearls from the drawer, sat on her bed, and stared down at her open palm.

Maven had been excited, but the pearl didn't look like much. Dull in color, it was the size and shape of a fat coin, with little indents like hair follicles covering its surface. There was something to be learned here. But she knew enough to be careful.

She took the cactus bud in both hands, between thumb and forefinger. Then, taking a deep breath, she twisted it to form a long crack along its surface. The flesh was wet and darker green. As soon as she broke the green skin, she wrinkled her nose. The fragrance drifting up was familiar.

That odor . . . there was something that it reminded her of . . .

Aware that scents in the air could have power, she carefully lifted the pearl toward her nostrils, prepared to swiftly drop it back down again.

The scent that greeted her was sharp and acrid. She jerked her head back. It irritated the back of her throat and made her eyes water. The pungent odor smelled like tar.

She lowered the cactus pearl down again.

The smell was more than familiar. She didn't know what the Weaver's Breath was; her teachers had never told her, and she guessed that it was a secret not many diviners knew. What was possible, however, was that even if the cactus and the Weaver's Breath weren't the same thing, they might come from the same family.

A sudden lightness in her head confirmed her suspicion. A gentle hum resonated in the air around her. The sensation wasn't as strong as that imparted by the orb on top of her staff, but it was noticeable.

The cactus was eaten; she remembered that much. People from the Imperial side knew about the potion, firewater. Yet she had never heard the cactus pearls mentioned by anyone.

It was a simple matter to break the cactus bud into two pieces, and then to break one of those pieces again. She was taking a risk, but Maven wouldn't have wanted them if they were a poison. What was it he had said? The cactus enabled someone to 'visit the realm of shadows'. What did that even mean?

As she wondered about what she was contemplating doing and whether it was a good idea, at the same time, she also saw a chance to learn something new.

A stern voice spoke inside her. She shouldn't do anything with the cactus. She should put it away.

But then what would she learn? Nothing.

She spent a long time staring at the quarter of the torn bud, squeezing it between her finger and thumb as a small amount of juice came out.

Then, summoning her courage, she put it into her mouth and chewed.

Juice burst out of the cactus, suffusing her mouth with a bitter, acidic flavor. She kept chewing. The taste wasn't foul enough to make her want to gag or spit it out, but was definitely strong enough to require determination to continue working at the cactus with her jaw. The sharp flavor grew stronger. Sour and harsh, it burned when it reached the back of her throat.

Meanwhile, she stared out the window, watching the stars as she concentrated on chewing.

She swallowed.

Nothing. It was just some—

Wait.

As she faced the open window, and glittering stars filled her vision, something strange was happening.

The stars were crying. Little lights dripped from them, trickling trails behind them as they fell downward. The sight was beautiful. She still felt in control, able to contemplate what was happening, and to know that despite the intense feeling, this wasn't a strong enough effect for her to be able to travel the gateways. The sensations she was experiencing were surprisingly pleasant. There was nothing in it that she could connect with anything like a realm of shadows.

More decisively now, she put the rest of the torn bud in her mouth, one piece and then the other. Her mouth twisted as she chewed, making sure to work at it with her teeth until she swallowed. She was in control. This was nothing like as powerful as the Weaver's Breath. She was a diviner, and had been tested beyond endurance to reach her position.

Reaching into the drawer in the bedside table, she retrieved the second of the cactus buds, placing it in a pocket in her gray dress, where it would be close if she decided she wanted it.

She sat on the bed, facing the open window. Trailing tears trickled down from the stars.

All of a sudden, everything changed.

A sharp kick slammed into her abdomen. Something tried to jump out of her stomach. Her head swam until she was reeling.

The world tilted, and then tilted the other way. She experienced herself being shaken, along with a lurching feeling in her mind, as if a giant hand had picked her up was throwing her around and around.

The part of her that was aware of what was happening was both horrified and curious; it told her to be careful—the strange sensations were only growing. She closed her eyes. But even with her eyes closed, dancing patterns became faster and faster.

Another kick struck her stomach, this one even stronger.

She realized she was leaning on the window frame, gripping it tightly, inhaling the sight of the stars. When had she stood up? It didn't matter; she could comprehend the weight and power of individual stars, rather than just see them as pinpricks of light. Her sense of awe was overwhelming. The moon, in comparison, was tiny. And yet it was close, so much closer than the stars, so close that she could reach out and touch it.

And so she did. She put out a finger and brushed it against the moon. Far below, underneath the moon, silver color flickered on the waves of the Emerald Sea. She understood the truth, deep in her bones. The moon didn't glow. It was her sun that was shining upon it, and the glow then reflected from the moon to light up the water and then reflected from the water to reach her eyes. She couldn't actually touch the moon. She was seeing her finger silhouetted and the two images blur together.

Everything in her vision was just a picture. Everything she heard was a vibration. The scents that reached her nose were little pieces of the thing they smelled like, so that when the salt from the sea drifted through the window, she was actually taking the salt in and making it part of her body. When she touched the fabric of her dress, she was experiencing the pressure the material applied to the sensitive parts of her skin.

A tiny, infinitely small part of her kept calling out, telling her that compared to the Weaver's Breath, what the cactus was now doing was much, much more powerful. And then that voice was gone altogether.

The walls began to melt. Sliding like waterfalls all around her, there was no apparent distinction between the walls and the things against them.

The floor was liquid. She was sinking into it. The bed, her feet, everything would soon be swallowed.

Then she was gone. There was no her.

The universe and her were one and the same thing.

She was going on a journey. She had no other option; she had to surrender herself to it completely.

✦

Bethany's eyelids fluttered and then her eyes opened.

Morning light poured through the open window. As she blinked at the clear blue sky, lit by the rising sun, for a time she didn't know where or even who she was.

She was lying on the bed fully clothed. When had she gone to sleep? She had no idea.

Then it came back to her. She clutched the pocket of her dress, letting out a breath when she felt the second cactus pearl still in her pocket. Her first immediate fear had been that she had decided to have another.

One had been enough.

A few remembrances were still with her. The universe was so vast that she was lost. And then the idea of being lost made no sense, like the idea of a droplet of water being lost in the sea. She was simply absorbed, part of the greater whole. She now couldn't comprehend all the intuitive feelings and new learnings, more profound than anything she had known before.

One question was stronger than any other. Was it real? Or did the cactus trick her into thinking she could reach an inner understanding of greater depth and meaning? Without being subject to its effect, she couldn't say for sure, and if she was under its spell, she wouldn't be able to intellectually analyze the experience while also journeying to the strange new realms. What was it Maven had called it? The realm of shadows? She knew what her teachers at the Observatory would have called it.

The tapestry.

The effect of the cactus made the Weaver's Breath look like a pale imitation. And yet, without doubt, they belonged to different branches of the same tree. After her senses blurred together, she had developed a heightened awareness of the pulse and hum of herself and the world around her. She had thought she could play the tapestry like a stringed instrument.

She left the bed and walked to the mirror by the dressing table. Looking into her own eyes, she shook her head. She looked exhausted.

Unfortunately, the cactus pearls weren't some secret source of strength. Perhaps she had made the wrong choice, when she fled the city of Gorvia, and she should have taken the firewater.

She frowned; something was strange. When she moved her body, her feet were squelching and wet.

She stared down at her feet. Somehow, her shoes were soaked through. How could that be? Surely she hadn't left her room?

A clawing dread churned at her guts. She looked quickly around the large bedchamber. Her staff . . . it was where it should be, but in a different position. Surely she hadn't left it at that angle; hadn't it been leaning the other way?

Could she really have gone outside? By all the stars alive . . . surely not.

If she had gone outside, she might have met someone. It had been late at night, but if she had, she would have been raving like someone gone mad.

She crouched down to squeeze her shoe. Definitely wet. They both were. And then she found something else.

She took hold of the dark wet fragment that was wrapped around her ankle to untangle it. Then her eyes widened as she held it up.

Seaweed.

She didn't remember anything—nothing at all—but in her crazed state, she had left her room and gone walking, all the way down to the harbor. She was lucky that she hadn't hurt herself.

"Never again," she muttered.

Some of life's secrets were best left as they were.

Chapter Twenty-Five

SAMARA LOOKED TERRIFIED.

Julian had been busy scrubbing the blood from his face and hands, but he stopped as soon as he saw his wife's face. He was in their villa's central courtyard, where he was cleaning himself at a wide stone basin, near a section of manicured gardens. He was weary, still in his armor after a full day of fighting on the walls, but from Samara's expression his troubles were far from over.

"What?" he asked quickly. "What is it?"

"You . . . You need to come with me."

Without another word she began to walk, and he grabbed a cloth to wipe his hands before hurrying after her. She climbed a series of steps, turning on the landing to ascend the next stairway, and then the one after, until she was leading him out onto the villa's open rooftop terrace. She turned to face him, chest rising and falling, dread in every part of her bearing.

A steady breeze tugged at her dark hair. The setting sun cast shadows from her body and lit up her fearful face. A few spiky plants in pots furnished the open terrace, along with stone benches and the occasional statue. Mosaic tiling decorated the low skirting wall.

Her choice in location meant that whatever she had to tell him, it was essential that they weren't overheard.

"Samara, tell me."

She waited until he was near, and then she held up her hand to display something: a rolled scroll, tied with a golden ribbon. She held it up so he could inspect the seal, the spider and star of Graystone, imprinted in the gray wax.

Samara was holding a message from her father, Lord Declan Quinn of Graystone.

Julian didn't like his own reaction. His stomach felt tight and constricted. Her recent warning was still fresh in his mind. Whatever was in the message, it couldn't be anything good.

"You know what the golden ribbon means. The scroll was given to me personally, by hand."

"Well?" He frowned, biting his lip. "What does it say?"

She brought the scroll closer to his face, making it clear that the seal was unbroken. "Julian . . . I can't . . . I haven't . . . "

"It's addressed to you?"

She gave a little nod. "It is."

"Then why wait? Open it!"

She was breathing hard; he had rarely seen her so panicked. "Julian, my father does not send me messages. He does not invite me to the home where I grew up. You know about our relationship. He refuses to even look at me." She turned the scroll in her hands, which were visibly shaking. "I don't want to know what it says." She met his eyes. "Please. Will you read it for me?"

"Fine," he snapped.

He snatched the scroll from her hand and broke the seal. Unfurling the paper, he read quickly. The message wasn't long; nor was there much in the way of flowery embellishment.

Samara,

Your mother is dead. Her grief became too much. Just this morning, she threw herself from the tallest tower of Graystone Abbey.

Julian glanced open-mouthed at Samara.

"What?" she asked. "What is it?"

He returned to Declan's cursive handwriting, which at this point became visibly tortured . . .

Whether this means anything to you or not, I do not know. You disappointed her. Bryan's death was not your fault, but you remain by the side of the man who killed your brother, our beautiful, beloved son.

Your mother's death now impels me to take action upon something I have learned, something terrible, something I can prove, but that I would prefer remains unsurfaced.

I know that our late emperor was poisoned, at your order, over a period of time, which I expect was done with your husband's full knowledge and consent. I also know that on the day our emperor died, when you went into his tent, you took a pillow, placed it onto Rigel's face, and you smothered him, pressing it down until he was dead.

Obviously, if I were to make this knowledge public, you would be killed. Quite horribly, one would think. Julian would of course meet the same fate, however I prefer to take another course of action. One must think of our empire, which as things stand, could barely survive such a crisis.

Here is what is going to happen. Tomorrow I will bury your mother. Before sunset on the following day, the sixteenth of Severen, Julian will announce his abdication. The process to find an alternative emperor will begin. Given our dire circumstances, a more experienced leader will take the reins of power. The decision will be for our assembly to make.

If Julian does not abdicate, I will recall the assembly and lay out the charges against both of you. This is not something either of us want, but do not test me, for I will do it.

I expect your prompt reply.

Declan Quinn, Lord of Graystone

"You . . ." Julian broke off, swallowing. "You need to read it yourself."

"What does it say?"

"Just read it!"

She held the scroll and took a deep breath, and then she was reading its contents. He watched her face as she put a hand to her mouth. And then, as she kept reading, she gave a little moan.

Her hand holding the message fell down. She was quietly crying, whether from the news about her mother or the horrific accusation, he wasn't sure. He reached out to touch her arm.

"Samara . . ."

"Lies," she whispered. "Such lies. But they will believe them. That is what makes it so hurtful." Her face screwed up, contorted with pain, which was frightening in itself. "I hate him, Julian. I hate him so much. They sent me to that convent . . . I was just a child . . . you have no idea what it was like. He hated me then. He hates me now." Tears were sliding down her face. "Please, my love. I need to know that you believe me when I say I had nothing to do with your father's death. You saw how sick he was. Please."

"I believe you." He opened his arms, and she came in, her head under his chin as he held her close. "I understand. I never thought . . . not in a thousand years . . . that he would do something this like this . . . not just to me . . . but to his own daughter." He swallowed again, still coming to terms with their plight, steadily understanding the terrible situation they were both in. "What do you think he means, when he says he has proof?"

"It isn't difficult to work out," she said hoarsely. "He is going to produce some person who pretends to know all, some cleric or maid or steward who will speak the words he gives them." She was shaking as she cried. "You have to believe me, Julian. You know me. I am your wife. I would never hurt your father. I would never hurt you."

The enormity of it all was still sinking in. He swallowed again, feeling like he might empty the contents of his stomach. She was right. It didn't matter what the truth was. The circumstances of the emperor's death were too aligned; everyone would believe Declan's story.

"Your mother . . . " he said.

"I'm glad she is dead. In her own way she was worse than him."

He released her and inspected her face, while she looked up at him with watery eyes. "As for this story . . . you and I both know the truth. But sometimes the truth doesn't matter, and this may be one of those times. We have all heard your father speak at the assembly. He is a persuasive man. If we don't do what he says, we could both lose our heads or worse. Samara . . . What are we going to do?"

"I don't know."

"Please. There has to be something. You always have an answer."

"All I know is that he wants us to suffer."

"It's me who he wants to suffer. You are at least his daughter."

This couldn't be happening; trapped in a nightmare, Julian was desperate to wake up. His mind jumped about, trying to find a way out, but even with Declan telling lies, he couldn't be allowed to carry out his threat. People would believe the worst, no matter what he and Samara said to defend themselves. And with the war going badly, people might be looking to believe, and find any excuse for a change.

"My mother's funeral," she said suddenly. "He wouldn't be able to deny me. I could go there and talk to him."

Julian gnawed at his lip and then nodded. She was right. There would be an opportunity—their last possible chance to change her father's mind. "And say what?"

"You know me. When it is called for, I can be very convincing. A funeral is a time to reflect on family, and I am now all he has left. I will throw myself on his mercy. I will cry. I will tell him about my regrets. This is the only way. We don't have any other options."

"But you know what he will ask for. He wants my abdication. He will want to know that we are going to give it to him."

"Abdication?" Although her eyes were wet; she wasn't crying anymore, and determination now filled her voice. "No, Julian. That is never happening. I will find another way. He wants reparations. I will give him what he wants.

"That may work for you . . . you are his daughter. But where does that leave me?"

"Let me go and find out."

"And if he refuses you?"

"If there is a way, I will find it. Believe me, Julian. This is what I am good at."

He shook his head, filled with bitterness and regret. Samara's brother had been a fool, and Bryan was a fool who deserved to suffer, to pay in blood for the things he said. But it was always Julian paying the price, over and over again.

This wasn't the first time he was forced to put his faith in his wife. But it was the first time that his life might be at stake.

"Very well. Do it. Go and talk to your father. See if there is another way. Every man has his price. He believes in the empire, we all know that. Remind him that the last thing we need is a crisis. We need our empire to be strong and whole. Find out what his price is."

✦

Kendrick watched another wave of the enemy charging toward the walls.

"Here they come!" he roared to the men around him. "Be ready!"

On the open ground in front of the small city, the enemy picked up speed. This next wave was the biggest yet; the Veldrians were committing everything as they surged forward on foot, crossing the dry desert plain to Narzin's gates and defensive wall. Kendrick kept his body half-crouched behind the parapet, only occasionally peeking out at the thousands of advancing warriors clad in protective leather armor. As they ran, the Veldrians brandished swords and screamed battle cries. Lifting his head, Kendrick counted a dangerous number of ladders, carried forward by their heaving numbers. Farther back, a thick battering ram made its way toward the main wooden gates. If the battering ram were ever allowed to do its job, without question, Narzin was going to fall.

He risked another glance. The enemy archers at the rear had their bows bent back, pointing them into the sky . . .

"Look out!" he cried. He ducked back down again. "Arrows!"

The rain of arrows forced him to bury his body deeper behind the low stone wall. He heard a repetitive clatter from the arrows striking the stone, but also screams and grunts and gurgles. Hoping the current volley was done, he again raised his head above the parapet.

Just a stone's throw separated the attackers from the bottom of the wall. If the defenders were going to employ their own archers, there would be no better time . . .

"Archers, draw!" Troy's voice behind him bellowed. "Loose!"

A great number of black shafts flew from the top of Narzin's tall outer wall, leaving holes in the mass of attackers whenever an arrow found its mark. It was now time for Kendrick to get to his feet, and he swiftly straightened.

"Ladders coming!" he shouted to the defenders around him.

A ladder slapped against the wall and two of Kendrick's men nearby used their pole arms to push it away. Teetering, the ladder finally tilted backward to fall back among the attackers. But then another ladder clacked against the stone, followed by another. An arrow slammed into the forehead of one of the soldiers carrying the pole arms; he didn't even cry out as he collapsed.

Already enemies were climbing to the tops of the ladders, to pour out onto the wall. The Veldrians in front were the biggest and toughest, some of them wielding two swords rather than one. To a man, they had the red-eyed, wild look of men in the throes of their potion.

A Veldrian came running, forcing Kendrick to block an overhead blow, turning his opponent's blade deftly before thrusting his sword into the man's chest. Moving into his next enemy, Kendrick sliced his weapon across the torso of one opponent, and then a second, taking both down in quick succession. As attackers kept climbing up the nearest ladder, he brought them down one after another.

Nearby, Troy bashed an enemy with his shield, before hacking down with his sword. In all directions, defenders fought hard, desperately trying to hold off the onslaught on top of the walls. Farther away, Caden, was in trouble as he faced an opponent twice his size. Caden dodged and parried, but the huge Veldrian had bloodshot eyes as he brought the half-moon blade of his axe far too close to Caden's head and body.

Kendrick despatched another warrior and then burst into a run. He slashed a Veldrian's leg from behind, and then dealt the man a finishing blow. Caden's struggles were becoming frantic. But before Kendrick could reach his son, two more Veldrians attacked him at the same time. Kendrick ducked and stabbed, bringing down the bigger man on his left. He crossed his sword in front of his face, arms tensed as his blade barred his enemy's, before he disengaged and cut the second warrior down with a hard slash across his chest.

Charging into the fray, he tore into another three warriors, dancing among them to hack and slice until the way forward was clear. He reached his son and found an opening, thrusting the point of his weapon into the huge axeman's throat. The Veldrian roared and reared back, exposing himself to Caden's subsequent blow. With obvious relief, Caden threw him a grateful look.

In a lull, Kendrick scanned the area. There were at least as many Veldrians as men to fight them off. Arrows flew past his vision, making him grab Caden and yank them both behind some barrels for cover—a group of enemy archers had found a position on the roof of one of the houses inside the wall.

He peered past the barrel. A bald man with a gray-speckled beard and a wicked scar on his face stood out in the open where any stray arrow could take him. Baden Lynch roared with his hands cupped around his mouth, giving orders to a distant captain. Meanwhile soldiers surrounded the lord marshal, weapons swinging as they found themselves embroiled. Kendrick's head turned in all directions. He made a quick decision.

"You all right?" he asked Caden, who nodded. "Come with me."

Kendrick burst into a run, evading enemies as he charged through another melee. With Caden close behind, he sprinted across the battlements, racing hard to reach the lord marshal. The fighting on the battlements ebbed and flowed, as the defenders momentarily cleared the area.

"Make way!" someone called, allowing Kendrick to approach.

Distracted, Lynch scowled in Kendrick's direction. With his collar buttoned up to his neck, iron spindle on its chain, zigzag scar and severe expression, there was no mistaking him for anyone else.

"Lord Marshal," Kendrick panted. "We can't hold much longer. We need to fall back. "

"You think I'm unaware, Conway?" Lynch's eyes were narrowed as he searched the walls. "Where is the emperor? We need him to give the order."

"Can't you give the order yourself?"

Lynch's nostrils flared. "I told you it has to be the emperor!"

Kendrick turned, eyes scanning. A heaving melee was underway, over where the wall was wider, above the city's main gates. "There!" he cried, pointing.

Julian was noticeable by his shining gold-trimmed armor as he fought in the thick of the battle. With him was his personal contingent of Imperial guardsmen in silver armor and white cloaks; together they made a powerful force as they fought hard to defend one of the areas most in danger of being overrun.

"I can fight my way over to him," Kendrick panted.

"All the way there?" Lynch asked. "The choice is yours. Good luck."

Kendrick turned to his youngest son. "Caden," he ordered. "Watch my back."

Taking a deep breath, Kendrick burst into another run, racing with sword in hand, gathering more of his men as he passed the section he was assigned to defend. As he left the area behind, another group of ladders struck the wall not far from where Troy and the other officers were coordinating the men from Esk. It was obvious that in seconds his eldest son would soon be under serious assault, but Kendrick couldn't worry about him now. He had to focus on his goal.

Surely anyone could see. The idea of holding the walls any longer was madness.

He sprinted at full speed, and whenever he collided with an enemy he slashed down but did everything he could to keep moving. Caden stayed with him, fighting hard as he defended their rear. Together they reached the scene of the most chaotic fighting, where Julian was slashing as he cut down the warriors who all wanted to be the man to bring down the emperor.

At last Kendrick reached Julian. Shoving his way closer, he grabbed Julian's shoulder to yell into his ear. "We have to fall back! Lynch asked me to tell you, and I agree! You have to give the order!"

Julian's glare was ferocious. "No." He shook his head vehemently.

Kendrick met him stare for stare. "We are losing men too quickly!"

"We are not falling back!" Julian shook off Kendrick's hand on his arm. "I will not give the order to retreat."

"Please, listen—"

"I am your emperor! You will do as I command. I order you to hold. Pass that on to the lord marshal."

Kendrick hesitated, but he had to think about his section of wall, where even now Troy was struggling.

"Very well," he said stiffly. He grabbed Caden to get him moving. "Come on! Let's get back while we can."

Kendrick didn't know if it would be the next wave of attackers, or the one after.

Narzin was going to fall.

Chapter Twenty-Six

JULIAN RUBBED HIS EYES. It was morning and he was tired. Despite the previous day's constant fighting, from sunup to sundown, he had once again barely slept.

Despite its vast size, the council chamber contained just him. If someone wanted him, they knew where to find him. Today was the day mentioned in Declan's demand: the sixteenth day of Severen. Fear was a constant presence, and even plagued his nightmares, so that the fitful moments of surrender were no escape.

He paced back and forth, clenching and unclenching his fists. Where was his wife? Surely she should be back by now. What if something had gone wrong? What if she was unable to see her father, and Declan pressed ahead with his plan? Before the day's end, Julian could discover that he was being accused of both patricide and regicide, of murdering his father the emperor. The accusation was leveled at Samara, but in truth it was targeted at him. Declan wanted him to fall. Whether he wanted his daughter back or not was a different matter.

Julian's jaw was so tight that tendons stood out on his neck. He tried to distract himself by moving to the window and looking down at the streets, where he could see the carts full of bodies that were still being cleared away. But the sight only reminded him of the perilous state the city was in. Which would fall first? Julian Malventus, or the inconsequential port city of Narzin?

"Emperor. They said that I would find you here."

Hearing a crisp male voice, Julian turned to see Lynch enter the council chamber. His lord marshal looked weary himself, but his bald head was smooth, his black and white beard was neatly trimmed, and the ever-present spindle still dangled at the base of his neck.

As always, Julian had been listening, but there had been no call to arms; the day's assaults had yet to begin. "Lord Marshal?" he asked, unable to shake off his dark thoughts.

Coming to a halt, Lynch gave Julian a grim stare. "I have inspected our defenses and spoken with the men. I am now advising you in the strongest possible terms. We must act now, while we can, before the day's fighting begins. This city is impossible to hold, as I am sure you can see for yourself. The walls are too low and the houses are built too close together. It is a miracle their archers haven't yet got numbers onto the roofs—but believe me, they will."

Samara's words of warning were still fresh. *No more defeats. You must show them you can win.*

"You must order the retreat," Lynch urged. "Meroy has stronger fortifications, and perhaps more importantly, the city is served by the Pillars of Dust. Let me be clear. If we do not choose to fall back, it will be thrust upon us anyway."

Julian looked down at his hands. His skin was tinged with red; no matter how he tried, he couldn't seem to scrub the blood off. While he watched, his hands were shaking. He wondered what to do. His lord marshal was both blunt and forceful. He knew what everyone would say, however, if he gave the order to abandon the city.

He had taken on the responsibility to hold the border at Lexia. He had failed. At Engel, he was supposed to turn back the enemy. He had failed. He had tried to hold the line at Narzin. Again, he had failed.

They wouldn't laugh at him; that time was past. He was a failure. They would want him gone.

"Also . . . " Lynch hesitated, but then pressed on. "I have to tell you . . . the truth is that even if we fall back to Meroy, we will not be able to hold the line there. It is my strong view that we have no choice but to abandon the Redlands altogether. We don't just need a stronger position, we need more men. I must ask you now . . . many nobles have promised us their men but we have yet to see them. Time keeps passing and tell me, where are the men? You are the emperor. Surely your nobles must do as you ask?"

Julian didn't answer. Something new was happening in the street below the window, drawing his attention. He leaned forward. A number of riders were outside the building. Among them was Samara, dressed in traveling clothes. She quickly climbed up the steps to the front doors and entered the building.

"Lord Marshal," Julian said. "I understand the situation and a decision will be made. Come and see me in an hour."

"An hour?" Lynch opened his mouth and then closed it. "Very well, Emperor. An hour but no more. I know you understand the urgency." He bowed and walked away, chin high as he stared straight ahead.

After the lord marshal was gone, Julian waited and paced. What was keeping her? She should be here already. What was she about to tell him? She had been gone for two nights and a day. Her visit to Graystone wasn't over quickly. That was a good thing, wasn't it? Had she managed some kind of reconciliation with her father? Had she begged her father to spare them the accusations Declan wanted to make? There would be a price. Declan would never satisfy himself until he had made Julian suffer. Samara was clever; everyone knew that. But by the Great Weaver, what price could leave him with his head still attached to his shoulders?

He faced the door, hands bunched into fists at his sides. He glared, staring and watching and waiting. He wanted to pray, but what could he expect? What outcome was it he was praying for?

Samara came to the door.

She was dressed in a forest green blouse, along with brown leggings and high boots made for riding. Her hair was glossy and fashioned with a number of jeweled clasps. She saw him, and her eyes widened with trepidation.

"Samara," he said, unable to wait any longer. "Well? What did he say?"

His fate was about to be decided. As his wife came up to him, however, his impatience shifted to raw, spine-chilling fear. She didn't say anything at first. Standing in front of him, she gnawed at her lip and wouldn't meet his eyes. He knew his wife, and whatever she was thinking, it wasn't anything good.

"What is it?" he asked, in a shakier voice this time. "What did you find out?"

"I saw the bodies on the way here." She searched his face. "You look tired. How bad was the attack?"

"Bad," he said. "Tell me. What happened with your father?"

She stood and looked down at her hands as she twined her fingers together and then she took a deep breath. "My father and I . . . we spoke at length. I said what I needed to say. I made reparations, if you can call it that."

He should have felt relief—she had accomplished that much—but his dread only grew; something bad was coming. "And?"

She allowed the silence to drag out. "Something was proposed. I will not say that it was agreed, but an offer was made."

"Now is not the time to dance with words, Samara."

"I am not trying to be obscure. I just . . . I hesitate to say it."

"What is it? What does he want?"

She still didn't answer immediately. "Husband," she said. She took another steadying breath. "You know how things were for me as a child. I had to make my own way in the world. I was the one to leave my family home. My parents . . . they kept my brother, the child they loved most. When Bryan died, my father turned his hatred on you. You stole his daughter—me—and then you stole the life of his son—"

"I wasn't the fool who—"

"I know how you feel," she interrupted, "and you know that I feel the same way. I am just trying to explain how my father feels . . . how he thinks. He thinks he has lost not just his family, but his entire legacy . . . now he has nothing to leave behind. After all, who will inherit Graystone after him? There is also the matter of what he calls the empire's sound rule. You know how he is. He fears the empire's eventual fall—"

Julian scowled. "I am aware. We have all heard about his ridiculous archive." He shook his head. "I know all this. And yet you spoke to him and here you are. Well, Samara? What was his proposal?"

She raised her head to stare into his eyes. "Do you remember when I told you that you needed to make peace with your enemies, that there must be a lasting settlement? I told you that this current situation cannot continue. You never had a coronation. Your support is ebbing away. And that is without my father's intervention."

"Of course I remember."

"When I went to Graystone, my goal was to make peace, to broker a truce and rather than opposition, to instead gain my father's support. My goal was to find out what price he would consider sufficient for us all to move forward. We need him to forget his false accusations. To instead reach a lasting agreement. He has a great deal of influence, and I set out to show him that by working with us, from the inside, he would be able to wield even more, as our ally rather than our enemy. That was the task you set me. If your enemies became your champions, you would never have to worry about your position again. Many more men would join the war here in the south."

"Samara . . . " he said in a low tone. "There is no time for this. I have to order the retreat within the hour. You know how that will look."

"Very well," she said. "This is my father's price. I wish he were here to deliver it, rather than me. You have to believe me . . . This will hurt me as much as you . . . "

His jaw, shoulders, stomach . . . his whole body was tensed, clenched hard as he waited. *Here it comes . . .*

"For you to remain emperor, you have to give your oath in blood that you and I will never bear a child. In my father's words, your line ends with you. The assembly will choose your successor, which we both know means that people like my father will nominate the next emperor. You and I . . . " her voice shook, and a distant part of him could see that this was difficult for her, "we will never have a child. That is the only price that will satisfy him."

He waited for the rest of it, and then his brow furrowed. "And that is all?"

"He also wants to be able to advise you in all things. You do not have to do what he says—we have an assembly after all—but he does want you to listen."

He frowned; he didn't like the sound of the last demand. "Advise—?"

She held up a hand. "In return," she continued to look into his eyes, "in return he will give you his full support. You will have your coronation. He and all the other nobles will bend the knee. You will be emperor until the end of your days. The Blues will immediately put their money and men into the war effort. This hostility will be over. Instead the Imperium and the Assembly of Nobles will be at peace. The empire will be whole. And together we will win this war."

His mouth was open as he listened to what she had convinced her father to agree to. There were some elements that he would want to change, but that could happen in time. In truth, she had accomplished everything he could have wished for.

But he couldn't help wondering why it seemed too easy. "Is that everything?" His brow furrowed. "There's something I don't understand. He says we must never bear a child. He might not always be around to monitor our agreement. With every oath or intention, how can it be assured?"

"Once . . ." She broke eye contact, and when she did, his guts gave a sickening squeeze; this was what she was frightened to tell him about. "Once, long ago, during the Holy Era, there was a compact, between the nobles and the emperors they chose to crown. Back then, it was considered an overwhelming urge for a man to try to found a dynasty, to see his offspring inherit power and privilege, and yet this urge was what the nobles wanted to temper. And so, in order to be crowned, every male emperor had to agree to never sire offspring. The outcome was that everyone wearing the crown would always be chosen by merit rather than inherit the crown by birth. This . . . rule . . . removed the chance of the empire being led by a tyrant, a madman, or a fool. Only the childless could become emperor—or empress. And once crowned, an emperor could never have a child again."

"You are not . . . you are not suggesting . . . "

"My father . . . he believes that what the empire needs is an emperor whose soul is pure. He . . . he wants you to undergo the Rite of Purification."

At last Julian understood, and he felt the blood steadily draining from his face. He felt weak enough to reach out and grab hold of the edge of the table nearby.

Samara still wouldn't meet his eyes. "Emperors have done it before—"

"Not for a hundred years—"

"Julian . . . these are my father's words, not mine, but I said I would deliver them faithfully. The Rite of Purification has worked in the past, he says, as a way to bring the empire's three pillars together. The head.. the body . . . the limbs. The emperor, corpus, and assembly. The rite demonstrates devotion, bringing the emperor closer to the Weaver. And the rite—"

He finished for her, speaking in a hoarse whisper. "—gives the assembly complete power over the succession."

"In my father's words, the rite is a noble sacrifice. An emperor gives up his ability to have a child, taking away any risk of a dynasty leading to tyranny . . . ensuring his successor is chosen by merit, rather than blood."

"You cannot be serious." Her hesitation, the dancing about with words, it all made a horrific sense. "No. Never. Not in a thousand years. I hope you laughed at him and walked away."

She was pale as she looked at him, revealing her terrible fear. "I am afraid that laughing at him is something we cannot afford to do. We are in terrible danger. The sword on your neck is there, even if you cannot see it."

After the shock, his anger rose, bringing tension to his body and heat to his cheeks. "They call it the Rite of Purification, but we all know what it is. He wants me to submit myself to castration . . . to be gelded like a stallion who must still share a field with the mares. A price . . . I see . . . it all makes sense now." He spoke with venom. "I will cut him into pieces. I will burn his home to the ground."

"He said that would be your reaction."

He stared at her, spittle coming from his mouth. "What about your reaction? You are my wife!"

She held his gaze, tears in her eyes. "And, if you do not agree, you know he will put in a motion at the assembly for an investigation. An investigation into your father's death. I discovered his body. They will accuse me of terrible things, in public, even if they are not true. These are the kind of accusations that can never be silenced. If my father is your enemy, rather than your supporter, what do you think his investigation would find?"

Julian had known there would be a price. The price was always going to be terrible . . . but this . . .

Samara pressed on. "If there is an investigation, and he brings out his so-called proof, what then would happen to us?"

An example would have to be set. They would both suffer a slow, torturous death. He might be skinned alive, or hanged, drawn, and quartered. Samara would probably be tied to a stake and burned while she screamed for mercy.

"We will be killed," she said simply. "Picture yourself, in that cell, waiting for the night to pass and the light to come up in the morning, knowing that you are seeing your last sunrise."

The image she painted was a vivid one, particularly when he had already had the same fear present in his nightmares.

"My love," she said, coming over to stand closer, "this is a shock to us both. I have thought this through from so many angles. If I knew another way, I would suggest it. Do this, and with his support, you will have a coronation immediately, and many more men for the fight. Without reaching this agreement, we will both be dead. I have to come back with a response immediately."

He shook his head, speechless, unable to manage words. When he returned his focus to the woman who was his wife, he looked her up and down.

"It isn't your body." His voice was both bitter and cold.

"I have always wanted children. Please. Believe me. This is hard for me too."

"But you could still have a child, with another man."

"I would never do that."

He knew her appetites. She was his wife, supposedly connected to his thread on the tapestry. But he didn't believe her.

"I made some enquiries," she said. "Even after this, our time in bed together would still be enjoyed. You would be emperor. I would be your empress. By your side. Forever. And you would become powerful . . . " her voice firmed, "powerful enough to one day have your vengeance."

He shook his head, slowly, but then with vigor. "No. I can't do it."

He heard the clatter of hurried footsteps. At the same time, battle horns began sounding the call to arms. A soldier burst in, his face red from running.

"Emperor," the soldier panted. "It looks like a full-scale assault."

✦

Several hours later, Julian again stood at the council chamber window, but this time he avoided looking down at the carts of bodies and stared toward the sea. The sky was darkening. At any moment, Baden Lynch was going to come in, and Julian knew what he was going to say. They needed to think of the wounded. There was no gateway near Narzin. They needed to think about the greater struggle. They had to save the army. They had picked the wrong place to make a stand.

Julian's father had experienced a great deal of campaigning, and yet Julian could never remember him speaking about the trouble he had dealing with so many bodies. After yet another day's fighting, the battlements had looked truly horrific. The fallen and wounded were sprawled in such numbers that it was difficult to walk from one place to another. They were going to have to dig a pit, a hole the size of a mountain, to fit all of the dead.

The fighting had been relentless. In the end, they had held the city, but at a terrible, unforgettable cost.

Everyone was now expecting the order to abandon the city. And when it came, they would know that the sacrifices they had made were in vain. If they were going to leave anyway, allowing Narzin to fall to the enemy, they should have done it a long time ago.

Julian couldn't win. If he had given the order days ago, people would have called him a coward. Now, they were already calling him a fool.

The sound of movement behind him told him someone had come to the door. He turned, expecting Lynch, but instead he saw Samara.

The sight of her made him think of only one thing. She hadn't been fighting—she had been resting, or perhaps refashioning her hair. For once, the sight of his beautiful wife didn't lighten his heart. Instead, her approach made his stomach churn in unsettling ways.

"This is it," she said, her expression utterly grave. "We are at the end." She stood in front of him, waiting for him to speak. "You and I both know the truth. There is no other option. We have to agree to his offer."

"Samara . . . " By the stars, his voice sounded weak. "You are my wife. What about us? It will change things. It has to."

"We will be strong."

He shook his head, facing the window again. "The coronation would be immediate?"

"That is the agreement."

He couldn't believe what he was contemplating. He had fought, but somehow he hadn't fought as hard as he should have. He had seen Samara's father bend his knee, but still that wasn't enough. In the past days of battle, he had killed countless enemies but always they kept coming. And even as he hacked and slashed and threw himself deeper into the fray, part of him worried and planned and tried to find another course of action.

He had to find another focus for his future.

Samara had mentioned vengeance.

He clenched his jaw. Once they had publicly applauded his coronation, he would make his own plans to crush them. He would destroy them in every way. Mercy would be the last thing on his mind.

"Tell your father I agree to it," he said. "Go. Right away. Meanwhile, I will give the order to abandon the city."

Chapter Twenty-Seven

THE GREAT IMPERIAL ARMY traveled with care, scouts and patrols fanned out in all directions. There had been no sign of pursuit, but that would come. For the time being, the invaders would be busy taking occupation of Narzin.

After a day's travel, the army reached a crossroads. On a distant hill, in the east, a large settlement with tall white towers and irrigated fields rose from the desert. However the army ignored the city of Meroy and headed west, toward their destination, the nearby Pillars of Dust. The white towers grew smaller at their backs, until they were all that could be seen of the nearby city.

At sunset, Bethany stood with Kendrick as they watched the busy scene at the gateway. Around them the barren landscape stretched on and on, red and dry, with scant patches of thorny scrub. The Pillars of Dust stood arrayed in a circle of seven, like tall anthills, each the color of dried blood. This region of the empire, the Redlands, was known for savage sandstorms, but despite the windswept marks on the pillars, the gateway still worked as it should.

Bethany glanced at Kendrick. He looked weary, even as he stood tall, with his armor cleaned and oiled. The defense of Narzin had been a brutal experience; he and his sons were lucky to have survived. With the fighting now done for a time, she could only feel relieved he had made it through. She didn't know what she would do if something happened to him.

He rested his eyes on her, and she thought she should say something. "I've never felt so pleased to be in front of a gateway."

He gave a short laugh. "I can't help but agree with you."

Flashes of light kept appearing between the pillars. The wounded were being taken away first, in gatherings of bandaged soldiers on foot and horses pulling stretchers on carts, all led by cloaked diviners taking them to a number of destinations. The assembled army was orderly, with each division bearing its own standard as the different groups waited to depart.

Kendrick turned to scan his own contingent. "And so here we are, Bethany. The emperor has made the difficult decision and now it is time to regroup. You may not have heard but levies from the Blues will now be joining us. Their numbers will make a difference, and when we return, we'll finally be strong and ready to turn back the enemy. We won't have long in Everlast. But I have good news—I've arranged it so you'll be able to attend the coronation."

"Attend the coronation?" Bethany's mouth dropped open. "My Lord . . . I am . . . honored."

He raised an eyebrow, clearly surprised at her formality. "Everyone important will be there, but that doesn't mean you have to go. I would advise it, however. You are young, and someone with your intelligence can rise high in the corpus. "

The last thing she wanted was to go to Julian's coronation. "I appreciate your efforts. I truly do. In this case it might be best, however, if I tend to some other things."

"You don't want to go?" He frowned, perplexed. "You never said why he wanted to see you alone. What is it? Does he frighten you?"

"Perhaps a little."

"As I said, he is the emperor, but he is also a man." He ventured a smile. "Until now, I would have said you don't get frightened by much."

She remained serious. "If it's possible, I would much rather see my mother."

"Of course. I understand. There is no pressure, Bethany."

There was silence between them for a time. And then she turned his way again. "What does it mean, this Rite of Purification? Everyone else seems to know."

From the way people spoke, she knew to ask quietly, so that no one else could hear.

Kendrick didn't answer her right away, his brow instead furrowed as he looked like he was trying to find the right words. "It hasn't happened for some time, but sometimes an emperor needs to demonstrate that he is more devoted to his duty than anything else. He has to prove that he is free of distraction. By undergoing the rite, he builds up his support, like a castle getting thicker walls and stronger fortifications."

"I don't understand. What does it entail?"

"Well . . . it isn't exactly my area . . . As I understand it, he is purified, with three days of ritual cleansing. You come from the corpus. You understand. He gives his oath in blood. Men can be distracted by many things . . . women . . . family . . . the advancement of their children . . . their own legacy. After the rite, an emperor cannot have a child. Instead, his successor will be chosen by merit, selected by the Assembly of Nobles. This choice . . . the sacrifice . . . gives him strength in the assembly, just as the act of purification brings him closer to the Great Weaver, and brings him support from the corpus."

A nearby mass of soldiers walked toward the gateway as they were called up. Armor groaned, harnesses jangled, and weary legs marched.

"Why is it he can no longer have children?"

"Your horse back in Esk is a gelding, if I remember correctly?" He waited for her to nod, and then spoke meaningfully. "That is how."

Her eyes widened, but Kendrick wasn't the type to jest. Julian had a wife, Samara, who was both beautiful and young. By the stars, how could he agree to it? Why would Samara?

In any event, everyone seemed to think that despite their numerous setbacks, the empire was going to regroup and come back stronger. That was the important thing. And Kendrick wasn't going to force her to attend Julian's coronation.

Another contingent was departing, and she wondered which part of the empire they were going to. As for her, she was more than eager to travel, even for a visit. Despite the fact that she would soon be back in Everlast, the Argent Arch felt like a vast distance away.

Kendrick harrumphed beside her. She felt a flash of guilt after turning down his offer to attend the coronation, which must have taken an effort to arrange.

"They are saying that everything will change now," she said.

He glanced her way; his thinking was often visible on his face. "Hopefully. We've been reacting this entire time, ever since our plan to dig in at Engel failed. From Everlast, we'll be able to come up with an entirely new strategy." He lowered his voice so that she had to strain to hear him. "And like him or not, we have to either support the emperor or put someone else in charge. It seems that everyone has made their choice and is now rallying behind him." He looked at her sidelong. "Yes, even my wife's brother. We'll have more men, more horses, more weapons, more mercenaries." He turned toward the distant city. With the light in the day fading, the tall white towers had taken on a golden glow.

"Unfortunately, we will have to abandon Meroy."

He continued when he noticed her surprise.

"We've learned from Narzin, Bethany. We need somewhere with proper fortifications. Most of the citizens are going to be evacuated, with some volunteers remaining. The city's governor is going to throw herself upon the queen's mercy. From what you've told me, she isn't the kind to butcher them out of hand. At least, that's what we're all hoping."

Bethany brought to mind Queen Zhuana's stony expression and her cold, calculating eyes. The queen had said she didn't want to burn Engel. But that didn't make her any less frightening.

"Meroy will fall," Kendrick continued. "But when we come back, we will come back twice as strong."

"Will you get to see Lady Anthea in Everlast?"

Kendrick nodded. "She is going to be at the coronation."

"Good." She thought about her mother. "Do you miss her?"

"Very much. I miss my wife and Isabelle too. I miss them with all my heart."

Chapter Twenty-Eight

JULIAN KEPT HIS BODY completely still. He couldn't be crowned emperor without moving sometimes, but at least for this part of the coronation he could hold himself in one position, seated high on an immense chair.

His wounds were fresh; his body felt tender, but he would be strong. The Rite of Purification was in the past, and that was what he kept reminding himself. He tried to keep his mouth closed and inhale through his nose so that no one would see the deep breaths he was taking. His mouth tasted bitter from laudanum, but he was on display, and couldn't risk becoming stupefied, no matter how much pain he was in. A sting climbed up to travel through his body, making him grit his teeth.

He was close now. It was nearly done.

He was in the Cathedral of the Hidden Source, the great sacred building in the Nexus, where the high confessor conducted the most important ceremonies and kept safeguard over the Crown of Blood and Gold. The structure was immense, tall enough to poke up from the Nexus complex so that its spire was visible from far away in Everlast—in fact there was a rule that no other building could be taller.

The cathedral had a grand entrance and multiple conjoined sections, with the coronation taking place in the main vaulted space in the center. A crowded gallery of guests filled every available seat, meaning that

Julian had a sea of faces turned his way. This wasn't like the fielding, where only people with a military interest attended. They were all here: every powerful noble, every high official from the corpus, along with the most senior provincial governors.

He would now have the support of his strongest adversaries. All of the embittered, the doubters, the hesitant, the old enemies and rivals; they would all fall into line and throw their weight behind him. Everyone would see his opponents here, in this place, applauding his coronation.

Dressed in a black robe with a symbol of woven white lines on the back, High Confessor Roman Valaeric approached until he stopped in front of Julian's throne. His gray eyes were somber, raised up to the ceiling. Light from high above glowed upon his smooth, pinkish skin.

The empire's heir was ready to be crowned.

Julian found himself thinking about his father's claim of a second child. The idea only made sense if his father had met a woman while campaigning in the Far Reaches. If something had happened in Everlast, the idea of keeping the liaison secret would be laughable. Julian had been busy with the war, but here in the capital he would be able to make proper enquiries.

After his coronation, he would learn from his mistakes, and do what had to be done to cement his power. He would find out the truth behind this story of another child. If there was one, he would see to it that he or she was dealt with.

Meanwhile, Declan believed that his false accusations gave him leverage. But what Declan didn't seem to realize was that his story was going to get weaker, after bending his knee not once, but twice, and after publicly proclaiming his support.

Julian would now wield the full power of his position. No one would be able to take it away from him.

A object was in the high confessor's hands. He was chanting as he held up the Crown of Blood and Gold, but Julian wasn't paying any attention to his words. The crown was heavy; Julian's father had let him hold it once when he was a boy. Made of solid gold, it bore huge rubies at regular intervals, with an exceptionally large stone at the front.

Its name—the Crown of Blood and Gold—was especially fitting. Julian had certainly paid in blood to be here today.

The high confessor's chanting reached a climax and then his steady, soulful voice trailed off. He held the crown dramatically high over the throne and Julian's head.

Past the high confessor's black robe, in the seating gallery, a multitude of eyes were on Julian, all focused on this one, significant moment. The tension increased. Julian's mouth was dry; his heart was beating hard. He had dreamed of this moment, from the time of his earliest memories, when he had been in awe of his father, the Dymantine Emperor, the most powerful man in the world.

High Confessor Valaeric lowered the Crown of Blood and Gold, to place it on Julian's head.

"Long live Emperor Julian Malventus Livius, the first of his name!" The high confessor called, the volume of his voice rising to fill the entire cathedral. "Long live the emperor!"

A powerful echo came from the seating gallery. "Long live the emperor!"

"All rise!" the high confessor called.

They all stood as one, all of his friends and allies, all of his enemies and haters. The high confessor raised his now-empty hands high and clapped. The staccato patter of hands coming together became louder, and louder, until the din of applause was deafening. From the cathedral's open entrance came a loud roar. The sound of a city and of an empire's acclamation was thunderous, filling Julian's head until he couldn't help it; he struggled not to smile.

There was someone whose reaction was more important than anyone else. Julian's attention moved toward the lean, high-browed face of Declan Quinn, Lord of Graystone, who was clapping as hard as anyone. Neither of them smiled, but Julian met Declan's gaze, and Declan nodded in return.

Declan thought that once they had won the war, together they would address the empire's apparent decline. Julian had simply said whatever he needed to say. He now kept his expression neither angry nor pleased. He had learned his lesson. He was able to hide his hatred.

His greatest enemy wasn't going to occupy his attention. Not now. Not today.

Julian tore his eyes from Declan, past Kendrick, his wife Anthea, moving from Baden Lynch to Tristan Benedict and Gavin Arturius.

There, facing him, was Samara, the woman he called his wife.

As empress, she was seated alone, directly in front of him, in a chair not quite as big and wearing a crown not quite as heavy. She looked as beautiful as ever, wearing a thick robe in purple and gold, with bright jewels at her fingers, earlobes, and neck. Her hair fell in the curling tresses he had always loved so much. When she caught his gaze, she smiled at him.

Strangely, he experienced a new emotion when he looked at her. She was beautiful, but her beauty masked a darkness in her core.

How much of what she did was only for herself?

All of a sudden, the high confessor nodded meaningfully at him. It was time.

Julian rose from the throne, and when he wobbled, he put a hand on the high confessor's arm to steady himself. A stabbing, throbbing sensation clawed up through his stomach; the laudanum he had taken was wearing off. The bandages were thick. The important thing was that he didn't tear his stitches.

He kept his face smooth and walked down from the throne, heading to the cathedral's great opening. As he tried to make a stately pace, the fabric of his long gold and purple robe trailed on the floor behind him. He couldn't help check—but no, no sign of blood.

Everything was planned in detail; Samara fell in behind him. Yet this was his moment; why should she share it at all?

He was able to shake off his irritation as he departed the cathedral and stood on the top step, to be greeted with a roar and rising applause. Out in the open, he raised a hand, smiling and waving to the crowd.

Veldon Marx, commander of his Imperial guard, stood at attention with his men arrayed behind him. Behind the guardsmen, the confessors, diviners, and clerics of the corpus were all in neat rows. There was a gap for Julian to walk through, where at the end of the path, a chariot and driver waited, ready for him to climb up and commence his parade of the city.

Julian descended the steps, heading carefully straight to the chariot. He wished he could have mounted a beautiful horse, but in his state, the idea was unthinkable. He climbed up to the platform, assisted by the driver, and winced as he took hold of the bar. Drawing a tight breath, he focused on standing tall.

All eyes were on him.

Samara climbed up to join him in the chariot, and he couldn't help noticing how easily she moved compared to him.

He was at the beginning of a long day. But he was proud of himself for his fortitude. He had sacrificed. But perhaps nothing gave a man strength so much as the idea of vengeance to come.

Chapter Twenty-Nine

BETHANY STOPPED TO TAKE in the Observatory. The complex was vast, and the hill that it straddled wasn't small. Within the walls were walkways, administrative buildings, and elegant towers with spires. The Crystal Dome crowned it all, lofty and ethereal, another reminder of the Eidar and all they had left behind. She had spent so much time under the dome she was facing, looking through the panes in the other direction.

A long time ago, her footsteps had brought her here, after the assessment at Speaker's Corner. At the time, she had wanted someone or something to shout at. But back then, after a few moments, all she had felt was envy at the people passing between the two huge doors that stood wide open at the Observatory's base.

Here she was now, with her copper hair glistening in the sunlight, hood back as she stood under a clear blue sky. She wore her diviner's gray cloak and had her staff in hand.

She had achieved her dream, in the end.

The Crystal Dome, like a crown upon a head, made her think about Julian's coronation. Declan . . . Julian . . . They had come to some new arrangement. Perhaps now they would be able to forget about her existence. This was where she belonged.

Rather than join the city in celebrating the new emperor's coronation, she had instead spent time with her mother. As they sat together and talked for hours, her mother had been as well as Bethany could hope for—unable to see at all, but using her cane to make her way around the dormus as she made cups of tea. When she did, her hands were barely shaking. And she said she wasn't in too much pain.

Bethany looked up at the Crystal Dome and smiled. It was good to be back.

Now she was going to see someone else. She pictured him now, tall and broad-shouldered, with pale skin, black hair curling to his collar, and a wide mouth with a wicked smile. She remembered his eyes, deep eyes like no one else's, warm and brown and flecked with gold.

She walked with purpose as she headed directly toward the Observatory's wide open doors.

✦

A long bench had half a dozen clerks behind it. As other people traveled farther into the Observatory, they ignored the clerks completely. The stone walls and ceiling were more than familiar. Even the smell was the same, cool and somehow wooly, like a warm winter coat hanging in a wardrobe.

Bethany headed to the nearest clerk, a plump curly-haired woman in a gray dress she wore buttoned up to her collar.

"Diviner?" the clerk asked politely. "May I be of assistance?"

"I am looking for someone. Diviner Xander—"

"Xander Cole." The plump clerk smiled. "I know who he is. He comes and goes all the time." Her smile fell. "I am afraid however that you are out of luck. There is a camp in Trent where they are housing refugees from Engel. Diviner Cole is there now, helping those poor people. I imagine it will be some time before he returns."

"Oh." Bethany's disappointment was so strong it surprised even her.

The clerk leaned forward, her kindly face sympathetic. "You can leave him a message, if you like?"

"Please." Xander was engaged to the corpus. She should have expected him to be busy, rather than simply waiting for her in Everlast. "Please just tell him that Bethany came to see him."

"Bethany . . . " The clerk pursed her lips. "Bethany . . . Sylvana?"

"Yes, just tell him I was hoping to see him."

"Wait." The clerk's brow furrowed as she pondered. "Diviner Bethany Sylvana, house diviner to the Conways?"

"Yes?"

As soon as Bethany nodded, the clerk stood up from her chair. "Please. Wait here, Diviner Sylvana."

The clerk waddled away, but she wasn't gone long, disappearing through a door behind the bench before she reappeared a moment later and closed the door behind her. This time she held something in her hand: a thick scroll.

The clerk raised the scroll. "This came for Lord Kendrick Conway. I assume Lord Conway is in Everlast for the coronation?"

"He is," Bethany said.

The clerk held out the scroll, but then brought her hand back up. "Diviner Sylvana . . . You know what the golden ribbon means? It is to go straight to the hand of Lord Kendrick Conway and no one else. Rather than use the Wheel, someone has paid good money to ensure that happens. We would usually send a message to Lord Conway asking him to come and get it, but now that I have you . . . You are his house diviner, after all." She offered the scroll again. "Here."

After taking the scroll, Bethany examined it. The paper was thicker than usual, and the scroll was strangely heavy. While it was wrapped in a golden ribbon, there was nothing she would call a seal. The name of its intended recipient was written in clear neat lettering: Lord Kendrick Conway of Esk. But without a seal, the name of the sender was a mystery.

"I can take it to him right away," she said. When the coronation was over, she would find the Conways at their city villa.

"And I will give your message to Diviner Cole." The plump clerk smiled, pleased with herself. "If there is nothing else . . . Diviner Sylvana?"

"No," Bethany said. "Thank you."

Before she left, she took one last look around, imagining three young students walking the corridors: Xander, Carina, and herself.

But time was always marching on, and she left the Observatory behind.

✦

Kendrick and Anthea's house in Everlast was tall and narrow, stuck between the houses beside it and facing a busy street. Kendrick much preferred Fernley Manor, and he didn't stay often.

Right now, however, there was nowhere else he wanted to be.

After a day on display, it wasn't until the front doors had closed behind him that he slumped with relief. He reached the main living area and yanked off his ill-fitting clothes. The tight coat went first, followed by the doublet, tossed on a nearby divan. At last, in just the tunic he had underneath, he groaned as he stretched. He then collapsed into the divan, to yank off first one boot, then the other. When he was done, he let out a long breath as he stared at the ground with knees apart and shoulders heavy.

Anthea watched, amused, with her blonde hair flowing and an embroidered crimson dress hugging her figure. "If an artist were to paint me the theme of weary, this is what I would expect."

A loud cry from outside made them both turn, but it was just the usual noise coming in from the city.

Kendrick rubbed his eyes. "I am exhausted, to be honest. And that's not just from the war."

Anthea came over. "Move along." After taking a place beside him, she turned to face him. "You are alive, and you kept the boys alive too. Of course you are tired, my love. You deserve some rest." She was close enough that her body was warm against his. "Kendrick, this time together is a gift. Do you have to leave so soon? Can't you stay, even for one more day?"

He rubbed at his chin, but then shook his head. "We have tonight but that is all. At least the boys are out carousing. I told you, everyone is expected to make their way to the Wheel first thing in the morning. My absence would be noticed."

"Yes, they will notice. But you will only be gone for a day." Reaching out with both hands, she rubbed his shoulder, moving to the back of his neck. "I've missed you, Kendrick."

"Hmm," he said pensively. His wife's touch was exactly what he needed. "Even if I was able to turn up a little late, you know I wouldn't be able to get the boys to do the same thing."

"I know," she said softly, as she continued to work the tight muscles in his shoulders.

"Hmm. I suppose the army has to get the army from the Wheel to Highguard Castle. At the rate they'll travel, they'll have to set up camp on the way. I'd have more than a chance to catch up."

"From what you've told me, Bethany has also been in some adventures. Perhaps she could also use some rest."

"Ha," Kendrick snorted. "You should have seen her when she came out of the desert."

"Just a day, Kendrick, and Bethany could enjoy some extra time in the city too. She could take the two of you straight to the Wheel, and before you know it you would be catching up with the others before they get to Highguard Castle."

Anthea continued to rub his neck, making him wince when her firm fingers felt the knots under his shoulder blade.

"All right," he said. "I can live with the consequences. I'll do it."

He lifted his wife's chin to kiss her. Breaking contact, he smiled and she smiled back. He knew how much he would enjoy their time together.

A knock on the door interrupted them. It was a tap, rather than an insistent pounding. With a sigh, Kendrick got up from his seat and walked over to the house's main entrance

He opened the door a little and then wider, surprised to see Bethany standing out on the threshold.

"Bethany . . . Please. Come inside."

Bethany had something in her hands as he gently guided her into the villa, before closing the door behind her.

"Bethany," Anthea called. She rose from the divan, crossing the room to reach Bethany and take her by the hand. "I know we saw each other yesterday but you seemed so worried. How is she? Your mother, I mean."

"She is well, My Lady." Bethany had stopped, rather than come all the way to the seating area. "I'm on my way back there now, but I thought I should give you this first." When she held up a scroll, wrapped in a golden ribbon, Kendrick eyebrows went up. "It looks important, so I thought it shouldn't wait. It's addressed to you, Lord Kendrick. It has to go straight to your hand."

"Thank you," Kendrick said, curious as he took the scroll. "I know what the ribbon means."

"Who is it from?" Anthea asked.

"It doesn't say." He showed it to her. "No seal. Just my name and the ribbon. It's heavy."

"I should go . . . " Bethany said.

"Wait." Anthea held up a hand. She nodded at Kendrick. "Aren't you going to open it?"

His brow furrowed as he looked for a knife, before heading to the sword he kept propped in the corner. He drew the weapon from the scabbard, touching the blade to the ribbon to slice it clean through. Returning the blade, he came back to Anthea and Bethany and unfurled the paper.

The scroll came in multiple pieces. The outer sheet of thick paper covered a cylindrical container made of leather, with a cap at one end to keep it well-sealed.

Setting down the leather container, Kendrick read the paper. There weren't many words to take in.

Kendrick, this is to be opened in the event of my untimely death. Otherwise, you may prefer to remain ignorant. The choice is yours. Do not reveal its existence to anyone. Declan Quinn, Lord of Graystone.

Kendrick let a long, anxious breath. "Read it. It's from from your brother." He handed Anthea the piece of paper, before picking up the leather container and turning it in his hands. "By the stars . . . " he muttered to himself.

Anthea swiftly read the message, even as Kendrick took hold of the container's cap. She looked up and made a startled sound. "What are you doing?"

"What do you think? I'm opening it."

"Kendrick, stop. Please. Do not open it."

Bethany spoke up, "I think I'm going to leave . . . "

Kendrick's hand was motionless, but he also didn't remove it from the container. "How am I supposed to go out there, as the senior commander of an army led by Julian, with Declan now part of it too, and not have any idea what it is your brother knows?"

She spoke sharply, incisively. "Do not open it. He only wants you to know if something happens—"

"And then what?" He held up the cylinder. "We all know it. If the wrong person finds out we have this, we could be killed, whether we know what's inside or not."

"Then we should burn it," Anthea said, scowling at the leather cylinder as if a snake might jump out and bite her.

"That might be a good idea . . . " Even Bethany was speaking up, which was unlike her. Her face was strangely pale.

"We all know that Declan was looking. And this now tells us he found something." Kendrick frowned. "I'll tell you what I am going to do. I'm going to open it. I will then read it. And based on what it says, I will decide whether or not to burn it."

Without another word, Kendrick yanked off the cap at the end of the container. He pulled out another, smaller piece of paper. This message was even shorter.

Kendrick read the message aloud: "Burnham Abbey, Malange." He let his hand holding the paper fall. "That is all it says."

It didn't take him long to make his decision.

"Bethany. Come and get me first thing in the morning. We will catch up to the army later. Bring your warmest coat. Make your preparations. I need you to guide me to Malange."

Chapter Thirty

KENDRICK BLEW ON HIS HANDS and stamped his feet. It had been a long time since he had traveled so far north. Bethany stood beside him on the abbey's threshold, and even with her copper coloring she was pale and shivering, with lips turning steadily blue. Past her, out in the open, snow steadily fell to leave a thick white coating on the ground. White powder covered their coats and dusted the hood of Bethany's cloak. The sky had no color at all.

As they both waited, their exhalations came out as mist. Kendrick pounded on the heavy door again. What was taking so long? Didn't they realize how cold it was?

The abbey was tall, narrow, and old. Sited on a hill where it overlooked the city of Malange, the only access was via a long climbing road. Its front door with solid, made of vertical planks of black wood. Iron bands held it together.

Back in Everlast, the morning sun had shone steadily from a bright blue sky. Bethany had opened her gateway at the Argent Arch, and then Kendrick stood blinking within the tall circle of the Statues of Malange. All of a sudden, he was far enough north that the sun was already up for hours. The disorientation was one thing but the shock of the cold was worse. At least the soldiers posted at the gateway could provide directions, and soon they were laboriously climbing the abbey's access road on foot. Kendrick spent most of the journey regretting not bringing horses.

Burnham Abbey was one of those places that rarely interacted with the rest of the world. There was a gateway nearby, but the Isle of Neska, where Malange was the most populous city, was a harsh place: mountainous, cold, and barren. If someone—or something—was to remain hidden, the abbey was a good place to do it.

Sounds of movement finally came from the door's other side and a panel in the center shot open. A pair of beady eyes examined first Kendrick, and then Bethany. The panel snapped closed. A moment later a sliding bolt screeched and clunked. The door gave a drawn out groan as it opened.

An old woman with greasy gray hair peered around the door as she held it slightly ajar. She wore a ragged black smock with a white stripe around the collar. "Our devotees live here in seclusion. Visitors are not welcome." She squinted at Kendrick. "What is it you want, My Lord?"

"My name is Kendrick Conway, Lord of Esk . . . "

The old woman made a sound. "Kendrick Conway . . . of the siege at Curran Castle?

He nodded wearily. "The very same."

Her eyes widened, before she recovered her cautious manner. "As I said, visitors are not welcome, Lord Conway."

"Be that as it may, can we talk about it inside?" Kendrick growled.

"I am afraid that—"

"Look," he said flatly. "Someone told me to come here. You might know the name. Lord Declan Quinn of Graystone."

"Oh." The old woman started. "I see. Well, then, that changes things. Wait here."

As the door closed with another creak, the clank of the sliding bolt told Kendrick it was locked again. He exchanged glances with Bethany, whose hands were under her armpits. Blowing on his palms again, he shuffled from side to side, lifting his left foot and then his right.

At last the bolt clanged again. The door opened a crack, and this time a different woman looked out at them. She was clad in the same style of black and white smock the old woman had worn, but she was young, careworn but pretty, with blonde hair and a heart-shaped face.

"My Lord . . . " she said, examining first Kendrick, and then Bethany. "Who are you? Why are you here?"

"We've come to talk," Kendrick said.

"Talk . . . " she trailed off.

"My name is Kendrick Conway. My brother-in-law is Declan Quinn of Graystone."

"Brother-in-law?" She sighed, her shoulders slumping. "I suppose you want to come inside?"

Kendrick struggled not to raise an eyebrow. "Yes," he said. "Yes, I believe we do."

With an air of resignation, she opened the heavy door wide, and Kendrick indicated for Bethany to enter the abbey as he followed straight after. The young woman blessedly closed the door behind them while he and Bethany stood rubbing her hands together. The chill was noticeably less painful inside, but that didn't mean the interior was warm. An antechamber greeted them, with walls, floor, and ceiling all made from the same gray stone. A corridor led deeper into the abbey, with another adjacent door nearby.

"This way." The young woman kept her head down as she walked. "Follow me."

She led them to the door nearby, opening it with an iron handle. Kendrick and Bethany entered a broad chamber, where high-backed wooden chairs framed a table and grimy glass-paned windows displayed views of the city of Malange, with the houses and streets barely visible through the falling snow.

The young woman turned to face them both. She took a deep breath as if to gather herself. "You are not here to kill me. Which means that it must be time."

"Time?" Kendrick asked.

"To atone. For what I've done."

Kendrick paused, waiting for her to continue. "Done? To whom?"

The young woman frowned. She glanced at Bethany and then back to Kendrick. "I don't understand. Lord Declan brought me here. He said that someone might come, either him, or you, Lord Kendrick. My name is Lorena. I was a cleric—"

"I remember you," Bethany frowned as she interjected. "You were taking care of the emperor."

Lorena nodded. "I was a cleric, but that is in the past. I now spend my days working for the abbey. I keep the floors clean and the fires burning. That is my penance and I will do it until I am cleansed. As for looking after the emperor . . . I told everything to Lord Declan . . . " She hesitated. "He didn't tell you, My Lord?"

"He said enough for me to come here." Kendrick cleared his throat. "Please. Just tell me what you told him."

She took another shaking breath. "Very well. I wasn't helping the emperor. I was doing the opposite." She lowered her voice to a strained whisper. "I was acting upon another's orders, but I still did it."

"Say it plainly," Kendrick said, fighting to keep his voice even. "What did you do?"

Lorena stared at the floor. "I gave him poison."

Bethany's gasp was audible.

Kendrick's mouth fell open. "You poisoned the emperor?"

He remembered the fielding, and Rigel's hacking cough in the high gallery. The emperor always rode in on a stallion, but he had barely managed with a chariot. And then . . .

"Answer me clearly. Who was it who asked you to do it?"

Lorena swallowed. "It was Lady Samara, My Lord. She asked that I make the emperor . . . ill. At first she paid me. It was a lot of money, and I did it. But then she wanted me to make him worse. I said that he might die, and I refused. And then some men broke into my mother's dormus. They hurt her and tore the place apart. Lady Samara . . . she told me that the next time they would do a lot more. She said it to my face. I was afraid. I did what she told me to do."

"You said this to Declan?" Kendrick asked. "That Samara had you poison the emperor?"

Lorena nodded.

"But why?" Bethany asked.

Kendrick glanced at her, "It's obvious, Bethany. To hasten her husband becoming emperor. He almost lost the confirmation vote. She couldn't afford to wait." He didn't mention that at the end, Rigel had been about to deny his son the succession, right before . . .

He met Lorena's gaze. "I need you to tell me the truth. This is important. Was Julian aware of what you were doing?"

"I only ever dealt with Lady Samara. But . . . My Lord, you still haven't heard it all. Julian came to see his father at the fielding, right after the knighting ceremony. They argued. Julian left. And then . . . and then . . . Samara ran in. I was the only one there. She told me not to move or my mother would die. Then she . . . she took a pillow and pushed it down onto the emperor's face. He was sick . . . and weak, but he . . . he kicked and struggled. I just stood there. I watched it happen. She . . . she murdered the emperor right in front of me."

Bethany had turned white. Kendrick stood stunned as he stared through the window at the falling snow. Samara's wailing had been so loud. She stopped whatever Declan had been about to say. And then Rigel's death . . . . his death had changed everything.

What Kendrick was hearing was the truth. He knew it with a well of certainty felt deep inside. Anthea . . . she had known. And he had also suspected . . . By the stars, everyone probably suspected. But without evidence . . .

Now here was the evidence, standing right in front of him. If the assembly heard her story . . . Great Weaver . . . Julian and Samara wouldn't just fall . . .

"Declan knows all this?"

"Yes, My Lord. I fled the fielding. I got my mother out of Everlast. I went into hiding with the corpus. I was terrified Samara would find me, but in the end it was him. It was Lord Declan who brought me here."

"Declan has always been thorough . . . Bethany? Are you all right?"

Bethany had her hand covering her mouth. "It's just . . . a shock . . ."

Lorena's eyes were tight and anxious. "Now that you are here, My Lord, am I coming with you? That is what he said would happen, if you came. My conscience will never be clear until I stand in front of everyone and reveal the truth."

Kendrick didn't have to think for long to shake his head. "Your name is Lorena—do I have that right?"

She nodded.

"Lorena, no doubt you understand that this has to be handled with the utmost care. What Declan and I both need is for you to stay here. Whatever you do, don't talk about this to anyone."

"Am I in danger?"

"You are about as safe here as you can be."

"The day will come, My Lord, when I can reveal the truth?"

"That day may come, or it may not. You are doing all that is within your control. Continue with your penance. Bethany, please come with me."

Kendrick's head was still spinning as he led Bethany from the chamber. He took it upon himself to open the heavy black door to the abbey, until he had closed it behind them and they were once again standing on the threshold, looking out at the pale sky and snow.

"What now?" Bethany asked.

"I don't know."

He rubbed at his face. What was Declan thinking? Early in the morning, while he was on his way to the abbey, the army would have gathered at the Wheel of Klare and begun the march to Highguard Castle. Julian would be leading from the front, with Baden Lynch at his side, along with Veldon Marx and the Imperial guard.

Kendrick's old friend Tristan would be there, as leader of the Wardens, responsible for the Blacks. With him would be hundreds of lords and knights, along with their levies, all from Kendrick's order.

Gavin Arturius would also be with the army, together with the great number of fighting men he was in charge of, all members of the Crusaders, the Reds.

And Declan Quinn would be there too. After all, he was in charge of the Blues, and had publicly applauded Julian's coronation as he and the other Guildsmen promised their levies to bolster the army's numbers.

"What is Declan's game?" Kendrick muttered. "He kept Julian on the throne, but why?" He came to the obvious truth. "He's still looking for this other child of Rigel's. Meanwhile he is keeping the empire functioning, even as he makes Julian suffer . . . "

Standing with him, Bethany looked frightened, echoing his own rising trepidation.

"We need to get back to the army. My sons are there. I know Declan. He may appear to be on Julian's side, but he will be looking for his opportunity, and as soon as it comes, he is going to strike."

"But this other child of Rigel's . . . they have been silent this long . . . Could they really change anything?"

He met her gaze. "This is going to reach a conclusion, one way or the other. We have to get there, as quickly as we can, before something terrible happens."

Chapter Thirty-One

THE WHEEL OF KLARE was one of the empire's most important gateways. Not only was it a key messaging hub, it was also located by a road that carved a straight path through the mountains, all the way north to Everlast. If the Wheel were ever taken, the empire's communications would be crippled and the capital would be exposed. Both the road and gateway had be held at all costs.

The Wheel's protection, fifty miles to the south, was Highguard Castle. A proud and ancient fortress, the stronghold had its back against the mountains and gaze fixed firmly on the plains. Past the plains was the Redlands, which, along with the Southern Provinces, had now been abandoned to the enemy.

Highguard Castle was where Julian would make his stand, and turn the enemy back, once and for all. The invaders would make no further progress north. He would rather die than let that happen.

Thinking about the days to come, Julian rode at his army's head on a dappled courser. The road was uneven, with frequent rocky stretches, and below his waist he was sore from all the bumps, despite his saddle's extra padding. And yet his mood was determined, filled with strength and purpose. He was at the front of an immense column of men and horses. His army was nearly twice the size. Nothing would stop him now.

The army he was leading had left the Wheel some time ago and now traveled in a southerly direction, through a region of hills coated in grass and woodland. Despite the road's condition, the terrain was at least open, mostly dirt or gravel, and the horses wouldn't have much trouble provided they traveled in daylight. Refreshed, renewed, reinvigorated, the soldiers drawn from across the empire marched toward Highguard Castle in good order. Scouts were out, but trouble wasn't expected.

Lord Marshal Lynch rode at Julian's side, dressed in brown leather buttoned to his collar and with his lips moving soundlessly as he held his T-shaped iron spindle. If his prayers earned them victory, then Julian had no intention of interrupting him. Arrayed behind them, Julian's personal contingent of Imperial guardsmen rode in formation, resplendent in white cloaks and silver armor, with their formidable commander up front. Following the Imperial guard, the army traveled in sections, and rather than three groups in total, there were now four, with the three orders each making up a block to follow Julian's leading section. As the knights of the realm traveled with their men-at-arms, foot soldiers, archers, stewards and other attendants, black pennants dotted the first group, followed by red, and finally the blue colors displayed by the Guildsmen.

For the first time, Julian had a large number of Blues as part of his army. And with his coronation applauded by all and the Marble Court now far away, this was a military endeavor. Veldon Marks and his guardsmen were utterly loyal, charged with keeping him safe and his position secure. Julian was away from towns and cities, far from any civilians. There would be no inconvenient votes. Out here, far from the capital, no one would disobey him or question his right to lead.

The sound of faster riding clattered on the rocky terrain, making him look over his shoulder. Samara's long dark hair, slender figure and elegant appearance was at odds with all the steel and might around her. She wore her dark green tunic, the color of the nearby trees, along with her brown leather leggings. Golden jewelry decorated her ears and throat, and her neckline was low, revealing her creamy light brown skin. She met his gaze with her smoky, slightly tilted eyes.

But her beauty didn't touch him at all.

He hadn't wanted her to come, but she had insisted, and already he regretted not being firmer. How did she do it? How did she so often convince him to agree to the things she wanted, rather than what he wanted for himself?

She was smiling, but her smile was strained. Meanwhile, he couldn't bring himself to offer her any warmth. Slowing her horse, she nudged it forward until she was beside him.

"There are not many of us wives, but I have just been speaking with Lady Judith—"

"Samara," he said coldly, and her eyes revealed anxiety that surprisingly brought him pleasure. When he spoke, he didn't whisper. "I am enjoying my present company. Perhaps you would prefer to continue as you were at the rear."

He knew it; he had publicly shamed her. She paled but didn't reply. Instead she turned her horse and rode away.

And he was relieved to see her go.

Lynch glanced his way but didn't speak, and Julian was content to continue in silence. Samara was the empress, but she had little in the way of real power. He was the one who had worked for his position, who had fought and suffered. No one else would bend him to their will, not while breath remained in his body.

Time passed as he led his great column through a thick emerald forest. The sun glowed on the treetops overhead, filtered by the wavering foliage. Farther into the woods, a stream glided lazily past. On the rolling hills, grassy clearings broke up the heavier woodland.

As the road began to climb, the horses snorted as the slope became steeper. Soon the forest opened up, revealing a broad landscape of forested peaks and valleys, before the terrain began to fall once more. The road curved back and forth as it wound down the hillside. In the distance, a gorge split the forest into two sections, with the white and brown cliffs indicating the location of the Swan River. And there, crossing the gorge, was the spindly form of Broadwater Bridge, an ancient wooden bridge with supports at either end.

Setting up camp would take time, and they would have to do it twice on the way to Highguard Castle. The three orders would raise tents in their separate areas, in the way they always did, with Blacks in one place, Reds in another, Blues somewhere different still. Even with some distance between them, it would be strange to share a camp with Declan Quinn. Everything bad that had happened to him could all be laid at the feet of—

His horse hit a hole and jolted his body on the saddle. Pain shot up from below his stomach. It took all of his concentration not to gasp.

"Emperor?" Lynch asked.

Julian steadied his breathing as he took control of himself. "I'm fine." He cleared his throat. "I was just thinking about our progress." He nodded in the direction of the bridge. "At the rate we're traveling, I should think we will make camp somewhere near Broadwater Bridge."

Lynch scratched the vicious scar on his cheek. "Best to camp just before the bridge. We can making our crossing first thing in the morning."

"The forest isn't too thick?"

"There are a few open fields, and it's thicker on the other side. It's an old bridge, so we won't be able to all cross at once. Better if we start first thing in the morning."

"Very well. That makes sense to me."

Julian looked over his shoulder to take in the long trailing column, when movement drew his attention. A different rider was traveling alongside the column to make his way to the front. His figure grew larger, until he was revealed as a steward, an older man, bald and olive-skinned, wearing a uniform in somber gray. He rode all the way up to Julian before reining in.

"Emperor." The bald man gave a deep bow. "I bring a message from Lord Declan Quinn of Graystone."

Even hearing the name made Julian's stomach tighten. "And what is this message?"

"My lord said he knows this region well. He suggests making camp on this side of Broadwater Bridge. There is fresh water and open ground on the near side of the river. He also asks if you will be hosting a strategy meeting before we arrive at the castle."

Julian kept his face expressionless, even as he was aware of Lynch nearby. He was the emperor, and yet Declan Quinn was making requests of him. Julian would be the one deciding the movements of his own army. If there was to be a meeting, why should Declan even come at all?

Samara's words came back to him. *He wants to be able to advise you in all things.* He again saw Declan's face at his coronation. *You are here because of the price I made you pay,* Declan's look had said. *In the end, I won.*

Julian stared straight ahead. He pictured it . . . sitting across from Declan and his dark, calculating eyes, listening to his lecturing, condescending voice. There were no proper chairs in a military camp. The folding chairs were always hard and uncomfortable. He would be feeling pain under the backs of his legs . . . he would wince and shuffle in his seat . . .

The scene in his mind changed without conscious direction. How good it would feel to secretly have his naked sword across his knees and ready. He would lift his weapon and lunge forward, stabbing, experiencing the satisfying rush of blood. Declan's eyes would go wide. The old fool would stare down at the blade in his chest . . . he would know his end was coming . . .

Julian was breathing hard. He had never longed for anything so much as the fulfillment of his vision. Deep down, there was something he couldn't change, no matter how hard he tried.

He couldn't live with the situation the way it was.

The time for vengeance wasn't in some distant, remote future. He had never had the power he had now. Why wait?

He could think of no good reason at all.

✦

It was night time as Julian stood outside his pavilion. His heart was beating fast. He was both nervous and excited. The mixture of emotions was strange, as if he were about to perform his first dance with a beautiful woman.

The moon was full and cast a silver glow on Broadwater Bridge, the wooden span at the edge of his vision. The army's sprawling encampment was everywhere else, where there was enough space for the Imperials, the Blacks, the Reds, and the Blues in the broad clearings within the forest. The Swan River made a constant rushing rumble below the bridge. A fresh wind blew at the nearby trees, shaking them as if they were agitated.

Julian was waiting, and finally, there she was. Samara had changed into a cream-colored dress that she wore with matching slippers. Her footsteps on the grass made no sound at all, masked as they were by the water and the wind in the trees. She had fashioned her hair into a flowing style. Silver circles dangled from her ears.

Julian held open the curtain at the entrance to his tent. "Go inside," he said curtly.

"Julian," she said as a greeting. Her expression was more than a little worried, but she said nothing more as she entered the pavilion.

"See that we are not disturbed," Julian instructed the pair of guardsmen nearby. "I don't want anyone getting too close."

"Of course, Emperor."

Julian made a last check. In addition to the two guards a dozen paces from the entrance, he also had a perimeter of soldiers surrounding the pavilion. Each guardsman stood far enough away for there to be no chance he and Samara would be overheard.

Satisfied, he turned and entered the tent.

Thick carpets lined the floor. Lanterns burned on the folding sideboard. Two divans faced each other across a low table, near a wall of canvas that partitioned the sleeping area behind. Another lantern burned on the table between the divans, along with some other, more important items.

Samara was frowning as she seated herself. She made a show of looking around.

"I don't know what you are talking about," she said. "There appears to be plenty of space for the two of us."

Julian took the other seat next to the low table, opposite her. "I have never enjoyed being away from civilized places, as you know. We have two nights at camp before we get to Highguard Castle. I prefer to sleep alone."

"You made yourself clear. And now we are far enough apart that you have to summon me with one of your guardsmen." She glanced down to where Julian had laid out paper, ink, a quill pen, and a stick of white wax. "Is this for me?"

His heart rate increased until he could feel the rapid patter in his chest. This was it. The time had come.

"You said I needed to have a coronation—and now I have. You said I had to make peace with my critics and I have done so. You said that to defeat the Veldrians I needed the full support of my nobles. I now lead a powerful army."

"We have sacrificed, but—"

"No," he interjected. "*I* have sacrificed, Samara. Not you. But you were going to say that the effort has paid off, and with that I agree. Everyone has seen your father and his allies applaud my coronation. Tell me, what would happen now, if he attempted his false accusation that my father was murdered, by none other than his own daughter, the empress, my wife?" He didn't wait for her to answer. "Do you know what I think? I think that no one would believe him—"

Her tone was skeptical. "He says he has evidence—"

"—to prove something that did not happen."

"Even if it is false, he can be persuasive—"

"People would be confused to say the least. Why be so supportive only to turn around and accuse me of my father's murder? It would look spiteful . . . vindictive . . . and fickle in the extreme. When he was openly an enemy, people would understand. But as my supporter? How would that look? People would assume I offended him or broke some agreement between us and now he is out for my blood."

She spoke quietly. "You sound like you have already convinced yourself of something."

He stared into her face. "Your father is going to die."

Her shock was immediate, in her caught breath and the swift widening of her eyes. "What did you just say?"

"You promised me vengeance, Samara. The fact is, I don't want to wait any longer. I have the support I need. And now the time has come—"

"Julian," she interrupted. "Listen to me. My father is a powerful man. The head of an order. He has too many friends and allies to simply—"

"You learned from your father, Samara. I learned from mine. Anyone can be a traitor. An emperor must always be alert for plots against him."

"But the Blues—"

"—are currently part of an army, with my guardsmen out in force. In any other place, they might have a chance to cause trouble. But my nobles are here with me, where I can keep an eye on them. There will be no rebellion. Not while I am watching."

"Julian, it is not just the Blues you have to worry about. He is related by marriage to Kendrick Conway. Kendrick Conway, Julian. A war hero. The man who saved your father at Curran Castle. The Blues and the Blacks together—"

He smiled. "Kendrick isn't here, Samara. He is away on leave. By the time he returns, it will already be too late."

"Julian. You have to listen to me. This is a bad idea—"

"You promised me vengeance," he repeated, narrowing his eyes. "This is what it looks like. You have told me a thousand times that you despise him. Or perhaps you have feelings for him after all?"

He waited, but she kept her lips sealed. Her face was pale as she returned his stare.

"Now," he said, "you are going to write your father a message, and then you will sign and seal it. Start writing, Samara. This is what you are going to say . . . "

Chapter Thirty-Two

CADEN'S DREAMS WERE FILLED with a magnificent castle, with walls of glowing sandstone and floors made of shining white marble. Golden flags decorated with the stag of Esk fluttered from the tall turrets, and strangely it was him giving the orders to the proud knights in shining armor. Stewards leaped to do his bidding, and a beautiful dark-haired woman beckoned him to follow as she led him to a bedchamber. She squeezed his upper arm and whispered his name: *Sir Caden. Sir Caden.* The squeezing turned into a shake. The shake became insistent . . .

Caden's eyes snapped open. His head turned. A bald older man, with dark skin, dressed in a gray uniform, was crouched by his bedside. Caden was in the tent that he shared with several others. Snores came from the other cots.

"Sir Caden," the steward whispered, releasing Caden's arm when he saw he was awake.

As Caden blinked away the last of his lurid dream, he recognized the steward. The bald man worked for his uncle, and the uniform belonged to Graystone.

"What is it?"

The steward put his finger to his lips. "You need to get dressed. Meet me outside."

The bald man left the tent, and Caden thrust his bedcovers away from his body to get to his feet. He found his trousers and pulled them on, and then searched for his light brown tunic. Once he had it on, he put on his boots. His companions were all fast asleep.

He left the tent. His uncle's steward was waiting outside. "Is everything all right?"

"My Lord Declan wants to see you."

The moon was full and shining from overheard. "Now? What time is it?"

"Near midnight. Please. This way, Sir Caden."

Caden followed the steward as the older man led the way. The surrounding tents were in orderly rows, and in the moon's silver light they had no difficulty navigating between them. Black pennants fluttered from several of the ropes, designating which section they were in. Soon they were entering the trees, and the rushing sound of the river became louder as they approached a different section of the camp, where the red flags of the Crusaders snapped in the gusts of wind. They passed along a long row of hobbled horses, who snorted and stirred as they both walked past.

At the late hour, everyone was fast asleep. As they plunged into the trees once more, Caden rubbed his eyes and stifled a yawn.

"Did he say what he wants?" he asked the steward.

"Not to me, Sir Caden."

The only people awake were the emperor's guardsmen, keeping watch from different locations in the camp. Caden and the steward now reached another collection of tents, were blue flags decorated the ropes of the pavilions. Caden lifted his head and frowned. Past the Blues' section of the camp, a screen of Imperial guardsmen stood in a distant line, maintaining a perimeter. Surely it wasn't usual practice for guardsmen to be out in such numbers?

As the steward continued to lead, Caden approached a large pavilion, with blue flags flying from every corner. It would be good to see his uncle. He had been so busy that he hadn't had a chance to talk to him for some time.

The bald steward pulled apart the pavilion's curtain, holding it so Caden could enter. "Enter. Please. My Lord is inside."

Caden entered the tent, where his uncle stood waiting with hands clasped behind his back, fully dressed, lit up in the glow of a half-shuttered lantern. The tent was larger than most, and he looked like he had been pacing.

"Uncle? You realize the hour?"

Declan gave a hint of a smile. "I know my reputation, Caden. I do like to work in the night, but I also realize that others prefer their rest. It

213

is good to see you, my boy. I assume that you were sleeping, and I am sorry to have awoken you."

"What is it?"

"I need your help." Declan revealed his hands, holding up a scroll, with its seal of white wax already broken. "I have received a message, a message that I must act upon." His mouth tightened. "It is from my daughter. She tells me she has information. . . something I will want to hear."

"Why not just tell it to you?"

"Ah, Caden . . . I will try to spare you the troubles that plague me. There are always plots afoot, my boy. Secrets within secrets. All I will say that if she knows what she says she knows, and feels the way that she feels, then she and I must meet in secret." He glanced at the clock on a nearby bench. "The time is nearly upon us. And that is where you come in."

Caden remained silent, brow furrowed, waiting for his uncle to continue.

"I would be a foolish man if I gave her my trust without thought. I want you with me as my witness. All I ask is that if requested, you stand out of earshot as my daughter and I talk."

"Why me?"

"To be honest, Caden, because of who your father is. Your father is a well-respected man, and belongs to a different order than the one I lead. With you by my side, I can rest easy knowing no harm will befall me. Will you do it? Will you come with me as my escort? I would ask your father, but he has yet to join the army."

Caden didn't hesitate. "Of course, Uncle."

"Thank you, Caden. Now we have some walking to do, to the bottom of the gorge and upriver." He checked the clock again. "The time has come. Are you ready?" He waited for Caden to nod. "Then let us get this over with, so that you can return to your bed."

✦

Caden and Declan walked upriver, following the bank of smooth pebbles. Declan's gaze swept side to side, constantly scanning and gazing up ahead. There was no way they could get lost or miss their encounter, for as long as they went against the current, there was no other way to travel. So close to the water, the rushing sound it made was loud enough to completely cover the crunch of their boots on the stones.

"Tell me if you see her," Declan instructed, speaking over his shoulder. "Your eyes are better than mine."

"Still no sign," Caden said.

All Caden knew was that Samara must be extremely frightened of being discovered in this meeting. They had been traveling for about half an hour with still no sign of her. Perhaps the meeting was no longer happening. She might have backed out, too anxious to go ahead with it.

Up ahead a huge boulder stood by the water, the size of a house and the shape of a lopsided cube. They continued to travel alongside the river, and then something moved up ahead, and both Caden and his uncle stopped moving.

A dark figure stepped out from behind the boulder to stand at the water's edge. He wore his cloak with the hood concealing his face, and the cloak was parted while he kept his right hand on the hilt of his sword. When Declan spied the stranger, he froze for a moment. But then he turned, and his head kept moving, eyes widening as he stared past Caden's shoulder.

Declan sucked in a sharp breath, hard enough for Caden to feel a chill prickle at the back of his neck.

Caden looked backward to follow his uncle's gaze.

Four Imperial guardsmen stood behind them on the bank, where they hadn't been before. The four soldiers had fanned out, and there could only be one reason—to block Caden and his uncle's ability to return the way they had come. They were huge men, clad in armor, with white cloaks on their shoulders. Each guardsman had his sword drawn, the bared steel glistening in the moonlight.

Caden and Declan had both halted where they were. Caden's ears became filled with the sound of his own beating heart, and his own hoarse, heavy breathing.

The stranger in black was walking toward them. Even as Caden tried to make sense of the scene, another four Imperial guardsmen appeared up ahead, near the boulder, also blocking the way upriver. On one side the gorge's tall wall was far too steep to climb. On the other side the river was deep and fast, with sharp boulders poking up from the current.

Caden and his uncle were perfectly trapped. And, unmistakable in the moonlight, Declan had an expression of horror on his face.

"Uncle . . . " Caden moistened his dry mouth. "What is happening?"

"I didn't . . . I . . . Let me talk to them."

The stranger in black continued to near. His hood still hid his face in shadow. With the river crashing nearby, he made no sound at all.

"Who are you?" Declan called. "Where is my daughter?"

Close enough now to talk to, the stranger in black stopped walking. He pulled his hood back to reveal his golden hair, calculating brown eyes, and downcast mouth. Caden recognized the emperor, Julian.

Julian had his eyes fixed intently on Declan. His chest was rising and falling, far too fast to be normal. "I am afraid that she will not be coming." He smiled. "I should rephrase. I am not regretful at all. In truth, I am pleased to be here instead."

With a slow, deliberate movement, Julian drew his sword. He raised the tip, keeping it pointed at Declan.

Caden's head kept turning. His eyes darted in all directions, but with four guardsmen behind, and another four blocking the riverbank ahead, there was nowhere he could run.

He had listened to his parents talk. Julian and Declan were enemies. But Declan was an important man, the head of the Order of Guildsmen. There had to be another explanation, other than the one that had terror shivering along his spine.

Perhaps there had been an attack? Could there be a plot against his uncle, and the emperor and his men were here for protection? His uncle's eyes were wide open, and his strong reaction was the most frightening thing of all.

Declan put out his hands placatingly. "I am here at my daughter's request."

"I am well aware." Julian flicked a glance at Caden and then back to Declan again. "You were supposed to come alone."

Declan visibly gathered himself, developing a firmer tone. "I brought a witness." He nodded toward Caden. "He is Caden Conway, the son of Kendrick Conway."

Julian watched Caden for a moment. A widening of his eyes told of his surprise. "I see."

"I should also have you know that if anything happens to me, his father will get certain information."

"Yes, yes. I am not as troubled by that as you think." Julian addressed Caden directly. "You should not have come, boy." He nodded toward Declan. "And he should not have asked you."

✦

Julian's blood was high and he was tense, ready for violence. He had planned this encounter in detail. But Kendrick's son was a complication.

Once again, Declan believed he had Julian in control. Declan wasn't as frightened as he should be, and his fear was what Julian wanted, more than anything else. Instead Declan stood with a combination of wariness and condescension, like a parent with an unruly child.

Declan kept his hands out wide. "Julian—"

"Emperor." Julian scowled, moving the tip of his sword closer to his enemy.

"Julian." Declan tried again. "Listen to me. I can see that whatever is between us is not yet finished. We can talk. You still need my support."

"I disagree," Julian said. "I have an army. We are at war. I just had a coronation, where my nobles openly gave me their allegiance. They each gave me their oath and bent the knee—and that includes you. Who would risk further division?"

"Julian, can't you see? If I told them what I know—"

"Lies. All of it lies."

"Ah . . . " Declan made a sound of realization. "I see it now. I miscalculated. You weren't involved . . . of course not. Which means . . . Great Weaver, yes, I have been a fool . . . She has you under her spell. My daughter was always good at that. However once the spell is broken, you see her for what she is. I am telling you the truth, Julian. Samara murdered your father. I swear it on my son's eternal star."

"Lies!" Julian snapped. "I have you in my power. You will say anything to escape. You will even risk your own blood." He sneered at Caden Conway, his sword point wavering from side to side like a snake about to strike. "The boy is your nephew. I can see that the two of you are close."

Declan continued, arms held out, showing his palms. "Julian," he said carefully, watching Julian's eyes. "Listen to me. As you said, you are the emperor. Nothing can be done with violence that cannot also be resolved by talking. The future of the empire is more important than either of us."

"I disagree. Many important outcomes are achieved by violence. What was done to me, for example. The loss of what makes me a man. The fact that I will never sire children." As Julian spoke, he brought his sword forward. "Don't tell me that wasn't a violent act."

"Your quarrel is with me, Julian. He is just a boy."

Julian's nostrils flared as he changed the angle of his sword and inched the blade closer to Caden Conway. His mouth tasted metallic. He moved his sword close enough to touch the razor sharp tip to the base of the young man's throat. As Caden swallowed, staring down at the steel, part of Julian screamed—what about Kendrick? But Kendrick wasn't even with the army. And perhaps Kendrick was too close to Declan anyway, which would make Kendrick an enemy too.

"Julian, listen to me—"

Julian scowled at Declan. "You lost your son then you lost your wife. Your daughter betrayed you and gave you to me. If I am honest, it brings me pleasure to cause you pain . . . "

Declan spoke in a hiss. "Get out of here, Caden. Right now. Run."

"I would have you know, this is the same blade that killed your son, Declan."

217

"Julian. Stop this! You know what his father will do."

"He does not frighten me. And right now neither do you."

Julian thrust, fast as a whipcord. He shoved his blade into Caden's throat and kept going. The young man convulsed, even as Julian pushed in hard to force his blade in all the way. With a savage grunt, Julian then yanked hard. As he brought his steel out of the wound, he twisted during the exit, knowing the thick veins were at the side of the neck. He then stepped back to avoid the following gush of red liquid.

Caden wrapped his hands around his throat. He made a rapid gulping sound, his lips working, perhaps trying to say something but then coughing red liquid out of his mouth. The blood came out in spurts between his clasped fingers, pumped hard by his heart through his severed artery. His eyes were wide open. He stared at Julian and then down at his hands. The blood grew while he watched. His knees began to tremble.

He took a step backward. And another. His boots entered the shallow water.

And then there was nothing left in his legs at all, nothing to hold him up. He crumpled. Falling to the side, his head slammed to the riverbank. His hands fell from his neck. Lying and turned toward the water, he stared at the river, as if he were watching it rushing past. Blood drained from his body to enter the river, mingling with the clear water.

Declan cried out. He raced over to throw himself to the ground. As he bent over the younger man, brushing away the boy's hair, Declan put his head against his, even as the lad coughed again and red liquid splattered from the side of his mouth to run down his face. Then Caden blinked slowly. He blinked again. And then his chest rattled, and his eyelids remained open as he died.

Declan raised his head to look up at Julian and when he spoke, his voice was ragged and raw.

"You will bring the empire to ruin. Everything I believed about you is true."

Julian moved the tip of his sword. As the blade dripped blood onto the smooth pebbles below his feet, he put the steel against Declan's body. "Get up."

Declan didn't even flinch. He climbed to his feet with naked hatred in his eyes.

"Now here is what is going to happen," Julian said. "You are hereby accused of exchanging secret messages with our enemy in an attempt to surrender the empire's south. Knowing I would never agree to it, you were plotting my assassination, after which you would install some puppet of yours in power." He nodded toward the young man's body, as blood washed into the river. "He is accused of the same crime. As is his father, your brother by marriage. The infection runs deep, but I will lance it."

Julian turned to look back over his shoulder, to where his four guardsmen waited upriver. He waved them over, and the four armored men approached.

"I am sure you know who Veldon Marx is. Tonight he is going to question you, and you are going to confess. In the morning, word will go out that you and Kendrick Conway were plotting my assassination and you have now paid the ultimate price. Your allies will believe it. They will all wonder which of their friends were assisting you, for they will know that they are innocent. They will be afraid and desperate to prove their loyalty. Your confession will be all the evidence I need."

"I will never sign it."

"Have you ever been tortured?" Julian asked. "My father always told me that like Veldon Marx, it is a blunt instrument, but an effective one. The fact is—yes you will."

Julian waited for his men to arrive. He then nodded toward Declan. "Take him to the commander." He pointed his sword at the body lying by the water. "Take the body with you. And find Kendrick's other son and put him under guard, but do it quietly. In the morning, we will get the army crossing the bridge early."

"You are a fool," Declan said in an ominous tone. "I have a lot of friends."

"I don't care. You pushed too hard, Declan. And now it is you who will suffer."

"Will you be joining us, Emperor?" one of the guardsman asked.

"No. You know what to do. I hope he doesn't make it too easy. As for me, it is late, and I need my sleep." Julian felt a lightness in his chest that he hadn't felt for a long time, perhaps not since when he was a child. "I have an eventful day tomorrow."

As the guardsmen seized Declan, he didn't even bother to struggle. Instead he stared directly into Julian's eyes. "In command of the empire we have a craven eunuch. At least your line will end with you."

"Whatever I am, it was you who made me this way. Goodbye, Declan. May you rot until your bones are dust."

Julian watched as his guardsmen took Declan away. He felt triumph but also relief, and a great deal of satisfaction.

Chapter Thirty-Three

KENDRICK RODE ALONG the uneven road. His fears kept him moving, and with Bethany riding beside him, he was relieved that she didn't seem to mind that they weren't taking many breaks. He and Bethany traveled light; they planned to catch up to the army before sundown.

He couldn't stop thinking about the package he had received from Declan, and his subsequent journey to Burnham Abbey. His biggest worry was that Declan thought he was in enough danger for something bad to happen to him. He and Declan needed to talk . . . and perhaps it might be time to involve some others, men like Tristan, who was both head of the Wardens and always someone Kendrick could rely upon.

There was one thing Kendrick was well aware of—only when they found Rigel's second child would they know if he or she could make an alternative emperor, someone the nobles could rally behind. Julian, without doubt, was not fit to lead the empire. By the stars, the man had poisoned his own father, all so he could seize power for himself before the opportunity was taken away.

Anthea hadn't wanted Kendrick to open Declan's scroll, but he had. Now he couldn't stop his whirling thoughts. This problem was too big for him alone.

Morning had seen him and Bethany depart the Wheel of Klare at first light, to follow in the army's tracks to Highguard Castle. Now, as the midmorning sun trickled through the treetops and glowed on the open hills, the sight of horse dung and fresh cart ruts meant they were clearly on the right path. The fair weather was holding so far, although up ahead, gray clouds looked to be gathering. The road curved like a ribbon, bending one way and then the other, as it navigated the hills and thicker woods, but always made its way farther south.

The sky gradually changed color. The sun vanished behind a thick blanket of darkening clouds. As the light faded from the day, all of a sudden it began to rain.

Bethany pulled up her hood, while he did the same with his own black cloak. His horse whinnied and blew. The rain began to harden and water droplets stung his cheeks. When Bethany turned her head, moisture was on her face.

"What do you want to do?" he called over to her. "Find some trees, wait for it to pass?"

She scanned the clouds. "It could go on all day."

"Keep moving, then?"

She gave him a slight smile. "I have no problem with a little rain, My Lord."

As if testing her resolve, thunder rumbled overhead. The rain soon pelted the road, filling the depressions with water, turning them into puddles. At least, in high summer, the temperature wasn't a problem. He and Bethany exchanged rueful glances.

"Just a little rain?" he asked.

She pulled her gray hood closer about her face. "I can take it if you can."

They were forced to slow their pace. At least the rain would impede the army more than it would him. The great host of men and horses would still be on their way to the castle, and would have to stop and make camp well before dusk. No matter what happened, he should be back with his sons by nightfall.

The rain settled down to a steady drizzle, and with the sky now completely gray, he and Bethany traveled the road in silence. His sons would be fine. They were just a couple of young knights, blessedly free from the struggles for power—just boys, really. People might call them men, but then they did something foolish or reacted with too much emotion. Neither had spent a lot of time from home. Troy was thriving, of course, but Caden could sometimes be needy. Soon he would see them again.

Bethany looked to be riding well. He could still remember the boys competing for her attention, but she was new then, and she seemed much older now. With her intelligence and spirit, he doubted either of them would be able to keep up with her. And a romantic liaison was the last thing either he or Anthea wanted. He supposed it was just interesting to compare such different people who shared a similar age.

The trees changed in nature, becoming sparser but also bigger: great evergreens, oaks, and cedar. His horse snorted as it climbed the road but then picked up speed as they reached a flat section, with hills on one side and fields on the other, and soon they were passing straight through an emerald forest. The air was fresh, wet from the recent rain. The road commenced a descent.

The rain stopped altogether, perhaps an hour before midday. They emerged through the other side of the woods, and their horses were forced to slow as they navigated the hillside and the road snaked on its way down.

Far ahead, the long winding gorge cleaved the forest in two. The Swan River followed the gorge, and the wooden span of Broadwater Bridge appeared in the distance; at the rate they were traveling, the bridge would soon be upon them. The gorge went out of view as the forest swallowed them up. But then the trees thinned, and as they followed the widening path and the ground leveled, there was the wooden bridge.

Long before reached Broadwater Bridge, signs of a camp were everywhere. The open clearings displayed flattened grass and black patches indicated camp fires from the previous night. Patches of torn grass became more frequent and the imprint of boots joined the indents of horse hooves. A tent rope had been left coiled around a tree trunk.

"The army stopped here last night," Kendrick said. "They will have crossed the bridge in the morning, one group at a time. Not safe to have everyone do it all at once."

He kept his horse moving and the bridge soon grew in his vision. The ground fell away at the gorge. The rumble of the river became louder.

Kendrick reined in, and Bethany pulled up beside him. His horse whinnied, irritated at the sudden stop. Bethany sawed her reins to walk her horse over to join him.

"What is it?" she asked.

As he wondered what it was he was looking at, he heard cawing, a moment before crows' wings fluttered above the middle of the bridge. Beside him, Bethany was staring in the same direction. She had seen carrion birds before, he remembered. And as for him . . . he had more experience of them than he wished to recall.

Someone had erected a basic structure in the middle of the bridge, made from a few timbers joined together. From the crossbeam at the top, two large objects dangled, a few feet off the ground, and with the structure's resemblance to a scaffold, the body-sized objects could only be one thing.

"Is that . . . ?" Bethany asked, before trailing off.

Kendrick frowned at the bridge, and the scaffold, where the crows continued to shriek. "Wait here."

He dismounted, watching the bridge as he handed Bethany his reins. He then walked slowly toward the structure, boots sinking into the mud while he scanned the area, alert to any movement. He kept his hand on the hilt of his sword.

The crows continued to caw, fluttering high above the scaffold, caught in flashes of black wings. He was about to reach the beginning of the bridge. The rush of water from the Swan River was now much louder. He never stopped looking at the pair of bodies, both dangling in the gusts of wind, turning around to face one way and then another. They weren't hoisted high, with boots just above the planks that made up the floor.

He stopped at the bridge's edge. The taller of the two bodies was bare-chested, and when the man turned toward him, something was written across his torso, but Kendrick wasn't yet close enough to read what it was. Kendrick turned back toward Bethany; she was still with their horses, partially obscured by the branches of the trees.

He decided to draw his sword.

The steel hissed as he gripped the hilt and pulled the blade from his scabbard.

He then stepped onto the bridge.

As he neared, he waved his blade in the direction of the crows, who squawked as they flapped away to land on a different part of the structure. Ignoring them, he kept walking toward the two dead men. The taller man was the older of the two, with blood-stained ash-colored hair. The two bodies continued to twist in the wind.

When Kendrick next stopped, he was just a short distance away. Another gust of wind swept along the gorge. The taller of the dead men turned to face him. There was an accompanying sound, a creaking of timber and rope.

The dead man had no eyes. Someone had plucked them out. He wasn't a man at peace. Whatever he had seen, whatever had been done to him, it had filled his last moments with horror. Lettering was carved into his chest, using his skin as a writing surface. There was just one word: *Traitor*.

The dead man was Declan.

The second body turned. The man moved slowly, coming round, revealing a head of light brown hair and a youthful face. His eyes were unharmed, but they stared straight into Kendrick's face, and directly into his heart. The young man's mouth was wide open. A horrific gash marred his throat. Blood stained the front of his light brown tunic, which was tucked into his trousers. His clothing was more than familiar, along with his boots.

"No." Kendrick's own voice was distant. "No." His vision tunneled in. All he could focus on was the body swinging on the rope.

He threw himself forward. He moved so fast that he almost slipped and struggled to keep his feet. He had to hurry. *Hurry!*

He reached the rope and hacked with his sword at the cord. In one hard stroke, his steel sliced it through. Caden's body hit the ground and rolled over. Kendrick's sword clattered to the bridge nearby.

He collapsed to the ground and pulled his son onto his lap.

Cradling Caden's head, he peeled back his son's hair. They had taken his boy. His boy . . . his little son . . . A distant part of him knew his son was dead, and yet he wiped the blood from Caden's face and rocked him back and forth. He wanted to scream. *Wake up!* The pain on his heart was agonizing. A fist was wrapped around it, squeezing hard, harder, with terrible, wrenching force.

"My son. My little boy. Oh no. No. Please. My baby boy."

Kendrick's mind was in pieces. Sitting on the bridge's wooden floor, he hunched over and hugged his son. He squeezed, tighter and tighter, knowing it would be the last embrace that Caden ever had. He tried not to look at his son's throat . . . at the gaping hole in his neck.

His little boy had barely lived. He hadn't fallen in love or seen the face of his own child. He had barely even gone to war. The risk was there, it always was at war, but this wasn't supposed to happen. It shouldn't have happened. It can't have happened. *But it has!*

Caden was his boy. He had rocked him to sleep as a babe, fed him soft porridge, taught him to ride a horse and hunt with bow and arrow.

Even now, with Caden somewhere far away, on his journey to becoming a bright light in the night sky, Kendrick loved him with every fiber, every sinew, every muscle, every bit of strength he possessed.

"Traitor!"

The loud bellow reached Kendrick from the bridge's far end. Through his blurred vision, three men were approaching, tall Imperial guardsmen in silver armor and white cloaks. Each guardsman had his sword brandished in front of him.

Another sound clattered on the bridge: heavy footsteps in the other direction. Kendrick looked back the way he had come, to see another pair of guardsmen heading toward him.

He gently laid down his son. His sword was on the bridge's wooden planking in front of him. He reached out to take it and slowly straightened, until he was standing tall and facing the three nearest men. None of them wore helmets, and he could easily see their faces.

The guardsman in the center called out. A big man with a thick neck, he appeared to be the leader. "We have your other son. Surrender your weapon and come with us." He nodded meaningfully at Caden's body. "Unless you want . . . " He paused and turned to the soldier beside him. "What was his name again?"

The man who replied had the squashed face of a brawler, with a square jaw and missing teeth. "Troy."

The leader nodded as he pointed his sword at Caden's body. "Unless you want Troy to suffer the same fate."

Kendrick looked once more behind him, making sure he hadn't missed any of them. "Five of you, eh?" He glanced toward Declan's swinging body. "Are you the ones who did this?"

"Throw down your weapon," the leader said. "I will not ask again." With just a short distance now separating them, he muttered to his companions. "Be ready to take him."

"I am no traitor. But I don't think that matters much to you."

The moment he finished Kendrick put both hands on Declan's body. He shoved hard, sending the heavy weight crashing into the leader and his two companions. Moving around the obstruction, he jumped forward to stab his sword into a guardsman's side, below his arm, where the armor didn't protect him. The man went down with a cry.

When the dangling body reached Kendrick on the backswing, he pushed it again to keep his enemies uncertain. He kept his weapon high and when the guardsman with the missing teeth hacked down at him, he blocked, disengaged, and then rammed the hard metal hilt of his sword into the big man's jaw. His opponent went down, and Kendrick followed up with a hard kick that sent him over the edge of the bridge. The man's cry was cut short with a thud.

The last of the initial trio, the leader with the thick neck, snarled and slashed at the rope holding Declan's body in the air. The body collapsed to the floor, to tumble beside Kendrick's son. The big man jumped over both bodies, charging fast with sword swinging.

Kendrick ducked. His opponent's blade whistled over his head. Kendrick brought the point of his sword up as he straightened, so that it entered under his enemy's chin. He pushed hard, and then used his shoulder to thrust his opponent away from him, to also send him tumbling from the bridge.

The last two guardsmen were already charging from the other direction. Kendrick leaped over the bodies, choosing less risky footing. He was panting as he waited in fighting stance, sword point held in the air.

The guardsman on the left was lean but wiry, his nostrils flaring as he went into the attack. Kendrick blocked and parried, until his opponent executed a thrust that almost scored Kendrick's abdomen. As Kendrick ducked back, he tried to keep his opponent moving so that he was in the way of the second man, but he wasn't facing common soldiers; these were Imperial guardsmen, and it showed in their skill and experience.

Steel clashed against steel, ringing throughout the gorge. Kendrick's arms kept coming up and down, blocking and then hacking in return, before he was forced to block again. The second man was going to outflank him, and he would be in trouble when he did . . .

Horse hooves clattered on the wood. Something long whipped through the air, as the end of a staff crashed into the second man's skull. As the guardsman at the back reeled, in the moment of distraction, Kendrick found an opening and thrust into his nearer opponent's torso. It was a risky move, but his sharp blade penetrated through, and the guardsman's eyes rolled back as he died.

With a final charge, Kendrick then sent the last guardsman over the rail, to plummet and scream until the sound abruptly cut off.

The fight was over.

Kendrick lowered his sword. He stood panting, as Bethany yanked at her reins, struggling to control her horse. She still gripped her staff, and looked surprised herself at what she had done.

Kendrick then turned back to his son.

Chapter Thirty-Four

KENDRICK HAD BLAZED THE TRUNK of the tree, so that one day he could find it again. It was a beautiful oak, with broad branches that spread over the riverbank, and the two finished graves now looked like long man-shaped heaps of collected stones. From his crouched position, he leaned forward to settle the last rock into place, and then he sank back to the ground.

He was aware of Bethany, standing and watching from the water's edge. She had wanted to help, but he had insisted that he be the one to bury his son and his wife's brother.

His chest was heaving as he blinked. With his work complete, he stared straight ahead, listening to the rushing river, while green leaves fluttered on the branches of the tree in front of him. Until Kendrick's return, Caden and his uncle would lie side by side, where they would share company under the shade and listen to the music of the flowing water.

Forceful feelings kept welling up. Shock. Pain ... terrible pain. Agony. Guilt overrode everything. He should have remained with his sons.

He pushed himself to his feet and stumbled to the water's edge. Bending down, he washed the blood and grit from his arms and hands.

He then filled his cupped palms to splash cleansing water over his face.

It was Troy who needed him now. Straightening, he turned back toward the tree and the pair of graves in front of it.

His sword was in its scabbard, on the ground nearby.

There were things that people had once said about him, back in his days of war. He had thought that a different life, past and long gone. But he had kept his blade sharp and his skill honed by regular practice—a skill once remarked upon as exceptional. It was hard to allow something that was such a part of his identity to fade with disuse. He was old, but he wasn't that old. When duty called, he had answered, and he had taken his sons to war.

Staring at the sword, with droplets trickling down his face, his entire body was tense. His grief led to anger. His anger became rage. The fierce, hot, energizing emotion helped him to fight the pain.

Julian had known that Declan would never stop working against him. But one thing holding him back would have to be Kendrick; after all, Declan was brother to Kendrick's wife.

Was Julian also aware of what Declan had learned? Did he know that Kendrick could now prove that Julian and his wife murdered his father?

One thing was clear, in any event.

Fresh from his coronation, Julian had used his own loyal soldiers to destroy his greatest enemy. He had taken a willful step across a line and murdered not just Declan, but Kendrick's youngest son. If Troy was still alive, he was a captive, and Julian had proclaimed them all traitors.

Many would be doubtful or confused—of course they would be—but what would they actually do about it? After what had just happened, who would have the courage to defy Julian now?

Declan was right. He had been right all along. He had always been sure of one thing: Julian should never have been allowed to become emperor.

Kendrick stared at his sword.

Who would have the courage to defy the emperor?

He would.

✦

Bethany rode at Kendrick's side, following the route to the south as it thinned to become a rocky trail. Bald hills now dotted the landscape. The sparse trees were gnarled where the road climbed toward a pass between the ridges.

There was no chance of becoming lost. The tracks left behind by an army were hard to miss.

Every time Bethany glanced Kendrick's way, his face was frightening. He was in a silent rage, forehead furrowed, bushy eyebrows framing a glare.

Bethany's own thoughts were dark. She would never forget the sight of Declan's tortured body, nor the wide-eyed stare on Caden's face. Caden was nineteen, a little younger than her. She couldn't understand how Julian had done what he had. He had used his newfound power to murder and butcher the two men. He had hung their bodies from a scaffold, laying a trap for Kendrick to spring, an ambush intended to destroy him as he grieved the death of his son. Julian had tortured his greatest enemy . . . making him scream . . . plucking out his eyes . . .

Bethany swallowed as acid burned the back of her throat. Her stomach was constantly churning.

After her and Julian's conversation at Narzin, when she had perpetuated the lie about her relationship with their father, what was it he had said? That if the Weaver was kind, he hoped to never encounter her again.

Her father's words came back to her, the last time she had seen him. I *have two children. My son is feckless, whereas my daughter is intelligent, brave, and resourceful. The past is but a memory. The future is what we are talking about now.*

If Julian learned the truth, what would he do to her? Would she become a broken body . . . a corpse dangling from a tree?

She still had the testament her father gave her. The piece of paper was with her, in the knapsack she always traveled with, although she had often wrestled with the idea of throwing it away. If the wrong person found it she would lose her life or worse.

As they rode, Kendrick wiped at his eyes, but he didn't emit a sound. She watched him and thought about his loss . . . and also about the future. She had to help him, in any way that she could. This was about more than just duty. She would support Kendrick and his family, no matter what was coming.

He had said the army would make camp before dusk, and that they would likely reach it late in the evening. What would happen when they did?

She remembered Xander's awe and Charlton's admiration when they spoke of Kendrick Conway and the Siege of Curran Castle. He was a war hero. If anyone could inspire a resistance to Julian, it was him.

Kendrick cleared his throat.

"You knew about him, didn't you?" he asked hoarsely, without waiting for a reply. "I never liked him, but I could tell that in your case it was different . . . you knew. I first noticed at Narzin, and then again when you wouldn't go to his coronation. I should have trusted you. And Declan.

I've been a blind fool. I can only blame myself."

She wished she knew the right thing to say. "Caden was always brave . . . whatever happened, he was only trying to help his uncle. No one could have expected . . . or known . . . " she trailed off.

The bitter expression never left his face, even as he glanced toward the sun, which was now halfway to the horizon.

"They were always fond of each other. Perhaps I didn't give Caden enough time. He is . . . was my son. He knew that. I loved him." After a pause, he shook his head. "Declan never went beyond the law—that would have gone against everything he believed in. He was never a violent man. What Julian did . . . He is burning down the house with him inside it. We may see the end of the empire, even without this invasion."

The vision he painted was a dark one, and she had to ask, "What happens now?"

He looked toward the south, in the direction they were traveling. "I have always believed the best moves are ones made slowly. A Warden protects and defends. That is what a fighting man should stand for." His voice firmed. "But sometimes change is called for, especially when the fate of our empire is at stake. And that time has now come."

"Kendrick . . . "

He turned her way. "What?"

She opened her mouth and then closed it. "I called you by your first name."

"I don't care about any of that. What were you going to say?"

"I was just going to ask . . . When we get there . . . what are you planning to do?"

"Getting Troy to safety is my priority. Then I'm going to gather my friends. And also a great number of Declan's. All they need is a leader." His tone became cold, as hard as stone. "A fighter. Someone who isn't afraid to stop him, before he destroys everything." He spoke in a menacing tone she had never heard him use before. "All they need is me."

Chapter Thirty-Five

KENDRICK AND BETHANY HAD REINED IN on high ground, under the shadow of a cliff, where they could watch the great camp below. The hour was late, and even with the moon high in the sky, the camp appeared as an orderly collection of pale tents interspersed with dots of flickering red. Old embers from fires lit up their surrounds, revealing the prone figures of men on blankets. The occasional canvas tent glowed, indicating occupants yet to sleep.

Kendrick spent time making his assessment. A stream followed a deep gully that divided the broad field in half. With the camp in two pieces, the Imperials occupied one side of the gully while the nobles occupied the larger of the two sections. The different orders usually camped in their groups, but in the moonlit darkness he wasn't able to make out the colors of the flags and pennants. Down below, however, within the bigger swathe of tents, he would find red markings to designate the Crusaders, blue to mark out the Guildsmen, and black to identify his own order, the Wardens.

Sentries kept watch along the camp's perimeter, all of them Imperial guardsmen. But while guards were out, the camp wasn't fortified; in this region, north of Highguard Castle, attacks would not be expected.

He could guess where Troy would be—with the Imperials on the gully's other side. Everyone would know what had happened by now. Julian would have concocted some story, and given the state of Declan's body, he probably had a signed confession. The camp looked calm from a distance, but its occupants would be on edge. Kendrick was well known. He was the man who had rescued the late emperor at Curran Castle. He had been granted the honor of hosting the fielding.

And now he was somehow a traitor?

People would be confused. Why would Kendrick risk everything to betray the new emperor? Was there something that Kendrick knew but they didn't?

Kendrick tore his eyes from the scene, instead looking toward a clump of large rocks on a taller ridge. It was a place his military senses told him would be a good meeting point as well as somewhere defensible if he had to make a stand.

"Bethany," he said, making sure he had her attention. "See those rocks? I want you to head over there and wait for me. If you see danger, do whatever it takes to get away and hide where they will never find you."

"I want to come—"

"Listen to me," he growled. "Do as I say. I can't be worrying about you too."

"Kendrick?"

"What?"

"What are you going to do?"

He gathered his reins and kicked his horse into motion. "Among other things, I am going to find my son."

He hoped that Bethany would follow his orders, but he had to put her out of his mind as he rode down toward the hillside toward the camp. He had to get his bearings and figure out what was where, and how the camp was divided among the different groups.

Keeping his distance as he rode, he soon figured out where the blue flags were, after seeing a place where a fire was still burning as it shot bright sparks into the air. And not long after, he spied the red flags, decorating the ropes of the tents in a location even closer to his position. Once he had seen the other two colors, it was easier to decide where the black flags were, with the darkest shade of all.

Before anything else, he had to get in.

After skirting the camp, he rode straight up to a sentry, an Imperial guardsman who stood near the part of the camp he had chosen. The guard's position had drifted, which was common enough. The nearest other sentries were located some distance away.

The guardsman was tall, with wide shoulders, curly hair, and a youthful face. When he spied Kendrick, a lone rider approaching on horseback, he put a hand on the sword he wore at his side and stepped forward.

"Who goes there?" the young guardsman called into the night.

Kendrick pulled on his reins, slowing his horse to a walk. He confirmed again that he was only facing the one sentry. The guardsman took another step forward, which was foolish, because then he was also in darkness.

"Who are you?" the guardsman demanded. "I will not ask again."

"It is just me," Kendrick said softly. "I have to ask a favor. Hear me out and you won't regret it . . . "

Kendrick kept approaching on horseback until he was bearing down on the guardsman. He didn't want to kill the man; the guardsman was young, perhaps as young as Caden, but Kendrick was going to get past him. Kendrick's hand was under his cloak, on the hilt of his already drawn dagger. The guardsman was wearing armor, but no helmet, leaving his curly head bare, which was the weakness he was going to exploit.

With Kendrick now close, the young man frowned, staring up, and then his eyes widened. Kendrick's hand on his dagger gripped tightly; the muscles in his arm bunched. The guardsman opened his mouth, and at the same time tried to draw his sword—

Holding his dagger upside down, Kendrick cracked the hilt like an axe against the young man's skull. The guardsman's eyes rolled back into his head before he crumpled without a sound.

Kendrick didn't stop moving. As was usually the case, a broad path had been left between the tents. He kept his horse quiet but walking as he rode past sleeping men clustered around the red glow of dying fires. A few people were awake and moving about, but no one remarked upon a lone rider on horseback. A soldier watched him, nodding back when Kendrick gave a casual wave.

Nudging his horse a little quicker, Kendrick passed row after row of tents, decorated with the color black. Shoulders tensed, heart beating fast, he searched the bigger pavilions—and there it was, a pavilion grander than all the rest. Kendrick yanked at his reins to turn his horse toward it, letting out the breath he was holding at the sight of the Wardens' shield emblem on the canvas flaps that functioned as doors. He swiftly dismounted, hobbling his horse by tying its legs together, and then went directly to the tent to pull the canvas aside and enter.

A manservant on a padded blanket blinked and opened his eyes. He made a startled sound. Meanwhile, Kendrick was already on his way to the next partition. "What—? Wait. You can't go in there—"

"If you value your life, be quiet," Kendrick snapped.

Kendrick pushed aside the curtain to enter the dim space beyond. A camp bed greeted him along with a collapsible table and two chairs. Kendrick's focus went immediately to the man who sat on a folding chair, resting his weight on the table.

Tristan Benedict, head of the Wardens, had a golden goblet in front of him, along with a wavering candle. He had a gold-tipped quill pen in his hand and paper on the table, but there was no writing on the paper at all. The lantern emitted just enough light to reveal Tristan's jowly face, which was drawn back in surprise. Usually he was heavy-set but elegant— now he looked to be wearing every one of his years, with gray hair disheveled, sagging cheeks, and shadows under his blue eyes.

"Kendrick?" Tristan let out a breath. "By the stars, man. I was about to go for my dagger. You're alive . . .? I thought you were dead, man. That's what we were told—"

Kendrick pulled up a chair and sank into it. "He killed my son, Tristan. My boy Caden. Declan was tortured . . . I buried them both." He stopped abruptly. "Troy, have you seen him? Is he alive?"

"I believe he's alive, but there's not much more I can tell you." Tristan's voice was hoarse. "I knew your sons were missing when we crossed Broadwater Bridge. At first, I thought you might have somehow returned and taken them with you. But then, not long after the crossing, Julian gathered everyone. He waved a piece of paper and announced a plot he said was initiated by you and Declan. He said you were already killed resisting capture, you and Declan both. The Blues are irate, as you can imagine. This army feels like it's about to destroy itself. We've all been wondering what to do. As for your sons, I was told Caden was missing, while Troy had more information Julian wanted—"

"Who are you writing to?" Kendrick interrupted, nodding toward the letter.

"My wife. We both know this can't end well. How do you—?"

Loud shouts split the night air. The commotion was enough to make Kendrick and Tristan stare into each other's eyes.

Kendrick swore. All of his plans were going to be ruined. "I had to take out a sentry to get in. Looks like I didn't hit him hard enough." He swore again, screwing up his brow, thinking furiously. "Get dressed and grab your sword."

"But Kendrick—"

"We don't have a choice. Quickly!"

Kendrick raced from the tent, and when he was out in the open, the scene was already changing. Around the tents and fires, some of the nearby men were up on their feet, turned to face the same part of the camp, toward the direction the shouts were coming from. The barked orders came from across the gully, in the area of the Imperial section. A powerful voice reached his ears: "Guardsmen! Form up!"

Buckling on his sword, Tristan came out of his tent, clearly agitated as he stared toward the commotion.

Kendrick grabbed his horse by the halter and removed the reins hobbling its legs. Events were rapidly spiraling out of control. He had intended to secure the support he needed before issuing any kind of challenge. With help from his allies, he would have had a better chance of initiating a plan to rescue his son. He was going to have to think on his feet.

He wore his armor and with him he had his sword and his horse. He was in the midst of his order, the Wardens, the group he had been loyal to his entire life, and who had promised to be loyal to him. He had a sea of tents surrounding him, as well as hundreds of campfires. These were his men: the nobles, knights, men at arms, and levies of the Blacks.

Putting his foot into the stirrup, he pulled himself back up onto his horse's back. There was nothing else to be done. He opened his mouth to suck in a deep breath. He was a commanding officer, and could make himself heard when he wanted to be.

"Wardens!" he bellowed. "To arms!"

Tristan shot him a frightened look. "What are you doing?"

"What I have to," Kendrick replied. "To arms!" he roared again. "Wardens! To arms!"

Raised voices came from all directions as others picked up the cry. Men raced out of tents, swords in hand, some in armor, others without. They saw Kendrick, up on horseback on the broad path between the tents, with Tristan standing nearby. Their numbers grew quickly. Kendrick heard his name spoken more than once.

"Wardens!" Kendrick continued to bellow. "To arms!" He raised his voice even louder. "Guildsmen! To arms! Soldiers of the Blues! To arms!"

Figures were rushing past the campfires, from the tents, and from even more distant parts of the camp. A young soldier raced toward Kendrick and then stopped and stared. "He's here!" he cried. "It's Kendrick Conway. He's here!"

As knights and their followers gathered in numbers, Kendrick had no choice; the time had come for confrontation. From his position on horseback, he was in the midst of an ever growing number of men. It wasn't long until a great crowd stood ready, surrounding him, waiting to hear what he had to say.

"Listen!" he called, sawing at his reins, moving his horse so he could take them all in. "Guildsmen!" he roared into the distance, in the direction of the blue flags he had seen. "I am talking to you too! Crusaders! This involves all of us! All of you, listen!" He paused to suck in another deep breath. "You know me. I am no traitor. But I have learned some difficult truths, and I say it clearly to you now, that I am against the man who currently calls himself our emperor."

He continued to turn his horse, keenly aware of the fighting men now gathered around him. "Do you know why Declan Quinn of Graystone is dead? He discovered proof, undeniable evidence that Julian and his wife poisoned and then murdered our emperor, after he turned against his own wretched son. I remember it. And you remember it too. We were all there, at the fielding at my estate in Esk. Cast your mind back. Think again about that day. Declan of Graystone was making an announcement. Do you want to know what he was going to say? He was going to tell everyone that Julian no longer enjoyed his father's support. Instead, you, and me, we all know what happened. We know who it was who delivered Rigel's death. She killed Julian's father to put her husband on the throne. Now Julian has murdered both Declan and my son Caden, a boy of just nineteen! What can we do about this? We can fight! This is what I need to know. Are you with me?"

As Kendrick sucked in another breath, he leveled his gaze on Tristan. His old friend was now going to decide what happened next.

"Wardens of the empire . . . Guildsmen of the empire. Crusaders of the empire . . . !" Kendrick bellowed. "We are all united in our love for our empire. A murderer now calls himself emperor. A twisted man who killed his own father. Now, I need to know." He enunciated each word in turn. "Are you with me?"

Tristan was pale, as he glanced at the assembled men and then back at Kendrick. Kendrick's stomach tightened. Surely his old comrade wouldn't abandon him now? The seconds trickled past. But then Tristan returned Kendrick's gaze with a nod, and his mouth opened wide.

"We are with you!" Tristan bellowed.

The cry was picked up from several quarters, called out from place to place. Men raced away, shouting as they went.

Facing Tristan, Kendrick had to roar to be heard above the din. "Get everyone mounted up. We need the advantage of horses. Hurry! We won't be able to hide it. We have to move fast."

Chapter Thirty-Six

JULIAN'S MIND WAS BUSY. If he tried to sleep, he would simply stare at the canvas ceiling, so he sat at a folding table and ran a smooth stone over the blade of his sword. He had always found the action soothing, as he circled the stone up and down the length of the blade, watching the light from the nearby lantern reflected in the polished steel. And as his father had always said, a skilled swordsman took care of his weapon.

Julian was more than pleased; he was triumphant. He had done it. Declan was dead. Back at the bridge, a trap for Kendrick had been neatly laid. And he had demonstrated his power to all, with the proof right in front of him, for his army was still together. He had even managed to go an entire day without having to speak to his wife.

The stone made a quiet scraping sound as he slid it over the metal. Tomorrow Julian and his army would arrive at Highguard Castle. Queen Zhuana was now basing herself in the city of Meroy, the most important city in the Redlands, but the castle now barred her progress; she would be able to go no farther. Julian would crush her and take back the Redlands and then the Southern Provinces. He would liberate Meroy, Narzin, Gorvia, Bavia, and Lexia. He would return to Everlast triumphant, and then rather than regain lost territory, he would move into the attack. He would expand the empire's borders until they were larger than ever before. He would overshadow his father's name, to become the greatest emperor in history.

A shout reached his ears, a frantic cry that made his head turn toward the tent's entrance. He frowned and his stone stopped moving. Tilting his head, he listened intently, and then he heard two more cries in quick succession. More raised voices echoed the growing chorus.

"Emperor—"

The canvas moved to the side, to reveal the brutish face of Veldon Marx. The commander fixed Julian with his icy stare.

"Emperor, Kendrick Conway is in the camp."

Julian's eyes widened. The danger was all too clear. He had to move quickly. Marx had thought five men would be enough, but it seemed the commander was wrong.

Julian was already dressed, but he grabbed his scabbard to resheathe his sword. "Fetch his son. You know what to do."

The commander nodded and left. Once he had his sword in place at his hip, Julian crossed the tent to head outside. The scene was frantic but there was order to the chaos. Soldiers in silver armor and white cloaks were gathering. Near the gully that divided the camp, the commander strode around, barking at his men, forming them up, getting them ready for conflict.

Julian strode toward the gully, where a wide wooden platform formed a makeshift bridge across the gap. At the commander's orders, the guardsmen were spreading out in a long line, where they would easily be able to defend their section of the camp.

Soon Julian was standing beside the commander, whose towering height would make any other man look small. Once in position, Julian lifted his sword a few inches from the scabbard, testing the sharpness of his blade with his thumb.

"Remove the bridge?" he asked the commander.

"No, Emperor." Marx's voice was deep and deadly serious. "Once we know what we are facing, we need it there so we can destroy your enemies."

✦

Kendrick reined in, just in front of the makeshift bridge. His blood was high, roaring in his ears as he faced the wide gully. He wasn't looking at the rows of white tents in the Imperial section nor the grand pavilions at the back. Instead, right in front of him, was a long row of Imperial guardsmen lined up on the gully's other side.

Kendrick couldn't easily compare the number of riders he had with him, but he was leading a sizable force. Would it be enough? That depended on whether fighting broke out. The emperor was well defended, with a solitary wooden platform the only access to his side. Kendrick's group was mounted, but couldn't use their horses to gain an advantage.

With his soldiers at his back, Julian was standing beside the huge commander of his Imperial guard. Neither Marx nor Julian had drawn his sword, but they both carried them: Julian's in a scabbard at his side and the commander's broadsword strapped to his back.

Julian's malevolent gaze moved between Kendrick and Tristan, who was on horseback at Kendrick's right. The drawn out silence continued.

Meanwhile, Kendrick couldn't see bows, not among either group. The gully, however, was a natural barrier between them.

Julian turned to say something over his shoulder.

A ripple of movement went through the guardsmen. And then Kendrick's heart squeezed hard. There was Troy . . . his son was alive. At the same time, Kendrick couldn't embrace him, nor offer any words of comfort. He didn't know how he was going to get through this.

Troy's clothing was torn. His flaxen hair was tousled and he had bruised and bloody marks on his face. His glaring eyes revealed defiance as two guardsmen herded him forward. Flanking him on either side, the soldiers gripped his upper arms, while his bound hands were visible in front of him.

Kendrick's chest continued heaving. Scowling at Julian, he raised his voice. "You have my son."

Julian called out, replying in a cold voice of his own. "He is a traitor, Kendrick. Just like his father. I am giving you a simple choice. Surrender yourself or he dies. Your plot was uncovered. I have Declan's written confession. Your youngest son has already paid the price . . . the price that all traitors pay in the end." He nodded toward Troy. "Your eldest son has confirmed the details and revealed all there is to know. "

"Father, that's a lie—!"

Julian snarled at his guardsmen. "Gag him!"

Someone produced a piece of white cloth, which a guardsmen wrapped around the back of Troy's head and tightened as it went into his mouth. Kendrick's nostrils flared. One thought overpowered all others. He had to save the life of his son.

"Let him go," Kendrick said as he stared into Julian's face. "He is just a soldier who fights in your service. We both know he had no involvement in any act against you."

"As I said," Julian continued, raising his voice, "upon questioning, your son revealed all there is to know. As will you, when you turn yourself in and we can finally put an end to your betrayal."

"Listen to me," Kendrick said grimly. "You go too far. Release him or there is going to be war."

Julian raised an eyebrow, looking past Kendrick, to the men he had arrayed around him. "War? With what army, Kendrick?"

Fear was clawing its way through Kendrick's guts, constantly rising higher. Julian didn't care. Nothing Kendrick said was going to have any effect. He had another course of action, however, and he called out now to the guardsmen.

"He killed his own father," he said, loud enough for all of them to hear him. "He murdered your true emperor, who didn't think his son was fit to rule. I can prove everything I am telling you now. That's why he wants me dead. Listen to the truth. If you don't turn him over, you will be destroying the empire. Turn him over. Do it now."

Kendrick waited and the seconds trickled past. Not a single guardsman shifted. Instead they all remained in place, eyes fixed straight ahead as they awaited orders. Veldon Marx leveled Kendrick with his pale stare. Nothing else happened at all.

"I told you I can prove it." Kendrick called out, raising his voice even louder. "You were sworn to protect his father. How can you call this man your emperor?"

Tristan spoke in a murmur. "Kendrick . . . We do not have a strong position."

Julian's expression became smug. "As I said. You have a choice to make, traitor. Surrender yourself. Or your son dies here and now. I will give you until the count of ten before you see his throat opened up in front of you." He paused to let his words have their intended effect, and then, to Kendrick's horror, a guardsman put his sword across Troy's neck, as Julian counted. "One." A brief pause. "Two." Another pause. "Three . . . "

Kendrick's eyes shot wide open. Any decision he made was going to be the wrong one, the choice that killed his son. He had to face the truth. As things were, there would be no saving his son.

"Wait," he insisted. "Wait!" He held up a hand. "Let him live." He indicated the riders he had supporting him. "We'll leave. There's no need to more blood to be spilled."

Julian considered, but that was all he did. "No. I am afraid that is not good enough. I want your surrender, Kendrick. Or stand ready to watch him die." He resumed his count. "Four." His pauses were now briefer. "Five. Six."

For once in Kendrick's life, he didn't know what to do. He had to surrender himself or Troy would die—but surrender would only mean that he would be tortured, in order to produce his own confession, before his son was killed anyway.

It was Troy who decided to act.

Troy wasn't a small man, and he had become a skilled fighter. He butted his head into his captor, the soldier with the sword to his neck. The guardsman lost his grip.

Time slowed, taken place in a series of images. Troy whirled and reached with bound hands to wrest control of his dazed captor's sword. He gripped it hard and ran the guardsman through. Turning quickly, he slashed his blade across the chest of his other captor.

Another guardsman came in. Troy whirled and slashed his opponent to bring him down.

But the shock of the moment was leading to action. More guardsmen were drawing swords, charging into the fray. Troy became surrounded by enemies.

Kendrick didn't consciously act. He moved without thinking and dug his heels into the sides of his mount. But Tristan was shouting something, and lunged forward to grab Kendrick's horse by the halter. The animal whinnied and reared back on two legs. Kendrick struggled to keep his seat.

Another image came, seen between the chaos: an Imperial guardsman hacking his sword into Troy's torso. Troy screamed. A second guardsman thrust into Troy's chest. More of them were stabbing his son, over and over again.

Tristan was shouting. "We have to go, Kendrick! Listen to me. Today is not the day. There will be another."

Julian cried out in a voice filled with venom. "Anyone who goes with him, I will destroy your families and burn your homes to the ground!"

"Come on!" Tristan pulled Kendrick's horse with his, so that they were turning away together.

As the large group of riders moved, heading away from the area in a mass, Kendrick's horse wanted to do nothing more than follow.

But something died inside Kendrick as he looked back, to see his son's broken body on the ground.

Chapter Thirty-Seven

THE SILVER MOON SHONE RAYS OF PALE LIGHT upon a rough camp. Chosen to be defensible, the site occupied a flat area with broken cliffs on three sides. The only approach was a steep slope that would tire any man or horse.

Campfires decorated the rocky terrain, where men sat around the flames or lay spread out beside them on blankets. Everyone had shared what supplies they had. Armor and weapons lay where they could be grabbed at short notice. Horses huddled in a group. There was no separation into the different orders. Blacks, Red, Blues—they were all on the same side now.

Bethany stood with Tristan. They were both turned the same way, toward Kendrick, who was apart from everyone else, sitting on a rock as he stared into the flames in front of him.

"I can only imagine . . . " Tristan said. For a moment he was silent before he glanced at her. "I am afraid, however, that we have important decisions to make, and we need to make them now. Julian will be sending riders to the Wheel, and our option of traveling the gateways will soon be gone. We have to call it what it is. What we have here is now a rebellion."

With them were perhaps a thousand men, spread out over the high ground, along with a multitude of campfires. And yet, what chance did they have, against Julian's much larger numbers? Rebellion meant one noble house at war with another, knight fighting knight, friend against friend. Who would be foolish enough to join them?

"We have to think of our families," Tristan said. "And right now, you are our only diviner. It is the leaders he will go for—Kendrick and I most of all. I can travel overland to Breanne. You will have to go to Esk with Kendrick, before the opportunity to travel the gateways is gone—"

"Riders!" someone cried.

Tristan turned his head as one of the men pointed at something in the distance. The bright moonlight revealed twenty or more riders, another group on horseback who had deserted the army to join them.

"Brave men, all of them, when they had the option of staying. I should thank them personally." Tristan hesitated, his eyes again on Kendrick.

"I'll talk to him about traveling to Esk," Bethany said.

Tristan nodded and then left her to greet the newcomers.

After he had gone, she remained where she was for a time. As Kendrick stared into the fire, he would be thinking about his sons . . . about his wife who was yet to know . . . about Isabelle . . .

Bethany's own father had been poisoned and then murdered by suffocation. Why? All so Julian could become emperor, as if nothing was more important than power, not family, not duty, not loyalty, not love.

She reached into the pocket of her dress, and her fingers closed over the folded piece of paper, reassuring herself that it was there.

Standing in place, she inhaled and then exhaled, letting her breath out slowly. If she did what she was about to do—when she did it—everything was going to change. But she was making this choice herself. Kendrick was strong, but he couldn't be strong all the time. This time, she would be the one to show her strength.

The time had come. She had to confront her past.

After another deep breath, she walked toward Kendrick as he rubbed his eyes and continued to gaze at the flames. Choosing a different rock, she sat down facing him, but he made no sign of acknowledgement.

"You did all you could," she said softly.

"It wasn't enough," he whispered.

"I need to ask you something."

He turned his reddened eyes upon her, but didn't say anything. He was suffering. This was her time to help him.

"This other child of Rigel's . . . What difference could they make?"

He cleared his throat. When he spoke, it was in a quiet voice. "Now? It is hard to say. They could make all the difference . . . or none."

She took the folded paper from her pocket. She opened it up, and spent a moment looking at it again, seeing the elegant bordering and swirls in the corners, and the Imperial emblem, the Crown of Blood and Gold, at the top. She read the long lines of text in spidery writing, and then her father's full name, Rigel Regus Livius, written in sloping letters.

"Here," she said.

He frowned, puzzled, as he took the paper from her. Looking down, he began to read her father's testament.

She watched the transformation of his face. She waited for a time and then spoke at the point when she guessed he would be finishing.

"When my father became emperor, his marriage to my mother was annulled. However I am legitimate. There will be records in the Imperial archives in Everlast. Witnesses too."

"You . . . I can't . . . ." He kept re-reading the statement. "This must be a . . . It's you?"

"You know that my mother raised me. My father was never with us. But he was always alive. Up until his murder, that is."

"You aren't . . . " he stared directly at her, "you aren't someone who would make this up."

"No, I am not. It was my father who forced Paxton to retire and made me your house diviner. You were hosting the fielding, and he was worried about what might happen. Rightfully, it seems." She steadied her voice, which was shaking. "I'm sorry. I should have told you from the beginning. You have to understand, I never wanted anything but to be a diviner. That and to help my mother. At the fielding . . . my father said he planned to reveal me to the world, but that was the last thing I wanted. My mother always said to never owe him for anything . . . to do everything I could to stay away from their world. I always tried to do that. I tried so hard—"

"But Bethany . . . surely you realize you could be something else entirely . . . ?"

"Don't you see? I've never wanted power, or wealth, or anything like that at all."

"By the stars . . . Bethany . . . what a secret to carry . . . "

He continued to stare at her. The nearby flames crackled but the night was quiet, other than the overheard snippets of conversation between Tristan and the group of newcomers. A distant horse gave a whinny.

It was a long time before Kendrick spoke again. "But why? Why now?"

"Because I want to help if I can. Because of what he's done and what he could do next. Also . . . because . . . " she trailed off, as he watched and waited for her to go on. "I have an idea, and my bloodline is what makes it possible."

He didn't say anything, simply gazing at her with a disconcertingly focused expression.

As she pressed on, she almost wanted him to look away. At the same time, her mother had wanted her to hide. She was instead going to stand tall. "This is my thinking. At the moment, everyone has a common problem—a common enemy, Zhuana." She watch Kendrick carefully, gauging his reaction. "What is it that Zhuana wants?"

"Lands in the empire . . . Security for her people . . . "

"And she has proven her strength. She will not be ignored. Compared to what she's already done, accommodating her now doesn't seem like such a high price. She wants lands in the empire. Why not give them to her, along with titles and whatever else would give her a stake in the future?"

He furrowed his brow.

"Think about it," she said. "Declan wanted an alternative, someone who isn't Julian. But perhaps what we also need is a future for everyone to rally behind." She stared into his eyes, hoping she was making as much sense as she thought she was. "Julian offers war. But what if we could instead offer peace? There's already opposition to Julian's rule. What if we found a new way forward? We could promise an end to the war, with no more fighting. The empire is broken. We could make it whole again."

Kendrick's expression told her he was thinking it through. "Zhuana has military strength. But she has far from conquered the empire . . . and, for her, there's no easy pathway to peace." He frowned, considering. "We could offer Zhuana an alliance. Together we bring down Julian, and when it's done, part of the new settlement is to give her what she's always been after."

She let out a relieved breath. He understood. "Do you think it could work?"

From his face, he was seeing her in an entirely new light. "You're Rigel's daughter. You're also a diviner, connected to the corpus. Our empire has three pillars, and that just leaves the assembly. Which is where Tristan and I come in." His voice was becoming firmer. "If Zhuana doesn't want to keep fighting forever, she should be more than eager to work with us. She has no claim to the empire. Even victorious, she would struggle to hold it all together. She would know that."

"What about Julian?"

He smiled grimly. "If we brought the right proposal to the nobles, Julian would soon find himself in a cell."

"It could work?"

"Yes . . . Yes, I believe it could."

Sitting with Kendrick by the fire, Bethany heard a voice and turned to see Tristan approaching.

"Kendrick . . . " Tristan hesitated. "We've been busy making plans. I can take everyone with me to Breanne, and we can base ourselves at my estate as we resupply. As for you, I suggest you get your diviner to take you to Esk so that you can get your family to safety. Time is of the essence—"

Kendrick interrupted, climbing to his feet, as Bethany stood along with him. "We've found a way forward."

Tristan frowned at Kendrick and Bethany in turn. "Very well." He smiled without humor. "I am glad that someone has."

"When you get to Breanne, I want you to continue to gather all the numbers you can. Wait for my message, but be ready."

Tristan's frown deepened. "And where is it we are going?"

"When the time comes, I need you to bring everyone to Meroy and join me there."

"Show him," Bethany said to Kendrick. "We don't have long. If we want to make use of the gateways, we have to leave right away."

As she walked away to gather her possessions, she couldn't help looking back over her shoulder, where Kendrick was talking animatedly to Tristan as he showed him her father's testament.

◆

A rising sun lit up the scene as Bethany paced in front of Fernley Manor, on the gravel outside the main entrance. Not far away were the two polished wooden doors and the sign above them that announced the manor's name.

Anthea sat on the broad steps that led to the landing with Kendrick close beside her. Kendrick's slender blonde wife had her eyes tightly closed. Isabelle was in Anthea's arms, held fast against her body.

Bethany was tense, biting her lip. She was tired, but wide awake in a nervous, agitated way. Time was passing. The Wheel would now have been alerted, and from there news would travel like wildfire. Across the empire, guards would be on the alert for any so-called rebels using the gateways, and among them a diviner named Bethany Sylvana. Soon none of them would be able to travel the gateways at all, aside from the gateways in enemy hands like the Pillars of Dust at Meroy.

And yet Kendrick and his family needed time. Anthea had just learned about the deaths of her two sons, as well as her older brother. While Anthea grieved, she would be trying to comfort her daughter at the same time.

As Bethany waited, a respectful distance away, she reflected on the frantic journey to the Wheel of Klare. She and Kendrick had traveled throughout the night, heading back the way they had come. They had crossed Broadwater Bridge and left the Swan River behind. When the road gained height, and they looked back, a dozen riders were in pursuit, armored men in the uniforms of Imperial guardsmen. After a close race, they had narrowly made it to the gateway and then to Kendrick's home.

As Bethany waited, fatigue merged with the lingering effects of Weaver's Breath, and she still had two more journeys to make. First she would take Anthea and Isabelle to safety. Then she and Kendrick would travel onward to the Pillars of Dust.

What would happen when they arrived? Her last encounter with Zhuana came back to her. What was it the queen had said? *There is something in you . . . something I have seen before . . .*

Bethany brought herself back to Fernley Manor. Feeling wretched, she headed over to the steps in front of the entrance.

"Lady Anthea . . . " She hesitated. "I'm afraid we need to think about moving on. Our enemies could arrive at the Star Temple at any moment. You and Isabelle are in danger."

Anthea stared at Bethany with moist eyes but a surprisingly fierce expression. "Just promise me, Bethany . . . promise me that you and my husband will do everything you can to bring him down."

Isabelle raised her head as tears slid down her freckled face. "We're all going together aren't we?"

Anthea spoke softly, "No, my love. It isn't safe for us where they are going. You and me . . . we're going to be better off somewhere else."

"Where?"

"I'm taking you to the Shrine of Lurian," Bethany said.

"And then?" Isabelle asked, turning toward her mother.

"From there, we will need to make our own way. It will be quite an adventure, my love. We will need to make our way by ship."

"I don't understand. Where are we going?"

"To the island of Ormont," Anthea said, meeting Bethany's gaze as she spoke to her daughter. "Ormont is an independent kingdom. Their gateway failed a long time ago. I know the king, Rafael. He is an old friend."

Kendrick harrumphed. "Bethany is right. We need to move on." He raised an eyebrow at Bethany. "Are you sure you don't need to rest?"

"I'll be fine."

"Very well. But first . . . " His eyebrows came together; what he was saying to her was important. "Julian is going to learn your identity. Your mother is going to be in danger. Do you have someone in Everlast you trust?"

She immediately thought of Xander and Charlton and nodded.

"Write a message—I can send it by rider to Sedgeford, and they can send it onward from there. As soon as you have it ready, bring it to me."

Kendrick turned back to his wife and daughter.

Meanwhile, Bethany knew she would struggle with what she was about to say.

Chapter Thirty-Eight

SQUAT AND BROAD, built from massive blocks of black stone, Highguard Castle had its back against the mountainside and defenses facing the plain. Holes for archers peppered every wall. The crenelated battlements formed long rows, facing every approach, tiered and overlapping so that even if a section of wall fell, the attackers would be looking up at still another wall to climb, while defenders rained arrows and scalding oil on those below.

After giving the castle a thorough inspection, Julian was satisfied with his choice about where to launch his counteroffensive. The army settled in. He had enough men to defend the castle or mount a full scale battle out on the plain.

Hundreds of soldiers soon manned the castle's battlements, keeping watch with bows in hand. In the open courtyards, others kept busy, making preparations for the battle everyone knew was coming. When people spoke they had to raise their voices to be heard over the clangs and clatters. Piles of weapons and supplies collected in rooms and corners.

Now, as Julian stood on the fortress's highest tower, with a harsh wind blowing under a cloudless morning sky, he had an opportunity to reflect on recent events. A pair of his personal guardsmen watched him dutifully from the distant stairway, as still and silent as statues. There was something his father had often said, and, back then, it had never made as much sense as it did now.

"Even in company, an emperor is always alone," he murmured to himself.

In the direction he was facing, at the plain's other end, Zhuana was in the city of Meroy, where she would be under the same sky. A lot had happened since Julian had defended Narzin and then abandoned the region to the Veldrians. His sacrifice: his so-called purification. His coronation. The growth of his new, enlarged army. The destruction of his greatest enemy.

He now had a number of nobles in open rebellion. He could almost feel the ghost of his father watching over him, whispering cruel words into his ear. After officially declaring those who had left traitors, he had no choice but to continue with his plan to deal with the invasion from the south.

He reminded himself—he was in a much stronger position than he had been in Narzin. His army was more powerful, and his proclamations ensured that everyone knew that the departed were sentenced to death. In time, they would be hunted down like the dogs they were.

And he would do it without qualm. Kendrick had inadvertently revealed the truth—that he and Declan had been colluding in their efforts, which made Julian feel more than vindicated for the events of past days. If Julian had done nothing, Declan Quinn and Kendrick Conway would have pressed on with building support against him, all without him knowing. Their charges would have seen Julian seized and locked up, ready to be delivered a torturous death, for there could be no other punishment after being condemned for patricide and regicide. Kendrick was his enemy, and had been his enemy, since long before Julian's blade opened up Caden Conway's throat.

Julian could see Kendrick now, filled with anger, calling out to tell Julian's own guardsmen that he could prove his accusation. The guardsmen were sworn to serve their emperor, and had remained loyal, but the experience had left Julian unsettled.

First Declan had leveled his charge, but that was in a message, and after Samara's reconciliation with her father, Julian had assumed the matter would go away. But then, just before he died, Declan had vowed it was the truth. And now, Kendrick had repeated the same story.

Declan had been Julian's enemy, and would say anything to save his own life. Samara was his wife.

But he had to ask himself, not for the first time. What if it were Samara who was lying?

If she hadn't made her ploy with the tax officials, and altered the outcome of the vote, he would have lost the succession. And if his father had lived, rather than died, then once again, he would never have become emperor. She was always committed to his rise to power, at least as much as he was.

She had been the first person to find his father's body. Putting aside the story about poison, which always sounded far-fetched, what if the rest were true? Would she do it? Could she do it? Did his wife have it in her, to murder the emperor, the father of her own husband?

What if everything bad that had happened to him, including this rebellion, had its cause in the actions of his wife?

The hard breeze blew straight into his face as he scowled. The wind drifted on the distant sands, air given form by the dust shifting on the landscape. These thoughts were ugly, but they also weren't to be shied away from.

There was something heard above the wind ... a faint sound, a regular beat that made him turn his head toward the stairway behind him.

Footsteps echoed in the tower's dark interior, growing louder before Samara emerged.

She was in a simpler dress than she usually wore, as white as pure snow, contrasting with her hair and the olive shade of her skin. She scanned the area and spied him near the tower's edge. Her eyes were sparkling, which made his frown deepen; he couldn't believe she was actually smiling.

She came over, casting a quick look back at the guards to check that she could speak without fear of being overheard. "I have been looking for you, my love." She searched his expression. "From your face, I can guess what is occupying your thoughts. I thought it might help if I put your mind at ease. Things are not as bad as you may think. Nothing is hidden anymore. All of your enemies are out in the open. "

He didn't immediately reply. Even now, as she stood in front of him, he was aware of how easy it was to fall into her spell. "Easy to read, you always called me."

"Not so much of late." She met his eyes, evidently hoping for a returning smile, but his face remained cold. "I know this has been hard on you, but I am speaking the truth. We are in a stronger position than ever before. Your enemies are now declared traitors, and no one who remains in this castle will question your command. You are free to crush your enemies, when the time is right, and no one will be able to stop you."

"When the time is right ... And when, may I ask, might that be?"

"When you are hailed as a savior for defeating the Veldrians. As a victorious emperor, when you destroy these rebels, everyone will cheer you on."

"And Kendrick's public accusation? What about that?"

She was unable to hold her smile, and it steadily fell away. "Julian, we have been here before. It is just a story, drawn up by your enemies to hurt you. Do not let them succeed."

"Many of my nobles have rebelled. Some at least believe it."

Irritation entered her voice. "Or perhaps they left because of what happened to my father. And to Kendrick's sons. You didn't have to do it. I told you the time wasn't right."

"Or perhaps, Samara, even after what your father did to me, you still thought that he should live—"

"That's not true—"

"Stop," Julian snapped. "Just close your mouth and stop talking."

Stunned into silence, Samara's lips pressed together. But then she took a deep breath. "Julian—"

"I have had enough of your unsought opinions. The Crown of Blood and Gold was placed onto my head, not yours. I have made greater sacrifices than anything that you have done."

"I realize that." She reached forward and took his hand, to place it on her breast, over her heart. "You are more intelligent than your father, and you are also stronger than he ever was. Believe me when I tell you that you have consolidated power like no man or woman before you. You only have a few hundred lords and their men-at-arms to deal with, deserters you will strip of rank and title, traitors whom no one will open their doors to. Everyone here is with you. And who is there now to speak against you? No one. You have total control. You will hunt down the traitors and destroy them. You will defeat your enemies. And then you will reign supreme."

He removed his hand from her body. Her honeyed words were only making him more angry.

"I also have news that will bring you joy," she said, meeting his gaze. Once again, she tried to smile, and to bring a smile out in him.

Instead he scowled. "Can you never be direct? What is it?"

"I am with child."

He couldn't have been more shocked if she had slapped him. "What did you just say?"

"You heard what I said." She bit her lip, the light in her eyes shifting to worry.

He turned away from her, unwilling to look at her face. He was actually hurting inside, with the pain of regret twisting at his guts. This was the end. The happy memories with his wife were soured forever. He saw her now for who she was, for the first time. Everyone had tried to warn him. "And now for the rest, Samara. Whose child is it?"

It was now her turn to flinch. "Yours, of course."

"No. We all know that is impossible."

"Julian," Samara's voice became sharp, "you do realize that it takes time for a woman to know?"

"Who is he?"

"My love, what are you talking about? We have always been together. When would I have time to steal away? Not that I would wish to. Please . . . you are being ridiculous. There is no one else."

He shook his head, unable to help a bitter laugh.

She came to stand even closer to him. "Julian. Listen to me. I am telling you the truth . . . I thought you would be happy. You are the emperor. You had to pay a price but you can still have an heir. No one can touch you. You are going to be a father."

She was such a skilled liar, that he almost could have applauded her. Instead he created distance between them, backing away. She came forward and he took a step back, holding up his hand, eyes narrowed so she knew not to approach any closer.

"After what they did to me . . . " he whispered. "And it was you who said I had to do it." When he stared at her in disgust, it was through a haze of red. "And now? After they cut me? You sought the arms of another."

"Julian, please." She was frantically shaking her head, side to side, in little increments. "I was always faithful. I can see that you are hurting. But I would never betray you. Nothing could be further from the truth. Why would I be so foolish? You know me better than that."

Julian sneered. She thought she was the one in power. She was always conniving, manipulating, shaping events to suit herself. She had always wanted a child. And now she was taking him for a fool.

It was obvious what she was, what she had always been. A snake. A woman of cunning, looking out only for herself.

"Do you remember the bargain your father insisted we make?" he asked. "That we would never have a child, and we would both be childless to the end of our days? Your father may be dead, but the agreement still stands, not just for me, but for you too." Her mouth was open, as the blood visibly drained from her face. "I am taking this away from you."

"No." Her eyes shot wide open. "Please."

"This feels fair to me. Then, Samara, we both lose something."

"Julian . . . Listen to me."

"I am done with listening to you. I told you that what you demanded from me would destroy us. And it has." He called out to the pair of soldiers. "Guards! This woman in front of me is a traitor. Seize her." When they didn't move, he raised his voice. "Now!"

The two tall soldiers came forward and grabbed Samara, one on each arm, keeping their faces impassive as they then waited for further instructions.

"Take her to the dungeon. I want her in a secure cell. She will try to escape, to convince you, she will even offer you her body. Listen to me carefully, and pass the word around." He pointed his finger, moving it from one soldier to the other, and back again, making sure that no one could mistake his intent. "I will crucify anyone who aids her escape, as well as your brothers, sisters, parents, children, uncles, cousins, every distant relation . . . they will all be hung up on a cross until dead. Do I make myself understood?

"Yes, Emperor."

"Julian, please . . ."

Julian put his back to her, returning to the view, as the guards led Samara away.

Chapter Thirty-Nine

BETHANY WALKED UPON the path of stars. She made incremental movements of her staff, brow furrowed as she thought about how the sky should appear at the Pillars of Dust. The taste of the Weaver's Breath was harsh at the back of her throat. The stars shifted position as she worked, until she looked back over her shoulder.

"Come a little closer," she said to Kendrick, her only ward, who silently obeyed her command. "Be ready to step out just behind me."

The time had come. Bringing her staff up, she sliced at the air, to open up a gash that she widened and shifted until she was facing a rectangular, shining doorway.

"Follow me. Keep walking until we are on the other side."

As soon as she finished the instruction, she took a step forward herself, and then another. She entered the black doorway and past it until she was once more back in the world she was used to. The sensation was like stepping through a curtain made of air. Her skin tingled and the hairs stood up on her arms.

Shift.

Dry heat made her gasp. The contrast was powerful after the sea breezes and tangled forests where she and Kendrick had left Anthea and Isabelle. A hot wind pushed up against her as she stood blinking, holding a hand up to the bright sky. The familiar red hulking shapes of the Pillars of Dust surrounded her.

Kendrick emerged behind her, and she raised her staff to twist it and close the gateway. The wind blew dust past the circle of rust-colored monoliths, only occasionally revealing the ancient symbols. Kendrick groaned, still dazed and uncomprehending.

And as expected, the gateway was definitely guarded.

Fierce-looking warriors watched in a row, just inside the pillars. With curved swords, bows, and quivers of arrows on their shoulders, they inspected Bethany and Kendrick with dark narrowed eyes. Bethany was in her diviner's garb. She held her staff in one hand and clutched a length of white cloth in another. Kendrick also had white fabric tied in a band about his upper arm. He wore his armor and carried his sword, and they both had packs, but there was no one else with them.

One of the Veldrians raised his bow. Nocking a shaft to the string, he pulled the string back to point his arrow directly at her. Bethany's stomach tensed. All he had to do was release, and his sharp arrowhead would slam straight into her body.

"Hold!" She held up her white cloth. "We bring an offer."

The Veldrian with the bow glanced at his companions. He called something in an unintelligible language, and one of the other warriors spoke back. The bowman then addressed Bethany in accented Imperial. "What offer do you bring, Graycloak?"

"Queen Zhuana knows me." As Bethany met the Veldrian's gaze, she projected a confidence she didn't quite feel. "Believe me. Your queen will want to hear what we have to say."

The bowman again spoke to his companions. The moments dragged out. Their fate was being decided.

At last he lowered his bow. "We take you to the city. You ride?"

Bethany nodded. "We both can."

The Veldrian called out to someone out of view. He then gave a cold smile. "If the queen not like what you say . . . " He drew his finger across his throat, even as some more Veldrians came over with horses.

✦

Bethany and Kendrick rode toward the city of Meroy, flanked by their escort of a dozen Veldrians. As they neared, the city emerged from the land around it, presenting a silhouette Bethany remembered from the last time she had passed through this area.

Meroy was a graceful city, with high walls and a cluster of pale towers like branchless trees rising from the center. The white stone reflected the bright daylight, giving the city a stark beauty compared with the harsher shades of the surrounding desert. With its own gateway, Meroy was a much larger settlement than Narzin or even Engel. After all of her victories, Queen Zhuana would be comfortably in command, even as she occupied one of the empire's most important cities and made plans with her council of druadan.

The massive gates came into view, while the hot wind continued to blow and the fiery sun climbed the clear blue sky. From his position on horseback, Kendrick glanced her way. His bushy eyebrows were concerned. No doubt, they were both worrying about the same things.

The queen believed she was winning the war. She would know that Highguard Castle blocked any farther encroachment, but at the moment, they were just two people. Kendrick didn't plan to send a message to Tristan until he knew they had an agreement. They were riding straight into their enemy's stronghold. There would be no easy escape.

But there was a time to reveal fears, and this was not one of them. Bethany kept her face as stony as Kendrick's as she brought to mind people from her past. She imagined Charlton squeezing her hands and telling her that difficult things were the only things worth doing. Her mother would say that she had tried to keep Bethany from her father's world, but she was a grown woman and her own person, and she loved her no matter what. Xander would give his crooked smile as he told her she might be foolish but no one could say she wasn't brave.

She raised her chin and rather than let her fears dominate she instead paid more attention to her surroundings. As her group traveled the yellow road that led the city, they passed a patchwork of fields where crops ripened in the sun, irrigated by channels that separated one green rectangle from another. On the final approach, a great camp encompassed her vision, all the way up to the walls. The road took her straight through the camp. A multitude of canvas tents spread out on both sides, where Veldrians moved about, not just men, but women and children too.

Meroy's broad gates were open, but they were forced to slow by the flow of people. Despite Meroy's conquest, there was no sign of recent fighting. Life in Meroy appeared to be much as normal. Women carried water urns on their heads. Men whacked donkeys pulling carts. Children played in the streets. Everyone wore loose clothing in pale colors to protect their bodies from the searing heat.

The flow of people thinned once they were through the gates and navigating the streets. Passing spiky trees and a mixture of Veldrians and desert folk, they traveled alongside a row of market stalls displaying fruits, vegetables, metal implements, and a range of clay earthenware. Old women haggled. Vendors announced their wares. Aside from the difference in clothing and climate, not to mention architecture, the scene wasn't that different from the Fabric District in Everlast.

As they headed deeper into the city, they left behind a white tower on their left and then another just as tall on their right. At the center of the cluster, another of the white towers drew her attention, and as the streets opened up, their destination was soon clear. A grand structure ahead was like a palace, filling the entire end of the road, and the tower at its center shot up to a height taller than any other in the city.

Bethany's heart rate picked up tempo. It appeared that the Veldrians were doing as promised, and taking them both to the queen. As for what would happen next, they were about to find out.

Tall gates led to a graveled area, where the leader of their escort called a halt. In front of them, broad steps climbed to a set of grand doors, where armed guards watched them silently.

A Veldrian horseman with a tattoo on his neck turned to frown at them. "Dismount. Both of you."

As Bethany followed the instruction, her entire body was tense with worry about the coming encounter. Kendrick climbed off his mount and some youths led their horses away.

More guards arrived, well-dressed Veldrians who were far less dusty. A slim warrior with a cap of curly hair inspected Kendrick and then Bethany, assessing them, resting his eyes on Kendrick's sword.

"Hand over your sword. You will leave your possessions here." He nodded at his men. "Search them both for weapons."

Without a word, Kendrick unbuckled his sword belt, passing it to a Veldrian, and then raised his arms to allow his body to be patted down. Another guard swiftly checked Bethany over, running his hands in a businesslike fashion over her sky blue dress and diviner's cloak.

The guard with Bethany glanced at the curly-haired warrior. "Take the staff?"

"It is a weapon as much as the sword. Of course." His tone was matter-of-fact as he addressed Bethany. "If the queen lets you live, it will be returned to you." He indicated for them to follow. "Come with me. The queen knows you are here, and she does not like to wait."

Chapter Forty

BETHANY HAD TIME TO THINK as she climbed, following endless steps that wound upward. Meanwhile the sound of footsteps echoed around the tower's interior and the dry air was cool after the fiery heat outside. What would Zhuana say to her and Kendrick's proposal? Did it make sense for Zhuana to ally herself with them? Was there anything they hadn't thought of?

A door was open above, and at last they emerged on the tower's highest level. The curly-haired guard beckoned them onward; accustomed to the climb, he was barely out of breath. He led them to a branching corridor and an arched entrance, where a thin man with a pointed beard, dressed in a robe of blue and gold, stood waiting. The curly-haired guard indicated Bethany and Kendrick, gesturing as he spoke.

The man with the pointed beard, a steward from his elaborate costume, held a gold-tipped staff that he pointed at them. "You. Approach." When they neared, he leveled his staff in the direction of the next room. "Pass through and know this. You are entering the presence of Zhuana, Queen of Veldria, Empress of the Redlands and the Southern Provinces. She has granted you this audience. Do not waste your time."

Hearing the titles, Bethany's heart raced even faster. Zhuana had laid claim to the south, and with her forces occupying several important towns and cities, it was a claim that she could justify. At the same time, pressing on with her war would only end when one side or the other claimed total victory, and the empire's armies had yet to be defeated. Could they convince Zhuana to relinquish her conquests, and to instead agree to a lasting peace?

The steward's frown deepened; he had his staff pointed toward the archway. Bethany and Kendrick had come with a purpose. It was time to see it through.

Keeping her back straight, Bethany passed through the archway. Kendrick's presence was reassuring at her side as they entered a vaulted space large enough to fill the entire top of the tower. The ceiling made graceful arcs as it rose and fell, with gaps between supporting columns that afforded a view of the entire city. Green plants in pots contrasted with the white color of the stone. Elegant bronze statues of men and women in robes framed the perimeter.

Zhuana stood near the rail, where she appeared to be contemplating the view. Dark-skinned and athletic, with long black hair woven with diamonds, she wore a striking dark crimson blouse, brown leather at the shoulders and breasts, and a pleated skirt that hung to her knees. She carried her curved sword comfortably at her side. She was as beautiful as ever, in her cold, frightening way, with ruby-red lips, high cheekbones, and fine features.

The weapon was no decoration. Bethany had heard the stories. Zhuana was a warrior queen. When the Veldrians fought, Zhuana fought with them, hacking and slashing, killing her enemies at will. There were guards in the room, but at the same time, Zhuana was the kind of woman who protected herself.

Zhuana's actions said enough. She had conquered city after city: Lexia, Bavia, Gorvia, Engel, Narzin, and Meroy. If the empire's respect was what she wanted, she had it.

Bethany's mouth was dry. What was she doing here? An image came to her: the diviner at the Star Temple of Esk, her scalp bleeding, skin removed. The woman had died. She had worked for Lexia's governor. A house diviner like Bethany.

No. Zhuana would never do such a thing herself. The diviner had said as much, sprawled out on the stone of the Star Temple at Esk. What had she said? *A message. From Maven Dresk, on behalf of the queen.*

Bethany knew who Maven Dresk was. She could recall his face easily, with his sneer and broken nose.

Her intuition about the queen had to be right. Zhuana had helped her escape. The queen was embroiled in some kind of power struggle with Maven Dresk. She had wanted Bethany to tell the empire that she had no part in Engel's burning.

Zhuana turned, and her expression was hard, even as her eyes steadily narrowed. Clearly, Zhuana recognized Bethany. She was wondering why she was here, returned of her own free will.

The steward called out. "Bow to Queen Zhuana! Bow down and show your respect!"

Kendrick bowed, and Bethany bowed alongside him. Zhuana gave no sign she had noticed; she was still staring hard at Bethany.

"Ah," the queen said, making a sound of realization. "They said there was a diviner. However I was not expecting you. Let me think." She frowned. "Bethany. Do I have that correct?"

Bethany nodded. "That is my name. And I remember you, Queen Zhuana. I remember that you did not want the city of Engel burned."

Zhuana's tone was puzzled. "And now you have returned. Why?"

Bethany had thought hard about what she would say. "We are here because we bring a proposal. We are here because we believe that your goal is not to destroy the empire. In the end, what you want is to join us in peace and security. You have shown everyone your power. But the empire is vast and is now waking up. Without a change of course, there is much more death to come, on both sides."

"The time when I should explain myself is long past. What we could not achieve by agreement, we will now take by force." Her gaze turned to Kendrick. "And you are?"

Kendrick gave another bow, shorter than before. "Queen Zhuana, I am Kendrick Conway, Lord of Esk. I represent a large number of the empire's nobility, and I can inform you that there has been a rupture, a division within the empire. If you have not yet heard, you soon will. Julian Malventus stands accused of his father's murder. We will do what we must to see justice done. We will restore the empire before it breaks into pieces and splinters into nothing, and a dark age takes over our world."

"Hmm," Zhuana said. "A large number group, you say? Very well. Where are they?"

"I can give you names and houses—we have a sizable group of nobles, knights, and men-at-arms—however right now I am here to make initial contact and gauge your interest in our proposal."

"Interesting. As you may or may not know, I have met Julian . . . met him and spoken with him at length. Tell me then. What exactly do you think he did?"

"He conspired to have his wife poison his father. Then, when the emperor was weak, his wife murdered the emperor in his sick bed. As I am sure you can imagine, people ask fewer questions about a dead man they thought was very ill."

"His wife killed his father? That is quite a story—"

"I can prove every word. He was about to lose the succession. The cleric who did the poisoning—"

Zhuana held up a hand. "Do not interrupt me again." Her eyes blazed. "Remember who I am, and where you are."

"Of course." Kendrick bowed again. "My apologies, Queen Zhuana."

Zhuana's attention moved back to Bethany. "And you? Where do you fit in? Or did your purpose end when you brought him here?"

Bethany stared straight into Zhuana's eyes. She had to earn this woman's respect. "No, my purpose does not end with my role as a diviner. Do you remember, Queen Zhuana, what you said to me when we last met? You said there was something about me you recognized."

"Yes. I remember . . ." Zhuana inspected her for a long moment. "And so now you are about to confirm for me what my heart was telling me then. I have a sense for these things. I have visited the realm of shadows many times. I know my own destiny . . . so tell me, young woman, what is yours?"

"You are a queen. The blood of a royal dynasty flows through your veins. I spent my life hiding from it, and it was something I never wanted, but I can no longer hide from the truth." Bethany raised her voice. "My father was the emperor, Rigel Regus Livius. He is a part of who I am. When Julian was born, his mother did not survive. Years later, Rigel met my mother, and they were married. I am the result. I was born in the capital, Everlast. My mother still lives there now. Julian is my half-brother. You may see some resemblance. After all, we share the same bloodline." She nodded at Kendrick. "Give it to her."

Kendrick put a hand on his breast pocket. "If I may . . . ?"

The queen nodded, and he withdrew the folded piece of paper, to pass it over. As soon as she had it, Zhuana unfolded the paper and read the contents. Her brow creased, and then she made a sound of surprise before staring straight at Bethany.

It was now Kendrick's turn to speak. "Everything you have just read can be confirmed in the empire's records. The marriage was annulled, but she is legitimate. If Julian were to fall, Bethany is next in line to inherit the Crown of Blood and Gold."

Clearly thinking hard, Zhuana lowered the piece of paper in her hands.

Kendrick continued, "Queen Zhuana . . . what plan did you have for the days after you conquered Everlast, assuming you might be successful? The empire is vast as you know. Who do you have on your side who can explain its inner workings? There are hundreds upon hundreds of noble houses. There is Imperial law, custom, and tradition. There is the issue of legitimacy."

Zhuana turned toward the view, as she stared at something other than the desert city. She then cleared her throat. "Very well. You have my attention. What is your proposal?"

"We will secure a place for your people in the empire, obviously, which I'm sure must be a part of any new arrangement. And in return, you would give us your help in bringing an end to this war. I don't want to fight my brothers, just as many would happily follow someone other than Julian. The most important thing is to create a vision for the future we can all unite behind. If we can remove Julian from power and crown someone else, we can make the empire whole again."

"Someone else," Zhuana said slowly. "And that would be her?" She nodded toward Bethany.

"Hear me out," Kendrick said. "You already have a powerful army. The empire fears you. I can muster another thousand men, a strong force of knights and men at arms. We know the empire. We know its strengths and weakness. But rather than take up the fight, there will be many on the other side desperate for another way. And yes, we also have someone we can unite behind." He glanced at Bethany. "As a diviner, she has a connection to the corpus, and would have strong support from one of the empire's three pillars. I can give you the nobles, which is another of our pillars. And she is her father's daughter, which makes her the next, legitimate successor. We are on the side of justice. When they find out about our alliance, they will see that there can be a lasting peace. A new empire, reborn. This war will be over. And Julian, murderer of his father, will fall."

Zhuana stood thinking, her eyes almost closed as she pondered. Then she called out, past Bethany's shoulder, to the steward with the pointed beard and staff. "Summon my council of druadan. Do it quickly." She returned to Kendrick and Bethany. "I ask that you remain outside until called upon. I will have refreshments sent while you wait. We have important matters to discuss, and I am afraid we must discuss them in private."

✦

"The queen will see you now."

Bethany met Kendrick's worried gaze, before they both pushed themselves to their feet to leave behind the pair of chairs and low table where they had been waiting. Bethany had been too tense to even taste the fruits, meats, and cheeses. Kendrick might not have even realized the food was there.

Together they followed the steward with the pointed beard to enter the vaulted space where they had last met Zhuana. This time the queen wasn't alone. Flanking Zhuana were the queen's council of nobles. But one man among them made Bethany's stomach tighten.

Maven Dresk, the bald and broken-nosed warrior who had captured her at Engel, watched her approach, and if he was surprised, his dark gaze revealed nothing. Aware that she was being watched, Bethany held his stare for a moment, allowed her own eyes to narrow just a little. What had he said to her? *You are a woman, a pretty one, and you are a diviner. Listen to me, girl. I am never letting you go.*

She had now returned to these people, as a free woman, and someone negotiating with his queen, rather than him.

However their alliance was far from concluded. If they were unsuccessful, and Bethany didn't gain the queen's protection, Maven would be free to exact his vengeance upon her.

As soon as they saw Bethany, murmurs broke out among Zhuana's council, although Maven remained silent.

Zhuana's incisive voice interrupted them. "This is her. Please." She nodded at Bethany. "Introduce yourself."

Coming to a halt, Bethany was the focus of all attention. "I am Bethany Sylvana of Everlast. Diviner of the Dymantine Empire. Daughter of Maryam Sylvana and Rigel Regus Livius."

Zhuana spoke up, "And this is Lord Kendrick Conway, the leader of this new rebellion." After Kendrick gave a bow, Zhuana addressed both him and Bethany. "We have decided upon our own proposal. We agree to your terms. We will relinquish our conquests, on the provision of suitable lands to call our own. However when it comes to the empire's leadership, important questions remain. How can we prevent any agreement being altered later on? You say your assembly has endured for seven centuries. Such a method of governance is difficult to oversee, and there would be much that would be new for us. We are not familiar with the way your assembly operates, and yet without our own place within it, how could we ensure we have a say in the future of our people? With no stake in the empire's reign, our position would be too weak. But we are not weak. This is something we have already shown to the world. We are strong."

Bethany fought to keep her breathing even. It sounded like Zhuana wasn't going to agree to their alliance at all.

Zhuana continued, "As I said, we have come up with our own proposal. I do not offer this lightly, and you shall soon see why." Raising her hand in the air, she clicked her fingers. "Where is my son?"

Zhuana's gaze moved, and Bethany turned her head to look over her shoulder. A young man was approaching, and she recognized Zhuana's son Garric from their brief encounter during her capture. Garric was younger than her, lean and somewhat handsome, with tousled brown hair, Zhuana's dark coloring, and sharp, regal features.

Bethany frowned. What was the queen doing? From Garric's proximity, he must have been waiting for his mother to call him out. But then Kendrick reacted as something occurred to him, drawing a sharp breath.

"I understand your motivations as well as your plan," Zhuana said. "We all want what is best for our people. I too desire peace, but not on the terms you have given me. You need someone to replace Julian, someone your assembly will confirm. You need to bring an end to our invasion." She leveled Bethany with her steady gaze. "How old are you, Bethany?"

"I am twenty." Bethany's brow was still furrowed. What was happening?

"My son Garric is nearly seventeen, but he is a man, and fights as a man. He is learning quickly, and to my mind it is clear he will make a good leader. Garric, this is Bethany. She is comely, would you not agree?" Garric took an obvious interest in her, his eyes moving from her copper-colored hair to her face. But when he didn't reply, Zhuana frowned at him. "Garric, say something."

"Lady," Garric said, turning toward Bethany. His voice was clear and refined, as he spoke Imperial with a noticeable accent. "I am Prince Garric of Veldria." He gave a small bow. "It is my pleasure to be meeting you. I hope our encounter will not be a brief one."

"Now," Zhuana said. "As we all know too well, I am a stranger to the empire. If I were to become empress, many would resent my rule. My son, however ... if he were married to the daughter of Rigel Regus ... Well, it would obviously bolster his claim. Garric would become emperor. And you, Bethany, would be his empress. What do you say? You could rule together. Two different sides of a coin, but a golden coin nonetheless."

Bethany's mouth dropped open. She looked again at Garric, seeing him in a new light. He returned her stare. They locked eyes.

"Queen Zhuana ... " Bethany began. What could she say? She had promised to do what was right, but she had never given any thought to the fact that her future would no longer be her own, extending to matters of the heart. "Forgive me. I have not had time to think about this proposal." She didn't finish the obvious thought that the last thing she had expected was a proposal of marriage.

Kendrick kept his head down and spoke in a murmur. "Bethany . . . This is obviously not what we planned. Think about what you want."

"There are some complications," Zhuana said, ignoring Kendrick. "But I believe these could be addressed. I would remain Queen of the Veldrians. I would also remain at my son's side, and reside in your Imperial Palace. Which means that you, Bethany, would be seeing quite a lot of me. What do you say, daughter of Rigel Regus? Will you agree to this union?" She turned to Kendrick. "And you, Lord Kendrick Conway . . . will you agree to the form that our new empire will take? Can you bring your allies over with you?"

Kendrick hesitated, still watching Bethany. "The choice is not mine, Queen Zhuana. Perhaps some time to think—"

"Wait," Bethany said. She spoke decisively. When she had first made her choice, she had known there would be no turning back. She had to think about what was right for the people she cared about. She could bring an end to the war. Julian would no longer be emperor. The man who had killed Kendrick's sons would never again be able to threaten anyone. "I agree to it. Lord Kendrick will help with the details, which will include the role of our assembly of nobles."

"Very well." Zhuana smiled. "It is agreed. You and my son will be married. Together you will rule the empire." She tilted her head at Kendrick. "Are you certain your nobles would agree to this union? Not only those in your rebellion?"

"I believe so . . . " Kendrick said with obvious reluctance, watching Bethany for any change in expression. "If you relinquish your conquests, I am sure that new lands can be found for your people, lands that you will be more than happy with. If everyone is in agreement, your son will be emperor, to exercise power jointly with his . . . with his wife and empress . . . subject to the votes of the assembly, as has been the case for seven centuries."

"It will be as you describe," Zhuana said. "My advisors will help to put this into written terms. However there is something we have yet to discuss."

"Go on," Kendrick said warily.

"We were fleeing a threat from the south. It must never be allowed to enter the empire."

He nodded. "I'm sure we can agree to that."

"Good," Zhuana said. "Then we have an understanding." She called back to the steward. "The lord and lady are our new allies. Find them suitable quarters, the best you can get. Give them anything else they need."

The thin man with the pointed beard bowed. Meanwhile Bethany didn't meet Kendrick's gaze. They had achieved what they had set out to do. But his eyes were on her, and she knew he was thinking about the cost.

Chapter Forty-One

JULIAN SAT ALONE at a polished table of black ebony, a golden goblet near his right hand, a golden plate in front of him. With a silver knife and fork, he sliced at the duck's breast on the plate, watching as blood welled from the rare meat. He cut a piece and ate it. He drank a sip of tart red wine. As he wielded his knife once more, a steward silently filled his goblet from a crystal decanter.

Some people liked music or conversation, but Julian wasn't one of them. He preferred to think. Once, there was a time when he and Samara would dine together, and he had never had the heart to tell her that her blathering wore at his nerves. Now he could do things just the way he wanted.

Nonetheless, while he ate his luncheon, he struggled to keep a grip on his restlessness.

He had made plans with his lord marshal, and they had agreed to force a decisive battle, a great confrontation to be unleashed on the plain. Crushing the Veldrians would enable Julian to move forward, giving him the ability to locate and destroy the rebels from his own side. He was more than impatient to lead his army to victory.

Instead he sliced off another morsel of red meat, chewing it to release the moisture.

Everyone at Highguard Castle was busy, preparing for the upcoming conflict. But a haze on the horizon was the first sign of something wrong, before growing winds delivered an onslaught of dust and grit to the castle.

Soon a sandstorm was raging, and all anyone could do was wait.

The quiet in the wood-paneled dining chamber meant he could hear the howling wind outside. The dusty gales had grown into sweeping clouds. A sudden shudder made him scowl at the shuttered windows by the table. Being part of an old castle, the shutters barely blocked the wind, which was forceful enough to keep the curtains fluttering like pennants on a sailing boat. While he watched, another flurry was actually visible as it brought fine particles into the room.

He frowned down at his plate. When he looked carefully, specks of grit now coated his food. His mouth twisted in disgust. Whether he was satisfied or not, it appeared that his luncheon was over.

His eyes moved to his goblet, and he picked it up to inspect the contents, before turning it over to upend it onto the floor. There was no way he was going to willingly drink dusty wine, even if it was good wine from Trent. He nodded to the steward. "More wine."

The wine steward came over to pour, gracefully avoiding the puddle on the ground, before he backed away. Julian then heard a hesitant voice.

"Emperor? The cleric you asked for is here."

By the door was a woman in white, standing by another steward. The cleric was square-faced and stocky, with her dark hair cut straight at her jaw. The sight of her eased some of his restiveness: the sandstorm may be keeping him from battle, but there was something else that required his attention.

After a sip from his replenished wine, he beckoned the woman forward. "Do you know what it is that I want from you?"

She nodded. "I can do what you ask, Emperor. There is risk—"

"I don't care about the risk."

"Very well." She bowed.

Julian drank another mouthful of wine. After swirling the liquid through his mouth and then swallowing, he spoke again, "The medicine you will give her . . . Is the effect permanent?"

"Sometimes. Sometimes not."

"Very well. That is all. You may leave. Be ready for my summons."

After the cleric left, Julian turned again toward the shuttered windows. The ebony table's surface was no longer glossy, and he wiped a finger over the dust to make a trail.

His introspection led in an obvious direction. What would he do with Samara now? She was his wife under the law. At some point, he had to either kill her or have their marriage annulled. She had murdered his father and betrayed his love; if she was dead he would feel little remorse. But was she more valuable to him alive—?

He explored his own feelings, and decided that once this task was completed, he would consider her price to be paid. They would be even, after what she had done to him. She could spend her days locked in a tower, for all he cared.

He now felt nothing for her at all.

✦

Julian stood in front of the cell, staring at Samara through the bars. Without all her usual ablutions, she looked dirty and unkempt. It was cold in the dungeons beneath the castle, and she hugged her body as she sat on a crude wooden stool. The thin white dress she wore appeared vaguely ridiculous, although she had none of her jewelry, which had been taken away to prevent her giving bribes to the guards. He wondered if she had tried any other powers of persuasion. If she had, she wouldn't meet with much success. He had been clear about the punishment he would mete out if she escaped.

She returned his gaze, barely blinking. "Why are you doing this to me? Julian . . . Listen to me. I am carrying your child."

He scowled. For once, it would be a relief if she would cease with all of her lies. "It is the child of another man. I cannot seed children, remember?" He sneered. "You always were insatiable."

"We can talk. You used to trust me."

"I did trust you, and it has brought me nothing but suffering."

"Julian, it is not too late. You can stop this. Wait until you see the child. You will know it is yours. Please. I am your wife!"

"And I am the fool who married a snake." He held up a piece of paper to screw it up and toss it through the bars. "As for being my wife, that is no longer the case. I had the scribes make this copy for you. Our marriage is now annulled. It is done, Samara. There is nothing at all you can do about it."

She glanced at the screwed up paper on the floor without picking it up. "I am telling you the truth. The child is yours. I swear it on my life."

"Swear to me something else." He stared at her as his nostrils flared. "Swear to me that you didn't kill my father."

She stared at him, imploring. "I swear to you now, on my life, that I did not kill your father."

"Liar!" He snarled as he stepped as close as possible to the bars. "You despicable creature. He was my father!"

"Whatever you think . . . whatever you believe . . . If he had not died, you would not be where you are now."

She broke his gaze to stare at the ground as her hair spilled in front of her eyes. Shaking his head, he was momentarily unable to speak.

He took a breath and beckoned at the woman in the white uniform, with her hair cut straight at the jaw. She carried a bag with multiple straps and pockets and stood patiently as she waited to begin.

"Cleric . . . come closer." As the woman approached, he jerked his chin toward Samara as she sat in the cell. "She is all yours. The guards will do your bidding. And they will help to ensure that you accomplish the task you have been set. Guards?" He now addressed two men, both middle-aged and burly, with grim expressions revealing that they knew exactly what they were here to do. "Give me your names."

"Roland Hale, Emperor."

"Myron Loxley, Emperor."

"Cleric?" Julian turned to the woman.

"Freya Carlson, Emperor."

Julian pointed his finger at each in turn. "I will remember you—all of you. Now get to work. You know what needs to be done."

He turned toward Samara again; she was watching him like a rodent caught in a trap. Her eyes were wide open. Her face was as white as the color of her dress.

"You may resist, but this is happening. You will drink what she has to give you."

"Please. The child is yours. Don't do this," Samara whispered.

"I had to pay my price. And now you are paying yours."

"You are an evil man."

It was now a relief, for him to see her clearly in the cold light and to know her for what she was.

"I will say the same thing to you, Samara, that I said to your father. Whatever I am, it was you who made me this way."

✦

A hazy morning sun rose in the east, gradually banishing the shadows cast by the tall stone walls. Waiting outside the city, Bethany stood with Kendrick, gazing ahead like he was, waiting to greet the newcomers. The wind was now even stronger and made her long hair flutter in front of her face.

Behind them, Meroy's gates stood wide open, leaving the city exposed as a sign of trust. Also at their backs, rows of Veldrian soldiers waited in formation, in matching leather garb as they made a formidable display for the Imperials. Each warrior held a spear upright, clutched in the same manner as the man beside him. If the heat bothered them, they didn't show any sign of it.

With still no sign yet of Tristan, Kendrick rested his eyes on her, strangely hesitant. He glanced over his shoulder, checking how far they were from the Veldrians. "Bethany . . . I know you keep saying the same thing, but I need to be completely certain. Are you sure this is what you want? Your marriage to Garric, I mean. It wasn't ever something we ever discussed."

"I've already told you. If you think about it, there isn't another way. This is just how things have to be."

"But they don't have to—"

"Kendrick," she intentionally used his first name, "do you believe Zhuana would let me be empress on my own?"

He hesitated, but it wasn't in his nature to lie. "No."

"And would Tristan and the other nobles ever want Zhuana to be their new empress?"

"No. Never."

"She is no fool. You can see that. And neither am I. A union is the only way we can make it work."

"But you still have your life ahead of you."

She tried to smile; he only wanted what was best for her. "And I still do." She met his gaze. "I don't claim to know Prince Garric, but I will in time."

"Bethany," he said in a low tone. "You may be convincing yourself, but you are not convincing me. Don't forget, I've raised three children of my own."

She replied quickly; his comment would have been accidental, and he would immediately think of his sons. "Isabelle once told me that you and Anthea were from different worlds, but you were married nonetheless."

"She said that?"

"Coming from different worlds isn't always a bad thing."

He continued to watch her, as she tried at the same time to conceal her worries about the strange future that awaited her. She hid any thoughts about Xander, and the kiss they had shared at the lake. She would now belong to a different union. When Xander found out, which he inevitably would, he was going to feel betrayed, like he never knew who she really was.

"Different worlds?" He again looked over his shoulder at the Veldrians, muttering under his breath. "You certainly have that right . . ."

A shout made him face forward once more.

They were here. Dressed in shining armor that hugged his heavyset frame, Tristan led from the front with a long row of riders on either side of him. They kept coming, row after row, all armed and armored, ready for whatever came next. A dust cloud followed in their wake.

In his message to summon them, Kendrick had provided the rough shape of their arrangement with the queen. Bethany had wanted him to explain every detail, but he had said that some things were best said in person. He had been confident, though, that he could win their allies over.

Tristan and his column of riders came closer until they were reining in directly in front of them. The sizable number of horses stirred, snorting, with white-flecks on their mouths and sweat shining on their flanks.

Blue-eyed and jowly, Tristan took in the sight of the assembled Veldrians, along with Meroy's wide open gates, and Bethany standing with Kendrick. He ruefully shook his head.

"Well, Kendrick, it's not every day that one gets to meet a queen." Tristan smiled and then turned his attention to Bethany. "Or an empress-to be." He put his hand on his heart and gave her a bow. "It seems there is hope for us yet."

"How many?" Kendrick asked.

"Straight to it, eh?" Tristan turned to look over his shoulder, assessing the group behind him. "Twelve hundred, give or take. I have a few more friends who aren't here, but I'm quite sure they will like your plan."

"Your family is safe?"

Tristan barked a laugh. "Unlike you, Kendrick, I have a castle." He scanned the area. "The queen . . . Where is she?"

"Not here, obviously, but you'll soon get to meet her."

Tristan paused to turn again, and this time he spend some time staring to the north, across the desert. "Any news from Julian?"

Kendrick shook his head. "Not yet."

"There's a sandstorm on its way. There won't be any fighting until it's passed. As for Julian, there's one thing we can be sure of. He's not going to be happy when he finds out."

Chapter Forty-Two

THE GUSTS WERE HARD BUT IRREGULAR. Wind slammed at the castle before an extended pause, long enough to get Julian's hopes up, before the howling grew louder and another burst rattled the shutters and flung the curtains in all directions.

If anything the sandstorm was growing, and after another ferocious clatter, Julian glared toward the flying curtains. Standing by the ebony table in his personal dining chamber, he returned to the wooden figures he had arranged in neat rows and columns.

The Veldrians' strength was in their horsemanship, and with almost all of them riders, the group on the left contained a large number of warriors on horseback. On the right, he had his own army formed up, knights up front and ready to charge, with different divisions behind them: archers, spearmen, mercenaries, and regular infantry.

The table's surface represented the flat plain where the battle would take place. There were some who thought Zhuana might try to defend Meroy, but Julian and Lynch were both in agreement. The tactics the Veldrians employed meant they fought best on open ground. As soon as they became aware of Julian's approach, they would ride out to meet him, resulting in the decisive conflict he was desperate to have.

Julian studied his deployment, trying to ignore the raging winds outside. Each figurine represented five-hundred men, which meant that there were dozens of wooden pieces. His own army was the largest, and there were three groups at his disposal who were critical: his indomitable knights, who would overwhelm any opposition; his archers, who would have to defend his army from the enemy's wheeling riders; and his spearmen, who would defend both his archers and his infantry. He moved several of the figures with bows, and then maneuvered some of the wooden men holding spiky spears.

Another gust of wind broke through his concentration, making him topple a piece, which also knocked over the one next to it. He scowled and picked each wooden figure up. When would this cursed sandstorm end?

He was re-settling the second piece when he heard a male voice in front of him. He looked up, startled; he hadn't realized he was no longer alone.

"You will soon have to add some more pieces on the other side." Lynch glanced at the figures that made up the Veldrian army. "I have some news, and it isn't good."

Julian straightened. He was surprised to see his lord marshal's expression. Lynch was usually cold, but he was always steady, and it was unlike him to reveal his worry.

"Well? What is it?" Julian asked.

"Does the name Bethany Sylvana mean anything to you? She is a diviner. Kendrick Conway's—"

"—I know who she is."

Lynch sounded surprised. "It's true, then? She is who she claims she is? To be honest, I was aware of the rumor that your father had another child—"

Julian flinched as if the other man had punched him hard in the face. "What did you just say?"

Lynch was frowning, clearly confused. "Apologies, I thought you said you knew . . . I've had a message from one of our spies, a steward who works close to the queen. This kind of news . . . well, it is not the kind of news that can remain quiet for long. This diviner . . . she says she is your half-sister. Your father married her mother while he was campaigning in the Far Reaches. When he became emperor, he had the marriage annulled, but she would still be legitimate. I assume that it's true, then—?"

Lynch broke off when Julian held up a hand, shaking his head from side to side. Part of Julian knew he needed to take hold of himself. For a moment, he didn't know whether to cry out in frustration or laugh at himself out loud. One thought was stronger than any other.

What a fool . . . what a splendid fool he had been.

But then . . . he couldn't blame himself . . . for if he had been blind, then so had everyone else.

The pieces fit neatly together. The tale could only be true.

His father had another child, a girl five or six years younger than him. She was the young woman with the copper hair, the one he had encountered outside his father's quarters at the Imperial Palace in Everlast. How could he have not seen it before?

In the end she had revealed herself. He had a half-sister. A half-sister! He had even met her . . . he had spoken with her in person.

She had been so close to him all along.

The second time he had met her, he had been confused to learn she was Kendrick Conway's house diviner. No doubt his father's influence had put a gray cloak upon her shoulders, and then helped her become house diviner to the Conways. She had worked her charm on Kendrick, playing a long game, her eyes always on the prize she sought.

She wanted what he had—she wanted the Crown of Blood and Gold.

By the stars . . . after everything else that had happened. What was it Lynch had said? They would have to add more pieces to the other side? She and Kendrick must have gone to the enemy. The additional numbers Lynch was referring to were the rebels, who would fight for Zhuana in order to bring about his downfall.

His enemies were now allied against him.

Lynch was watching, waiting for him to speak.

"It is true," Julian slowly said. "We will deny it, of course. But yes, it's true. It appears that my father sired another child while he was in the Far Reaches, leaving his infant son—me—back home in Everlast."

"She says she has proof. And there will be records, back in Everlast. The annulment, her birth—"

"—Records can be destroyed."

"They can, but she was born in Everlast. Her mother might still be alive. People will know them both."

Julian scowled. The girl was playing with fire, and everyone she cared about was going to get burned. "Perhaps I was not making myself clear. I won't just go for records. I will destroy every sign she ever existed."

"Even so, our problems do not end there. They have made an agreement, a union. She is going to marry Zhuana's son. The rest is obvious. They intend to claim the Imperium, with Zhuana's son representing the Veldrians and his wife—a diviner—representing both the corpus and your father's line."

Julian could now understand Lynch's concern. "You fear that more rebels will now desert us to the other side."

"Yes," Lynch said bluntly. "That is exactly what I fear."

For a long moment, Julian stared into the distance. "Then we both know we have to act fast. As soon as this sandstorm is over, we ride to battle. We face the same rebels and the same number of Veldrians. When we defeat them all on the battlefield, the end will be the same. That is all you need to be thinking about. How go the preparations?"

"We are as ready as we can be."

"Good. And when conditions change, we are certain they cannot go around us?"

"They would have to cross the worst stretch of the Red Desert, and we would see them doing it, which means we would be able to ride out to meet them."

"Very well. Keep watching the enemy, and inform me if anything changes. Meanwhile, I need to find Veldon Marx. I have some matters I must attend to."

Chapter Forty-Three

IT WASN'T XANDER'S FIRST TIME in the Fabric District, but that didn't mean he knew his way around. He followed a broad avenue and turned into a narrow road. Passing shops and markets, where weavers, dyers, fullers, tailors, and seamstresses plied their trade, he walked with haste, worried eyes constantly searching.

Horses and carts clattered along the cobbled streets. Passersby thronged the paths, ignoring the refuse and the loud cries of the hawkers. The morning sun brought rising heat and the unpleasant blend of odors that collected in such a populated area. Farther away, dozens of tall compounds surrounded the central maze of markets and alleys, looming and somehow sinister, despite their worn appearance. Massive structures, the compounds contained level upon level, divided into each little dormus like a beehive.

Xander stopped in the street. This wasn't working. He needed directions. He raised a hand at a long-faced man in fine clothing who scowled at him and simply kept walking. His luck with a dusty laborer was no better. Everyone looked busy, like they had somewhere important to be.

He waved to get an older woman's attention; she had a ruddy face, and her footsteps would take her right past him. "Madam? The House of Healing on Dyer Street—do you know it?"

She jerked her chin past her shoulder. "Back that way. Another block. Turn right."

He squinted. There was another junction between roads, and Dyer Street might be the one perpendicular to the street he was on. He opened his mouth, but the ruddy-faced woman was already gone. A bell pealed somewhere, and he picked up his pace again, walking with long strides toward the junction. He couldn't help it; his walk changed until he was almost running.

Please. He couldn't fail. Not now. Surely he still had time.

Bethany's message had come when he was away from home. Slid through the slot in the door of his dormus, he hadn't discovered it until he returned from his duties in Skollard to arrive back home in the morning. Once he read it, he left immediately, still wearing his diviner's uniform.

Xander,

I need to ask you for a favor. It is better if I don't tell you why.

I need you to go to the House of Healing on Dyer Street in the Fabric District. Find a cleric named Charlton. I trust him. He knows where my mother lives.

Tell her to gather all of her money. Then, as soon as you can, take her to a gateway and guide her to the Temple of the Infirm at Laurel. Explain to her that I love her and I will find her.

Say nothing to anyone but Charlton. If questioned, you and I are not close, and this was just a minor favor. Destroy this message.

I am sorry to cause you such trouble.

Bethany

Xander swiftly turned into Dyer Street. Speeding along the side of the road, he scanned each shop and any signs he could see. He passed a tailor followed by a dyer, and then a baker's stall. The aroma of fresh bread wafted over as he kept himself moving fast.

Outside one of the last shops in the row was a sign, and at last he read the name he had been searching for—*The House of Healing*—along with the symbol of an open hand with a droplet in the middle.

Xander went straight to the door, grabbing the handle to haul it open. He strode inside, searching, but so early in the day there were just two people waiting on the benches. At the back of the room, a junior cleric sat at a desk, her eyebrows raised at his disruptive arrival. He was breathing hard after his frantic journey.

"Diviner? May I help you?"

"I'm looking for a cleric . . . . Charlton."

The young cleric went to the inner door that led to the chambers farther inside. She pulled it open to call out. "Charlton! A diviner is asking to see you."

Xander waited impatiently. Soon an old cleric appeared, calling something back over his shoulder. As he approached, the cleric's manner was calm, despite Xander's obvious agitation. He had unruly graying hair and bright blue eyes, with a kind, careworn face.

"Diviner? How can I help?" the old cleric asked.

"Cleric Charlton?"

The old cleric nodded, tilting his head. "Yes?"

Xander cleared his throat and nodded toward the main front door. "Can we speak outside?"

Without another word, Xander turned to leave the building, relieved when Charlton came with him. He moved to a space on the side of the street where they could talk away from the passersby.

"My name is Xander. I'm a friend of Bethany's."

Charlton furrowed his brow; Xander's obvious tension was making him worried. "Is something wrong? Where is she?"

"She sent me a message . . . " Xander hesitated, but Bethany had said he was to be trusted. "She didn't exactly say she's in trouble, but I think she might be. She said she trusts you. And she told me that I can trust you."

Charlton stared seriously into his eyes. "And where Bethany is concerned, you can."

"Do you know why Bethany's mother would be in danger?"

"Maryam?" Charlton's tone was puzzled. "No. Not at all."

"Bethany wants me to get her mother to safety. She said it's important. Do you know where I can find her?"

"I can take you to her right now." Charlton's frown deepened. "Are you sure you can't tell me what this is about?" Xander shook his head. "Very well. Hold on. I need to arrange someone to see my patients."

As Xander waited, Charlton bustled back to the House of Healing, opening the main door to call out to the young clerk. "Myra? Something important has come up. Ask Cleric Ren to see my patients. Tell him I am asking as a friend." After waiting for a reply, he closed the door.

"Very well, Xander. We can go together. Maryam lives in Compound 12C. It isn't far. Come with me."

◆

Xander met Charlton's gaze as the cleric stared grimly back at him. After climbing four flights of steps, they stood at the entrance to the dormus. The door was wide open, as if someone had stepped out for the briefest moment and would be back at any time. A heavy silence hung in the air.

Charlton was the first to step inside, with Xander close behind. They both raised their voices out as they entered.

"Maryam?" Charlton called.

"Is anyone here?" Xander asked.

Xander felt a heavy weight sink into his stomach when he didn't hear a reply. Perhaps Bethany's mother might be away buying groceries, or visiting the gardens, or seeing a friend? She could be in the washroom?

But why would she leave the front door wide open?

In the corner, a pair of armchairs faced each other by a low table, but the mug on the table lay on its side in a pool of brown liquid. Xander crossed the room to set the mug straight, before turning back to Charlton.

The cleric was frowning as he looked around the room. "Her cane is gone," he said. "She needs it to get around."

"Is it like her to leave the door open like that?"

"No. Not at all. She may be blind, but her mind is as sharp as ever. Her medicine makes her sleep . . . " He trailed off. He was staring at a bottle on the main dining table. A vial filled with liquid sat on the table, a small bottle with a stopper like the kind often used by clerics and apothecaries.

"Is that her medicine?" Xander asked.

Charlton went over and picked up the vial. "It is," he said as he tilted the tiny bottle from side to side. The vial was at least half full.

A coat hung on a hook on the back of the door. The corner bench used as a preparation space was neat and orderly. Xander could picture Bethany sitting on one of the armchairs, sharing her mother's company. He turned; there was something on the ground, below the nearest armchair, and he went over and crouched to retrieve the object. A moment later he was holding up a blanket, small in size, with Bethany's name woven into the material in childlike letters: a memento kept by her mother. He set the blanket down gently on the chair.

Charlton continued to call out Maryam's name. As the cleric headed deeper into the dormus, Xander hurried to follow him. Xander glanced into the washroom, seeing a basin and clay jug. He and Charlton moved to the last room in the dormus, a bedroom containing two beds. One of the beds was perfectly made; the other was made but rumpled. A clothing chest lay open with its lid up, displaying the contents: folded stacks of clothing in an array of colors. The bedroom looked like it was ready to be used, and would contain Bethany's sleeping mother when nighttime came. But how long had it actually been, since the dormus had last been occupied?

Having completed their search, Xander and Charlton returned to the main living room. As Xander stood in the middle of the space, he anxiously wiped a hand over his face. If Bethany's mother had just stepped out, she would have been back by now. Neither he nor Charlton were calling Maryam's name anymore. Instead they were both staring into each other's worried eyes.

This was Bethany's home . . . the place where she grew up. As for Bethany's mother . . . she was gone, nowhere to be seen.

"Do you think . . . " Xander broke off and then tried again. "Do you think that someone took her?"

His stomach was now churning. Bethany had known her mother was in danger. He was the one she had gone to for help. But he had failed her . . . and her mother was already gone.

"I honestly don't know. I'm sorry. It . . . it does appear that way."

"But why would someone take her?"

Charlton let out a breath as he shook his head. "It's the same as asking why Bethany asked for your help. Maryam doesn't have her medicine. Her cane is gone. All I know is this doesn't look good."

"But who would take her?"

"I couldn't even hazard a guess. Please, Xander. You have to tell me. What was it Bethany said?"

Xander hesitated. "She wanted her mother to gather all of her money. She then asked me to take her mother to the Temple of the Infirm at Laurel."

"Hmm. Somewhere she would be cared for, then . . . where she would be able to remain for some time. When did you last hear from her otherwise? I haven't seen her since before the coronation."

"She tried to see me at the Observatory but I was away in Trent. As for where she is now . . . she's house diviner to the Conways. I expect she would be with the army."

Charlton sighed, and then as he looked around the empty dormus, he turned again to face Xander. "Listen. I know quite a few people in the Fabric District. I can also talk to Dahlia. She helps Maryam and might know something. Leave this with me. I'll make some enquiries and I can find you again through the Observatory. At the moment, there is nothing else we can do."

Chapter Forty-Four

THE GROUP OF IMPERIAL GUARDSMEN reined in on the road, half a mile from Meroy's broad gates. As they waited, in their silver armor and white cloaks, although their number was fewer than twenty, they were bold enough to remain in place. When challenged, they asked for Bethany Sylvana by name. They would only deliver their message when they spoke to her in person.

Bethany was now approaching. She was on horseback, and Kendrick rode on one side of her, Tristan on the other. Meanwhile, a flanking escort of eighty armored knights would be more than a match for the guardsmen if it came to trouble.

She shielded her eyes from both the sun and the dusty wind. Soon she was able to make out the group of figures up ahead as they waited for her on the broad yellow road. As she kept her horse moving, the fierce wind blew into her face, making her grimace. The sandstorm's strength was fading, but it had some power left, and the sky was a dirty yellow. The row of guardsmen became larger, revealing individual horsemen, and they had fanned out in a way that marked one of them as the definite leader. This was the rider she focused on.

He was huge, a massive man in armor of steel and gold, wearing a white cloak draped from his shoulders. Mounted on a powerful warhorse, he had his reins in one hand, held casually on his lap while he waited. He had a sloping forehead and heavy jaw, with deep-set icy eyes and close-cropped white hair. The hilt of a broadsword jutted up from one of his shoulders, with the oversized weapon worn on his back. He carried something on the saddle in front of him: some kind of bag or sack.

Julian's message could address a number of different topics. Clearly, he had learned who she was faster than anyone expected. There was no use worrying; she would soon find out what he had to say. No matter what she told herself, however, the nearer she came to the guardsmen, the faster her heart was racing.

As Kendrick had told her, the guardsmen weren't carrying any bows or other projectile weapons, but he had also asked that she keep her distance.

"That's close enough," Kendrick muttered from her side. "Rein in."

There was now silence as the two groups faced each other. Bethany tried to moisten her dry mouth. The wind howled over the desert. The sun beat down from overhead.

Kendrick spoke in a low tone. "See that man in front, the big one? His name is Veldon Marx. He commands the emperor's personal soldiers, guardsmen like the ones with him. This is as close to him as you ever want to get."

Tristan called out to the other group, raising his voice to be heard over the shrieking wind. "We are here. What is your message?"

Leaving the rest of his men to remain where they were, the commander, Veldon Marx, kicked his horse forward. He halved the distance between the two groups and then after stopping again, he tilted his head back, sucking in a breath to bellow.

"Traitors! I deliver a message from Emperor Julian Malventus. No reply is required."

The commander paused, scanning the group of knights and men-at-arms, gazing at Kendrick and Tristan and finally fixing Bethany with his stare. There was no emotion in him, but she couldn't prevent the chill that climbed up her spine. He then took his sack and tossed it to the ground in front of them. He yanked his reins, turning his horse around.

Bethany heard a man's voice.

"Fire upon them, Lord Kendrick?"

"There's no use. Let them go."

As the commander reached his men, he spurred his horse on to greater speed. The group of riders turned together, picking up pace until they were leaving at a gallop. Soon their figures became smaller as they followed the yellow road away from the city.

Everyone who remained had only one thing left to focus on: the dirty brown sack on the ground.

Kendrick glanced at Bethany, and then dismounted. His face was hard and expressionless as he crossed the distance to the sack. As he crouched down beside it, he hesitated as he prepared to take the edges and open it.

Bethany only watched for a moment before sliding off her horse's back. As he peeled the sack open, she walked over to join him.

He growled at her. "Stay away."

"What is it?" she asked, ignoring him and continuing closer.

"I don't know. Just stay back."

He opened the sack and looked inside, hiding the contents with his body. She waited for him to recoil or gasp. Instead, if anything he looked confused. He reached in to pull something out. A moment later, he held up a length of wood.

"Does this mean anything to you?" he asked.

He was holding a rod: black, smooth, and thin but strong, with one end curved to make a handle. It was an ebony cane, and Bethany did know it well. She was the one who had bought it. She had seen her mother use it a thousand times.

"Give it to me," she whispered.

He passed her the cane, but as she took it, Kendrick looked at his hands.

His palms were red and sticky.

Bethany found herself holding the cane in both hands . . . her mother's cane. She could feel how wet the cane was, how it stuck to her hands like it was coated with some adhesive. She could heft its weight, which even now was familiar. She remembering last seeing it in her mother's hand, as her mother said goodbye when Bethany visited during the time of the coronation.

She didn't want to think about what had happened. But she had to. She couldn't just push this away.

There could be no denying it. She couldn't help it. She pictured her mother somewhere terrible, in a dungeon or in a pit. Big men surrounded her, or perhaps it was just one man, maybe even the huge man with the icy stare. Her mother was blind. She wouldn't have known everything that was happening to her. But she would have felt the blows.

Over. And over. And over. Until something broke inside her and she died.

Bethany fell to her knees. And yet it wasn't over. Kendrick was pulling something else from the sack. Something that tinkled. He withdrew a pair of dangling earrings, like acorns on metal thread. Both were coated with drying blood.

When he looked at her, he knew. "I'm so sorry," he whispered.

But Kendrick wasn't to blame.

She was the one who had done this.

✦

Grit covered the wooden figurines, as well as the table itself. The ebony surface was no longer glossy, it was covered in dust, and until the sandstorm was over there was no purpose in wiping it clean.

Julian had no choice but to ignore the wind, the ratting shutters, and the curtains that danced in a frenzy. Standing over the table, he took three clean wooden knights from a pouch and added them to Zhuana's army. Reports were that Kendrick and Tristan now commanded more than twelve-hundred knights and men at arms, and even though his own number of knights was far greater, the pieces would make a difference when the fighting started.

Both Kendrick Conway and Tristan Benedict were veterans, and provided Zhuana listened to their advice, the knights they led would be positioned at the front of her army. Frowning as he worked, Julian made a few adjustments, and finally straightened to examine his work.

There was nothing in the terrain to provide an advantage. Was there anything else he might have missed? Julian's force was larger, but in every conflict so far, the empire's fighting men had paid the higher price.

His own knights now had an obstacle: the knights on the other side. Without the obstacle, he would usually order the charge right away, but his knights would get ahead of the rest, even as those in the middle found themselves embroiled with the rebels. Perhaps he should explore the idea of dividing his knights in half, placing each group in his army's wings? There was a pincer movement, effectively used to subdue the highlanders from Gila back in the early days of the empire. The idea was something he would have to discuss with Lynch.

The shutters rattled with another ferocious gust, making him tear his gaze from the table. How would Veldon Marx be faring? The commander's journey to Everlast had met with early success, and he had made a swift report before heading to the south to deliver his message.

"Emperor." Lynch entered the dining chamber. He was scratching at his wandering scar, which was something he did when he had bad news. "It has happened again, I'm afraid. Great Weaver curse them all."

Julian's eyes narrowed. "Deserters?"

"Lords Pascoe and Rodgers, as well as a few hundred men. They left the castle in the night, snuck out of the eastern gate. We were able to follow their tracks for a time, but the winds make it impossible."

"And let me guess. They weren't just fleeing for their homes."

"They were traveling south."

"Hmm."

"You should also know. Commander Marx has returned. He said he delivered his message."

"Good. You never know. She may now panic and run."

"Marx also said that the winds are calmer in the south. It may be—"

"Wait." Julian held up a hand.

The shutters were still. For the first time in what felt like an eternity, he couldn't hear the wind at all. He intently watched the curtains, alert to the slightest sound or sign of movement. The material fluttered a tiny amount, but then lay still.

The eerie silence continued. He now listened to his own rapid breathing.

"The Great Weaver has answered our prayers," Lynch said. He lifted his iron spindle and kissed it.

"Come with me," Julian snapped. "Quickly!"

He headed straight for the door and his lord marshal fell in behind him. Reaching a corridor, Julian traveled its length, before making another turn. Another hallway of black stone led to the curling stairway within the castle's tallest tower. The clatter of his and Lynch's footsteps bounced off the wall, echoing like competing drum beats.

Even as he climbed the stairway, he picked his ears, trying to hear any sound of the wind. His calves ached, heart racing as he made his rapid ascent.

He burst from the tower's stairway, out into the open air. Now under the open sky, he walked straight to the tower's edge, where the plain lay spread out in front of him.

It was late in the day, and a fiery sunset cast a blood red glow on the terrain.

The sands were no longer shifting. There was barely any wind at all. He stood where he was, panting, as Lynch came up to join him. They watched together, and they both knew the time had come.

"Give the order," Julian said. "Spread the word far and wide. Two hours before dawn, I want our army ready to leave this castle. It is time for us to crush our enemies, once and for all."

Chapter Forty-Five

BETHANY FOUND KENDRICK on the open rooftop of their shared villa, where a mosaic pattern decorated the floor and terracotta urns lined the stone rail. The morning air was still for a change, neither cold nor far too hot. Kendrick stood alone and gazed toward the plains, at the streaks of yellow and reds that filled the dawn sky.

After a glance at his face, she also watched the sunrise. His eyes were shadowed. She doubted she looked any better. "How long do we have?"

The news had arrived the previous evening—one of their allies had carried it from Highguard Castle as soon as the order was given.

With the sandstorm over, Julian wasn't waiting. He was leading his army toward Meroy. Zhuana was already planning to take her own forces to meet him.

Kendrick spoke without turning. "They would have already left hours ago to avoid the heat. There won't be much waiting. My guess is the fighting will start an hour or two before midday."

She drew in a deep breath. "Do you think we can win?"

"In truth? I don't know. Either way, a lot of people are going to die."

"What about our proposal for peace? Can't we convince Zhuana to wait?"

"I've tried, Bethany, but I have no influence here. If she waits too long, she increases the chance of defeat. These Veldrians' strength is speed, holding the initiative. I hoped we had more time. But Julian is trying to destroy us before there is much of a chance for talking."

He turned to face her, bushy eyebrows covering his sorrowful gaze. "I still hold hope. More allies keep coming to our side. We've all suffered, and I have to believe that the Weaver wouldn't let it all be for nothing." His voice came in a low rumble. "Did you find her, last night?"

She shook her head. "Not yet . . . I looked . . . "

She tilted her head back to look up at the sky, but all the stars were gone. No. Not gone. It was just too bright to see them. The stars were always there. Always watching.

"Believe me, Bethany, you will search and search, and then one night, when you are not expecting it, your mother's star will appear in the sky. And then you will know that she is looking down on you, with all the love she has. She will never forget you, just as you will never forget her."

She nodded, even as she kept her fingers on her lips for a moment, gathering herself, so that when she spoke her voice was steady. "I keep thinking about my friends in Everlast . . . the ones I asked to help. I don't even know if they're alive."

"My wife would say you should only worry about what you know. Anthea believed in the fates. You have to trust that they are well."

"I can't do that. I can't just hope and watch the stars. I should have done more, back before . . . " she swallowed, "before all this happened—"

"No. Whatever you do, Bethany, don't think like that. You didn't do anything wrong. Promise me you won't take responsibility for something done to you by an enemy. You didn't do this. He did. Do you hear me?" She nodded and he stared into her eyes before he was satisfied. "I understand. I really do. You never wanted power. But sometimes it takes power to keep the people you care about safe. We find ourselves in one of those times."

Kendrick let out a sigh and returned to frowning at the dawn. A hint of the sun's orb appeared, just above a sandy ridge in the distance. A new day was on its way.

Bethany cleared her throat. The hours, minutes, and seconds were always passing. There was no time to wait. If she was going to take action, she had to do it now.

"There's something I want to talk to you about . . . an idea." As she spoke, he quickly turned toward her. "I don't know much about power . . . about how to make it work for you rather than against you. What I'm best at is being a diviner. This idea . . . it's something bold . . . something new." She strengthened her voice. "It's something that could make a difference, even in the time we have. I'll have to do some tests. But I think I know a way we can end this without a lot of people dying."

He stared hard at her. "Tell me."

✦

It was later in the morning as Bethany hurriedly navigated through the camp outside the city. Despite the early hour, everywhere there was movement. Veldrian warriors led horses, lugged weapons and armor, and pushed carts containing feed for their animals. The accompanying sounds of the camp were just as frantic, as fighting men and women called out in loud voices. A lean woman with tattoos on her shoulders hugged a bawling babe to her bosom, before handing the infant to an older woman as she wiped at her eyes. A bearded man hoisted a young girl high. A husband and wife, both armed and ready, leaned into each other with foreheads pressed together.

Reaching a different area, Bethany began to encounter more druids, noticeable by their furs and lack of weapons. Their movements were just as frantic as they gathered flasks and called out to one another. She earned a few curious looks, but people were generally too busy to give her much attention. Meanwhile her eyes were tight and anxious as she navigated the tents. What if he wasn't here? Everyone was busy, and he would be busier than most.

She leaned forward to look along the space between the next row of tents. She released a breath of relief. There it was—a tent much larger than any other, with an animal's skull above the entrance. She put on speed to head straight over. There was no time to wait, and she peeled the canvas aside, peering in as she tried to make sense of the interior.

The first thing she noticed was the smell. The stench was sharp and bitter, heavy in the air so that it stung the back of her throat. An array of furnishings filled the space: benches and tables, sideboards and stools. Black iron pots bubbled as they rested in beds of coals raked out on great dishes of stone. Flasks lay arrayed in neat rows and columns. Bowls displayed powders in shades of red, yellow, and green.

A skinny man, lean enough to be skeletal, faced one of the cauldrons, hurriedly tearing green leaves into the large steaming pot. With close-cropped graying hair and gaunt cheeks, he was concentrating as he counted under his breath. Strangely, he was wearing furs, but he wasn't sweating at all, despite the glow from the coals and the pungent smoke in the air.

While she waited for her eyes to adjust, a puff of desert wind pressed against her back, shredding the smoke but leaving the powders undisturbed.

"Close it," the skinny man snapped. "Quickly now. In or out. Make your choice."

She stepped inside and yanked the canvas to close it behind her. Meanwhile the druid remained at his cauldron, not even bothering to look at her.

"If you know what is good for you, never do that again."

He said it matter-of-factly, with just a frown to reveal his annoyance. She inwardly cursed the wind. If he was who she thought he was, she didn't want him irritated; she was here to ask for his help.

He spoke again, just as curtly, "Well? What is it? I know who you are, Lady, but as for why you are here, I could not hazard a guess."

"You are the druid Alric?"

He never ceased what he was doing as he tore his leaves into the cauldron. "And you are the diviner who carries the emperor's blood. I am busy, as you can see. Every flask of firewater will save many lives. What is it that you want?"

She moved around a long bench to approach his position. "I need your help."

He grunted. "As I said, I am busy—"

"Then stop and give me the attention I deserve."

He was stunned enough that his hands stopped moving as he raised his head to look at her.

"This could be the most important thing you have done in this war. I need you to tell me about this." She reached into the pocket of her dress to show the druid the last of the cactus pearls she had taken from Maven Dresk.

He arched an eyebrow. "We call them pearls. They are the flower buds of the harbinger cactus. They must be picked at a certain time and soaked in a special solution to remove the poison. Well? Is that all?"

Everything depended on his answer to her next question. "I need to know. Can you get more?"

"If you know anything about them, you will know they are not for the faint of heart. We give them out only after careful consideration."

"You haven't answered my question. Can you get more of them?"

"I can . . . " he said slowly. "Unlike some of our other components, the pearls are relatively common. It is a tradition among our warriors to take them to hone the mind, just as honing a blade maintains the edge."

"Do many of your warriors take them?"

He nodded. "However they confer no special powers, whatever you may think. The effect is more . . . profound."

"And you say you have more?"

Swiftly finishing his task with the leaves, he brushed his hands against his clothing. "Why do you ask?"

"I need your help with a test. If it works, it could change everything."

"What kind of test? You do realize that I understand very little about what you do? I have my knowledge, Graycloak. You have yours."

"I'll explain when we get there, but I'm telling you the truth. This test could win you this war. And all it needs is you and me. That is . . . assuming you can cope with the effects of the cactus?"

He snorted. "If anyone can, I can."

"Then gather more pearls, as quickly as you can, and meet me at the Pillars of Dust."

Chapter Forty-Six

BETHANY CROSSED THE VAULTED ROOM at the top of Meroy's tallest tower. Kendrick and Tristan stood together on one side of the queen. On Zhuana's other side were the druadan, the queen's council of nobles. Faces were grim. The tension in the air was palpable. Julian's army was on the way; time was passing swiftly. Whatever was being said, all conversation halted when the queen saw her coming.

"Ah, here she is," Zhuana said impatiently. "Well, Bethany? You asked that we gather and here we are."

Bethany came to a halt. Standing tall, staff in hand, diviner's cloak on her shoulders, she made sure to reach everyone with her gaze. "I know how we can win this war without a great number of people dying."

"That is what Lord Kendrick said, but conflict is now inevitable," Zhuana said. "This is going to be decided on the battlefield one way or the other."

"I know it feels that way. And I agree with you that today will decide the fate of the empire. Julian's army is much larger than it was before. However so is yours, Queen Zhuana. More allies keep joining us, and our plan has always been to present a clear path to peace, which is why Julian wants to force us to fight. There is only one way to stop him. And that is to show we have already won."

Zhuana's eyebrow went up skeptically as murmurs broke out among the members of her council.

Bethany raised her voice, bringing their voices to an end. "When a diviner like me leads a group through a gateway, the minds of our wards—the people we guide—are stilled and they become compliant. For me, however, the situation is very different. My staff delivers the Weaver's Breath, which means I can see the tapestry with my eyes wide open. This isn't always easy, because Weaver's Breath alters the mind, and the experience must be tamed like a wild animal."

A member of Zhuana's council, Dan Hewin, a stocky man with oversized ears and a bushy beard, spoke up. "Alters the mind in what way?"

Rather than reply, Bethany opened her palm, to display a handful of the cactus pearls. "These create a state similar to Weaver's Breath. In truth, the effect is more powerful still." She glanced from one Veldrian to the next. "You have taken them?"

Zhuana nodded. "I have. We all have."

"The druid Alric and I performed a test, and the result is what I hoped for. If someone is under the spell of the pearls, their mind is not stilled in the path of stars. Like me, your warriors could travel with their eyes open. What this means is that when they emerge through the gateway at the other end, they won't be weak and easily subdued. Instead, they would be conscious, prepared, and . . . " She paused for effect. "Alert and ready to fight."

Maven Dresk made a sound of surprise as his mouth dropped open. "This is it. I knew it. This is the answer I was searching for."

Bethany glanced at Kendrick. It was his turn to speak.

"The empire is ruled from Everlast," Kendrick said. "Within Everlast is the Nexus, the area that contains the Imperial Palace, the Marble Court, and the Cathedral of the Hidden Source, home to the high confessor. As any diviner will tell you, there is a gateway inside the Nexus: the Portal of Polaris. Not many outside the corpus know it exists, and it is always well-guarded. Usually any enemy would be dealt with immediately."

It was Maven who spoke up, "But if we were in good fighting order, we could battle them on even terms. We would then be able to seize the Nexus," he smiled grimly, "and the heart of the Eternal Empire."

A long silence greeted his words. Zhuana appeared to be thinking, working through what she had learned. "This plan means only Veldrians could go." She hesitated. "I mean no offense, Lord Kendrick, but the pearls would have you raving like madmen."

"I agree, Queen Zhuana," Bethany said. "However there is more to this plan to come. Even seizing the Nexus still leaves Julian and his army unaccounted for . . . " She turned again toward Kendrick.

Kendrick leveled his gaze upon them all. "At the same time that a smaller group takes control of the Nexus, as we were already planning, the rest of our combined forces will ride out to meet Julian's army. The two armies will face each other across the plain . . . "

Zhuana leaned forward, waiting to hear. "And then . . . ?"

"Then, as is tradition, there will be an opportunity for parlay. Tristan and I will ask to meet Julian, but there is no love lost between us, as he well knows. We've thought this through. We'll ask that we meet with Julian along with the lord marshal, Baden Lynch, and Gavin Arturius, the leader of the Reds."

Zhuana frowned. "And if Julian refuses?"

"Our envoy will make his request out loud," Tristan said. "Julian won't spurn his lord marshal, and to tell Arturius to remain where he is, while possible, is unlikely to say the least."

"Very well. Go on."

Kendrick nodded at Tristan. "Along with Tristan, and the Blues whose support we already have, Arturius from the Reds gives all three of the noble orders. We meet at parlay, perhaps to discuss our surrender . . . "

Zhuana was listening intently. "They will want to hear what you have to say . . . "

"And that is when we deliver the news. With your army at our backs, Queen Zhuana, we will announce that we have already seized the Nexus. It is done. The palace has fallen. If there is no new agreement, all of Everlast will soon be under your control."

The druadan were exchanging glances. A few of them began to mutter, until Zhuana held up a hand. "But to have any effect, they have to believe you . . . "

Kendrick nodded. "We are now at the crux of the plan. When we tell them the Nexus has fallen, the empire's leaders will be shocked—and that is when we deliver the final blow. They only have to use their eyes, when you, Queen Zhuana, advance, at the head of your powerful army. When they see what you are wearing: the Crown of Blood and Gold, taken from the Cathedral of the Hidden Source at the Nexus and brought back through the Pillars of Dust, then how can Julian call himself emperor, without a capital, without a palace, and without a crown?"

"Ah," Zhuana said, her eyes lighting up.

Kendrick continued, "Everyone knows that you hold at least three of the empire's gateways. But now things have changed—you have solved a problem no one has solved before you. As a result, not only have you seized the Nexus, but as long as you have a diviner working with you—" he glanced at Bethany, "—all the empire's gateways are yours to use to seize. Why just stop with the Nexus? To them, it won't be just the Nexus that will have fallen, but the entire empire."

"The empire's strength becomes its weakness," Maven said, nodding to himself in satisfaction.

"The other side now has a choice. You can keep the crown as the empire's conqueror. Or they can support a new union. The Veldrians are to be accommodated as citizens of the empire, but other than that, what we want is unity and peace. We will make the empire whole again. All we ask is that Julian—the man who murdered his father and allowed his palace and crown to be taken—is rightfully removed from power."

After finishing, Kendrick and Bethany waited, while the druadan watched Zhuana.

"You will be saying all of this while Julian is right in front of you," Zhuana said. "You cannot expect him to do nothing."

Kendrick answered with confidence. "You have to understand the devastating impact it will have to know that the palace has fallen, along with the Marble Court. And just as critically, the empire's gateways. Even if Julian rages and tries to order the attack, his nobles will realize there is no use fighting anymore. They will be worried about their homes and families. They will be thinking about the empire's future. They will be desperate for a peaceful solution, and we will be the ones to give it to them. I know these people. A lot of them would love a reason to remove Julian from power and make the empire whole. We just have to give it to them."

Zhuana continued to ponder, before turning her attention to Bethany. "This gateway inside the Nexus . . . You have used it before?"

"I can get there, Queen Zhuana, even if I haven't traveled there before."

Zhuana's frown deepened. "But for you to be involved in the palace's capture . . . " She shook her head. "No. The risk to you is too great. There will be fighting from the moment our warriors arrive. Without you, there could be no lasting settlement, no union between us and the empire."

Kendrick raised an eyebrow at Bethany. As they both knew, Zhuana was surely correct about the Veldrians being attacked the moment they stepped through the portal. But there was a simple solution.

"I can hold the portal open. I don't have to leave the gateway to allow your warriors through."

"You can do that?" Zhuana asked.

Bethany nodded. "I can. But we still need the crown—"

"There will be diviners in the Nexus?"

"Yes," Bethany said. "Many."

"Then when we have the crown, another diviner can open the way to the Pillars of Dust."

"Will that work?" Kendrick asked, waiting for Bethany to nod.

Zhuana let out a breath, showing uncharacteristic relief. "Then we have a plan to end this war." She smiled. "Our forces are going to face the Imperials, but we may yet win the day without joining battle. We will take the empire's heart and show it to them. And with not much time to act, we now have work to do. Dan Dresk? I would like to speak with you alone. The rest of you may leave."

✦

Zhuana regarded Maven, who narrowed his eyes as he waited for her to speak.

"We have had our differences, you and I," she said.

"Regrettably, we have."

"What do you make of this plan?"

He sounded surprised. "You want my advice?"

"I want your opinion."

"The plan is sound. Bold but sound. We strike at the empire's heart. We capture their crown and at the same time use it to show them what we have done. We ask for terms and agree to peace, while their leaders see that many others have already joined us."

"I am pleased. It gives me hope that you like it." Zhuana cast her mind back to when Torian Varlish had brought his army to Veldria, and she and Maven had worked together to learn about their enemy. "You are a strong leader and a renowned fighter. The warriors who seize the Nexus . . . I would like them to be led by you."

He frowned as he pretended to consider, even though what she was offering was a valuable prize. He would forever be the man who had captured the emperor's palace and seized his crown. His name would live on in legend.

"We are close to victory. All you must do is seize the crown and deliver it back to me. There is no other I would entrust with this most important task. We have had our disagreements, but something that unites us is that we both remember the way the empire humiliated us. I want you to take this Nexus and their crown. Let no one else near the palace until I am able to enter myself."

He nodded slowly, as she had always known he would. "What will we do about the darkness, Queen Zhuana, once your son is emperor?"

"We will build walls and fight it off, even as we learn more about it. It is the only way to be safe." Even as she spoke, time was running out. "Will you do this, Dan Dresk? Will you save your people in our time of need?"

He stared into her eyes. "I will, My Queen. I will do what you have asked of me, and I will prove that I am worthy of your trust. Others may have failed you, but I will keep take this Nexus, deliver their crown, and keep the palace safe for your arrival."

Chapter Forty-Seven

As MORNING LIGHT CAST LONG SHADOWS in the Fabric District, Xander once again found himself outside the House of Healing. He paced back and forth while clatters came from shuttered shops where workers opened doors and windows for the day ahead. Carts trundled past on the busy road, pulled by teams of snorting and jangling horses. Vendors bellowed from the direction of the nearby market.

Xander frantically scanned the faces of everyone he saw, moving from face to face, from the laborers heading to their workshops or storehouses, to the common people who lived in the area. A skinny woman headed down the street, dragging a reluctant boy. A scowling lady in a crimson gown carried a dress draped over one shoulder. An old man grunted and groaned as he pushed a handcart along by the handles.

Bells had already sounded the hour. Xander clenched and unclenched his fists. He had come to the right place. Charlton . . . where was he? What if something had already happened to him? Xander had no other way to find him than to head to his place of work.

A newcomer drew his attention as he approached from farther up the street. He was a gray-haired older man in a white uniform, and Xander immediately stopped his pacing. Then, becoming certain, he put on speed, until he was almost running. Charlton had the same careworn face, blue eyes, and unruly gray hair. Lost in thought, walking with bowed shoulders, he held a key in his hand as he prepared to open up for the day.

When Charlton saw Xander charging his way, his eyes widened as he braced himself. Xander almost collided into him, grabbing the cleric's upper arm, to move them both until they were closer to the nearest wall.

"What—?"

"You remember me, don't you?"

"Of course—"

"We don't have much time." Xander turned his head to look over both shoulders, checking over the street. "Listen to me carefully. We are both in danger." He lowered his voice, staring into Charlton's face. "Don't speak. Just listen to what I have to say."

It was now Charlton's turn to check the people on the street. "What happened? It's about Bethany, isn't it? Tell me."

Xander's tone was grim. "Some men came to my dormus last night— they were in the emperor's colors, but believe me, these were not nice men. They asked me questions, about how well I know Bethany. In particular, they wanted to know if she had ever mentioned her parents. I said that I knew about her mother, and that her father abandoned her when she was young. That's when they told me . . . If I heard a story, they said, about Bethany, I wasn't to believe it. Not a word of it was true, they said. Then they asked me again if I knew anything special about her. I said no. They told me I wasn't to leave my dormus until they returned, not even to do my work. They wanted to speak with some other people. They said if I was hiding anything, they would find out. When they left, they asked me one last question . . . "

Xander checked the area again. No one gave him or Charlton any special attention. They were just a diviner and a cleric, talking at the side of the street.

Satisfied for the moment, he continued. "To get into the School of Divination, we all had to have a sponsor. They asked me if I knew who Bethany's sponsor was. They would find out for themselves, but it would save them time if I told them."

Charlton's brow was creased with worry.

"I assume it was you?" Xander asked.

Charlton nodded. "Of course."

"I obviously didn't stay in my dormus. I went to see a friend. She's always vague about what she does, but she works at the Nexus, and she knows about everything that's happening in the empire. I asked her if the name Bethany Sylvana meant anything to her. Her reaction told me enough . . . " Xander trailed off. He still couldn't believe it himself.

"Well?" Charlton asked. "What is it?"

"I only just found out . . ." Xander cleared his throat. "Queen Zhuana has found herself a rival, someone to challenge Julian for the crown and bolster her own claim. She plans to marry this woman to her son and install them as emperor and empress. Charlton . . . the woman . . ." Xander broke off, shaking his head, struggling to find the words. "She is a diviner, from Everlast, and her name is Bethany Sylvana."

Charlton's eyes shot wide open as the remaining color drained away from his face.

"Charlton . . . Did you know?" Xander asked. He kept his voice quiet as he searched the older man's face.

"No," Charlton said. "She never told me. I never knew. At the same time . . ." He shook his head. "Stars alive . . . She was always hiding something. But this . . ."

"I was hoping you might be able to tell me I'm going mad."

First Xander had received Bethany's carefully worded message, and then her mother had vanished . . . Nothing though . . . nothing could have prepared him for this. Kendrick Conway had been declared a traitor . . . Bethany was his house diviner . . .

"It's true then?" Xander asked.

"It has to be. Especially after what happened to her mother . . ." Charlton hesitated. "There's something you should know. Maryam's body . . . we found it . . . not far from her compound. I went to the Observatory but they said you were away, and it wasn't something I wanted to put it in a message. Maryam . . . she was a friend. I knew her well. We gave her a decent burial. Everyone pitched in. The people in the Fabric District . . . they know Bethany and her mother . . ."

Xander was desperate to sit down, but all he could do was listen to what Charlton was telling him. He remembered the knocked over mug of tea . . . the blanket with Bethany's name written in childish letters . . .

Bethany had relied on him to get her mother to safety. He hadn't known the truth about the extent of the danger she was in, and he had come as soon as possible, but it didn't change what had happened.

"Xander, listen to me. You can't blame yourself. Trust me . . . that line of thinking will get you nowhere. And as for Bethany, her troubles are far from over."

Xander was still struggling to match the two images. There was the Bethany he knew well, with her intelligence and dedication to her craft, her occasional sweet naiveté and her sense of duty to the people she cared about. And there was the Bethany who was a rival to Julian and might become empress instead, in a union with Queen Zhuana's son, Prince Garric of the Veldrians.

"It's clear now what Julian is doing," Charlton said. "He will do everything he can to bury the truth."

Xander again looked over his shoulder as the sense of urgency returned with force. "You need to leave. We both do. That's why I came. Get out of Everlast and find somewhere to hide. If he did that to her mother . . . Burn it all . . . she is his half-sister . . . "

Bethany had needed him . . . needed his help, and he had failed her. But she had lied to him, the entire time he had known her.

Had she really? At first, they hadn't known each other. What could she have said, that her father was the emperor, and she was his secret child? That one day her older brother might do everything he could to destroy her?

"First you have to tell me something," Charlton said. "What are you going to do now?"

"My friend told me something else . . . I don't know if I should tell you . . . "

"I've had a full life," he said sternly. "I can handle whatever it is."

"There's going to be a battle. A big one. It's going to decide the fate of the empire."

Wherever she was now, Bethany would be frightened. Xander had made his decision, even before he had found the cleric. "I came here to warn you, but I've done that now. After all this . . . I have to go to her. "

"You care about her, Xander?"

He answered without hesitation. "I do."

"I'm no diviner, and I can't do the things you can. But I know healing, and I believe that I know Bethany. We will travel together. Wherever you're heading now, you're going to take me with you."

Chapter Forty-Eight

KENDRICK RODE AT THE LEAD of a broad swathe of armored men on horseback. Hooves thundered on the yellow plain. Heat blazed at an angle from the sun, which was now halfway up the azure sky. Tristan traveled at Kendrick's side as they both stared straight ahead, attention fixed on the horizon in front of them. Together they led the great mass behind them, row after row of horsemen, numbering well over a thousand.

The end was coming. Julian's army had now been sighted. A final conflict loomed but Kendrick planned for it to be one of words, rather than blood and death. In just a few hours, Julian, the man who had killed both his sons, was going to fall. And when an emperor fell, he fell a very, very long way.

After a gap, the Veldrians followed behind. Kendrick's group of knights and men-at-arms was sizable, but he had an entire army in his wake. When Kendrick looked back past his shoulder, the dust cloud made by the Veldrians stretched all the way across his vision.

Through the haze, he could just make out the Pillars of Dust, where some of the distant people were still recognizable. Bethany's familiar figure was in the midst of the pillars, clad in her diviner's cloak and holding her tall staff. Zhuana was saying something, probably issuing some last instructions. A short distance away, Maven Dresk and his hand-picked force of warriors waited to enter the gateway that Bethany was about to open.

Kendrick returned to facing the direction where Julian and the army would appear. He scanned the distant horizon. Gripping his reins tightly, he kept rehearsing the details of their plan, searching for weaknesses. When they heard what Kendrick and Tristan had to say, and when they saw Zhuana wearing the Crown of Blood and Gold, everyone would know the war was over. Their choice would be to fight it out on the plain, to kill and maim and die, or to depose the emperor so many despised.

The decision, he hoped, would be an easy one.

✦

Bethany stood in the middle of the Pillars of Dust, a little apart from everyone else as she closed her eyes and focused on her breathing. As she worked to calm her racing heart, Zhuana spoke nearby.

"Remember," Zhuana said, addressing Maven. "Everything depends on what happens after you go through the gateway. Do this, and you and I will have a fresh start. I will raise you up above all others."

Bethany opened her eyes in time to see Maven's stern face as he nodded. Maven then left the queen to gather his men, assembling hundreds of his handpicked warriors until they were massed within the sand-colored pillars. Maven got them into rows and columns, and then a druid came forward with a flask.

The druid traveled from warrior to warrior, giving each a draught of firewater from the flask. He emptied one flask and then another as he ensured that every man had imbibed a quantity of the liquid.

Maven addressed Bethany. "The pearls. When do we take them?"

She grimly returned his stare. "Now."

Each warrior put a pearl into his mouth and chewed. They all did it together, the large group of warriors, all armored in leather. To have so many, all under the effect of the cactus . . .

"Ready weapons!" Maven growled.

A clatter and multiple snickers filled the air as Maven's warriors drew their swords.

Bethany faced forward, even as her back itched. Behind her were so many men, all ready to commit violence as their vision began to shake and quiver . . .

She was also about to have her familiar battle with Weaver's Breath. And this time, she wasn't going to have docile wards who would follow her every instruction. At least Maven appeared to have them in firm control.

She again met Maven's eyes. "It's now time. Are you ready?"

His pupils were larger than normal, but he nodded. "Ready."

As satisfied as she could be, it was time to prepare her staff. She turned her orb one way and then another until she heard the faint click. Taking another deep breath, she then raised her staff up high.

There could be no turning back now.

She brought the staff's base onto the ground.

The familiar stench of tar washed over her. The onset struck her in a rush. All of a sudden she was light-headed, like she was floating. The world around her began to hum. The hum became a vibration as she connected with the gateway, sensing it resonate along with the tapestry.

Wielding her staff, she brought it up and down, across her body, faster and faster until she was matching the pulsating of the world around her. Her skin tingled. In and out, up and down, everything was moving in increments. The world around her thrummed like the strings on an instrument. The tapestry was ready for her.

She cut her staff down in a slashing stroke. The air in front of her tore open in a flash of light. She used her staff to slice deeper, widening the hole, peeling it apart, lengthening and shaping until she was standing in front of a glistening black doorway.

The portal in front of her flickered and shone, like polished black glass.

"Stay with me," she called. They all had their instructions, but she was going to have to manage a large group of fighting men, all with blood high, ready for battle. "This is it. You know what to do. Follow me!"

She took a step into the doorway.

Shift.

Darkness enveloped her, broken up by glimmering points of starlight that shot past her at terrible speed. She walked on the path of stars, trying to ignore the trails of light darting past her on both sides, above her and below her feet. Maven and his warriors came with her, staring around themselves in awestruck wonder.

With the Weaver's Breath holding her tightly in its grip, she fought to keep her focus. Breathe in. Breathe out. It was so strange, so different, to have people who were alert here with her. Even as she walked forward to create space on the ethereal road, more warriors kept coming up behind her. Soon she was at the lead of a column of Veldrians in leather armor, swords bared as they exchanged wide-eyed glances. Still more of them came from behind the group.

"What is this place?" Maven asked.

She checked once more behind her to see that all the warriors had entered. She twisted her staff and closed the gateway at the Pillars of Dust.

Maven was craning his neck to look in all directions. "This is what you call the tapestry?"

"The tapestry is always with us," she said. "We're just experiencing a different view of it. I need to concentrate now." She called back, "Stay with me as I walk."

It took some effort, but she calmed her racing heart, while the flying stars slowed as she maneuvered her staff. She imagined the sky above Everlast . . . where the stars would be, along with the objects in the sky above. She had never traveled to the Portal of Polaris. But she knew Everlast well, and there were only small adjustments to make compared with the Crystal Dome.

She continued to walk, using her staff to alter what she was seeing. She paused; she needed to make a slight shift. There. At last, she studied the black expanse around her, the constellations, the planets, the moon.

"I am now going to open the gateway!" She called back as loudly as she could. "Be ready!"

"You heard her!" Maven called. "You know the plan! I want a defensive ring around the gateway. We are taking the empire's heart. Our names will live on in legend!"

Bethany brought her staff up. She stared up at the metal orb at the top as her heart gave loud, thumping beats. With both hands, she sliced the orb at the darkness in front of her. As soon as she had made her first opening, urgency fired through her; anyone on the other side would be able to see what she was doing. She swiftly turned the gash into a portal, holding the gateway open. She took a long step to the side.

"Go!" she cried.

"Men! With me!"

Without hesitation, Maven jumped through. Warrior after warrior streamed past to leave through the portal and follow him, knowing that they needed to gain the swift advantage of numbers.

Bethany was able to see through the doorway she had opened. The Portal of Polaris was different from most other gateways. Most were in the open, but the gateway that served the Nexus was buried in an underground chamber. Dozens of broad stone columns, each the size of a mighty tree, supported the stone ceiling. The floor was arranged in a series of tiers, with the portal on the lowest of all, in an open space that made it the focus of the area.

Maven and his warriors fanned out. The Veldrians with bows had arrows fitted to strings as they searched for something to aim at. Others held swords out in front of them.

One fact was obvious right away. There were no guards, nor any other people at all. She heard sounds of surprise from the Veldrians.

"I expected it to be guarded," one man said.

"Why guard it when no one would be foolish enough to come?"

Maven called out. "You all know what to do. We find the cathedral first . . ."

Bethany couldn't remain in place; she had to return. She twisted her staff to close the gateway. Immediately the view through the portal vanished, to be replaced by a starry black void. Once again she walked on the path of stars, and at the same time, she maneuvered the world around her, working until she had positioned herself to emerge at the Pillars of Dust.

Her head was pulsing, this time with the pain of a headache. Steeling herself, raising her staff, she grunted and sliced opened the gateway. She formed the opening into a door, and stood in front of a shining rectangular mirror.

She took a deep breath and stepped out.

Shift.

Immediate heat pushed into her from the yellow sun that hung in the morning sky. The light was bright and blinding. Dry air pressed up against her skin. With another movement of her staff, she closed the gateway behind her.

And then it was done, and she stood panting after her efforts.

Zhuana stood alone within the circle of pillars, waiting for her return. "Well?"

"It is done."

"Excellent. Now come, Bethany. Julian is with his army on the plain, and we must be there to meet him, crown or no crown. This is your destiny as much as mine. Let us now ride together."

Chapter Forty-Nine

XANDER STEPPED THROUGH THE PORTAL he had just opened in the Pillars of Dust. The change of environment was jarring. Savage heat from a fiery sun shone down upon him as he found himself in a dry desert landscape completely devoid of plants. With Charlton just behind him, he closed the gateway, even as he became aware of a number of bowmen with arrows drawn to their cheeks, ready to let them fly. From their leather armor and tattoos, they could only be Veldrians, tasking with guarding the gateway.

"Wait!" he cried.

He raised his staff high to display the length of white cloth tied around it. The archers paused, and time passed with heart-wrenching slowness. Meanwhile Xander braced for the worst.

Charlton stood dazed and uncomprehending as he recovered from the journey. Other than Xander's staff, neither of them carried a weapon. Surely the Veldrians would give them a chance to talk?

"What is it you want?" The Veldrian who spoke had long black hair tied back behind his head. He didn't lower his bow.

"We are friends of Bethany Sylvana," Xander said. "I need to know where she is. It is very important that we find her. Please. Bethany Sylvana. Where is she?"

"Gone," the Veldrian said flatly.

"Gone where?"

"With the army."

The Veldrian lowered his bow, and his companions slowly followed, one by one, until Xander's stomach muscles relaxed. The long-haired bowman then nodded toward something in the distance.

Xander warily climbed to higher ground in the direction indicated. He shielded his eyes, and then he saw it: an immense cloud of dust, spreading out across the landscape.

"Xander . . ." Charlton spoke in a soft voice. The cleric was coming up to join him, and after the travel, it was taking an effort for him to talk. For a time he looked toward the dust cloud. "What is happening?"

"Horses." Xander called out to the long-haired Veldrian. "We need horses."

"No."

Xander reached into the pouch he wore by his belt. He grabbed a handful of coins and opened his palm to display them. "I can give you money. Silver."

The long-haired bowman stared hard at the silver coins, thinking and scratching his chin. He then nodded. "Good." He put his fingers to his mouth and whistled, and soon a boy came their way, leading a pair of horses.

✦

The Veldrian army maintained position. Numbered in the tens of thousands, the vast collection of riders made a great milling mass, an immense host of warriors waiting on horseback. Meanwhile, in multiple rows of knights and men-at-arms, the rebels had also formed up. A cleared space, a stone's throw in distance, separated the two groups, with Veldrians behind and rebels in front.

Bethany rode with Zhuana alongside the Veldrian army. They both had their attention on the horizon, where another dust cloud was approaching: the Imperials led by Julian.

A frantic cry made Bethany look over her shoulder, back the way she had come.

Zhuana's head turned as well. As the shouts became louder, two riders appeared out of the haze, one clad in white, the other in a gray cloak, both working hard to catch up to her. At first the words were indistinct, carried away on the wind, but then the subsequent shouts were clear.

"Bethany! Wait!"

The pair of riders grew larger, and then Bethany's mouth dropped open. No. It couldn't be. For a moment she forgot all about Zhuana, and Julian, and the desperate plan to remove him from power.

One of the riders was Charlton, dressed in his cleric's uniform, with disheveled gray hair, blue eyes, and wrinkles. The second man was tall, with black hair all the way to his collar, a wide mouth, sharp features, and a diviner's cloak worn over his tunic and trousers.

The sight was strange . . . impossible. At the same time, a powerful feeling of relief washed over her to see them alive and well. Neither Charlton nor Xander appeared harmed in any way. Without conscious thought, she was already sawing at her reins to turn her horse around.

Zhuana's face was cold. "Bethany? Who are these people?"

"My friends," she replied. "I have to talk to them."

"You know how important this is." With great dexterity, Zhuana pulled at her own reins and drew her horse to a sudden halt. "Be quick. I will remain here. Do what you must to be rid of them."

Bethany finished wheeling her horse to meet Xander and Charlton. They both reined in and she did the same. For a time they all stared at each other. She was smiling, but then gradually her smile fell away.

"What are you doing here?" she asked. They were alive and well, but they shouldn't have come here, to this place. They should be anywhere else.

"We've come to ask you the same thing," Xander said. "By all the stars alive . . . what are you doing, Bethany?"

A short distance away, Zhuana's horse was pawing at the ground as the queen waited impatiently. "I have to go with her. Both of you need to leave."

"Bethany, why?" Charlton asked quietly. He met her eyes with gentle but worried expression. Great Weaver, she had missed him . . . missed him and his constant kindness. "You are planning to be in a battle?"

"You have to trust me. There isn't going to be a battle. We can end this war. We're going to bring about a lasting peace."

Xander nudged his horse closer, so that his position was right next to hers. "Are you sure this is what you want? Are these the people you belong with? This prince . . . do you even know him?"

When she didn't reply, Charlton spoke up, "What you are doing is dangerous. Please, Bethany . . . think about your life ahead. I know you. You're not an empress. You're a diviner. That's what you always wanted."

"We can go somewhere else, together," Xander said. "All you have to do is come with us. With me."

She shook her head. "If you know anything about me then you'll know that I can't simply leave. I have to see this through."

Charlton hesitated. "Your mother—"

"He killed her. I know."

"Very well. Then I understand why you want to stop him. I buried her, Bethany. Believe me, I know. But what would your mother want for you? Are you sure this is worth your life?"

Bethany's throat caught, but she remained firm. "Yes. It is."

Xander was staring straight at her. There was pain in his deep brown eyes. She remembered the lake and their kiss . . . their shared laughter at the fielding . . .

Charlton glanced at Xander. "Then we can only be here to support you."

"No." She frowned. "I don't want either of you here. I don't have a choice. But you do. Both of you. You need to go."

"I'm not leaving," Xander said. He didn't take his eyes off her. "I know you and what you want, even if you don't know yourself." He raised his staff. "This is what you want. I'm not going, Bethany. Not until you've convinced me you want this other life instead. And at the moment, that's something you haven't done."

"You can't get rid of us that easily." Charlton managed a smile. "You should know better. That isn't what good friends do."

Bethany didn't know what to do. She had tried so hard to separate her two lives. She had wanted to protect these people from who she was— even when she asked Xander for help in her message, she had done everything she could to hide the truth and to explain as little as possible.

"Go," she snapped. "Both of you. I told you. I don't want you here. Leave the way you came."

She dug her heels hard into the flanks of her horse, turning her mount to head back over to Zhuana. But as she and the queen resumed their journey, she looked back over her shoulder, and her heart sank.

Xander and Charlton were still following.

✦

Kendrick sat astride his warhorse. The animal stirred but he kept his reins pulled tight, holding them with white knuckles. He stared straight ahead and couldn't stop dwelling on the same thought, over and over again.

Everything came down to this moment. The empire's fate would be decided by what happened next. Along with the empire's fate, that of his wife, his daughter, his friends, his home . . .

Two armies had gathered. As a rising hot breeze blew across the yellowed dirt and gravel, horses whinnied, leather strained, buckles clinked, and armor groaned.

A long distance separated Kendrick's wide formation of riders from the Imperial army in front of them. Nonetheless, Kendrick was able to take in the great number of mounted soldiers on the other side. Without Zhuana's support, he would never dream of facing the force in front of him. His greatest fear now was that fighting would break out before talks could begin—even with the Veldrians behind him, it was impossible to say who the victor would be. He would be forced to battle his former comrades, against his fellow noblemen and their sons, against men who were only following orders.

From horseback at his left hand, Tristan spoke up, "Any word about the crown? The time is now upon us."

"Not yet," Kendrick replied.

He turned, searching for Bethany. Everything depended upon her skill and how she had fared with the Nexus. He struggled to swallow his tension, and as the moments passed, the rising heat was fraying his nerves. He watched hard, scanning for movement, for anyone riding rather than remaining still.

There. He let out a breath. There was Bethany on her horse, riding alongside the army, heading straight toward him. He then spied two mounted men following her: a tall diviner with black hair, and an older man with a mop of gray hair, a cleric from his white uniform.

Bethany gave him a determined nod, which did a little to ease the tension in his shoulders. It appeared that there hadn't been any problems with her plan to travel to the Nexus.

"It worked? They got in?" he asked as soon as she was near.

She reined in, her horse snorting, blowing hard after her ride in the heat. "The Veldrians are in the Nexus. It won't be long now. The queen is with her army, ready and waiting."

As the two other riders pulled up behind her, Kendrick raised an eyebrow. "And they are?"

"My two friends . . . the ones I told you about."

She had barely finished speaking when a trumpet blasted from the other army.

"We can't wait any longer," Tristan said, resting his gaze on Kendrick. Without waiting for a reply, he opened his mouth to bellow "Envoy!"

The formation parted to allow a young rider to approach. With sandy-colored hair and a determined cast to his face, the envoy held his chin high as he waited for his orders. Rather than a lance or sword, he carried a flag on a pole, gold in color, with a three-pointed star in its center. The colors of the three points represented the three orders: black, red, and blue.

"You know what to do," Kendrick instructed the envoy. "Offer the other side an opportunity to talk. I want Baden Lynch present, as well as Gavin Arturius. No one is to be armed. Everyone is to meet on foot."

The young man nodded sharply. "I will do as you command, My Lord."

The envoy spurred on his mount, heading alone at a gallop toward the distant Imperial army. Kendrick tracked him with his eyes, still clutching his reins tightly.

Julian could refuse to engage. He might order an immediate attack. If Julian wanted to meet with Kendrick alone, Kendrick would have to say no, for he needed to speak past Julian, to Baden Lynch and Gavin Arturius.

Time passed. The sun climbed as the day's heat became increasingly fierce. Kendrick blinked sweat out of his eyes.

He shielded his eyes. There. Finally. At last the envoy was returning, coming in fast. Soon the young soldier's was pulling up, breathing hard after his hurried ride.

"My Lords—" he panted.

"What did he say?" Kendrick demanded.

"He agrees to the meeting. But there are conditions . . . " The envoy broke off, struggling to regain his breath. "My Lord," he addressed Tristan, "he says he understands you and Lord Conway to speak with one voice. He asks that you remain here."

Kendrick and Tristan exchanged glances.

"Also," the envoy continued, "he says that you may be leading your rebellion, My Lord, but it is another who wants to be empress. He insists that she must be present too."

"No," Kendrick said. "Impossible—"

"Wait," Tristan interrupted, returning to the envoy. "He agreed to the rest? Lynch will be with him? And Arturius?"

"Yes, My Lord. They both said so, to my face."

It was Bethany who spoke up. "I want to be there." Seeing Kendrick's scowl, she held his gaze. "I want to see his face when he realizes he's lost everything."

"Remember, Kendrick . . ." Tristan said. "Julian may suspect a trap. A man in your position would be out for blood. This gives us what we want."

Kendrick scratched his chin. "But the trap could be laid for us. Julian . . . Lynch . . . Arturius. Three strong men, even without weapons."

"What do you suggest? We can't keep asking to increase our relative strength."

A throat cleared as the older cleric, the man with the graying hair, spoke up, "May I make a suggestion, My Lord?"

"Go on."

"My diviner friend and I could come with you. A diviner and a cleric wouldn't pose much of a threat. But I promise you that if there is trouble, we will make sure that Bethany gets away in one piece."

"You would do that?" Kendrick addressed both the cleric and the diviner.

"Wait—" Bethany attempted to interject.

"Yes, My Lord," the black-haired young man replied. "We would."

Kendrick gave a reluctant nod. "Very well then. Go and tell them," he instructed the young envoy. "I assume they won't have any problems."

The envoy departed again, just as swiftly as before. The searing wind picked up as they waited. Fortunately it wasn't long before the young soldier was once again pulling up in front of Kendrick.

"It is agreed, My Lord."

Kendrick glanced at Tristan. "Well, this is it."

"Well then. I suppose it is." Tristan reached out to offer his hand. "I know we are past shaking hands, brother, but today it seems somewhat called for. Good luck. May the fates be kind."

As Kendrick took his companion's hand, he remembered visiting the House of the Wardens in Everlast and discussing the vote and the fielding, and sharing stories of campaigning in days gone by. Stars alive . . . so much had happened since.

"Remember, Kendrick, our side holds the Nexus. In the beginning, that is all they need to know. We offer peace and a unified empire. All Julian offers is war."

Kendrick nodded grimly. He stood up in his stirrups, turning to address the formation of knights and followers. "I go now to bring peace and unity to our empire. Upon my return, you will know that our work here is done. May the fates smile kindly on us all!"

Loud cheers in unison greeted his words. After sinking back into his saddle, he nodded at Bethany and her two companions. "Dismount. We will be walking out to meet them."

Kendrick's sword was in the scabbard by his saddle, and so he was clad in armor but without a weapon as he dismounted. He checked on his companions, and together they began to walk. They made a strange group: an aging fighter, two young diviners, and a careworn cleric. Bethany and her black-haired companion both carried their staffs. Kendrick led from the front.

Out of the haze, the Imperial army became sharper, more distinct. Individual men on horses stirred but maintained position, armored riders lined up side by side in a similar arrangement to the group he had left behind.

Deciding he was about halfway between the two forces, Kendrick came to a halt.

Up ahead, three men were approaching. Kendrick checked quickly, but as agreed, none of the trio were armed.

All of a sudden, Kendrick only had eyes for the man in the center, clad in glistening armor and a white cloak, his golden hair shining in the sun. There was nothing Kendrick could do to slow his heart, which was pounding with loud, steady, thumps. More than anything, he wanted this man dead. He wanted him to suffer, and to suffer more than any man before him.

As Julian approached, his gaze was on Kendrick in turn, a gleam in his eye and an upward curve on his lips. Then Julian's head turned, and his eyes lit up—he was now watching Bethany, the cause of so much trouble.

Kendrick could guess what he was thinking. Julian's expression was confident. If Kendrick wanted to talk, what else was there to talk about, other than the terms of surrender?

Everyone stopped walking. For a long time there was only silence.

Kendrick faced Julian, and all of his raw emotion took hold of his heart. He remembered Declan's tortured face, and Caden's body swinging back and forth on the rope. He again heard the sounds . . . the creaking of the ropes and branches.

He saw Troy's crumpled figure on the ground. He had a vision of Bethany kneeling on the ground, holding a bloody black cane in her hands.

He was desperate to see Julian humbled. When it was all over, there could be only one final end. Julian's head would soon be leaving his shoulders.

Kendrick opened his mouth, but it was Julian who spoke first.

"Your plot has failed. The Nexus is safe." He glanced at Bethany. "As is my rightful crown. You have lost, traitors. And now all of you are going to die."

Kendrick's world came crashing down around him.

315

Chapter Fifty

THE UNDERGROUND CHAMBER WAS COLD, a place of dim light and dark shadows. Stone made up the featureless walls, the high ceiling, and the floor formed in concentric tiers. From the vast room's layout, it was designed to focus all attention down on the rectangular doorway, where Maven and his men had emerged after their journey from the Pillars of Dust.

Faced toward the climbing tiers, Maven's face was impassive, but as he scanned the area, he was awestruck at what he was seeing. The upright stone columns appeared like a forest of broad gray cylinders. The only light came from flickering torches on poles, placed on either side of the Portal of Polaris's stone frame, lending the area a garish uncertain glow.

Maven had traveled to Engel, Narzin, and Meroy, but even their governor's residences and villas had nothing that rivaled this vaulted chamber for sheer mystery and grandeur.

Zhuana had been generous indeed to entrust him with this task. Generous, or perhaps foolish; the answer depended on what happened in the coming days. He would fetch the crown, as agreed, and get it swiftly back to the queen. But once he and his hand-picked men held the Nexus, he would have an opportunity to take control of the empire, and what happened next would be largely up to him.

The lack of guards was strange . . . against everything he had been told to expect. He was an experienced warrior and leader, and he knew enough to be wary.

"Stay together," he said in a low voice. "We have arrived and we now hold the gateway. Together, on my mark, we will move to the first set of columns."

Holding his sword out in front of him, he lifted his gaze. There was supposed to be a door at the back of the space, but he had yet to see it. After arriving, his men were packed tightly together.

"What was that?" a warrior hissed nearby.

"Hear that sound?"

"Wait," Maven instructed. "Listen . . . " he trailed off.

The sound was now audible to everyone. It was a repetitive crunching, growing louder with each passing moment. Soon Maven knew what he was hearing . . . the heavy sound of footsteps, the noise made by many men marching together. The regular thump and clunk of soldiers in heavy armor surely couldn't be a coincidence.

As soon as he had the thought, Maven's blood ran cold.

Around him, his men were exchanging fearful glances. What had been a strength now became a weakness. Maven had hundreds of his warriors, all in a close, tight group. The small force of guards he had expected to overwhelm was entirely absent. Instead they were trapped, rats stuck at the back of a nest, as their captors poured hot oil inside . . .

There was only one answer he could see. As he continued searching the area, eyes roving, part of him reluctantly admired her. She had waited her moment. By the Mother, how she had waited. She had used him when she could, outmaneuvered him when she couldn't. And then, when the time was right, that cold-blooded woman had betrayed him.

A boom accompanied a burst of daylight as a door opened somewhere at the far end of the vaulted space.

"Men!" Maven roared. "Swords up! Be ready! This is a trap. Prepare to fight for your lives."

Looking up over the rising tiers of the floor, Maven tried to see what was happening. He blinked, trying to dispel the effects of the cactus pearls. He had been confident, expecting an easy fight against unsuspecting opponents. Now he had to give his all and fight at his very best, or he was going to die.

And then something terrible happened, as archers stepped out from behind the stone columns.

In matching Imperial uniforms, armored in chain mail that left just their faces showing, they already had bowstrings drawn to their cheeks. More of them kept appearing, bows already drawn, arrows already pointed. The stone columns made for perfect hiding places.

"They're already here—" a warrior screamed.

In one great volley, the archers loosed, cutting off the man's cry. More arrows slammed into Maven's warriors as the Imperials bent back their bows, selecting their targets at will. Warrior after warrior convulsed when arrows appeared in their bodies. The Veldrians in front tried to turn back and flee, so that the next arrows struck between their shoulder blades. They swarmed against Maven and knocked him down. One of his men collapsed on top of him. Another followed. And then another.

Bowstrings kept snapping and arrows thunked as they struck flesh. Maven found himself under a pile of bodies. Gritting his teeth, he held his breath. There was a chance that he might still survive this.

After all the creaking of bows, the thrumming of strings, the grunting and screaming of dying men, the aftermath was strangely silent.

He stared up, into the fabric covering a Veldrian's torso, wondering what was happening. He had a young man's face in the other direction. The warrior eyes were sightless. Blood seeped from the side of his mouth.

"We still haven't found the bald one, the one with the broken nose," a crisp voice called. "Keep searching until you find him."

The bodies shifted. Maven still clutched the hilt of his sword, but when he tried to move his sword arm, he was pinned down, completely unable to move. A patch of light appeared as a body moved away. Another dead man followed suit.

"I've found him!"

Maven stared grimly up at at an Imperial guardsman, a blond, square-jawed soldier with a triumphant look in his face. The guardsman showed something to Maven: a sharp dagger, the blade glinting in the torchlight that was also reflected in his eyes.

There was nothing Maven could do. He struggled under the weight of the bodies.

"Queen Zhuana sends her regards," the soldier said. "She says to tell you that this is for Barrix."

The soldier reached forward and punched his blade into Maven's throat. At first, Maven felt nothing. But then, as he tried to breathe, liquid instead filled his mouth; he couldn't even wrap his hands around his throat, no matter how much he wanted to.

All that came from his mouth was a gurgle, the last sound he heard as he died.

✦

"You have lost, traitors," Julian said. "And now all of you are going to die."

For a moment, Kendrick stood in shock. What could have gone wrong? Everything had gone to plan.

He had been about to tell Julian the Nexus had fallen. He was about to explain about Zhuana's newfound ability to use the gateways. Zhuana would ride up, wearing the Crown of Blood and Gold. It was Julian who was supposed to fall.

Julian smiled; he looked like he was enjoying himself. "You are wondering why . . . how . . . The fact is, I had a wife, but she betrayed me." His expression changed, becoming bitter. "I was telling the truth, Kendrick. I played no part in my father's death. He was my father. It wasn't me. It was all her." With obvious effort, he calmed himself. "At any rate, after ridding myself of Samara I became an emperor without an empress. And then, just like that, my new wife made me an overture. She is not just any woman, she is Zhuana, Queen of the Veldrians. You see, she possesses many attributes, among them beauty, but also wisdom. Your plan was always foolish. She came to me and here we are. We will welcome her people into our empire. She will be empress at my side and her son will succeed after me. Our enemies will all be crushed. And after your fall, Kendrick, you will have your wish granted, for our empire will be whole once again."

Kendrick looked at Baden Lynch and Gavin Arturius, but they stared straight ahead rather than meet his eyes, and both remained stony-faced and silent. He turned, hearing a rumble; something was happening behind him.

The Veldrian army was distant, but it was getting closer, bringing with it the thunder and dust of its approach. Compared to the two armies, one in front of Kendrick, the other behind, his thousand rebels were like grains at a mill, ready to be squeezed between two blocks of stone. They were outmaneuvered. Their numbers were tiny compared with those arrayed against them.

Zhuana had betrayed them all.

Julian was right. Kendrick was going to lose everything he had ever cared about. He had lost both of his sons, and now he had lost his wife, his daughter, and his home. The life he had enjoyed with his family was gone forever. His plan had failed. He was now going to lose his life.

Sensing the change, Tristan and his long line of riders attempted to turn to face the Veldrians. But the Veldrians were at their backs, close enough to pose an immediate mortal threat. Kendrick heard a panicked cry, and then another, from the direction of the friends and allies he had left behind.

The Veldrians were archers. Their powerful bows fired quicker than any Imperial-made weapon. Kendrick heard Tristan's bellow. Tristan and his knights drew swords. But even as they did, countless arrows filled the air; at such a short distance, the sharp arrowheads would pierce the strongest armor. Kendrick's allies fell. Holes in the formation appeared with horrific frequency. Horses screamed. Rolling animals thrashed upon the ground. Another hail of arrows flew from the Veldrians. More than half of the knights and men-at-arms were down. Gaps appeared, gaps that widened as more and more horsemen fell. A final cluster remained, and then there were none; they were all just bloody lumps on the ground.

Tristan was gone. Kendrick's old friend had stood with him in his time of need. And now he was dead.

Kendrick's eyes were stinging; water blurred his vision. He couldn't breathe. His chest was tight, squeezing so hard it hurt.

In front of him, Julian turned his head to stare coldly at Bethany, "Goodbye, half-sister," he said. "This is your end too. I could take you all prisoner, but it is going to be cleaner this way. Be sure to give my regards to your mother."

Chapter Fifty-One

THOUGHTS CYCLED OVER AND OVER in Bethany's mind. Along with the thoughts came images. The images brought emotions.

Her mother, singing as she carried buttered flatbreads from the market into their dormus . . . Her mother, blind, beaten to death with her own cane . . . Charlton's sad blue eyes as he told her that he had buried her. Julian's cold smile . . .

Kendrick at his manor, issuing instructions to his family, working hard for the fielding to come . . . His despair as he held Caden's body in his arms . . . His hollowed stare into the flames of a campfire after Troy was taken as well . . . His stunned expression when he saw her father's legacy, written in such neat letters . . .

Xander's kindness as he taught her about the Eidar, and all the other things she didn't know . . . His arms wrapped around her as they waited under the Crystal Dome for Carina to reappear . . . The heat of their kiss by the lake . . . His raw expression as he told her wasn't going to leave her . . .

Charlton's stern admonishment that the books he was giving her were hers; they were a gift . . . His grave face as he promised to take care of her mother . . . His look of astonished pleasure as he saw her for the first time in the clothing of a diviner . . .

With every passing second, every part of a second, every part of a part, she knew that she had lost. All of her pain, all of her joy, it no longer mattered anymore.

The effects of her recent travel to the Nexus were still with her. Time slowed until each thought was in its own tiny space. As well as the world of words and power, of hatred and injustice, she could still sense the vibrations of the tapestry. The reality of her situation sank in, and her emotions pulsed along with the ground beneath her feet. She felt like a blood-soaked cloth, being squeezed dry in a strong fist, over and over again.

Zhuana had betrayed them all. This shouldn't be happening but it was. It wasn't just Kendrick here with her, but Xander and Charlton too. Everyone she loved was trapped, about to be crushed between two unstoppable forces. They would be peppered by arrows, sliced by sharp blades into gruesome pieces. There was no way to survive what was coming; they were all about to be killed.

She had been toyed with, played like the fool she was. Charlton's words were still with her. She was a diviner, not an empress. He knew her better than she knew herself.

Time was space and space was time . . . that was what the diviners always said. Now, it was as if time had nearly stopped altogether. The wind that fluttered at hair and clothing did so in slow, noticeable movements. The bright sun hung in the cloudless sky, completely frozen in place. Julian was staring at her, the curve of a smile on his lips, which were moving imperceptibly slowly. Kendrick looked utterly grief-stricken. Charlton had his hand clasped around the chain he wore at his neck, with the wedding band on his finger visible as he held the locket containing his dead daughter's hair. Xander was turned toward her, revealing his deep brown eyes, but they were panicked, showing too much of their whites.

Her emotions pulsed along with the tapestry's vibrations. In comparison, each heartbeat was eternally distant from the next. Where was the humming coming from? She was on a flat plain. There was nothing sizable around her—no monoliths or statues, no mountains, rocks, or temples. Instead, as had happened before, she could feel the pulses given off by people.

Julian, her half-brother. Kendrick, her protector. Charlton, her mentor. Xander, her friend.. her confidante . . . perhaps her lover.

How had it come to this? She cast her mind back to her assessment at Speaker's Corner, as the director sternly addressed all the gathered people: *Time is everything. It is the great unstoppable force. Time is space and space is time. You cannot travel through the gateways and have others entrust their lives to you without an understanding of time.*

But what *was* time, and where was space? If they were the same thing, then how did events happen one after the other? And if space could be manipulated, as traveling the gateways implied, what did that mean for time? There was also the perception of time. Right now it was moving incredibly slowly, but soon it would speed up, and quicken, and Julian would give his orders, and she would die.

There was a moment when she had felt close to reaching some kind of new understanding. Back then, she and Xander had been together by the lake, standing together at the water's edge. She had been so excited to be discussing the things she thought about late into the night. She hadn't realized then that he had probably been thinking about something other than the mysteries surrounding their art. She closed her eyes, experiencing the memory in barely any time at all, as she heard her own excited voice.

"What if gateways are just there to help us? To make something difficult a lot more achievable? If we can orientate our position ourselves . . . if we can sense the passage of time, and know the season and the stars and the exact location of our world compared to the sun . . . if we can warp the tapestry not by weight, but by the fact that we have agency, and we are living creatures who all have an outsized effect on the world around us. Maybe then . . . maybe we wouldn't need gateways at all . . . "

After smelling the fresh, fragrant air by the lake, and Xander's warmer, muskier scent, she opened her eyes.

She was abruptly back in the present. The wind was blowing harder on her skin. The sun beat down from above. Julian had just finished speaking.

Staff in hand, she stepped forward. Facing Julian in front of her, her position was protective, with Kendrick, Charlton, and Xander a little behind her.

She reached into her pocket and her fingers found an object: the cactus pearl, still in the same place she had left it. She wrapped her hand around it and then lifted it to put it into her mouth.

"Have you come to beg, Bethany?" Julian asked.

She didn't answer. Instead, she chewed and swallowed, and as she stared directly at him, she thought about everything she had learned. A young girl witnessing a demonstration at the Argent Arch had developed a dream. A worker in a shop in the Fabric District had tested for divination school. An emperor's forgotten daughter had shown she could graduate with no help from anyone else. She had been captured and escaped, endured suffering but survived. She had challenged established ideas. The diviners didn't know the truth. They didn't even understand the gateways.

She could sense Charlton without looking at him. He was sad but stoic; steadiness was always his way. Charlton, her champion and supporter, her mentor, the man she owed so much to.

Kendrick's aura was strong; his emotions were so dark she could point to his exact position. He had said that as long as she was his house diviner, she was a part of his family. He was responsible for her. No harm would come to her as long as she was under his protection. His despair came off him in waves. He had failed his family. He had failed her. He had failed himself.

Xander was horrified about what might happen next. Here they were, in front of an army led by an emperor who wanted them dead. She knew he cared about her, but what she felt pouring from him was so much stronger. Why had he never told her?

And then there was Julian.

She remembered him accosting her, challenging her, sneering at her as she waited outside their father's chambers. She saw him at the fielding, stunned as he accepted the oath of fealty, still in shock from their father's death. She heard his sinister, playful tone when he mentioned her joining her mother.

Julian was hurting so much that all he could do was cause pain in others in an attempt to make himself feel better. He would continue until someone stopped him.

And yet they also had a connection.

Time had slowed. But then it sped back up again.

She raised her staff into the air. She slammed it down. Hard.

She tasted Weaver's Breath in her nostrils. The full force of the pearl slammed into her at the same time. Trusting her instincts, she whirled her staff. Part of her was already in the stars. Another was conscious of the vibrations emanating from all the people, but especially the three people behind her: Kendrick, Charlton, and Xander. It was this connection that she focused on and held onto, finding the correct rhythm with her staff, the hum and vibration that made each person unique and connected to her.

Finally she remembered.

She saw herself standing on a beach, under a glorious golden sky. In her view were strange trees, of a kind she didn't recognize, with long spiky fronds and brown nuts the size of a boy's head. The trees swayed to a balmy breeze. Sand was beneath her feet and warm water was above her shoes, soaking them through. A piece of seaweed wrapped itself around her ankle.

The place she had left was in darkness. The stars had been crying. But then she had seen the naked truth for the first time, and gone to open a doorway to a new place, so far away that it was in daylight and the feel of the sun upon her skin was like nothing she had felt before. It was with a sense of sad longing that she had gone back into her mirrored doorway, to re-enter the path of stars and return to her bedchamber in the villa in Narzin.

This wasn't the first time she had done this.

The part of her standing on the plain saw Julian begin to retreat, watching as he stepped backward without turning around. He stuck his arm straight up into the air. She heard him bellow. "Archers!"

The same part of her heard a multitude of creaking bows.

She sliced at the air, at the same time making a loud cry.

There was no time. This was the end of time.

Directly in front of her, her gateway peeled open.

Kendrick shouted something. She yanked her staff backward, twirling it at the same time. She widened the hole until it was as big as she could make it, and then she pulled the black mirrored surface toward her.

The gateway swallowed them all up: her, Kendrick, Charlton, and Xander.

And then it closed behind them.

Chapter Fifty-Two

JULIAN MALVENTUS LIVIUS and Zhuana Arianus Livius stood together, under the span of the Argent Arch, waving to the immense crowd that spread in all directions, filling not just Imperial Avenue but a dozen other streets. They turned as they waved, and each time they did, another rolling cacophony of powerful cheers enveloped the Imperial capital.

Fluttering color filled Julian's vision. Flags streamed from every tower in sight. Gold and purple banners decorated Imperial Avenue, the main colonnade that led to the broad gates of the Nexus. The immense arch, made of marble and granite, stood high and proud on its hill, placing him and his new empress always in view.

The wedding was done. The agreements were signed. The assembly had cast its votes and they had passed—not that there would be any dissent, with such a powerful emperor to oversee the proceedings.

Julian's marriage to Zhuana was one for the stories. He wore the Crown of Blood and Gold, and she wore a new crown that she had designed, also set with rubies—they were already calling it the Crown of Fire.

"The people are joyful, are they not?" Julian asked.

"There is food and ale on every corner. There is peace. Of course they are joyful." Zhuana paused, to regard him with the unsettling stare she sometimes gave him. She looked beautiful in her purple and gold dress . . . beautiful, stern, and frightening. "Julian . . . "

He didn't like her tone. "What?"

"Before the day is done, there are things that we must discuss . . . more preparations that we need to make."

"Can it wait?"

"No. It cannot."

"Your son will be heir. It is all agreed."

"That is not what I wish to speak about. And I think that you know this."

"Then what?" He turned again, waving in a different direction. "Can we not enjoy this moment?"

"I have not yet saved my people."

"I disagree. I would say that you have."

"No. There is still work to be done. This darkness . . . It is not enough to keep it away. We also need to understand it."

Julian continued to smile, but his mouth was straining. "You are going to be a strong empress. I can tell."

She smiled, revealing a glint in her eyes. "If you keep your wife happy, your life will be the same. Be sure that you never forget it."

✦

Isabelle played in the water gardens, chasing a ginger cat as the agile creature raced along the stone paths. Skipping past one pond and then another, each filled with lily pads and rainbow fish, she tried to snatch the cat as it dashed down some stone steps to vanish behind a collection of statues.

The isle of Ormont was warm and humid, with ferns and exotic flowers draping over bubbling streams where water trickled and pooled. Swimming in the sea was like taking a bath. Nights were balmy. Some people called it a paradise, but the loveliest place could become a jail cell; the most beautiful surroundings could fail to stir joy.

Disturbed by the commotion, Anthea turned to watch her daughter, but Isabelle hadn't yet noticed her. Isabelle finally stopped when she saw Anthea. Meanwhile the ginger cat paused, casting worried eyes back in Isabelle's direction, before racing away altogether.

Seated on a beach by the pond's edge, Anthea turned away so that her daughter wouldn't see her face. She took a linen cloth from a pocket in her dress to dab at the corners her eyes. She had been staring into the murky water, thinking murky thoughts.

"Mother?"

"Hello, Isabelle."

"Are you all right?"

Anthea put away the cloth. She didn't want to cry in front of her daughter. "Not really," she said, giving a tremulous laugh without a hint of humor. "Come here." She put out her arms.

As Anthea hugged her daughter tightly, she kissed the brown hair on top of her head. She drew in a slow breath, eventually releasing it as a long sigh. "As long as we are together, my love. As long as I don't lose you too."

Anthea wanted her pain to go away, even as she couldn't let go of it. Had it been painful, when he died? Or was it quick? Were his last thoughts of her, and of their loving years together? Or had he been filled with terror and despair?

The stories varied, depending on the source, but they were some things they all agreed upon.

Kendrick, Tristan, and their allies, along with Bethany Sylvana, were all dead. Kendrick Conway, hero of the Siege of Curran Castle, had led his rebels into a final ill-judged battle on the plain between Highguard Castle and the city of Meroy. But unbeknownst to Kendrick, Emperor Julian had brokered a union with Queen Zhuana. Anthea's husband, the father of her children, had been caught between the two armies. And that is how he had died.

However there were places where the tales differed. Most said that after being trapped between the two forces, the rebels had been struck down with arrows, to form a mass of corpses on the sunburned plain. Other accounts were more fanciful. They told of the Great Weaver's wrath that the emperor had been disobeyed, and a black fist that closed over Kendrick Conway and Bethany Sylvana and squeezed them into nothingness.

Months had now passed. Anthea and her daughter were in exile, somewhere they hoped they would be safe. Julian and his new wife were married, with Zhuana crowned as empress. Anthea's grief had been overwhelming, and still was now. She had lost the three men she loved most. Her pain was a raw wound that was never going to go away.

"Ohh . . . my love . . . " Anthea murmured as she held her daughter.

"I miss them too. I miss them all the time. But please Mother, don't be sad. Rafael told me we will be safe here."

Anthea's heart went out to her daughter, who was only trying to make her feel better. Giving Isabelle another hug, Anthea knew she needed to be strong, if not for herself, then for her daughter.

"You certainly are," said a pleasant, male voice.

Anthea turned and there he was: their host, Rafael, King of Ormont. With a swarthy complexion, curly dark hair, and a charming smile, he stood with his thumbs hooked in his belt. She swiftly wiped her eyes on her wrists; there was no time to pull out her cloth. Putting on a smile, she climbed to her feet and smoothed her wrinkled blue dress with her hands.

"For as long as you remain here, you are both under my protection. We both know that Declan was like a brother to me. The empire has fallen to darkness, but at least here in Ormont we are free. A safe place is the least you deserve."

"Rafael," she said, "I was not expecting you."

"Nor would I expect you to expect me," he said with a grin. "I have been looking for you. I am hosting another feast tonight. Will you be there?"

"Of course." She smiled. "It would be my pleasure."

He smiled, even as he moved his gaze to Isabelle. "And you, Isabelle?"

Anthea hesitated, opening her mouth, but Isabelle spoke first.

"Will there be dancing?" Isabelle asked.

"Always," he said with a broad smile. He took Isabelle's hand, lifting it to kiss the back of her palm. "What banquet would not have dancing at the end? Perhaps one of my nephews can show you some steps, my dear."

Isabelle clapped her hands together.

While no one was looking at her, Anthea took hold of the spider she wore on a necklace. But then she let go, allowing her hand to fall.

The fates had not been kind.

She knew not to trust them anymore.

Chapter Fifty-Three

FROM A ROOM AT THE TOP of the Tower of Testing in Everlast, Samara stared up through the bars of a window too high for her to see anything but the sky. She watched as a bird flew past, screeching as its wings swept up and down, a reminder of her stolen freedom.

She was never one to give up hope, however. Julian had annulled their marriage and was now wed to another woman. But she still had her beauty. She still had her friends.

The bird was soon gone, leaving her with nothing else to focus on. Being stuck in the tower gave her too much time to think, and most of all, to reflect upon her past, and on the choices she had made.

There was a time in her youth, a period of her life for which she had concocted an elaborate narrative, a plausible weaving of tales. She had been seventeen when she escaped from the cruelty of the convent school her mother and father put her into. When she came back to the empire's Inner Provinces, to eventually introduce herself to the court in Everlast, and then to the emperor's only son, she had been twenty-five years old.

Eight years was a long time, especially for a girl who had to forge a new life with no money, no support, and no possessions other than a few changes of clothing. She had to be careful with the way she treated those eight years. She veered somewhat near the truth—one never knew what people might uncover—but she certainly didn't travel too close. As for Julian, she gave him the same story she gave everyone else.

First she gained sympathy for the harsh treatment she had endured from her parents, who valued their son but never their daughter. Her tale then involved her years of hard work, first as an assistant animal trainer with a traveling troupe, then as a tutor for a merchant's children. As she learned from the merchant by observation, she left his service to invest the money she had saved into jewelry from distant parts of the empire. Her business flourished, to the point that soon she was helping wealthy customers find the rarest pieces from among the empire's latest fashions. As a beautiful young woman, soon wealthy in her own right, it was logical for her to make her way from the Inner Provinces to Everlast itself, to the ladies who belonged to the most powerful noble houses of all. And, as expected, her profession made her many friends.

That was the story she gave, which evoked a favorable mix of sympathy and admiration for all she had done.

The truth was the more interesting tale, and there was only one man she had ever shared it with.

✦

"I think I am in love with you," Samara said. She allowed a smile to creep up on her face. "It's true. I love you."

From a deep, satisfied slumber, she had opened her eyes to see Haniken Ruhn, the Ice King of Tar, standing fully clothed beside the sumptuous bed. Morning light peeked through the heavy curtains nearby. The air was colder than she was used to, but there was always a chill so far north.

Haniken was about two decades older than her, in his early forties, and as fit and healthy as a man could be. His skin was perfectly pale, as white as the snow that covered his island kingdom. He had straight, short-cut hair, high cheekbones, and was tall and slender but with muscular definition in his shoulders, arms, and torso. He wore a black tunic, trimmed with gold, tucked beneath a golden belt, with matching leather trousers and high boots. As he watched her he had his hands clasped behind his back.

Haniken was smiling. But rather than share her pleasure, she realized with a gut-wrenching sensation that he instead was revealing amusement.

"No, Samara. You merely think that you do. What are you . . . twenty-two? You have yet to learn what love is. Save your words of devotion. I have enjoyed your company. However I was about to say something quite different. The time is now approaching for you to move on—" he broke off as he saw her face. "Now, please. I have little time for theatrics. Surely moving on is something you are used to?"

She sat up, holding the bedcovers against her breasts. "Only because I have had to." She bit her lip. "My father—"

"Yes, yes. I have heard plenty about your father."

As Haniken stood over her, she blinked frequently as if confused, and stared up into his eyes. By the stars . . . he was handsome, and powerful, and a king. There was no one to stop him doing anything he pleased, anything at all, and he knew it. She wanted him. She was desperate for him to want her in return . . . like nothing she had wanted before.

"I do love you." She shuffled the slightest bit, so that the linen slid from her left breast, even as she pretended not to notice. "Please. Let me prove it."

"Oh?" He didn't attempt to hide his mirth. "And how might you do that? You are attractive, but so are other women. I am a king. When I found you, you were—"

"You didn't find me," she interrupted. "I found you. I told you everything about me. I could have hidden it but I didn't. You know that I come from a powerful noble house—"

"—which you turned your back on in order to become a woman of your own means." He said the last words with heavy irony. "I was listening, Samara." He pretended to think. "Was it a troupe master who was first, or was he an acrobat?"

"I was seventeen. I helped with the animals. I left as soon as I could—"

"You had an education, and so you were able to sell your services as a tutor in a noble house, using a false name. The family treated you well. And what did you do? You had to leave after sharing a bed with the lord of the manor—"

"I told you. He forced himself upon me."

"You then looked for a way to regain your former wealth and privilege, and then you met an older woman, elegant and prosperous. She took you in. You thought she cared about you. Ah, but it was only later that she asked you to share your bed with one man, and then another. You argued with her. She would not release you from her service. And so—"

"And so I poisoned her. And I would do it again." Samara didn't regret telling him about what she had done—the Ice King of Tar was a man with few scruples to say the least. People from the empire called him a butcher for a reason. "I can be useful, Haniken. I can make my way in many different circles. I have killed before, and I am willing to kill for you. And I promise you—I can give you something that no one else can."

He raised an eyebrow, curious. "And that is?"

"I can give you the empire."

He snorted, but she continued to stare into his black eyes, telling him with her expression that she was deadly serious.

"Listen to me," she said. "Give me enough money and I will get myself into court, no matter what my father says or does. I will be your spy. I will make sure that everything the empire does works to your favor. Let me prove myself. Please, Haniken. Everything I do will be for you."

✦

Samara had climbed so high, and come so close. It wasn't over yet.

A twitch inside her belly returned her to the Tower of Testing. Her abdomen looked almost normal, the same way it always appeared—she had lost weight since her imprisonment. But as she put a hand over her stomach and experienced another movement, the life inside her was real.

She still had her beauty. She still had her friends. And within her, she still carried her and Julian's unborn child.

Julian should never have underestimated her powers of persuasion.

There had been three of them in the cell with her, the cleric with the severe hair, cut to her jawline, and the two guards, one tall and the other short, both middle-aged men who had heard Julian's threats and were doing what they had to in order to survive. The cleric had her potion—medicine was definitely the wrong word. The guards were prepared to hold her in place . . .

✦

After Julian left the cell, Samara had waited until he was out of earshot. Then, with calm, confident movements, she smoothly climbed to her feet. When she addressed the two guards and the cleric, she spoke as equals; she was deadly serious and they needed to hear what she had to say.

"Roland Hale. Myron Loxley. Freya Carlson." Samara looked at each of them in turn; she had been listening when Julian asked for their names. "If you value your lives, I suggest you listen to what I have to tell you."

"We have our orders," growled the taller of the two guards, Loxley, a bearded man with a bald head.

"And if you do not follow them, you fear he will hurt you. Let me tell you something. From now on, your lives are in danger no matter what happens next."

Loxley exchanged a quick glance with the shorter guard, Hale. Even the cleric hesitated, looking to the two guards for guidance.

"Let me tell you a story about Julian," she said, meeting each of their eyes in turn. "Once, when he was thirteen, he visited the famous hot baths at Malange. As you may know, the baths in the north are shared by both sexes, and so he chose to time his visit late at night, when no one else would be there. But then an older woman slipped off her clothes to join him, and when nature took its course, his body revealed his arousal. The woman noticed, and unthinkingly, she laughed."

Despite the content of the story, no one found any humor in it. Samara's ominous tone gave a hint about what was coming.

"Assuming the woman was laughing at his manhood, Julian was filled with shame. More than anything, deep inside, he didn't want the woman spreading tales, and he knew of only one way to silence her. One of his guards was present for his embarrassment too, and he ordered the guard to hold the woman's head under the water until she was dead. The guard initially refused. But Julian was adamant, and when he threatened to go to his father, the frightened guard did as he was told. And do you know what Julian did then? He calmly dressed, took his dagger, and stabbed the guard in the back, before pushing his corpse into the water. He later said that he had intervened in a rape, with the woman too drowned to be saved. There was no one to say otherwise, for there was no one to tell the tale other than Julian himself."

A horrified silence now filled the cell. No one was looking at anyone else.

"Julian once trusted me enough to tell me this story, one of many from a childhood unlike anything we could relate to. But he is unpredictable. He thinks that I am carrying another man's child. He is wrong, but that is what he believes. Would you say that is something that would bring him shame? According to him, the three of you are the only ones to know about this secret. What might the three of you do with what you know? Perhaps you might tell someone that he allowed his wife to become impregnated by another man? Will you reveal that he asked you to end my pregnancy so that no one would ever know?

The cleric, Freya, swallowed. The two guards—burly men who weren't frightened by much—were now wide eyed. Loxley was breathing hard.

"There are some things we can all agree on," Samara continued. "You are the only ones who know what he has asked you to do, which means that you share his secret. Do you know what men like him do to the people who carry their secrets? You are all going to die. No one will be able to protect you."

"None of us have a choice," Freya said, almost in a whisper. "We have to do as we are ordered."

"There is always a choice. Let me present it to you now." Samara checked all of their faces; they were listening; she almost had them. "I have been an empress, and a princess, and before that a dealer in fine jewels. Before I met Julian, my business was my own. Did I give all my wealth to Julian? No. He was the emperor's son. Why would I do such a thing? Instead all of it is out there, in the place where I keep it safe, just waiting for someone to take it."

The expressions on the three people had changed. She had watched their emotions oscillate, since even before Julian left. Julian's direct threats had them frightened. Her own talk of secrets had them terrified. There was a way out. She now had them thinking about escape, about a life of luxury, ease, and pleasure.

"I can make you all extremely wealthy. All you have to do is tell Julian what he wants to hear, that you have accomplished the task he set you. It will be you, Freya, he expects to hear from." Samara met the cleric's panicked eyes. "Tell him in coded words, publicly, somewhere he cannot immediately act upon the news. This is your opportunity. All three of you must then flee before he has you silenced. Remember, this is his plan, to silence you, even if you do what he has asked you to do. Your lives are at stake. You must go to immediately to Everlast, to the place I tell you, and then the gold will be in your hands."

"How much gold?" Loxley asked.

"Enough to live out your days in wealth and comfort."

Thoughts crossed each of their faces as they imagined a staggering amount of gold. And Samara actually had it, kept safe for a moment like this.

"Even if you go ahead with what he has asked you to do, you are dead. This is where we find ourselves. I am afraid that you do not have any good options. Take my money. Get your freedom. Get away from him, and from me, and from all of this trouble forever . . . "

✦

The bird outside Samara's cell window screeched as it passed again, bringing her back to the present. And then it was gone, and she had nothing to look at except for the blue sky and the cell at her back, and the bare walls she knew too well.

"Lady."

Hearing a male voice, she turned from the barred window to look at the guard who had spoken. He was the simple kind, with piggish eyes and a jowly face, his body plump with muscle gone to fat. He watched her from the opposite side of the iron bars that kept her from her freedom.

He called out to her in a tone both low and gentle. "I have a message, Lady Samara."

As he pushed something through the bars, she crossed the small space to head over. She met the guard's eyes, smiling her appreciation as she took the sealed and folded piece of paper. She then went back to the window, pretending to need its light to read the message. The paper was tiny, the same size as the palm of her hand. As soon as she finished reading, she tore a piece off it, screwed it up, and ate it. She continued in the same way until all of the paper was gone.

Behind her, the guard was still watching.

She went back over to him, with her arms out, as if she wanted nothing more than to embrace him. But all she could do was push her hands through the gaps between the bars. He reached out and held her hands. She squeezed. He squeezed back.

"The note," the guard asked. "Another message from your family?"

"It is," she lied. "They tell me to hold on. Help is coming."

He scowled. "We will get you far away from here, Lady. He should suffer for what he did to you."

She smiled. "As long as you are with me, when I get out of here. Then I will be happy."

He glanced over his shoulder, toward the stairs that traveled down the tower. "I have to go," he said regretfully. She squeezed his hands one last time, and then he let go. "Have heart, Lady." He smiled, touching his breast, above his heart.

"I will be able to, thanks to you." Returning his smile, she placed a hand over her own breast.

After he left, she returned to the window, looking up as she tried to see any birds outside. There was little else to occupy her attention, and time passed in the same strange way that it always did, moment by moment, hour by hour, day by day.

She was still at the window when she heard something different: a low whistle, followed by a thunk. A man grunted. A heavy weight collapsed, somewhere nearby. Footsteps sounded on the steps that climbed the tower's interior. She turned, just as a clang reached her ears.

Her cell door creaked as it opened.

The man holding the barred door had the high cheekbones and coal black hair of Tar. He gave her an elegant bow.

"My name is Larken," he said. "King Haniken sends his regards. Please, Lady. Come with me."

Samara followed her rescuer out of the cell. As she descended the stairway, she stepped over the flaccid body of the guard who had delivered the message she had long been waiting for.

She smiled. Haniken Ruhn, the Ice King of Tar, had gone to a great deal of effort to rescue her.

That, in itself, told her something.

Chapter Fifty-Four

A COLD WIND DRIFTED across the windswept hills, carrying snow and bits of dried grass. Scavenger birds wheeled in the sky as they searched for creatures brought down by cold or thirst. The moon was low, just above the horizon, with no warmth in its light, only chill. The wind made no sound. The birds were silent. The silence was all-encompassing, stretching from hill to hill, to the withered forests and distant ranges, where mountains like old men with snowy crowns told of a land forgotten by time.

But then a ripping, sizzling sound crashed across the landscape. From the few gnarled trees, black birds burst into the sky, frightened by the premonition of lightning. Lizards dashed under rocks to hide.

A bright light flared, somewhere above the ground. The light faltered but then sparked still brighter, elongating like a tear in the air itself. The opening peeled apart, revealing utter blackness that shone as slick as boiling oil.

✦

Bethany slammed into the ground, rolling, coughing, choking. Her senses were overwhelmed. A cacophony of sounds came from all directions, loud and mingled so it was difficult to tell one from the other. Male voices cried out. Bodies thunked one after the other as they struck the hard dirt. The impact was forceful enough to cause her to wrap her arms over her head as she rolled. Somehow grit entered her mouth and even her throat and lungs. Hurting everywhere, for a time all she could do was wonder where she was injured and how badly.

Prone on the ground, she coughed and tried to clear her lungs as she checked herself over. After a few moments, she decided the pain wasn't strong enough in any one place to indicate something broken. She raised her head. A ragged male voice was calling out.

"Is anyone hurt?"

The voice belonged to Kendrick. Summoning all of her strength, she tried to stand, but kept lurching from side to side.

Her vision was too blurred to see. She swallowed and put her hand over her mouth, which tasted like tar and cactus, even as her stomach churned with nausea. She didn't know where she was, nor how she had come to be here. The last thing she remembered was Julian telling her she was going to die.

She turned, confused, scanning her surroundings. She kept blinking, and then the wavering figures gained focus. Kendrick was in his armor, crouched over Charlton and helping him up. In the other direction, Xander was groaning as he rolled, but then he staggered, one hand on his chest, until he managed to get up to his feet.

Along with his armor, Kendrick wore a long-sleeved tunic, trousers, and high boots. Xander was in his diviner's cloak with crimson underneath. Charlton was standing, dusting off his white cleric's uniform.

Finally she remembered. The opening . . . the portal. It threw them all to the ground. She knew she had created the doorway, although she had no idea how she had done it.

Where was she? Wherever this was, it was utterly unfamiliar. It was dark, nighttime, but she had just come from scorching sunlight, where it was morning, with a fiery heat beating down. She shivered. Now she was more than cold; she was freezing.

In the distance a range of mighty mountains loomed, but unlike any mountains she knew, these mountains were tall and sharp, with snowy white caps.

"Bethany?"

She turned. Xander was watching her, his face concerned. And there was Charlton, turned toward her with an awestruck expression on his face. No one said anything. They were all staring at her, including

Kendrick.

"What happened?" Kendrick asked. "One moment we were all dead. But then a hole opened up and swallowed us."

"She saved us," Charlton said. "We all saw it." He never took his eyes off her. "We would all be dead if she hadn't done it."

Kendrick had a hand on his temple. "But how . . . how is it even possible?"

It was Xander who answered. "The truth is . . . it shouldn't be."

"But then what happened to us? How are we still alive?" Kendrick asked Xander.

"All I can tell you right now is that we aren't in the same place," Xander said.

Kendrick turned around to stare in all directions. "Then where are we?"

"Look," Xander said.

He had his head tilted back and to examine the night sky. Stars were out in a glittering multitude that twinkled down at them. Bethany rubbed her temples before joining everyone else to run her eyes over the constellations. The sky was familiar; she was under the same stars, but there was something else . . .

She stared at Xander, and he stared back at her.

"What?" Kendrick asked. "What is it?"

"They are diviners, Lord Conway," Charlton said. "The stars are in their blood. They can use them to navigate . . . to know the time of year . . . and it seems . . . "

"Well? What is it?"

Bethany answered, "This isn't the same sky we are used to."

Xander and Charlton both looked relieved to finally hear her speak. Meanwhile Kendrick was still confused.

"What? We're on some other world?"

"No." Xander shook his head. "This is our world. But the stars . . . "

"The constellations are upside down," Bethany finished.

"I don't understand. What does that mean?"

"The empire lies in the top half of the world," Bethany said. "Wherever we are, we're now somewhere in the bottom. And also . . . "

Xander spoke up, "Some time has passed." He glanced at Bethany. "Can you guess?"

She shook her head. "Perhaps with more time to study . . . "

"Wait." Kendrick frowned. "Are you telling me that we haven't just changed location, we've also moved somehow in time?"

"Yes," Xander said. "That is exactly what we are saying."

"How long? Months? Years?" Kendrick scowled. "I need to know. My wife and daughter are out there."

"My Lord, the important thing is that we're here," Charlton said. "Somehow, we are all still alive."

"I would guess months, rather than years . . . " Bethany said slowly. "Which means that everyone must think we're dead. And Julian will think he won."

"That's true . . . " Kendrick said, before trailing off.

Rather than finish, he stared up at the sky, where countless tiny bright lights looked back down at him. Bethany watched Kendrick's face. Somewhere, up there, were his two sons, Troy and Caden.

Somewhere up there was her mother.

Kendrick visibly gathered himself, straightening and squaring his shoulders, "However, because of you, and what you have done, Diviner Bethany Sylvana . . . "

He brought his gaze back down, to stare directly into her eyes.

"We are still here, which means that this is not yet over after all."

* * *

The Third Volume in the Gateway Saga is Coming!

In the meantime . . .

The Dance of the Dead

A standalone heroic fantasy by best-selling author James Maxwell, set in an entirely new world of magic and darkness.

Malgannis Vandryden, the greatest general of his age, is doomed to be a shade in the underworld and atone for a life of bloody deeds.

For Princess Coraline Vandryden, Malgannis is a tragic hero from another age, a man who lives on in legend. Then her world is torn apart by a brutal conqueror, and a black priest brings her an opportunity to make a bargain—he can deliver her the help she needs, if she is prepared to sacrifice the most valuable thing she has.

For who could win her a war better than her great-grandfather Malgannis? Perhaps unholy bargains are called for when desperation demands it . . .

Out on Amazon 17 June 2025.

Acknowledgements

First and foremost—thank you Alicia, my wife and the bedrock by my side.

And to Mark and Peta: once again, your feedback has been much more than helpful, and your support and friendship even more so. Thank you!

Thank you Marcus for your keen and critical eye where it's needed.

As always I am ever grateful to my readers Amy and Amanda, and my wonderful editor Niki.

And to my amazing readers: my everlasting gratitude to you for your support over the years, for your generosity and feedback and for taking the time to leave reviews of my books.

May the threads of the tapestry connecting us all be forever strengthened and woven together.

Printed in Great Britain
by Amazon

62764280R00201